SILENCE IN
EDEN

SILENCE IN
EDEN

Jerry Allen Potter

Thomas Y. Crowell Company

Established 1834   New York

FIRST EDITION

Designed by Janice Stern

Library of Congress Cataloging in Publication Data

Potter, Jerry.
  Silence in Eden.
    I. Title.
PZ4.P867Si [PS3566.0698]   813'.5'4   77-18639
ISBN 0-690-01742-1

78 79 80 81 82 10 9 8 7 6 5 4 3 2 1

for Prebble

PART I

Chapter

1

Mary Hyde lay small and thin, her depleted body barely discernible beneath the heavy blankets. Frank and Jonathan had moved the big bed into the living room to the heat of the fireplace. They kept the fire burning day and night. "We can only try to make her more comfortable," the doctor had said as he replaced his tools in the black bag, "as much as possible." And Frank had tried, though until two days ago she had known little comfort. The pain tore into her and the thing ate and sucked the life out of her. She knew what it was, and was brave, until one night as Frank dozed on the small canvas cot beside her bed he was awakened by the sound of her crying. She whimpered. That was a week ago, when the agony tore into her and made her scream until, weakened, she wept softly. She slept little, and never soundly. And then yesterday morning the pain left as suddenly as it had begun.

Frank called Doctor Herman, who once again listened to her heart, felt her wrist, took her temperature, and said simply as Frank followed him out onto the porch: "Just a matter of hours now, Frank. Tonight or in the morning. I'm sorry." And as the old man turned Frank could see his eyes fill with moisture. He walked toward his car; his white head bent down and his shoulders slumped. Frank, knowing that it wasn't because of the wind and the cold, hurried toward him, caught up with him, put an arm around the aged doctor's quaking shoulders. The doctor extracted a clean white handkerchief, shook out its carefully ironed folds and wiped his streaked face with it. He turned toward Frank. "Yes, Frank?"

"Listen, Ben, you've been mighty good to us. You've come day and night, left medicine. Really helped us. I want you to know we appreciate it, we're beholden to you."

"I know, Frank. Thanks. I guess I'm just getting too old to keep this up much longer. I've been in this country too long and lived with these people too closely not to be affected by what's happened. Mary's coming to this end just seems to top it all off, Frank. Seems the land's dead. All Oklahoma's just dryin' up and blowin' away. Every day seems somebody's movin' off, leavin' for good. Sam left yesterday, Frank; I don't think you knew that. Bank took his farm."

The weight inside Frank became just a little heavier. His feeling of helplessness came flooding back, sickly engulfing him. He thought of the debt against his own farm, felt weak, leaned against the doctor's car, then thought again of Sam Benner. "We were in France together, in the war...."

"I know, Frank. He said he'd ought to come by, but didn't want to burden you with it. Asked me to say goodbye for him. I wouldn't have brought it up now except your boy will surely find out about it in school."

"It's okay, Ben."

Doctor Herman placed his bag on the seat of his Model A, walked around front, grasped the crank handle, and pulled hard. She sputtered but didn't kick over.

"Here, Ben, let me get her." Frank cranked once and the old machine came to life noisily as Frank adjusted the throttle wire and idled the old girl down.

"Always did say you had the strongest arms in the territory." The doctor revved her up, slipped her into reverse and backed out the Hydes' long drive, fine yellow dust billowing up; then blowing back toward the car, stinging the old doctor's face with bits of sand.

As Frank Hyde watched he saw a familiar but unwanted sight: another family headed West crept by in an old rattletrap truck loaded to the top with decrepit furniture, trunks and boxes,

4

chicken coops, and children. "There goes another one. Goddamn, there goes another one." The doctor's Model A waited for the tired old vehicle to struggle by, then backed on out and headed for town.

From her bed Mary watched as Frank turned his back on the highway and its refugees, watched him gaze slowly out over the land that had once been green with new crops thriving in the fertile earth. Slowly his eyes traversed the now parched brown distance. The sky was brown and the earth was. Every green thing had died with the last hope of rain. Here and there a small tuft of long, dead, yellow grass had survived the constant foraging of lean and hungry stock. To the south, toward the great rock mound, an ancient cedar bent away from the wind as if to bend away would offer some respite from the cold, drying blast. Even the cedar wasn't green but a dull rust color. No rain to speak of for over three years, and even the snow was holding off till late this year. It seemed to Mary that there was no more God in Oklahoma, that he had forgotten; that maybe he'd left the land to shift for itself. It had not fared well under a truant divinity.

That was what Frank had called her God before she became ill, a truant divinity. "Out for lunch is another way of putting it," he'd said whenever he and Brother Tarler argued religion. Frank would bring up every major tragedy that had ever been recorded, and at the end of his delineation of each grim statistic, memorized as a defense against the onslaught of "unreasoned fanaticism," he would look the preacher or other would be soul saver right in the eye and ask quietly, "And where was your God then?" Without a flinch or a waver he would say it, then with the sheer power of his own unbending conviction would stare down his adversary, anger building up like steam in a thrasher.

The first time the Reverend Tarler visited the farm, years ago, right after he'd taken the church, they sat on cane-bottom chairs on the front porch talking about the weather and fishing and whatever else it is the preachers and prospective converts talk about until the preacher gets the divine nudge or mobilizes enough courage or gall to press his case about religion.

So he acquiesced to the divine nudge and said, "Mr. Hyde, I

5

soon hope to be able to address you *Brother* Hyde for I dearly pray that you will forthrightly mend your past, straighten your path, and yield to Jesus."

Frank Hyde didn't say anything right off. He was taken aback just a little by this preacher's short speech, memorized probably, and for this very occasion. But he wasn't taken all that far aback because he too had prepared for just such a delivery. He knew that preachers didn't come messin' around unless they wanted either your money or your soul. So when Mary mentioned, upon returning from Sunday services, that the new Reverend and his wife would take Sunday dinner with them, Frank retired to his library, the one-holer out behind the barn where an old icebox was filled with "reading material": *The Age of Reason, The Jefferson-Adams Papers,* the works of Shakespeare, Montaigne, Marlowe, Gibbon, Aristotle, and other assorted wizards of wit and worldly wisdoms. And there he sat with the best physic in the world, a good book, touching up his knowledge, checking his verses, memorizing to do brain battle against the stilted minds of medievalism.

So while Frank was somewhat taken by surprise by the preacher's sudden, almost impetuous outburst, he was not himself altogether unprepared. He didn't answer the preacher, just didn't respond. Just sat there rocking and grinning.

Three minutes slunkered by. The Reverend became uncomfortable. But Frank Hyde had calculated well ahead of the man of God and to him the silence was amusing. He smiled. Tarler didn't see the twinkle in his gray eyes or the amused quirk at the corner of Frank's mouth. Tarler had expected either the usual weak promise to attend church in the coming weeks, or a brief excuse for not doing so as regularly as is desirable. Either would have released Tarler from his divine obligation to God and Frank Hyde's immortality. He would have done his ministerial duty and pressed his claim on the farmer's soul. That would have been sensible and tactful enough for one day, the first day.

Why, then, was this prodigal so visibly unruffled, so certain, so sure of himself? The preacher saw Frank Hyde as an adversary, as were all unbelievers who were self-righteous in their unbelief. And because of this he could not accept Frank Hyde as a social or

6

intellectual equal. He was prohibited by his own spiritual inse-
curity from accepting this man's challenge to his faith, a challenge meant by Frank at first to be only a bantering flex of his
mental muscle, a fire-for-effect trial of his own logical ammuni-
tion. And had the preacher been secure enough in himself to
accept Frank Hyde as a thinker and an honest student of life they
could have enjoyed many years of frank and honest discussion of
mutually troubling and universally disturbing issues. But the
preacher, exhibiting the lack of candor ubiquitous in the breed,
was not open for conjectural conversation. His mind was a closed
book, a box nailed shut long ago, absolutely void of thought and
conscious mental efforts. The answers were already settled for
Tarler. Frank turned to look into the eyes of the unnerved face
attached to the corpulence that sat uneasily before him. "Mr.
Tarler, you are apparently unaccustomed to being ignored."

The preacher laughed nervously, shifting his bottom on the too
small chair. "No one likes to be ignored, Frank." Frank suppressed a fleeting sense of imposition at the so soon and unwar-
ranted use of his first name, which he felt was usually an attempt
to gain an unearned intimacy.

"And yet," Frank said, smiling, "I shall continue to ignore you
as long as you persist in your unwelcome attempts to persuade
me to abandon my mentality."

The preacher studied Frank Hyde intently, as if first seeing him
just now. "I ask you not to abandon your mind, Frank, only to
consecrate it to the Lord. 'For to be carnally minded is death; but
to be spiritually minded is life and peace.' " And with this Tarler
could sit still no longer. He gathered up his great bulk and paced
the porch, stomping his heavy feet and pounding his fist into his
palm for emphasis.

"Because," Tarler continued, booming, "the carnal mind is
enmity against God, for it is not subject . . ."

"Don't do that, Mr. Tarler. You'll likely bring on a stroke or
scare hell out of the chickens."

The preacher stopped in midquote and just stared at the
grinning fool sitting happily there before him as if hell were a
joke.

"Besides, preacher, you won't get anyplace with me by quoting

7

the Bible. Doesn't carry any weight at all with me."

"You don't believe the Bible?"

"Don't believe it's infallible, or the word of a god." He let that soak in. "Especially your god."

"You don't believe in God?"

"Not too sure about God. Sometimes I think 'yes,' sometimes 'no,' but certainly I don't believe in your god."

"Mr. Hyde, you've already abandoned your mentality. You've given mind and soul to Satan himself. As it says in the Word, 'But their minds were blinded. . . .' "

"Just a dead Jew," Frank seemed to mutter to himself.

"What?" Tarler stammered. "What did you say?"

"A dead Jew, just another poor dead Jew. Just one more poor, murdered son-of-a-bitch."

Tarler turned to the window. "Minnie, bring my coat and come," he stammered. "I can't continue casting pearls before swine."

"Sit down, preacher." Frank spoke low and steady. The preacher searched his face, was uncertain what he saw there, but obeyed when Frank repeated, "Sit down!"

And Minnie remained in the house, uncertain exactly what to do. Mary Hyde spoke to her quietly, apologetically, "He's really a good man, Sister Tarler. He's just always been mixed up about religion. Thinks it's all in your head and all."

Suddenly Minnie knew exactly what to do, when in doubt, pray. "Well, then, let's pray for him, Sister Hyde, and for my husband, that God may bless him with light and wisdom." So they knelt at the sofa and prayed, nervously buzzing away like flies, to the Lord of hosts.

Frank continued, "Reverend, you are welcome in my home any time you like. And my table is yours any time you and Mrs. Tarler want to come. I recognize that you are the minister of the church my wife and little boy attend." All this he said very kindly, then he continued gravely, "But when you feel moved, after my uncommon hospitality, to convert me to a god . . . " at this Frank grinned and maliciously continued, "to a god who was his own father, to a man who by your very Bible went to bed with his own mother . . ."

8

"Mr. Hyde! That's actual blasphemy. My good God in heaven, how on earth could you possibly say it?"

And the Reverend Mrs. on her knees said, "Oh, my good God!" and Mary said, "Oh, my good God."

Frank grinned, fully enjoying shaking the foundations, "Preacher, all I did was *say* it. You are asking me to *believe* it."

"I asked no such thing."

"You are asking me to believe the Bible."

"Certainly, as it is written."

"You are asking me to believe that Jesus is God?"

"Most assuredly."

"You're asking me to believe that Jesus' mother, Mary, was impregnated by God?"

"By the Holy Spirit, Mr. Hyde."

"Father, Son, and Holy Ghost, they are not three gods, Reverend, but one?"

"Absolutely!"

"Then if they are one and the same, then Jesus was his own father."

"Mercy!" breathed Mary.

"Mercy me!" gasped Minnie.

"Mr. Hyde, you are a fool and I think God will surely be unhappy with me if I waste any more of His Sabbath day on the likes of you." He was angry. He rose to go.

"Okay, reverend," Frank said slowly. "I'll make you a deal. I'll go hear you preach next Sunday morning and I'll drop a hundred-dollar bill in the plate."

The reverend sat back down.

"On one condition, "Frank continued. "You're supposed to be a preacher, Mr. Tarler, a reverend, a minister of the Gospel. . . ."

"I was ordained by Bishop Adonijah C. Herter on July 11, 1901, to preach the Gospel of Jesus, and I do it, been doin' it faithfully lo these twenty-five years."

"And you presumably have undergone a strenuous regimen of ministerial studies?"

"I was graduated from St. Luke's Seminary May 30, 1898."

"And you have studied the Bible diligently lo these twenty-five years?" And when he said "lo these twenty-five years" he

9

dragged it out long and slow, shaking his head pedantically. His eyes twinkled.

"More like thirty years, I must admit."

"Then you must know quite a lot about the Bible."

"Cover to cover, read it twenty-two times, then studied it daily on my knees in the early hours, poring over it, searching out the message."

"Then what I propose to do is ask you three simple questions from the Bible. Questions from the Book itself. If you get all three correct then I'll readily and without reservation fulfill what I have just promised."

"You'll come to church this Sunday and put a hundred dollars in the plate."

"Correct."

The reverend looked out over the Hyde place and marveled at its rustic beauty, the promise of a bountiful wheat harvest thriving in the expansive fields, the herd of young Herefords in the feed lot, the freshly painted barn, the prim flower garden in the front yard, the glistening white porch they sat upon.

Frank had watched the preacher's eyes roam his farm. "I really haven't got all that much money, reverend, just keep the place up."

"Was just admiring the beauty of it, best-kept place in the county from what I've seen," he said. "I was reared on a farm in the eastern part of the state, near Poteau. Would have been there yet if the Lord hadn't called me to preach."

And Frank thought, "Or if the work hadn't been too hard."

"Here's the first question, preacher. Now listen carefully. In the Book of Judges, first chapter, Judah fought against the Canaanites and Perizzites and defeated them, but their leader fled. Judah's men pursued him, caught him, and cut off his thumbs and big toes. Who was . . ."

"Adonibezek." Tarler snorted and felt again the glorious Spirit descending upon him.

"Very good, but don't become too overconfident. The next one is harder. In fact, I have asked this question of a dozen preachers, maybe more, and only one could answer it and he only after I gave him a clue."

10

"That was Brother Williams," Frank heard Mary whisper to Minnie. "He was here before you."

Frank continued. "That was Reverend Williams, the young man who pastored the church here before you came. Extremely intelligent . . ."

"And extremely liberal," Minnie whispered.

"Yes, I've heard of him," Tarler retorted. "Just out of one of those modernist universities. Let things go here that should've been stopped long ago—kids dancing, picture shows, sin of all sorts, card playing. Heard he even drank liquor."

"Wine," Frank said, then softly, "like Jesus."

"Jesus drank only unfermented grape juice, Mr. Hyde."

"Did you know that the Reverend Williams used wine when he served communion, Reverend Tarler?"

"Sin in high places, sin . . ."

"Never mind another sermon right now. Here's the next question. In the ninth chapter of Second Samuel, King David entertained the grandson of an old friend. Who was the friend and who was the grandson?"

The preacher sat pondering. He closed his eyes and leafed through his scriptured brain to locate Second Samuel, then trod through nine chapters meticulously.

"Take all the time you need," Frank comforted. "I'm in no hurry."

When the preacher did not answer in several minutes, Frank, sitting next to the screened window, heard Mary get up and walk to the bedroom, where he knew she would find her Bible, bring it back, and locate the passage. He heard her return. The pages rustled and a subdued voice confessed, "Here it is, Sister Tarler, Mephib . . . Mephibosheth."

Frank thought he saw Tarler's eyes wince as the name was pronounced, but couldn't be certain that the man had heard, for he was a good ten to twelve feet away from the window. "Need a clue, a hint, preacher?"

"No, no, just give me a few more moments. I know it. Just being certain."

"I'll bet," Frank thought.

"Mephibosheth, grandson of Saul and son of Jonathan."

Frank thought he looked guilty. Could it be his imagination just because he didn't like the bastard? "I thought you weren't going to know that one."

"I must admit that I didn't know it immediately, Mr. Hyde, but the Lord helps me remember. Seems he whispers to me at times and blesses me with wisdom beyond my own. Bless the Lord." He took a big yellow handkerchief out of his right hip pocket, honked his moist red nose, and wiped his upper lip.

Now the bastard thinks he's hearing voices. The stupid son-of-a-bitch believes it! "One more question." He paused to run the last question through his mind to be certain he was putting it exactly right. It matters how you say it, this last one. Mary and Minnie were still whispering. Biddies. "Mary, you and Mrs. Tarler don't have to listen through the window. Come on out and join us. Nice day out."

They appeared immediately. "We weren't really listening, Frank. We were talking after we did the dishes." They took their spectator seats in the porch swing but didn't swing. They sat silently, both praying that the Lord could somehow bring this one off.

"Reverend, this is a real crippler. Nobody has ever answered it correctly. You might, considering your special help and all, but I doubt it." He gave the two women a shriveling glance. They both looked away.

"Now here it is. What biblical deity established the practice of human slavery in Canaan?"

Silence. The reverend sat still with his eyes closed, breathed a noiseless prayer, then bent over in his chair, placed his elbows on his knees, head in hands, and awaited the gift from on high.

"I think he's going to make you sweat for it this time, Reverend Tarler." Frank said softly. "I don't believe you'll hear any angelic voices on this one." He looked at the ladies' pale faces. He noticed that Mary's face was frozen in a hurt, kind of bewilderment, as if she did not at all understand her husband.

"Preacher, your Big Buddy ain't comin' through for you on this one. But, by your own eager testimony, you've read the good book at least twenty-two times, possibly more. I shouldn't think for a question of this sort you'd need any divine assistance."

12

"I must admit, Mr. Hyde, you've asked me a hard question. No chance you'd be joshing me, would you? I mean, it is a legitimate question?"

"You injure me, reverend. Of course the question is legitimate. Do you need a hint?"

"Let me think on it, pray on it some."

The ladies fidgeted. Mary knew the answer but dared not speak. If only there were some way to get the answer to Reverend Tarler. It would actually help Frank to help Reverend Tarler get the right answer. It would do Frank so much good to go to church. He hadn't been to church for years. He would hear Reverend Tarler preach. Such a good preacher, too. It would impress Frank if he thought the reverend was smart enough to know the answer. And then she knew. "I'll make some tea, some nice ice-cold tea," she announced and flitted across the porch, avoiding the interested eyes of her husband.

"And I'll help," Minnie offered as they both disappeared.

"Preacher, when I was a young man, before the war, I worked my way around the world to see what I could see of it before I settled down. I made it a point to talk to all the people I could about important things, how they felt about things. That was my college. That was my education. Books I could read any time. Still read. But talking to people, living with them, living like them. That's the way to learn about the world." Frank had the strange, empty feeling that he was wasting his time talking to this man. He was just as closed-minded as most other preachers he had known. But he was into it now and would continue to see if he could make a dent in the fortifications built around this preacher's blind faith.

"But you haven't learned about God, Mr. Hyde. In all your learning you left out the most important part; you left out God."

"That is just what I was about to say, preacher. In all my traveling I tried to learn about how different peoples felt about the concept of God and how they felt about other people's gods." Frank stopped momentarily and focused his mind on the past, back to his travels, to an old man standing on the frozen tundra in Alaska, to an old fakir in a ruined temple in India. "I once spoke to an old Eskimo about God when I was searching for truth. He very soberly assured me that the earth sprang forth from the armpit of a Great White Frog."

"How ignorant," Tarler grunted.

"I told him that he might be right, that I had no way of knowing for sure, and he looked at me as if I were a fool not to believe.

"In India an emaciated old fakir told me that the universe is one-legged and that leg rests firmly upon the sound of nothing and that silence is Truth and God."

"Faker is right." Tarler grunted.

"So I told him also that he might be right, that I had no way of knowing for certain, and he looked at me as if I were a fool not to believe. I told the Eskimo and I told the mystic that I was born among a people who learned from an old book to believe that the world was made in six days by a nearsighted old Spirit who made more children than he could handle so he drowned them and he burned them. . . .

"The Eskimo and the mystic both looked at me as if I were a fool to have been born among such a people, and I myself began to wonder about the good sense of a one-legged universe and the armpit of a Great White Frog."

"I don't think I understand exactly what you are trying to say, Mr. Hyde."

"I didn't think you would."

A shrill whistle came from the kitchen.

"We'll have that tea soon now, Reverend Tarler. Should perk you up some. You seem to be having some difficulty with that last question."

"Can't quite get a bead on it. Doesn't ring a bell."

"Slavery, reverend, human slavery. Which Old Testament tribal deity commanded it? One of the most despicable orders ever passed down the ecclesiastic chain of command. What old god was demon enough to command his people to take slaves and own them and pass them down from generation to generation?" Frank's voice was a little colder now, somewhat clipped and short. It always angered him that preachers knew all the good sides to their diverse gods and never the bad.

"This must be some kind of trick question, Mr. Hyde, because, I

14

dare say, if it were plainly stated in God's word that such and such false god said, 'Go get slaves,' I would have known about it, so it must be some kind of hooraw kind of question. Tryin' to embarrass me. Not very fair at all."

"Well, if it is a trick question, maybe you can come up with a trick answer like hear another voice or something." Frank grinned maliciously.

"Mary," he yelled into the house, " 'bout got that ice tea fixed? Gettin' thirsty, preacher?"

"Be a minute, Frank," Mary answered. "Where'd Jonathan Alexander get off to?"

Frank looked toward the barn then to the line of trees hiding the creek about half a mile out into the golden wheat. "Can hardly see that kid when he's out there. Hair's same color's the wheat and he's 'bout the same height of it. And when he doesn't want to be found he can disappear like a ghost in a snowstorm."

"Seems like a fine boy," the preacher offered. "Sat quiet and listened well during preaching this morning. Shook my hand big as life and said he enjoyed my sermon. Said he's gonna grow up to be a preacher. Seemed right serious." Tarler looked to Frank as if for confirmation of the boy's intentions.

But Frank appeared to concentrate his gaze on the dark line of trees where the small golden figure of a boy bobbed swiftly before them, then disappeared into the sea of grain.

"He's comin', Mary. He's been down to the creek."

"You tell him he could go down there after dinner?" Mary appeared at the door. "He still got his good clothes on, Frank?"

Frank ignored the question. " 'Bout that tea, Mary."

"Be a minute." And she scurried back to the kitchen. She knew he was angry with her, bringin' the preacher to dinner. But it was her duty, she thought. It was her duty to her son and her own soul, not to mention Frank's. She didn't want the circle unbroken. She wanted Frank to be a Christian. So she knew why he was so short with her, ignoring her, hurrying up the tea. He didn't much like Reverend Tarler and he near hated Mrs. Tarler. If only Frank wouldn't try to embarrass them. If only Brother Tarler could answer that last question. It would impress Frank so. And suddenly she had a plan. A design sent from on high.

Then Frank could hear the women buzzin' in the kitchen and he wondered why they were buzzin' and not talking in normal tones. . . . He caught part of a phrase . . . "be really wrong, would . . . buzz buzz, buzz . . . should we . . ." Frank grinned. He looked at the preacher. He didn't think the preacher heard them. Damnfool women.

Still looking into the wheat, Frank saw the little head bobbing now closer, should break out of the turn row, then come round behind the barn, dust off his clothes real good, and wash his face and hands like he'd never been to the creek without permission.

Frank wished his son would not tell people about wanting to become a preacher. He was too young to know what preaching and religion were all about. But it was Mary's glory: her son a preacher. But Frank knew he'd once told Doctor Herman he'd be a doctor. Told Sam Benner he was going to be a farmer. Hates animals; how's anybody hates animals going to be any kind of a decent farmer? Tell anybody anything to get on the good side of them. Damned embarrassing. Frank worried about the boy more lately. Bright enough, strong and handsome, but Frank had seen a side of the boy's nature that even Mary was unaware of. It was more than just a small boy's natural inclination to kill snakes and shoot birds with air rifles. It was a calculating intent to cause hurt and to enjoy doing it.

Frank had first suspected one afternoon when he had gone up on the barn roof to replace a few shingles that had split. He noticed Jonathan standing near the tool shed, a small wooden leanto structure between the house and the barn. The boy was standing still, quietly observing a point on the ground three or four feet away. Frank could see nothing from the roof. Then the boy began to move slowly, walking carefully, stealthily, still watching something a few feet away. Eyes intent on his prey until he approached what Frank could see now was the ant mound toward the rear of the yard near the brush.

A sense of fatherly pride crept over him as he watched what he thought was his son learning about the small creatures. The farmer ants. Little red fellows hard at work gathering grain for winter.

But the thrill of witnessing his son's apparent fascination with the small creatures struggling with the huge kernels of wheat and the mammoth kernels of corn was shattered by a terrible guttural chuckle of the small boy as he watched the ant battling the last few inches toward home. The boy bent down and picked the ant up. Held him close to his face, then crushed him between two pink fingers. He opened his fingers and inspected the utter damage he had done and he laughed again, louder. He turned and kicked the mound, shattering it, then he stomped the fleeing refugees and ground them with both feet. Then he stepped back from the crawling red fiery danger of the angry survivors and watched them scattering wildly about as if some cruel god had just signaled an end to their world.

"Jonathan."

The boy froze at the voice behind him then turned slowly with smiling face and cold eyes to meet his father's angry stare. "I'm getting rid of this old ant bed for you, daddy."

Frank was as troubled by the boy's quick recovery as by his destruction of the ants. "There are other ways, son."

"Yes, with fire, gasoline and fire. Let's burn 'em out. Shouldn't have 'em in the yard like this." He was excited. They had burned out one colony last summer.

"No."

Then there was the thing with the rabbit. The Sunday-afternoon thing with the rabbit in the dried-up creek bed. That morning at church a visiting evangelist had preached on the subject of the crucifixion. He spent fifteen minutes explaining why God had to draw blood to satisfy his sense of justice and to assuage his anger at the "body of sin in man." He screamed an hour-long, tear-filled peroration on the gruesome details of the terrible deed itself.

The boy, seven years old, sat transfixed through it all. He winced when the thorns were applied and when the Roman spear was thrust into the side of the "lamb of God." And the boy could clearly see God's lamb spread-eagled on a cross. The preacher took pride in his powers of description and, noticing the boy's eager anticipation of every grisly detail, he outdid himself in exploring each hideous torture with the fake, sad voice of every hell screamer that ever lived.

17

Jonathan ate little of that Sunday's dinner and was silent through it. He excused himself from the table early.

"Eat the rest of your dinner, Jonathan," Mary urged. "Clean up your plate. We've got strawberry pie for dessert."

"Not hungry, mother. I don't want any pie."

Mary felt the boy's forehead, then, satisfied that he was not ill, she gave in. "Well, if you are going out to play, take the rabbits that bundle of lettuce scraps. At least *they* eat *their* food." Jonathan only smiled, kissed his mother's offered cheek, took the bowl of lettuce, and went out the back door.

He selected a white buck because there were many white bucks and one wouldn't be missed immediately, if at all. He stopped by the tool shed and picked up a claw hammer, which he carried in his belt, and a handful of small nails. He put the nails in his right overall pocket with his knife, for he carried the rabbit hugged to his left side in the crook of his arm.

He crossed the field behind the barn, being careful to keep the barn between him and the house. He looked back once or twice, and satisfied that no one had watched him, he entered the protection of the line of trees and descended into the small depression that was sometimes a creek and sometimes a bed of sand. He felt the beast tremble and he trembled too. "Crucifixion is one of the most painful of all deaths," the evangelist had said, "and for this reason it was chosen in God's plan for the death of Christ. He could not die an easy death. He had to suffer."

The boy stopped at a small rise in the creek bed: "Golgotha, the place of the skull." He knelt there and placed the frightened rabbit on the sand, placed one knee upon it to hold it prone, fished out a piece of twine from his left pocket. He cut the twine in three lengths. With one he bound the rabbit's front feet, then he tied the hind feet, left it struggling in the sand and went to the bank. There he found two sticks about the size of his arm. He held them together to form a cross, then tied the cross with the remaining string.

As he stepped back into the sand he noticed how good was its coolness against the bottoms of his bare feet, almost blistered by the trip across the hot field. He did not notice the breeze that began as he laid the cross on the sand and placed the squirming

18

animal upon it. His hands shook as he fumbled with the string around the front feet.

Frank sat in the porch swing reading when the breeze came. He felt its coolness on his cheek and knew that it had come from rain. He smelled the rain and searched the sky. "Gonna rain, Mary." He watched the black-based white pillars build up in the southwest. He loved to watch the storms come in black and violent, but cool and blessed to the summer earth. The summer storms were the life of the land.

With dish towel in hand Mary appeared at the screen door and looked out. "Soon's I finish I'll sit with you and watch it." She liked to sit with him on the porch when the storms came, four or five times a summer before the bad times began, not so much to watch the storms as to be near Frank when they came; for she feared them, feared the sky-shattering thunder and the searing bolts of lightning. She turned to finish up in the kitchen, then remembered Johnny and turned back to the door, "Where's Jonathan, Frank?"

"He's playin' somewhere. He'll head in when he sees it comin'." But Jonathan heard only the thunderous voice of the holy man that morning. "They laid 'im down on the cross and one of 'em grinded his knee into his arm to hold it still on the wood. . . ." Jonathan placed a small knee on the arm of the white beast. "And one of 'em took a huge square nail and placed it in the palm of that sweet hand that had so blessed . . ." And Jonathan placed a tenpenny nail on the small quivering foot. "And he took a large iron mallet and he struck the nail deep, through the precious flesh and into that sacred, terrible tree." The boy's hammer struck down, the animal shrieked. The boy heard again the voice of the preacher. "The Saviour's blood gushed out to stain forever the hammer-wielding hands of His persecutors, yet they spiked His other hand and they laid one weary foot onto the other and put a sharp spike in the tender flesh and pounded, *pounded* it down, blow after agonizing blow. And the Lamb of God writhed in agony."

The lad drove the small nail through the crossed hind feet of the terrified creature. Its eyes were wide. The little rabbit bit out at the bloodied hands that so hurt him but could not reach them.

19

"Then when the soldiers had done with their pounding a centurion commanded other soldiers to lift up the cross and its piteous cargo, and they lifted it upright and moved it to a hole dug into the rock, and they pushed it into the hole and the weight of the Master's body tore at the spikes in His hands and the spikes in His feet. The blood flowed down the post and into the earth."

The boy stood the weighted cross up and wedged it lightly between two stone slabs.

"And there he hung on the cross for my sins and for yours." Jonathan was transfixed in fascination at what his hands had done.

And the voice of the preacher came out of the approaching storm. "And from the sixth hour there was darkness . . . and one of the soldiers with a spear pierced his side, and there came out blood and water." The first drop fell lightly and the sky became dark. The breeze became a cold wind and the thunder roared. And yet the small boy stood transfixed by the shining red eyes pleading into the cold gray stare of its tormentor.

The sky broke open and the rain pelted down in sheets. Jonathan could hardly see the ghostly white figure in the darkness and still he stood before it.

The water ran off the small hills and off the fields and into tiny streams, and the thirsty creek bed became a small brown river.

Frank stepped onto the porch where Mary was waiting. "I've looked everywhere. He's not on the place."

"The creek, Frank." The thought of the raging creek turned her white with fear. She jumped off the porch and ran toward the creek. Frank darted after her, grabbed her, "I'll go, Mary. Go back to the house and build a fire. We'll be soaked to the skin." She hesitated. "Go on, Mary. Go back." He didn't wait for an answer, but turned and ran toward the faint dark outline of the trees. Mary watched him go, then hurried back to the porch, where she stood and waited.

Frank saw the lightning strike the great cottonwood that stood on the high bank. The powerful thunder crack that followed set off a ringing in his head. Out of the thunder, beyond the ringing, came his son's scream. He ran toward the old cottonwood. He lost his footing, hurtled down the creek bank grabbing roots and tree

20

limbs. He caught an old stump wedged into the roots growing out of the bank. He held on there, the water swirling around him in brown foaming torrents. Then through the rain and through the dark he saw and heard the screaming figure of his son crouched wild-eyed and frenzied on a rocky island in the raging stream. And above the boy, above his terrified golden-haired son, stood a crude wooden cross, and from that grotesque invention sagged the small bloodstained form of a . . .

When he saw the small white beast dead on the cross, Frank screamed and shook with horror. The boy heard, turned, and saw him, "Daddy, daddy, daddy, I can't get off. Daddy, daddy."

Frank fought to control himself, to think, to think and not to think. He scrambled back up the slick clay bank, holding on to grass that pulled loose by the roots, then bushes that finally held. He fought wildly through the undergrowth and made his way upstream from the island, then let himself slide down the bank and into the stream. He swam for the island and was slammed against it; he tried to hold on but was torn away by the rushing water. He grabbed again, caught a root and pulled himself up.

Jonathan fell on him and clutched at him, holding on, holding tightly, crying softly. Frank lay there for a moment sucking in air, trying to repair strength to hold on and courage to go back into the water. After a few moments he struggled to his knees and worked the boy around to his side and onto his back. "Hold on, Johnny, hold on as tight as you can." The little arms reached around him, the small hands digging into the man's flesh. Then Frank let himself and his small burden into the water and kicked furiously for the low bank. With the help, again, of branches and roots, he pulled to safety, the shivering boy still grasping tightly, the small burden still holding on.

As the months passed by the small burden became a larger and larger one. Frank watched the boy grow and suffered in silence, never revealing to Mary what he had seen the day of the storm. It would do no good for Mary to know about the strangeness in her son. He tried to talk to Jonathan about it a few days later, but the boy seemed not to remember it. Frank let it pass, not certain what else to do.

Frank shook himself out of the past when he heard the ladies

21

approaching with the tea. Mary carried a tray with four full glasses, and Sister Tarler followed with a full pitcher. Frank moved quickly to get the door for them. He noticed that they were silent, no buzzing, Mary did not look at him, but turned her back to him to let the preacher's wife pass. "Does Mrs. Tarler look nervous? Or am I just suspicious," Frank thought.

He went back to his chair by the door and watched the preacher take the glass Mary was offering him, and he marveled slyly at the quizzical inspection Tarler was giving his glass, holding it away from him as if better to examine some foreign, puzzling something on it.

"The old fart's half blind, or nearsighted." Frank examined his own glass. "Nothing unusual." Mary leaned the now-empty tray against the wall and went to her perch on the porch swing. Sitting down and looking toward Frank, she smiled, then pulled her glance away. Frank thought Minnie Tarler had tapped the preacher's vest pocket as she leaned over to fill his glass to the brim. When she turned to pour more tea into his own almost-full glass, and the preacher reached for his spectacles, Frank grinned at her knowingly. She looked frightened. "Skittish as a field-mouse," Frank thought.

Tarler examined his glass again. This time the light of recognition dawned on him. Frank could see that another miracle had occurred; God had struck again!

Jonathan appeared quietly from behind the house, hopped up on the porch. As the reverend removed his handkerchief and wrapped it around his dripping, frosty glass, Jonathan Alexander said, "Brother Tarler, what was that writing on your glass?" The reverend spit iced tea all over himself, took a fit of coughing, and when he finally gathered his partial wits, with red-rimmed eyes he wheezed, "N . . . nothing, Jonathan, not a thing."

"Looked like Jehovah, reverend, or something like that. J E something. Jehovah means God."

"That's what it means, boy," Tarler said. "Minnie, we'd best be going soon's you finish your tea. Time we were headed back to church." He extracted a watch on a gold chain. "Evening service starts at six-thirty." Mrs. Tarler drank fast, rising and handing her glass to Mary and turning toward the car.

"No need to rush off now," Frank urged. "If what Johnny saw was really there, preacher, then looks like God was trying to tell you something again. If he could write on stone tablets, don't see why he couldn't write his own name on an iced-tea glass." He chuckled maliciously. "Ever see any writin' on those glasses before, Mary? Stranger things have happened. You must be a real favorite, reverend, a real favorite."

In red-faced silence the preacher and his wife turned to leave. They jumped off the porch without using the two white steps, and they started for their car in the driveway. Halfway there the preacher stopped abruptly, turned, and pointed a heavy finger toward Frank's face. Frank could see the blood pounding through the veins on Tarler's neck.

"Hyde, God will smite thee and thy suffering will be unbearable." He trembled and his voice rose to a feverish pitch. "You should be forewarned that God sometimes strikes down a man's family to reach the heart of a stubborn man."

"I've heard of that happening, reverend. Maybe that's why I think you have such a kind and wonderful god."

Tarler shook his head; tears of anger shook him.

It wasn't good between Frank and Mary for weeks after. Frank was somewhat put out about Mary writing the answer to that last question on the iced-tea glass and Mary, embarrassed about getting caught, was angered further by his engineering the whole argument in the first place. But Mary, admitting her guilt both to Frank and to God, became her old sweet self again, and after two weeks of abstinence she rendered unto her man her marital favors in the warmest fashion. Frank could not remember such conjugal warmth. He forgave and never said another word about that afternoon with the preacher and the preacher's wife.

But now, ten years after, as she lay in the welcome respite from her pain, she remembered that afternoon with the Tarlers and the words the preacher spoke: "God will smite thee!" And he had. He had smitten the whole land for Frank's sin, and all men's sins, the preacher said. "Famine is the scourge of God!" he'd said over and over. He'd called the brethren together to pray for rain and the heavens to bear storms, but God was deaf and the winds came bearing not water to the thirsty lands, but dust and more dust and sand and heat and more dry, dry wind. Then Mary fell, smitten with the tumerous growth and dying daily.

Even Jonathan had hardened to the Lord. Mary had seen it happening to the boy slowly. He shied away from spiritual things little by little till now at eighteen he hadn't been in church for a year. They had seen the hardness in his eyes, the distance there from what he had been and could be now.

Frank's step was heavy on the creaking porch. His face was old as he entered the room. His hand was unsteady as he closed the door carefully and quietly. He turned and kept his eyes from meeting hers as he asked, "Can I get you anything, Mary, some warm milk?"

"Come here, Frank," she said weakly, but he was relieved that he caught no despair in her voice.

"Sit down here and hold my hand." He sat carefully on the edge of the bed and lifted her hand; he placed it in his, covered it with his other hand, and allowed the skeletonlike frailty of it to wound him.

"Frank, the pain is really gone. This morning when it stopped I was afraid it would come back again, but it hasn't. What time is it?"

"About two o'clock, I'd say."

"Then it's been four hours now since it stopped. What did Doctor Herman say?"

Frank didn't look right at her. "He said to get some food into you."

"I saw him smiling, Frank. When I saw him smiling I knew I was healed."

Frank winced inwardly, looked at her eyes and saw a light shining there that he hadn't seen in months.

She continued, "Yesterday, when Brother and Sister Tarler were here and you left, Frank, I wish you had stayed. He told me that God had been talking to him about me, that I could be healed if a man with great enough faith could touch the throne for me, and he prayed the most wonderful prayer. Sister Tarler prayed too. Liked to raised the roof. But oh how he prayed." Mary's voice became louder and louder; her eyes were like blue fire.

24

"Don't tire yourself, Mary. You should settle down now and rest awhile. I'll fix us some broth. Both of us. Broth'd do us both good."

"Frank, I'm healed. Praise God I'm healed. The cancer's gone." It was the first time the word had passed between them since they'd learned what it was. "And God's done it."

Frank got up and moved slowly into the kitchen. He leaned against the oaken table and silently nursed the blinding anger boiling up. "That son-of-a-bitch preacher and his goddamn fancy words. That stupid, goddamn son-of-a-bitch. I'll beat the fat bastard's pink face to a pulp. When Mary's gone I'll smash that fancy mouth of his, and his smiling goddamn wife's."

When Mary dies. When Mary dies. With trembling hands he opened the cupboard door and began to prepare the broth.

Chapter

2

Jonathan Hyde discovered sex at thirteen while on a Sunday-school picnic. It was more of a Boy Scout overnight outing than a picnic, but it was called a picnic by the preacher and old Brother Sapsis who organized it every two or three months. They took the boys to Glass Mountain to a cookout, a fireside prayer service, and a sleepout.

Billy Risedale was fifteen. Billy Risedale knew all about sex, babies, and jackin' off. . . .

"What?" Jonathan asked.

"Jackin' off." Billy declared with an air of superiority. "Doncha know what jackin' off is? Aincha never jacked it off before?"

"Jacked what off? What are you talking about?"

"That wee thing you got down there between your legs."

"My thing?!"

"Your goddam dong, you stupid shit. Doncha even know what your goddam dong is?" Billy and Jonathan had been commanded to go hunt firewood and they were considerably out of earshot and out of sight of the camp, but Billy's smart-aleck expression gave way to one of caution as he looked slowly and importantly in all directions before reaching down to his own thing, unbuttoning his trousers, and pulling it out, all of it, announcing proudly, "Now *that's* a goddam dong; that's really something to jack off."

"You're not supposed to do that?"

"Do what?"

"Play nasty. It's wrong."

"Who the hell said it's wrong?"

"Mama."

"How does she know? She ain't even got one, 'cept for your daddy's to play with every night."

"You shut up." Jonathan was as large as Billy. Billy just looked at him. Then he began pulling at it and flubbing it around.

"What're you doin'?"

"Jackin' off, stupid. Sure feels good."

"What's it feel like?"

"Try it yourself. You'll see. Feels goddam good. Better than anything in the world. Go on, try it. Get yours out."

"No."

"Come on. It's fun."

"No." But Jonathan stayed and watched. Billy leaned back against a big rock. The thing was large and red. He took it in his fist and pumped faster and faster. Johnny saw his face get red; his breath came fast; in a frenzy of jerking up and down, up and down, his face became frozen in a grimace; ugly eyes glazed unseeing; neck veins large and visible. Then, with a long, painful groan, Billy stopped pumping, stood up stiffly, pointed it alive and pounding toward Jonathan, who stood spellbound watching the milky white oozing from the small dark slit and splatting in the red dust at his feet. The dust swallowed it up and it made beads of dust.

"Now it's your turn, Johnny." Billy leaned back again against the rock, slowly milking his new shrunken, still red toy.

Jonathan turned and walked stiffly, swiftly away. His hands were shaking and sweaty and he felt a strange quiver in his stomach.

When Billy came back into camp he looked at Jonathan and grinned. Jonathan ignored him, and tried to ignore the strange feelings within him.

That night at the prayer service around the campfire Billy sat cross-legged on the ground next to Jonathan. While the preacher was reading from the Bible, Billy nudged Jonathan with his elbow. Jonathan ignored him and scooted over away from him. When the preacher commanded them all to kneel down, Billy knelt as close to Jonathan as he could get. Jonathan scooted and

27

Billy scooted. Jonathan scooted as far as he could without running over little Buster Wiggins, then stopped. Billy came closer and in the middle of the preacher's wailing prayer said softly into Jonathan's ear, "You're a queer." Billy pushed him harder this time. "You're a goddamn queer, Jonathan. You *can't* do it."

"Shut up!"

The preacher stopped, then started again, wailing his request of the Almighty as if the Almighty, if He wanted to, couldn't hear a whisper.

But Billy kept on. "I think you're a coward, Jona . . ." Jonathan caught him in his bent-over stomach with a hard put elbow. He put everything into it. Billy wheezed and started to fall forward, clutching at his middle. "Goddamn, Johnny, you didn't have to . . ." Then Jonathan grabbed Billy's shirt with both hands, whirled him around and threw him backward into the fire, fell on him and held him there and let him scream until he felt the preacher's big hands lift him up and off his adversary. Billy jumped up, beating at the fire on his clothes. He ran away from the fire, screaming and beating at it. He stumbled and fell and old Brother Sapsis fell on him and smothered the flames. Billy whimpered, then yelled, "You goddamn queer son-of-a-bitch, Jonathan Hyde!" Sapsis put his hand over the boy's mouth and picked him up and carried him down the mountain.

Brother Sapsis took Billy to Doctor Herman and the preacher took the other boys home, Jonathan last so that he could have Jonathan by himself. Jonathan explained it to him, said he was sorry, and bowed his head while the preacher prayed over him. The preacher let Jonathan out of the car at the highway then continued on into town to Doctor Herman's.

Jonathan felt a strange pleasure in his genitals. This was not the first time he had felt it and not the first time he'd wanted to touch his penis—and he had touched it once, at the creek. He had even taken off all his clothes. Exhilarated by the breeze and thrilled by the naughtiness of it, he lay back on the cool wet sand that day and, contrary to years of motherly concern, fondled himself and watched it grow by little pulsing jerks until it was the swollen, ugly little charger his mother always feared her little boy would come to be.

28

But this thing Billy had done was something else. Fascinating, like his father's bulls and boars, to spew out of that red faucet the stuff of life. Terrifying. Exciting.

So when Jonathan left the preacher's car that night he knew exactly what he was going to do. If Billy could make it do, so could he. He closed the car door as quickly as he could. The house was dark as he walked down the long driveway. The gravel crunched so he moved to the quiet grassy center. "Wonder if they are doing it now." He felt himself and was satisfied. It was already straining at the front of his pants, young worm come to life, demanding attention, desiring a separate ludicrous identity as the ruling root of existence.

In the hayloft he removed his clothing, all of it, and spread it on the loose straw, lay down and touched his thing. It was hot. He looked at it, a little white ghost erect against the darkness.

The barn was hot. Sweat drenched the boy's body as he labored heavily, both hands caressing, pulling, tugging, anything to keep the pleasure pouring over him like soft waves of warm water.

Then he started pulling the foreskin up and down, up and down, as Billy had done. It hurt when he tried to pull the skin all the way back. It was tight and painful, but the pleasure exceeded the pain and he pulled it on back, again, again, again, faster, faster until his arm could move no faster, until his tired fist could grip no longer and he stopped, breathing short, quick drafts of hot, musty air.

He tried his left hand, but it wasn't as good. He rested, fondling easily, softly, without exertion until his arm was rested.

Then he got up and pushed the loft door open and stood in the moonlight, felt the cool breeze on his hot body above the barnyard. Straddle-legged and jutting forth he pumped again as fitfully as before until the pleasure and the pain and his charging pulse all merged into one violent explosion. And above the world, balanced precariously between childhood and manhood, he spewed forth.

He held on to the edge of the loft door, slid down to seat himself, legs dangling out, then lay back to view with awe the wee potentate's proud demise, the sated monarch's quivering

29

transformation into just another boy's thing again, harmless and wrinkled, benign little wetter in slumber.

Billy Risedale wasn't burned badly, but he wasn't at church the next Sunday morning. The preacher, Reverend Tarler, looked for him at the front door even after Sunday school had begun. He was especially concerned that the boy was absent, for he had prepared his sermon specifically for Billy Risedale and all the Billy Risedales of the world who had learned how to have a good time with their lower natures.

Jonathan wished he had been as smart as Billy, for Tarler, having no Billy Risedale to nail with his verbal hammering, chose Jonathan. He was still uncertain what had occurred between Jonathan and Billy on Glass Mountain Tuesday afternoon so he couldn't take any chances.

"Brethren," he began his sermon, "this Sabbath morning I shall deliver a message on a very terrible and distasteful subject; but before I begin let me assure you that I preach not of my own accord, but according to the bidding of God himself." He paused and his eyes caught Jonathan's and found in Jonathan's face a fleeting sense of fear, and Jonathan thought he saw satisfaction in the hard eyes of the big man looming there above him like some fat angel. Jonathan looked away toward the open window and noticed that all eyes had followed the preacher's to himself. He felt the hurt of their accusing weight.

The preacher continued: "I have always been sensitive to the touch of the Spirit, and last Wednesday night I became aware that the Spirit of God was trying to speak to me about a practice that has touched our youth." This time he didn't look at Jonathan, but at Billy's parents, then at Mrs. Hyde. Jonathan felt his mother stiffen beside him.

"I was hesitant about preaching on such a matter because of its necessarily delicate nature and had almost decided to preach on something else when in a miraculous way I came across a scripture that shamed me back into submission to the blessed Lord. I was sitting in my study reading the Bible and praying when a gust of wind, and it was a still day, a gust of wind rushed through the room and blew the pages of my Bible. I reached over to try to hold my place, but it had blown the pages so that, when my hand fell upon it, the index finger of my right hand was pointing directly at the scripture I now take as my text. It is from I Corinthians, Chapter 6: 'Know ye not that the unrighteous shall not inherit the Kingdom of God? Be not deceived: neither fornicators nor idolators, nor adulterers, nor effeminate, nor abusers of themselves with mankind.' "

It was Jonathan's turn to stiffen. He looked down. Everybody in church knew that something awful had taken place on Glass Mountain. Whispering and giggles followed the reading of the text.

The preacher said, "And now let us pray that during this God-given message the blessed Holy spirit will convict those hearts guilty of fornication and lasciviousness and bring them mercifully back to Jesus." He bowed his head and began his booming, beseeching prayer. When he had finished Jonathan was gone. He went back to that church only once again in all his life.

Frank looked at his son again silently, and Jonathan retorted: "I don't do things like that."

Frank was sorry that the boy felt he had to lie. "I'm not trying to pry into your personal life, Jonathan. I just wanted to tell you that the preacher is wrong about masturbation. I have told you before that it is not bad and it won't hurt you. I know what he says. I know how the damn fool talks to the church boys. But it won't make you crazy and it won't blind you. You know that."

But Jonathan still worried about it. Sometimes he'd have nightmares and then feel dirty for days afterward. He longed for the days when he could go to church on Sunday and feel good and clean. When he had sinned in those days he'd just wait for a revival and "get saved" again. Like the time after the rabbit thing he'd gone to the altar and gotten forgiveness for it. "Got his soul home swept clean" was the way his mother had put it.

But he hadn't felt clean since he started it, and since then he'd had no will to quit. So he accepted the preacher's certain knowledge that the devil owned most people and they were virtual slaves to him. He tried not to think about it, tried not to think about hell and eternal darkness; but he wouldn't quit the thing

31

that all boys do and are sorry for but do anyway. And mothers who have no penis, and fathers, guilt-ridden, impressed with their God-given authority to keep people straight, make life hard on a boy who does it in the closet and in the barn and in tall cotton and behind trees and in trees. The boy, guilt-ridden and half crazy with fear of getting caught, thinks everyone he looks at can see it in his eyes and read it in pimple patterns on his face. He washes his hands a lot, doesn't sleep at night, worries about his sanity, and goes right on doing it. Because it feels good.

So Jonathan at thirteen and fourteen and fifteen became a stranger to his mother, a puzzle to his father, a near disaster in school, and contemptible to himself.

At sixteen his studies improved and he began again to talk to his mother, to spend more time with her and impress her. She thanked God. He had little to do with his father. He was civil, yet offered nothing. He'd learned to be unconcerned with his sin, pushing the guilt down deep so that it only came back to haunt him occasionally. Rarely did he worry about it.

At seventeen he'd forgotten guilt entirely, did without benefit of clergy painlessly, was kind and considerate to his mother so long as she didn't ask him to go to church and so long as she did not pray for him in his presence, and she did not. And at seventeen he began to feel that his father was a damn fool, and that no one on earth was quite as smart or half as tough as Jonathan Alexander Hyde.

The girls were mildly afraid of him. The boys feared and hated him, and with good reason. They knew what he'd done to Billy Risedale about a year after the Glass Mountain incident. Billy had spread it all around that Jonathan had in fact made advances that day of the campout, and that as far as he was concerned "Jonathan Hyde was nothing but a goddamn queer." And Jonathan hated him more than he hated even Reverend Tarler, more than he hated his father. Billy never crossed his path at school, never said a word to him directly, only about him. Then one day Billy let it be known that he wanted to fight Jonathan again, in a fair fight, not like at Glass Mountain.

When Jonathan heard about it he was still for a long time, then he smiled, and the snot-faced little boy who relayed the message saw nothing humorous in Jonathan Hyde's smile.

So the next Sunday afternoon Jonathan left the house and walked into town and through town to the place near the highway where the Cimarron River makes a sharp bend and sometimes leaves water holes in the sandstone big enough to swim in for a month or two after the rain.

Jonathan heard their voices as he approached. At the sound of Billy's deep laughter he slowed, tensed, and listened carefully, hoping to hear Billy say just one more something about him, just one more excuse for what Jonathan was about to do to him. Nothing. Laughter. Boys swinging out on a long rope and splashing into the brown water on a hot day.

Jonathan continued slowly toward the river and quietly peered down upon the boys, Billy Risedale naked, swinging long and lazily over the water, then dropping like a rock into it. Several other boys, some naked, some with jeans, were enjoying the fun. Swinging, jumping, then crowding back in line to swing and jump again. Only Billy didn't wait his turn. He charged in ahead of all the other boys, took the rope, and jumped again. Jonathan noticed that none of the boys protested.

Jonathan retreated silently, keeping low until out of sight and earshot, then headed quickly toward the highway, crossed the bridge, and made his way through the cedars to the edge of the red dirt bluff overlooking the river. He stood looking down at them until they saw him standing there above them, his legs spread wide apart, the sun right behind him, giving his head an aura of flame.

"Who is it?" one of the boys whispered. They couldn't tell who it was for the blinding sun. "Who in hell is that?" "Who's that man up there?" They all were still, quiet. Then they heard him and they knew.

"I found out what a queer is, Billy Risedale."

"Goddamnit, Jon Hyde," Pete Dill said. Jonathan marked which one it was. "Later," he said to himself. Pete looked to Billy for help. Billy supported him. "He's not just a son-of-a-bitch, he's a goddamn queer, a fuckin' goddamn queer."

Jonathan felt his palms sweat, felt the maddening sensation of hair stiffening on the back of his neck. He sprang forward and

33

hurled himself off the bluff, landing upright, both feet on the soft sand. Arms before him he struck Billy Risedale in the chest. The boy fell back into the water.

"You dirty bastard." He charged up out of the water swinging and cursing. Jonathan met him with a boot in the face then picked up a piece of driftwood and stood waiting for him, breathing hard, eyes hard and shining.

"Come on, you sniveling crybaby." Jonathan raised the wood and brought it crashing down upon his enemy's head. The boy fell back again, dazed and shaken.

Jonathan stepped down into the water, grabbed Billy's hair and poked the boy's head down into the water.

"I don't like you, you lyin' son-of-a-bitch. You're goin' to pay for your goddamn mouth." He reached into his pocket and produced a large pocket knife, opened its brown blade, and half carried, half pulled the now terrified Billy to the sand. Billy tried to get up, keeping his eye on the knife, but the grip on his hair would not falter.

"Kneel down, Risedale." He pushed Billy down in the sand in front of him.

Billy was frantic. "Help me, you guys. Get some help! Go get my daddy!"

Jonathan turned to them. "One of you guys moves I'll cut him." They stood frozen. Little Terrance Hendrick was crying softly. Jonathan turned back to Billy. "Now I'll show you what a queer is, Billy Risedale. I didn't even know before that day on the mountain. Now I know. You know, Risedale?"

Billy's face was white: he was shaking. "This ain't a fair fight, Hyde. Kickin' and that wood and that knife. I meant I wanted a fair fight with you."

Jonathan loosened his grip on the boy's hair, stepped back, flicked the knife shut, and dropped it into his pocket. "Okay, Risedale, get up."

Just as Billy stood up, Jonathan's hands darted up toward the older boy's head—he grabbed his hair again and crashed Billy's face down on his own swiftly rising knee. Billy Risedale crumpled backward; blood spurted from his nose. He held his face and screamed in agony.

34

Jonathan, breathing heavily, excited now by the blood and the pain he had inflicted, once again grabbed Billy's hair and wrestled him to his knees. "Now what's a goddamn queer, Risedale?"

Billy was silent. Jonathan looked at Terrance Hendrick. "You know what a queer is, Hendrick?"

Terrance, still crying, shook his head. "Pete, you know, goddamnit."

Pete said quickly, "Somebody 'at sucks cocks."

Jonathan smiled. "Now, Risedale." Jonathan unbuttoned his trousers and took out his swiftly hardening dick. He shoved it into Billy's face, holding the boy with one hand.

Billy's eyes widened with terror. He shrank away, putting up his hands and pushing against his adversary, but Jonathan held him firm. With his other hand Jonathan retrieved the knife. "Come here, Hendrick!"

The little boy hesitated. "Come here, damnit, I won't hurt you." The boy stepped forward. Jonathan handed him the knife. "Open it."

He watched the child's troubled eyes as he meekly obeyed. "Don't do it, Terry. I'll kill you, Terry," Billy screamed. Terry's hands trembled as he struggled to open the big blade. He handed it to Jonathan, who held it point first at Billy's neck.

"Now, suck it!" He pushed the knife firmly against the tender flesh below Billy's ear. "Suck!" Billy stiffened. Jonathan pushed the blade harder. "Suck it, Risedale. You know what I'll do to you after all you've done." He twisted the blade a little. Its point pricked the flesh and a thin trickle of blood mixed with sweat traced down his neck.

Billy shuffled futilely then opened his mouth and Jonathan entered him. "Easy does it, Risedale. That's good. You really do know how, don't you? Where'd you learn Risedale? That's it, sweetheart, just keep suckin'."

The other boys had gathered close, all straining now to see every last detail. All now feeling safer and fortunate to witness such a thing.

Jonathan's breathing became short and shallow and his hips pumped and quivered. Billy still struggled to flee from the red, steel hands, but could not until Jonathan pushed him away and

35

to the ground, then rained the foul stuff onto the face and chest of his thoroughly beaten, thoroughly broken enemy.

He turned to the others, brandishing blade in one hand and red, dripping pecker in the other, "Who next?" They were gone in a second, leaving their clothes behind them. "Billy Risedale, there go your friends. That's what you need friends for."

Looking down at the weeping, shattered boy he grinned, feeling more powerful and more wonderful than ever before in his life.

Chapter

3

Jonathan first saw Enola Vinson about three months before his mother's death. He was sitting on the steps of the high school when he noticed her getting out of an old Ford at the curb. She leaned back into the car to say something, then hurried toward the school. An older woman, about forty, got out of the old car and hurried toward the girl. Enola turned to face her. "Mama, I told you I can go by myself. I don't want you to go with me."

"Ashamed of your mother?" the older woman asked.

"Well, I'm not a baby!"

"You are a baby, more than you know." She walked along with her daughter.

Jonathan eyed the girl as they approached the steps. She was handsome. Not beautiful. Not really pretty. Pretty would be too delicate for her. Strong. Her hair was blond, long, and had just a hint of wave. It fell to her shoulders. Her eyes were gray-green feline angles, shining, angry, straight ahead, embarrassed by the presence of her mama looking after her at seventeen like a baby in first grade. She wore the same kind of flowered dress her mother had on, both new. He watched them go by him and up the steps.

When they had disappeared into the building Jonathan waited a few seconds, then deliberately walked over to the old Ford, a 1919 coupe. Texas tags. Tires were bad, no, one good. Right front tire good, almost new. A little tag under the license-plate holder said "Simpson Chevrolet" in wavy silver letters. He walked slowly past the window and peered in. On the seat were two envelopes. He could see the top one, addressed to Mrs. Bobby Vinson, Perryton, Texas. The address was crossed through with a big black "X," and scribbled out beside it was "Rte. 1, Box 49-C, Fairview, Oklahoma." Jonathan smiled and returned to the steps.

When Enola's mother approached the door to leave the building, Jonathan Hyde was standing there. He opened the door, smiled, and said, "Good morning, Mrs. Vinson."

She stopped, visibly surprised. "Why, thank you, young man. But how do you know who I am?"

"You're our new neighbors, ma'am. We're the Hydes. Own the farm just over the creek southwest of you." All this softly, carefully calculated to exhibit an air of youthful politeness.

"Well, you're a nice boy, Mr. Hyde." Her eyes explored him appreciatively. The boy saw something in them that excited him.

"Jonathan, my name's Jonathan, Jonathan Alexander Hyde, eleventh grade, ma'am."

"Well, that's a very regal name, Jonathan Alexander. My daughter is in the eleventh grade."

"Yes, ma'am, I'll introduce her to the other kids, Mrs. Vinson. She'll enjoy it here."

"I do think she will. Good day, Mr. Hyde." Jonathan watched her go. He smiled. He was pleased with himself.

Enola Vinson liked the looks of the boy she noticed was watching her in class, in the hall between classes, and on the campus. He was tall and reddish blond, almost handsome, even if a little gaunt, with slightly hollow cheeks and high cheekbones. His countenance expressed his self-confidence and usually carried a slight smile which might have been born of good humor, but his eyes said not.

She liked his looking at her and sometimes she would meet his eyes; he wouldn't look away immediately, but boldly continue testing her a few seconds more, then look down into his book or away to the window, smile gone. Then she'd catch him looking again and she'd feel a warm, uneasy stirring within. She liked it.

The boys at Perryton had looked at her, but she hadn't liked it. They stared at her breasts and everything else they wished they could get their filthy hands on. They'd heard about her mother, and Enola was convinced they figured she was just like her. Then came Charley Stipes and they knew what she'd do and what they could get, and after they got it she didn't like the way they looked at her, like at the brassière page in a Montgomery Ward catalog.

But this boy wasn't looking at her like the others and if he wanted what they wanted it wasn't because of what he'd heard from somebody's filthy mouth. It seemed like he liked her, not just her body.

She liked him.

That she had smiled at him was among the reasons Jonathan Hyde was attracted to this girl, but it was by no means the most important. She was good looking, yes, but of more use to Jonathan at this stage of his life was that she was a girl and because her father was in prison and her mother worked away she was alone most of the time and lived on the old place less than a half mile from the Hyde farm. Because of this, when Jonathan Hyde got ideas about Enola, as he did from time to time about most of the girls, there was the added factor of proximity and at least a measure of possibility. So, while he engaged in his nightly fantasies, Enola Vinson, blonde and bosomy, became more and more the unknowing guest of honor. She was always naked in his mental carousings or soon to be, always hungry for pleasures which it seemed in his forays could only be supplied by Jonathan Hyde.

But at school when he looked at her he was careful not to let her know he was interested in anything other than her long blond hair or her handsome face. He had already gained the first good graces of her mother and was certain that Mrs. Vinson had brought him to Enola's attention.

Mrs. Vinson was also pleased with Jonathan Hyde. A piece of luck to meet him like that.

"Have you met the neighbor boy, Enola?" she asked one day after school. Enola sensed the extra interest in her mother's manner, and as usual became immediately wary of anything that might follow.

"I don't know. Who is the neighbor boy, as you call him?" She looked at her mother sitting across the supper table, wondering where she had heard of Jonathan Hyde.

"The Hyde boy. Lives across the creek toward town. The big barn. You know where it is."

Enola continued eating, eying her mother carefully.

"It doesn't matter, Enola, I just thought he was a nice boy. I met him at school one morning." Enola's silence was not unusual. She had exhibited the small sullenness at Perryton. She had good reason, wondering that her mother knew anything at all about nice boys.

But Enola was sure Jonathan Hyde was a nice boy, and she thought of him as her nice boy about whom she could dream infatuated dreams of adolescent devotion and she did, constantly, until he became in her dreams more than her platonic Adonis. He became rather her secret lover, the kind, satisfying antithesis to Charley Stipes. While Charley was quick and rough and sneering, Jonathan was careful and sweet. And Jonathan was quiet. In her imaginings he did not tell the other boys anything.

So, charged with the physical wants of youth and blessed (or cursed as it may well be) with the uninhibited imaginations of juvenile immaturity, they both laid plans, she to master him with feminine charm, make him adore her, then gradually transform him as a sculptor shapes clay into the silent lover she'd wanted ever since she'd first touched herself in bed at night, alone.

Jonathan's plans were short range, simple, to fuck her as soon as possible, with her consent, if possible, in hopes of repeated meetings; but without consent if necessary. So Jonathan's dreamings took on a furtive note, a quiet fucking by force, and the more he thought about it the more it seemed the best route, by far the quickest and the least demanding.

So he began to devise a method to get her alone in the dark to insure his anonymity. He remembered the outdoor toilet behind Enola's house, a good thirty yards back, with Johnson's grass and bushes behind and to one side of it.

So Jonathan Hyde went one night to Enola's and waited behind the outhouse, hoping desperately that she would show up. He thought of waiting inside the toilet but decided against it for fear of Mrs. Vinson's coming. He made a place in the grass, lay down and waited.

The moon was just showing through the tops of the dry scraggly elms across the road to the east. Jonathan knew that in a few moments the path would be dangerously light, yet he waited. He could see into the outhouse from behind it, and the thought of seeing Enola pull down her pants and lift her dress was already exciting him beyond repair, so he lay still in the dusty grass and nurtured his dream. Even if he couldn't do anything to her because of the moon he might still see her and would jerk off behind the little building.

But she didn't come. Maybe she was not even home. Where the hell was she? Goddamn. Maybe she didn't go outside at night. Maybe she used a bed pot. The vision of Enola squatting naked over a night potty weakened him. Oh, shit. To hell with this goddamm waiting.

Jonathan kept himself in the shadows and worked his way through the trees and weeds, being careful to stay out of the moonlight until he was as close to the lighted window as he could get. The window had a shade which was pulled down, but it had a tear in it. Jonathan watched the window until he saw movement behind it, then crept up closer to it. That the old car was not in the drive gave life to hopes that Enola was in the house by herself.

As he moved nearer the window the hair on the back of his neck prickled up from excitement.

He had to approach from a slope, so that to see into Enola's room he had to stand on his toes and stretch. He could barely reach it, but could not see in because the rip in the shade was too high. He looked around for something to stand on. Nothing. As he hurried around the side of the house, he did not see a length of loose pipe sticking out from under the house till he had caught it with his foot and sent it clanking against a concrete block and pounding like thunder into the underfloor of the room next to Enola's. Jonathan froze, his heart pounding, his breath in his throat. Then he dropped to the ground and slid under the house. He felt sick as his shaking hands groped for the pipe. He found it and lifted his body over it and crawled further under the house.

Footsteps! Bare feet. Boards creaking. On the ground under the girl's room he saw streaks of light shining through the cracks in

41

the old floor. The sound of a lock clicking. Bare feet. Silence.

His nausea subsiding, he realized how difficult it would be to rape her. Locked doors, high windows—he'd have to kill her to keep from getting caught. He lay back in the fine dust under the house and closed his eyes. He saw her there again naked inside his head, offering herself to him, smiling, then begging him for it. "Please, Jonathan, please let me have it. I want it, please, Jonathan."

He lay quietly under the house.

He stroked himself, opened his pants and brought out the part of him that gave him the most pleasure and the most misery. Its hunger was insatiable, its desire for attention constant, but the reward it gave was unmatched as its fruit drizzled out unseen into the dust and he dreamed visions of a dozen willing maidens and Enola most beautiful in the midst of them.

Afterward as he inched silently out of the cramped darkness, he wanted to hit her, to kill her for making him grovel under her house. She should come to him begging for the magnificence he could slide into her. Begging. Absolutely.

The next morning while dressing for school he couldn't locate his billfold. He checked again the pockets of the jeans he'd worn last night, and the realization of where it might have fallen paralyzed him. The fear of discovery churned in his stomach. He sat down heavily on the bed, turned instinctively to the window, and looked out over the dry field and into the woods toward Enola's house.

It was during these few moments of fear of being discovered that Jonathan Hyde could least reconcile his two beings, the Jonathan Hyde good and the Jonathan Hyde bad. He could easily live with the knowledge of his own sin if only he alone knew of it, but he could not bear for others to know the truth, that the devil led Jonathan Hyde around by his balls. And that Jonathan Hyde enjoyed every minute of it.

When he left the house he did not go to the road to await the school bus. He headed instead toward the creek, trying to walk casually, swinging his books jauntily by his side, so that if his mother was watching him from her sickbed in the front room she

42

would assume that her son had decided to walk to school that morning. But as soon as he got to the trees he hurried into them, ran down through the creek bed and up into the elms, where he slowed and cautiously progressed toward the house. The old coupe wasn't there and the bus would already have come by for Enola, so as he approached the house his eyes were scanning the yard, finding nothing but dry weeds and old boards.

It wasn't on the ground near the side of the house. Jonathan squatted down on one knee and peered into the dark under the house. No billfold. It could have fallen out behind the pipes and boards, so he crawled under the house and over the pipes and boards and found nothing. When he turned to crawl out he saw Enola bending down looking under the house at him. She was grinning. In her hand she held Jonathan's leather billfold.

Jonathan froze, searching her face. She smiled. "Did I scare you?" she asked.

"You scared me. Where'd you find that?"

"Right where you lost it. Right where you're sittin' lookin' so funny."

Jonathan stared at her a few seconds longer then began slowly working his way toward her over the old boards and the pipe. When he was near the edge she stepped back and held the billfold behind her. "Can't have it back." She giggled. He darted out from under the house like a snake and grabbed her ankle. He caught a glimpse of her white panties as she went down wailing gleefully into the dust and weeds.

Jonathan was surprised by her laughter and excited at the thought of her lying there helpless on the ground before him. He pounced on her, grabbing for the wallet. She clutched it to her bosom. He followed it there and his hand felt the breast and the breast felt the hand. She stopped laughing and lay still. Her eyes were soft on his face until she saw the blood dripping down his cheek.

"Jonathan, you're bleeding!" Her hands held his face. He held still while she brushed back the red strands that had fallen down across his sweaty brow. "Your head is cut. Your forehead is cut right here."

43

He got back up on his knees. He touched his forehead, then examined his hand. "I didn't feel anything." He wiped his wet fingers on his shirt.

"Don't wipe it on your shirt, Jonathan. Come in the house and I'll clean you up and put a bandage on it."

"Your ma here?"

"She's never here." She arose, straightened her clothes, took his hand, and looking at his wound turned toward the house.

He looked for whatever had cut him. "That wire there. And I didn't even feel it."

In the house she washed his cut. "It's not as bad as it looked. Just a scratch really. Does it hurt?"

"Can't even feel it." He hadn't expected her to be kind to him. She should be angry. "I got your dress dirty."

She brushed at it. "I'll make a bandage." She turned to go. He held her hand.

"I don't want a bandage."

"You should have something over it."

"No." He could more easily explain the scratch than a bandage. Running through the trees a dead limb caught him. His mother had seen him hurry into the trees.

"Jonathan." She turned back to him. "Why were you here last night?"

He dropped her hand, looked away. She saw his face redden. It thrilled her. She took his hand again. "You don't have to tell me. I think I know."

He jerked. Looked up. "You know?"

"I think so. You came over to see me, tripped over some junk out there, and got chicken."

"That's right," he said. "I was going to ask you to go someplace with me."

"I will. Do you mean it?"

"Sure I mean it."

"You mean like a date?" She pulled him up and led him toward the sparsely furnished front room.

"Like a date. Saturday afternoon to the picture show."

They sat down on the wornout sofa.

"Jonathan, ever since I first came I've been wanting you to ask me for a date." She still held his hand. He was a prize and she had captured him.

He said nothing. It was unbelievable. He had come last night to rape her and now here he was alone with her and she liked him! "God," he thought, "I wonder if there is any chance she'd . . ."

"Did you know that?"

"What?"

"That I wanted you to ask me."

"No."

"You act nervous, Jonathan. Don't worry, my mother won't come back."

"But what if she found us here alone, and not at school?"

"She'd think bad. But if she drove in the front we'd run out the back. She'd never see us."

Jonathan thought of the woods out back and the creek bed. "Well, let's go out there now anyway."

"What on earth for, Jonathan? She won't come back. She's working."

"I'd feel better anyway. Where's she work?"

"Enid."

"All the way to Enid?"

"Sure. You know what she does at work, Jonathan?"

"No, what?"

"I'll tell you but in my own good time. It's bad, but you should know about it. You got a right."

His breath came quicker. He wondered if she could tell it. "Let's go outside and walk down to the creek."

"You goin' to school at all?"

"Nope, not at all. You?"

"I should. Mama'll raise hell if she finds out I skipped. I didn't mean to say that, Jonathan."

"What, hell? You can say it. I say it. I say worse than that sometimes."

"I'll bet you do too!"

"Don't worry, we'll write a note."

"You mean fake a note?"

45

"Sure. I do it all the time. 'Dear Miss Burley, Jonathan Alexander had to remain home yesterday due to the illness of his mother. Frank Hyde.'"

"Really?" She squealed. "That's neat. Let's do it now."

"Do what?" he jerked.

"The note. Then we'll go outside if that'll make you feel safer."

"Get some paper," he said, then got up and walked back into the kitchen. She disappeared and returned with her school notebook and her fountain pen.

"Not that," he said. "Something else. Does she ever write letters?"

"Sure."

"Then get some paper she writes letters on, and a pencil. Never use what you use at school."

She giggled. "Oh, Jonathan, you really have a racket going, don't you?"

"You bet." You bet I got a racket. And I got something else too. He could visualize her again, sprawled out on the grass, tied to four stakes, wide open and screaming.

She brought the pencil and a tablet of writing paper and put it on the table in front of him.

"I'm not going to write it," he said. "You are."

"Oh, Jonathan, I shouldn't. She can tell my writing."

"No, she can't, I'll show you." He took one sheet from the tablet, folded it neatly and deftly tore it into two equal sheets. On one he wrote:

Miss Burley,
Enola was unable to attend school yesterday as I was ill with my heart and she just insisted on staying with me.

Mrs. Vinson

He showed the note to Enola. She laughed. "Jonathan, you are a genius."

"See how it looks in my regular handwriting? Now see how I change it." He wrote it again. The script was backhanded and larger. "See how it's different? The capitals are printed, even. Never guess I did it. Now your turn."

46

"Are you sure she won't know?"

"Try it. Take another page. Go on, write it in your regular hand." She did. It was a large, flowing, beautiful hand. "You write pretty."

She put her hand on his shoulder and squeezed. "Thank you, Jonathan."

"Now try it again. This time write small and straight up. Cross the t's with a short cross." She did.

"Think that'll do it?" She pushed it over to him.

"Perfect. Now to get rid of the evidence." He went to the stove and took a match from the box, took the paper with his writing and the first with Enola's and together they ran out the back door and toward the toilet, where he ignited the notes and watched them fall to the bottom of the pit and burn themselves out.

He looked at Enola. She was beaming. She still held the bogus note and the tablet. "What'd you bring that for?"

"We still have to write your note."

"No, I write mine on the back of a feed-sack tag. More authentic. And I won't take a note tomorrow."

"Why not?"

"Because two notes from us might look suspicious. Especially if Miss Burley knows where we both live."

"Jonathan Hyde, you are quite an operator."

And to himself he said, "You bet I am."

He turned and started into the woods. When he realized she hadn't followed he turned and looked back. "C'mon, let's go to the creek."

She hesitated. "Jonathan, maybe I shouldn't."

"Shouldn't? Why not?"

"Well, you know, mother would raise cain if anyone saw us."

"No one'll see us. No one's ever down there."

"I don't know, Jonathan."

"Scared to?" He had to get her down there.

"No, of course not," she said, a little angry.

"Then put that tablet down and let's go. I'll show you some places where no one will ever come. Some secret places I go to all the time."

47

She came forward. He turned and she walked beside him into the brown scraggly wood.

"I used to have secret places too, where we lived before," she announced.

"Perryton, Texas," he said without looking at her.

She winced and stopped walking. "How did you know?"

"I know lots of things," he looked at her. She was troubled. He grinned. She grinned back if somewhat weakly. "What else do you know?"

"About you?"

"Yes."

"You came from Perryton in a Ford you bought at Simpson Chevrolet. On the way from Perryton to Fairview you blew a tire and had to buy a new one. Your father is in prison in Texas. His name is Bobby. . . ." He looked at her.

"What else do you know?"

He had regained his courage and his self-confidence.

"Don't worry, Enola, I won't tell anyone."

"Tell anyone what?"

"About your father. What else?"

She was silent, but turned and started walking again.

"You can't help it about your father, Enola, and it's nobody's business."

"How did you find out?" She stopped again and turned to him. Her eyes were wet.

Good God, she's really upset about that.

"How did you find out?" she repeated.

"By accident. The mailman put his letter in our box by mistake. We have forty-eight and you have forty-nine. I just left it in the box and he picked it up the next day and put it in your mail box."

"When?"

"Right about the time you came to school first, I guess. I didn't pay any attention to it."

"But you remembered that my father was a convict." She was visibly hurt.

"Look, Enola, I'm sorry. I didn't mean to hurt you. I just like to learn things about people." Then softly, "Okay, Enola? Cheer up."

48

She looked at him and smiled. "The other things, how did you know?"

"Your car has a brand-new casing on the right front. Brand-new. And on the back of the car a little tag says 'Simpson Chevrolet'!"

"You are a spy." She grinned. She was relieved.

"But I'll never tell, Enola," he said. "Not on you."

"We didn't buy the car, Jonathan. That's not the way we got it." She watched his response.

He smiled broadly, "You swiped it."

"No, silly."

"How then?"

"Someday maybe I'll tell you."

"Tell me now."

"Say please."

"Please."

"No, not now."

They walked on without talk. The woods became dense and darker. He moved in front and picked up a stick to clear the way of spider webs.

"Goodness me, where are we going?"

"You'll see." Already his insides were beginning to churn with anticipation of what might take place.

When they reached the creek bank he turned and reached for her hand. As she gave it to him she looked at his face and into his eyes. She wished she could really talk to him. Tell him everything. He was so strong. He would listen and care and understand. He would love her.

"Not far now," he said. "Just up ahead."

She looked down the creek bottom and saw where the banks narrowed. They were twenty feet high on both sides. Red sandstone.

He stopped and listened. "Hear that?"

She strained to hear. "Water?"

"A spring. C'mon."

He ran ahead. She ran after him. He disappeared around the bend where the banks narrowed. She followed, into the narrows, and there he lay stretched out on a huge boulder beneath which gurgled a small stream.

"Comes out of the ground right here." He pointed under the boulder.

"But I thought this creek was dry."

"It is. The water fills up this hole here, runs around the next bend and goes down another hole right in the sandstone. After that all the way to the Cimarron it's dry as a bone."

Already she had sat down beside it and was taking off her shoes. "I'm going to put my feet in it."

"Not right there. Snakes might be under the rock. Go to the other side where the sun's shining on it. You can see if any snakes are in there."

She put her shoe back on. He laughed. "Jonathan Hyde, you're mean. There's not any snakes in there!"

"Water moccasins come for miles around to get water."

"No kidding?"

"No kidding."

She moved to the other side and took off her shoes. He sat up. "You're not afraid?"

"Nope, you?"

"No."

"Then come on."

He stood up and walked to the end of the boulder, then turned and ran three great steps, made a giant leap, and landed beside her.

"You'll break your neck."

"Not me." He sat down beside her. They took off their shoes and put their feet in the water. Enola jerked hers out.

"It's freezing," she gasped.

"Not quite, but it is cold. Comes from deep down in the earth."

"You know about everything, don't you?" She didn't say it sarcastically. She was impressed. He wanted her to be. She carefully let one foot, then the other slowly submerge.

"You were going to tell me how you got the Ford," he said.

She was quiet, thoughtful. He tossed a twig at a water bug.

"I want to tell you, but I shouldn't. It involves a lot more than you'd think." She looked at him, searching his face for a hint of understanding.

"It's okay, Enola, you don't have to. It's really none of my business." Now she'll tell me, he thought. She was looking back into the water at the perfect reflection of the sky and the deep green branches of a cedar high on the bank above them.

Jonathan watched her face. She was troubled about more than just that damned old wreck of a car. Then she turned her face toward his and said softly, "Jonathan, can I talk to you personal?"

"Sure, Enola." He waited.

"I feel like I can talk to you. The way you looked at me at school. It seemed like you could see right down inside me. It seemed like you understood exactly what was there."

He looked into the water. A feeling of power crept over him. He was strong and important. She needed him and was dependent. He liked the feeling.

She spoke again. "It might sound silly, but, Jonathan," she paused, "I feel something for you that I've never felt before." Her voice was quivering. He saw her hands holding each other were white from the grip.

He placed his hand over hers and squeezed. They were cold. She looked up at him. There were tears in her eyes. "I know how you feel, Enola. I feel the same way." Then he watched her as she turned her face up to his. As she smiled he brought a hand to her face and touched away a tear. She reached for the hand and held it in hers. His arousal was immediate; this was far more than he'd hoped for, far more, and he'd make the most of it. "In fact, Enola, ever since the first time I saw you I haven't been able to get you out of my mind."

"Me too, Jonathan. You were so nice. Really, Jonathan, do you feel that same way about me?"

He nodded yes.

"Can't sleep at night for thinkin'. Like that, Jonathan?"

"Like that." He wanted to pounce on her to throw her back on the rock. He wanted to make her know he was a man. He wanted to do it. His pleasure became pain from desire, and his nuts began to ache as if some steel hand had them in its grip.

She turned to him and put her hands on his face then she reached up and kissed him on the cheek. He held her there and found her mouth and kissed her mouth and knew for the first time the sweetness of a woman's mouth.

51

He looked again at her. Her eyes were closed, but tears ran down her face. She was laughing and crying. He smiled and looked at her swelling breast and wished that the pain in his groin would wait a little longer.

He stood up and pulled her up. She pressed against him and kissed him again and her belly felt him hard against her. She looked into his eyes and he knew that she wasn't afraid of it.

"We'd better go back to the house." She turned to pick up her shoes. "I'll bet you didn't eat any breakfast at all this morning, did you?"

"Nope." He grinned.

"Then let's go."

While Enola made sandwiches she knew he was watching her. She liked it. With Jonathan it was somehow different.

"Tell me about the coupe," he said to her as she placed the sandwiches on the table.

"Not now, Jonathan."

"It's really about your ma, isn't it?"

"Yes."

"Then I already know about the car."

"How do you know?"

"It figures."

"Jonathan, sometimes you scare me. You scare the livin' daylights right out of me."

"What do you mean?"

"Knowin' things and all. How do you figure things out like that?"

"Just listen and watch careful. People tell you everything by not tellin' anything." He picked up a sandwich and bit into it. With his mouth full he continued, "Now you didn't want to tell me anything about your ma, which tells me quite a bit without you sayin' it. See what I mean?"

She didn't answer. She searched his face for evidence of any real feeling about her mother. If he knows she's a whore why doesn't it bother him?

"What's the matter?" he said. He stopped chewing the sandwich. "Why you lookin' me over like that?"

"If you know about my mother why doesn't it bother you?"

"It doesn't."

She was silent. He continued eating and wondering how to go about it. The pain was more severe and he imagined how it would be. Maybe on her own bed . . .

"My mother went to bed with Mr. Dougherty."

He stopped chewing again. "She what?"

"The coupe. She went to bed with Mr. Dougherty that owns the car lot where we used to live and he gave her the car."

"You mean she did it with him, let him do it, and he gave her a goddamn car?"

"Not just once, silly, several times. You're supposed to know so much about everything."

"Not everything." He finished the sandwich and washed it down with a huge glass of water. "I've never known a real . . ." he paused and looked at her, "I mean . . ."

"Whore."

"Well, I didn't want . . ."

"You can say it. Only don't ever let her hear you say it. C'mon." She took his hand and led him into the living room, where she sat him down on the couch and sat beside him and leaned over close to him. "Kiss me again, Jonathan."

He glanced toward the screen door.

"Still worried she'll come home?"

"Maybe."

"She won't. Sometimes she'll be gone two or three days. Kiss me."

He kissed her. He noticed her nose was cold.

"You can put your arms around me, Jonathan, if you want. Sweethearts do that, you know."

He lifted his right arm. She leaned back against him. His right arm was around her middle and his hand below her breast. She could feel him hard against her back. She put her arms around his neck and pulled him down to her lips and kissed him and felt his fever.

"Have you had a lot of experience with girls, Jonathan?"

"Tell me about your mother."

"Answer my question, silly. Have you?"

"Enough. She been doin' it long? I mean just since your pa got sent to prison?"

"Before they were married."

"While they were married?"

"No. How much is enough, Jonathan?"

"Just enough."

"Have you ever gone to bed with a girl?" She asked quickly and watched him closely. He hesitated.

"Yes," and looked into her eyes. "And you? With a boy?"

"No." She said without hesitation. He watched her a moment.

"You're lyin'," he said.

"And so are you," she said.

"No, I'm not. Tell me about it."

"You first. You tell me about yours first."

"My what?"

"See, you haven't, you don't know anything about it. That's why you're askin' so many questions about my ma."

"Tell me about her."

She pulled herself up to his lips again and kissed him long and hard, then her tongue began exploring his lips. He was startled at first. He hadn't ever dreamed that this was part of it. Then he parted his lips and she went in and found his tongue. His heart was pounding and he felt her hot breath coming faster. The pain in his groin was so intense he thought he might burst.

She pulled away. "You really haven't had a girl before, have you, Jonathan?"

He looked into those green eyes, half closed now and visibly hungry.

"Say you haven't, Jonathan. Say you haven't." Then she pulled up close to him and pressed her firm breasts into his heaving chest. She said softly, "Say I'm the first, Jonathan. For you I want to be the first."

"You are, Enola. I was lyin'. I didn't want you to think I didn't know what to do." Darn her, he thought. He didn't want to admit she was first. It gave her a kind of ownership. To hell with that.

"And the only one, Jonathan. I want to be the only one. Ever."

"Okay, Enola." So what?

"Then admit you really don't know anything about it."

"Teach me."

She kissed him again. He parted his lips for her right off. Then he used his tongue. She pulled away. "You learn fast."

"I am not stupid," he said. She laughed.

"C'mon," she said. She got up. "To the bedroom, my bedroom, Jonathan. It'll be better in there."

"No," he said and got up. "Not here."

"Why not, Jonathan?"

"Too dangerous. We get caught and all hell will break loose. Your ma'd kill me and if she didn't my pa'd skin what's left of me."

She knew her ma really wouldn't care all that much. He had money. His pa had the nicest farm in the area and he loved her, but best to do what he wanted. "Then where?"

"Back at the spring."

In the dark red shadow of the canyon wall as Jonathan Hyde watched the girl reveal her breasts to him, large and firm, he felt the driving surge of power that only a man can feel. The blood gushed out of his pounding heart into his flushed temples, down into his belly, and the grand god thing that ruled him sensed that this was the day of its baptism. Priapus rose up. The boy's hands reached out and cupped her breasts. The nipples hardened under his fingers. He knelt and kissed them. She pressed his face into them, pushed them into him, rubbed them over him. His mouth opened and he sucked like a babe at first breast. She unbuttoned her skirt and dropped it around her feet. He pulled back to view her. His hands fell to her hips, found the top of her pants and rolled them down, giving truth to his dreams. She was as blonde there as above and so beautiful. He touched the hair, then found the cleft. His trembling fingers, sliding down into the hot wetness, entered. She cried out softly, "Yes, Jonathan, deeper!" So deeper still he pushed and found no ending.

She knelt and lay back on the cool rock, pulling him over her. Her legs opened and his hand still probed and kneaded and felt the smooth warm wall contracting. She pushed hard against his hand, arched her body upward. Writhing mightily, she gasped. She pulled her legs together and brought her knees up to her

55

breasts. She bent her neck up toward her hugging knees, every muscle taut and quaking. Then she fell back, exhaled heavily. She opened her eyes and smiled at him as the glorious shivering in her loins gradually gave way to rested peace . . . for a moment, and then he had shed his jeans and was upon her, thrusting and searching for entrance. She reached down and grasped it, thrilling at its great girth. Then she guided him in, and when he had thrust his full length she clutched him to her. "Now go, Jonathan." And when he had thrust his length a second time the god shook him and drew every muscle in him toward his lower belly, and he spilled.

In the cold spring water she clung to him. She straddled him and pressed her breasts into his chest. He pulled her to him and pushed himself into her open crotch.

"He's wakin' up. Comin' to life again," she said. She reached down and grasped it, realizing happily that her hand could not reach around it. "You've got the biggest one I've ever seen."

"How damn many you seen? Sounds like you seen a real bunch."

"I have." Then she watched him. He was silent.

"Not like you think, Jonathan."

"You said you'd done it before."

"I didn't say it. I said I hadn't and you said I lied."

"Ya did lie."

She placed her cheek on his chest. "I did because I didn't want you to know. I'm not proud of it, but I knew you knew anyway." She guided him into her and began making slow, gyrating motions. "I should be ashamed of myself, Jonathan, carrying on like this." She giggled. "I would be with anybody else in the world, but with you it's different."

"Were they good, Enola?"

"Who?"

"The others. The other ones you fucked in Perry. . . ."

"Don't say that word." She pulled away from him, but he held her arms.

"Isn't that what it is, Enola?"

"No, it shouldn't be that word. That's the word men use with a whore. I'm not like that."

"Then I'm sorry and I won't say it again."

"It makes me go all cold inside. I can't help it."

"Then I won't. I'm sorry." He pulled her close again, "Okay?"

"It's just I don't like that word." She opened again and slid onto him again.

"There are other words for it," he said, stroking slowly deep into her.

"I know, and I don't like them either."

"What do you like?" he asked with a powerful thrust.

"That." She looked up. "You."

"No, I mean for doing it. What do you call it?"

" 'Loving.' When I do it with you I call it 'loving.' "

"And with somebody else? With the boys back in Perryton, what?"

"Jonathan, there was only one back in Texas. Just one," she lied, "and he wasn't a boy. He was a man, one of my mother's men, and he made me do it. He was drunk and he had a knife, and he made me."

"Was he as good as me?"

"No. He wasn't as large and he came too quick."

"You were being raped and you complain it was over too fast?"

"Not exactly raped, Jonathan. He just made me."

"But you enjoyed it."

"Yes, some of it, when he was kind."

"You did it lots of times."

"Yes. Does it matter so much, Jonathan?"

"Nope, not really, not now. Might make it easier with you knowin' so much already." He thrust deep and hard again. She held him, arms around his neck and legs locked around his back.

"I know enough to know you're good and going to be better," she said.

And so he did, and they did upon every available occasion make love. She taught him many things, and still he quizzed her unmercifully, always wanting to know more about the boys in Perryton and more and more about her mother's men. At every opportunity he would go to her house after school, staying out of sight until he saw the pickup was gone then going to Enola's window and calling her softly. She let him in and they immediately undressed. It was then that he would ask about her mother's men and she would tell him. There was a way she could watch, she explained; her mother's closet and hers were back to back, and by removing one plank in her own closet she could see through a huge crack in her mother's closet wall, and most often, because Mrs. Vinson's closet door was seldom shut, see right into her bedroom.

"She won't let 'em unless she's drunk," Enola explained.

"Won't let 'em what?"

"Won't let 'em even in the house, and then they have to be quiet and leave right away soon's it's done, so's not to wake poor little me. Mama don't know I know she's doin' it here. Just started last week. And three of 'em came already. Really two, one twice."

"Damn!" he'd say. And she'd give it to him play by play, knowing very well it would drive him wild and get him started again no matter what he'd done already. She loved it, so she related every detail and made up some of her own.

"Damn!" he'd say, and she'd tell him about her mother's men again in terms so real he'd wonder whether it was her mother or herself she was talking about. But it didn't matter; he wanted to see it.

So late one night Jonathan slipped out of his room and let himself out the back door. It was almost pitch dark, but by now he'd made the trip so many times he had no difficulty navigating the barnyard and crossing the now dusty fields. By starlight he made out the old Ford in the Vinson yard. No other car was there yet, but maybe later.

He scratched Enola's screen lightly with his finger. Instantly the screen opened; she'd already unlatched it. He reached under the house and pulled out an old apple crate, stood it on end and stepped up on it. At that moment they heard a car on the gravel road behind him.

"Hurry, Jonathan," she whispered. "Hurry."

He looked back. Too late, they'll see me, he thought; but just then the car's lights went out, the motor was cut off, and the car glided down the road and pulled in at the driveway on the other side of the house.

"Damn, that was close," he whispered as she helped him into the window.

"Did he stop?" she asked.

"Yes."

"Then let's hurry and get in the closet while she lets him in." She took his hand and led him toward the closet. She had already pushed all the clothes back so there was plenty of room for them both to sit down facing each other.

They heard a loud tapping on the door, then Mrs. Vinson's bed squeaked and they heard her walking softly across the floor.

In a moment the soft glow of a lamp lit up her room and Jonathan could see her, dressed in a long flannel nightgown, her blond hair streaming down over her shoulder.

"Quiet now, Paddy. My kid's asleep."

His speech was slurred, and as he came into view Jonathan saw he was holding a bottle in his hand and a half-filled glass in the other, "I've heard about your kid, I have."

"You've heard what?" Mrs. Vinson's voice growled, challenging.

"Heard she's already a full-grown woman mighty near," he said.

He raised the glass and downed all of it. He poured another glassful and lifted it to his lips, then paused, "Wouldn't be she's reached the age o' funnin', would she?"

"You dirty son-of-a-bitch."

"Now, now woman, don't get your ire up. Just thought how nice it'd be having two as good as you."

"Shut up," she snapped as she pulled the nightgown over her head.

Jonathan drew in a quick breath. His already-hardened member pulsed. The woman wore nothing beneath her gown, and her breasts were larger even than Enola's. She stood erect and pushed them toward Paddy and she smiled.

"Now that's what I came for," Paddy growled. He set the bottle and glass down on the dresser quickly and ran his hands over her breasts.

She pushed him playfully away. "Not until you put something

59

else down on that table, Paddy love," she said.

"Oh, for love's sake, Ellie, for once for love's sake. I'm broke, honey, and I love ya."

She reached for the nightgown and started pulling it over. Her eyes were on his face.

"Hell, woman, you're too much for the likes o' me." He grinned sheepishly, pulled out his wallet and shelled out three bills. Placed the wallet back in his trousers.

"One more, Paddy."

"It's three there, woman."

"Yes, and it's after midnight. One more, Paddy."

"Hell, woman, you're a Scot for certain. Not a bit o' Irish in ya." But he laid down one more. "When a man wants a woman he don't take no thought on what time it 'tis."

"When a man wants to fuck he don't take no thought to nothin'. That's the god's trouble with this world, Paddy."

She lay back on the bed and spread her legs while Paddy undressed without taking his eyes off her. Nor did Jonathan. He could see into her crotch. He reached over to Enola and felt her. "Take off your clothes," he whispered. She did so with considerable difficulty and he did the same, dropping his clothes to their feet. He found her cleft and kneaded it, and she pleasured him softly with shaking hands.

Paddy finished undressing and stood before her. Jonathan and Enola could see that he was ready for her. Yet he stood over her then stepped back and got the bottle and drank from it deep and long. "Drink, woman?"

She took the bottle from him, turned it up, and sucked from it. "Now, c'mon, Paddy, on with it, or in with it." She chuckled.

Paddy took the bottle from her and downed its remaining contents. He set it on the dresser and turned to her. "I want it the other way this time, Ellie," he said, stroking his swollen staff appreciatively. Then softly he added, "Like the other time, Ellie."

"I thought you liked that," she purred, sitting up in bed. "Just a minute, Paddy." She left the room and Paddy sat on the bed, then lay back and smiled.

Jonathan felt Enola's hand on his, squeezing it. He understood the signal. She was on the edge, so he stopped. He was almost there himself but not yet. He cupped her breasts in his hands and squeezed them.

As they watched, Mrs. Vinson returned with a washbasin and began to wash Paddy's penis. Jonathan still did not know what Paddy had meant by "the other way."

She grasped it, then rinsed it off. "I think you're so drunk you wouldn't know which hole you had it in, Paddy."

"Never, woman. I'll tell quick enough once you get 'im in."

Whereupon the woman knelt at the bedside and put it in her mouth and began working it there, to the moaning joy and slow writhings of the great bulk beneath her.

Enola felt Jonathan's hand reenter the warm, wet area of her crotch. His finger explored and found its waiting friend.

When Paddy's groans reached a certain peak the woman drew her face away from him, flicked his penis swiftly a few times with her tongue, then aimed it into a towel.

As Paddy unloaded so did Jonathan. Enola felt the hot fluid spurt against her belly and her breasts and she came then, hard and long, and as she came Jonathan thrust two fingers into her and wrenched them violently as he had learned to do for her.

The next day after school, after they had bathed in the icy waters in the pool in the canyon, she laid him down on his back and in the shadows performed upon him as her mother had upon the drunk Paddy. She took him into herself that way and gave him the grandest physical pleasure a man can know, for she loved him and he was her man and she gloried in it.

They watched often after that as Mrs. Vinson had men at the house, and always afterward they would experiment with any new thing they learned from their unwitting teachers.

To Enola, Jonathan Hyde was the sweetest, kindest prince in all the world. To himself he was the grand stud of all time. But to his father he was a still spoiled child shirking his responsibilities. It was about this time that Jonathan and his father quarrelled, for the first time as men, and Jonathan almost killed him.

Mrs. Hyde was asleep in her bed in the living room, but Frank still spoke quietly as he asked Jonathan to go down to the barn with him.

"What for?" the boy asked.

61

"I want to talk to you, Jonathan."

"What about?"

"About your mother." Jonathan glanced toward the living room. He shrugged, pushed himself away from the table, wiped his face on his sleeve, stood up and walked out the back door. Frank watched him saunter toward the barn, and he shook his head slowly.

In the barn Jonathan leaned up against the doorpost. He picked at his teeth with a sliver he pulled off the post. He looked at the ground and gave no notice of his father's approaching.

"Come on into the barn." Jonathan followed slowly. "Sit down on that crate there, Jonathan; this might take a spell."

Jonathan sat and Frank did. Frank looked at his son's face and tried to read it, but could see only scorn written there as the boy stared sullenly at the ground.

"Your mother's sick, Jonathan."

The boy looked up quickly. "I know that. Do you think I don't know that?"

"She's bad sick, son."

"I know she's bad sick. I see her wastin'."

"Doc says she's dyin'."

The youth continued to stare at the ground.

"Your mother's dyin', boy. Mary's got a cancer in her," he said quietly, thinly, "eatin' on her." Frank's eyes filled and his voice failed him. "I . . ." He stood up, walked a few steps, then turned back. "I want you to spend a little more time with your mother. She needs it."

"She talks religion."

"You can put up with that, goddamnit; she's your mother."

"You don't put up with religion."

Frank stepped closer. "I do. I overlook it. I don't believe it, and I don't like it, but for the past few years I've let it be. I respect your mother so I let her religion be."

"Okay." It was the thing to say. "Okay." Jonathan stood and started to go.

"That's not all I want to talk about, son. There's more." Jonathan returned to the crate and sat down heavily. It creaked under him. He waited for his father to speak.

When he spoke he spoke slowly and softly, but deliberately, for he had thought a long time about what he was going to say to the boy, and as long about whether to say it. And even now he paused so long that Jonathan looked up to see if he was going to speak at all. Frank sat on a crate opposite Jonathan and spoke: "There are two things we need to talk about, Jonathan. The first is the work around here. I just can't keep up with the farm work and do everything that needs doin' in the house and for your mother."

Jonathan cringed inside. "Here it comes," he thought. He had managed to get out of everything since his last run-in with his father over a year before. The farm and its stock, its fencing, and plowing had never interested him. *Goddamn farm.*

"I haven't said anything to you because I didn't want to upset your mother over having to force you to do it. And I'm not going to tell you to help me. I'm just askin' for your help."

Oh shit.

"Man to man, Jonathan. I need your help." He wished he could say, I need you; I want us to be good to each other. But he knew better. The boy would laugh in his face. His strange son would turn up his cold face and laugh at him. So he said only, "Will you help some?"

Jonathan only chuckled, waited a long moment, then slowly raised his head and gazed out over the dry fields. Can't be all that much to do on this goddamn place. Then he asked, "You're not going to make me?"

"No, son." He smiled and his heart beat faster. Maybe now the boy would come around, "Nope, I'm just askin'."

At this, Jonathan looked squarely into his father's laughing gray eyes and said in a voice barely audible, "No." And he watched with cold satisfaction as the unbelief spread over his father's face and tears of hurt welled up in his eyes, and then he continued, "I hate this place, this goddamn farm. I'll be glad when they run you off it."

"You're so cold," Frank said softly, "So cold. Jonathan, I wonder how it must feel not to feel at all."

"I feel," he retaliated. "I feel about things you don't know anything at all about."

"How do you feel about that girl?" Frank asked and his eyes narrowed as he watched his son's startled reaction.

"What girl?" He didn't look up.

"The Vinson girl, Enola." At this Jonathan got up and started to walk away. "Sit down," Frank said. "Goddamnit, boy, sit down," he roared.

Jonathan turned around. "You want me to sit down, goddamn you, make me." His eyes narrowed, he leaned forward and motioned with his right hand, "C'mon." His left fist was doubled tightly. He was larger than his father now, taller and heavier, and he had long thought he could beat him.

"You're a fool, son, a child to act like this."

"Just c'mon. Shut up and come on. Your askin' don't seem to work. Maybe your makin' is some better."

Frank moved slowly toward the boy and stopped an arm's length from him, "I'm through askin' and I'm through makin'. You're none o' mine by your own doin'. I wanted to ask you to help me cut wood with winter comin' on." He paused. "And I wanted to ask you to be careful about going to Vinsons' place so much."

Jonathan turned and placed both hands on the top of the stable rail and gripped hard. "Why?" he asked.

"Not because of the girl, but because of her mother."

"What about her mother?" Jonathan asked with his back to his father.

"The woman's a common whore, Jonathan. I don't want you to get mixed up with her. Best to ask the girl over here 'stead o' you goin' over there."

A slow rumble began to build up in Jonathan's gut; a thunder began to roar in his head. His hands gripped the rail and shook with fury as the screaming rage within tore him and shook him. This damned man behind him always seeing. Always knowing, reading into him, searching out secrets known to no one. The wave of raving hate broke him loose from all that is civil and human.

And it was an inhuman thing that Frank saw whirling toward him. Too late he saw the pitchfork in the boy's hands. He lifted his arms instinctively to ward off its blow and then the shank of the fork crashed down on his skull. The handle cracked and the fork buried its tines in the barn's hard floor. As his father crumpled to the floor at his feet Jonathan hurled the remaining handle away from him.

He stood wild-eyed and still shaking with rage over his father. Blood trickled from the shock of graying hair. Jonathan turned, took a pail from its place near the water trough, filled it, and splashed it over Frank's head. He stood for a moment watching; then when he saw the man move and bring a bruised hand to his head, the boy viciously threw the pail down, turned, and left the barn. He did not again speak to his father or allow himself to be near him until the day of his mother's death.

Chapter

4

Ellie Vinson was born Ella Beth Corrin in the back room of a bar owned and operated by her father and her mother, from whence her mother happily departed as soon as she was able, running off with a good-looking liquor salesman who had the good sense not to return for over a year. By that time Ernie Corrin's temper had cooled considerably, so that all Ernie did when Harold Flint called upon his establishment again was slap him mightily across the side of his head with a full bottle of cheap bourbon. When the salesman came to and staggered to his feet Ernie handed him a shot glass filled with the same cheap whiskey and thanked him for taking the bitch off his hands. "She wasn't no damn good at washing glasses anyway."

Ellie Beth was too young to remember that episode but she would always remember the bar, the dirty glasses, the filthy floors, the pool table that always needed brushing, and the tough, tired coal miners who struggled into the place every night after the whistle and stayed there drinking and fighting and telling lies by the thousands until late in the darkness when their sensibilities dulled to gray void, they stumbled home, some to wives and some to cold, lonely beds for a few hours of dead sleep before descending the next day into their burrows in the Kentucky hillsides, which swallowed them and squeezed the life out of them.

When the whistle blew at six the hole in the earth would belch them out and like bile they spewed out over the countryside. Some of them wound up at Ernie's, where for most of what they'd earned that day he would pour into them the brew that was able to help them forget what they were or help them to believe, for a time, that they were still alive.

And these men in her father's place of business formed Ellie's earliest memories. They fed her and burped her and rocked her to sleep; they carried her into the little back room, and they put her to bed there and changed her diapers and worried after her when she cried.

When she was a tawny-haired, blue-eyed toddler they bounced her on their knees and rode her piggyback on their sweaty, tired shoulders. And some of them secretly thought they could see in her face and her mannerisms a residue of themselves, remembering a swift tryst with her mother behind the outhouse or in it or on the bed in the back room during the hours after closing time when Ernie had drunk himself asleep. Several had even calculated down to the day, they thought, when the child had begun, and they loved her. And she them, especially those who were kind to her and gave her pennies and brought her ribbons and peppermints and pretty stones and crystals brought up from the mines.

But if there were those who loved her there were also those who watched with somewhat less or more than fatherly affection the quality of her physical growth. In her fourth and fifth years she began to show the first budding of an extraordinary beauty, and by eight or nine she had begun to take unusual interest in certain aspects of the stories she overheard, and she learned the meanings of words and phrases at ten that most women would never learn.

At eleven she was doing most of the work in the bar, even sweeping the floors and serving the drinks. She tended bar and racked the pool balls and brushed down the pool table.

As Ellie became older and more able to run the place, Ernie, owing to his increasingly sodden condition, became less able.

And then Ernie took up with Marie, a ne'er-do-well aging barfly. And from watching Marie and her father alone in the back-room bedroom Ellie sneaked-peeked her way into a fairly full knowledge of the differences between male and female and the fun ways of sharing those differences.

When Marie moved in, Ernie put up a thin partition between

his bed and Ellie's cot in the corner of the back room, but it wasn't enough to keep Ellie from knowing absolutely everything that went on. And, when Marie began sneaking out of bed at night shortly after the drunken Ernie had passed out, Ellie watched her as she opened the latch on the bar's side door and let in this miner or that. She watched as Marie satisfied the man on the floor or on a table or on the bar. And her eyes grew big when the man would give her money.

From that time Ellie began to feel that strange and wonderful warmth in her business end, and it felt good when she touched it. It felt wonderful when she rubbed it. Her first self-produced joy was a conversion, a glorious escape from the drab and thankless existence she'd followed for thirteen years.

For six months she satisfied her growing hunger by herself, rising high on the grunts and groans of her father mounted upon the woman in his bed. Then she plummeted to the blissful valleys of perfect peace while watching Marie and her customers from her bed in the darkened back room.

She began to see that men noticed her and that they couldn't take their eyes away when she leaned over to wipe tables in her short, outgrown dresses. She could feel their eyes crawling up her long legs and felt them boring into her. She liked it when they looked.

But one man more than looked, the whiskey salesman. He still came through Harlan and stopped longer now at Ernie's place. He knew who the child was, for he'd watched her grow up. But now he saw that the kid was her mother made over yet more beautiful. He ached to touch her and see her body and to plant himself into her. And Ellie knew it. She saw it in his eyes as he sat at the corner table alone, throwing down drink after drink, tipping her each time. Tipping was a rare thing at Ernie's, and even when it did happen Ellie dropped the coin in the tin plate behind the counter. Ernie had long ago taught her that tips weren't for her.

But tonight Ernie had gone to a dance with Marie, so she put the dimes in her own special little kitty that neither Ernie nor Marie even suspected. So she didn't care so much if he looked at her legs as she bent over to wipe tables, and she didn't mind his holding her hand and stroking her arm after he had pressed the silver coin into her palm.

When there were no more drinkers and she was alone with him he called to her and her heart beat faster and her breath was short.

"Just one more beer, Mr. Flint, then I gotta lock up," she said as she approached his table and set the beer down before him. He looked at her; it seemed to her he was not as drunk as he should have been. His gaze was clear and his words were "How old are you now, Ellie Bee?" He spoke softly.

"My name's not Ellie Bee," she said, grinning, "but I like it. I like that name. Just Bee. I like that best."

He smiled. "You're fourteen now or goin' on."

"Fourteen."

"You look eighteen." He took her other hand and held both of them tight in one of his while he poured his beer. Her hands were sweaty, yet cold and trembling.

"It's two, Mr. Flint." She tugged gently. "I have to lock up now." She knew he wasn't finished with his beer. She also knew that he really didn't want the beer at all.

He released her hands, "Then lock up, Ellie Bee." He watched her eyes. There was no fear there, and he saw a decision in them.

"I can't, with you still here." She waited for his answer.

He sipped the beer, then said, "Bee, have you ever been to bed with a man?"

Electricity went through her and her lips trembled as she said softly, "No."

He smiled again, his best smile. "Do you want to?"

Visions of the dark-haired Marie, legs wrapped around the back of a powerful young miner pounding away at her. Sounds of Marie groaning in unrestrained pleasure under Ernie's slowly grinding bulk. Memories of a hundred nights she had reached that joy by her own hand. But all she could bring herself to do was reply weakly, "I don't know."

"Come here," he said evenly. She obeyed, stepping toward him slowly. He turned his chair away from the table and sat facing her. She stood before him, holding one hand tightly in the other, waiting. He reached out and placed his hands behind her knees

69

and slowly moved them up under her dress past her firm round bottom, until he reached the top of her panties. Then he hooked his thumbs under the elastic and walked them down. He felt her open slightly as he pulled them down out of her crotch. And when he brought them all the way down to her feet she lifted her right foot and stepped out of one side, then the other. Then he moved his right hand slowly up her leg, whispering past calf and knee and expertly delving into the fine, silken down, which received a single probing finger. Back and forth upon her button the welcome finger slowly moved until her tormentor, seeing her eyes close and feeling the eager wetness, smiled, removed his hand and said simply as he started unbuttoning his shirt, "Lock the door."

When Ernie Corrin returned to his bar next morning he found his daughter standing behind the bar wiping it down. She smiled at him as he and Marie came dragging in.

Despite the tender soreness left by her first man, she felt good. Instead of being angry at them for staying out as she would have been under normal circumstances, she was glad they'd gone. Wished they'd go again.

Ellie Bee Corrin was a woman. She felt like a woman.

That night after Ernie was asleep she announced to Marie that she was cutting in.

"You little bitch! Ernie ain't gonna like this. He'll beat your goddamn brains in." Marie was furious.

"He'll never know."

"You think I won't tell him?"

"He might beat me, Marie. He's done that before. But you, he'll likely throw you out if he don't kill you."

And so for six months the child participated in Marie's little business, becoming a full partner and pursing half the take.

When Ellie had packed up more money than her father made in a year, she left. As she crawled out the window over her bed she heard the drunken snores of her father. "You'll never even miss me," she said. And she felt better than ever before in her life.

Enola lay alone in her bed, aware that the sound that awakened her was her mother putting out a man whose old truck spat and sputtered as it backed out into the gravel road. The dawn was an early red. The old quilts were a warm cocoon. As sleep sought to reclaim her, she was jolted alive again by the violent backfire of the old truck heading somewhere home; to what, she thought, to whom?

She sat up on the edge of the bed, swept the hair away from her eyes, and watched the cloud of brown dust billow up over the road outside. The red sky gave it a pink glow, and a slight breeze began moving it over into the trees to make them browner than they had been.

"Red sky in the morning," her father used to say. A sign of rain. How she prayed for rain. The pillow beside her own still held the shape of Jonathan's head from the night before. She must fluff it before morning, she thought. If rain doesn't come, Jonathan's family will lose their farm and have to move out. Where? "Somewhere," he'd answered, "and the sooner the better. That damn farm is better off dead. I've always hated it."

"But, if you move, what about . . . What about your mother," she had asked, wanting to say, "What about me? What about us?" But she could only say, "What about your mother?"

"She's cured," he said, not looking at her. "Healed."

"Healed? You mean she's well? Up and around?"

"Not yet. She's still weak, but she says she's healed. She felt it, like a bolt of electricity all over her body."

Enola was silent. Then, "How long before she's well?"

He didn't answer. His mother's sickness somehow caused him guilt. It was somehow a punishment for his sin. And now with Enola, God, how he'd sinned.

The preacher had said it, how sometimes God brings sickness and even death on a person's loved ones to wake that person up to his sin. He'd preached that many times. Doc Herman had called his preaching "criminal"; Frank Hyde had simply said, "Bullshit, I'd rather burn in hell than be in heaven with that man's god."

71

But Mrs. Hyde had said to Jonathan after that sermon, "If it took my life I'd gladly give it to bring you and daddy to the Lord."

He'd never told Enola that. He was beginning to feel the same old guilt again and she was part of it, most of it. But he couldn't help it; his dick led the way. He could but follow. He wanted to.

She thought of their loving; God, how she loved it. His grand thing filling her up. It made her shudder. She pulled the quilts up over her and watched the top of a great orange sun push up behind the brown dry stems.

She lay back again and placed his pillow between her legs. "How long? How long can this go on? Does his father know he comes here at night? Does mother know? Does she know we do it? No, they'd say something. Do something." It was a comfortable thought, that they didn't know. It was a warm safe truth.

But Mrs. Vinson did know. She knew all about Jonathan and Enola. She knew that they'd met often down at the spring, and then when winter came she knew he was crawling in and out of her window three or four nights a week. And she reasoned that he had to have learned from Enola how she made her living.

Ella Vinson lay still, smoking a cigarette and watching the morning sky brighten. She had heard Jonathan come in last night. She hadn't heard him leave, so for all she knew "he might still be in there right now on top of her. Lot o' room I've got to worry about that."

She didn't know what to do about Enola and Jonathan. The boy hadn't turned out like she'd thought. At first he was mannerly and kind, and on top of all that his father was known to own one of the better farms in the county. A nice match, she had thought. If she's that crazy about him, why not?

Then she'd seen him change, or at least she'd seen the real Jonathan Hyde come through. Sullen, lying, smart-aleck smile, eyes that called you names and laughed at you and accused you. She grew to hate him, but she was aware that while she hated him she was attracted to him. What an animal he was. How beautiful. A real prick. An A-number-one bastard, but a beautiful bastard. Ellie knew he'd watched her. Once he'd come over early in the morning to catch the school bus with Enola. He was sitting at the table drinking coffee with Enola when Ellie awoke and got out of bed without anything on. She didn't know he was sitting so that he could look into her room right at her as she stood at the mirror brushing her hair. When she looked up and saw him he didn't avert his eyes. He just stared, caught her angry gaze, then stared back. She turned from the mirror and walked toward the door of her bedroom slowly in full view. Then just as slowly she closed the door.

This morning, remembering Jonathan staring at her like that and knowing of his hunger for her regenerated her almost constant need for a man, and her thoughts turned to Bobby. Good Bobby. Good dumb Bobby. What would prison do to someone like him, soft and tender on the inside, hard as bone outside?

He had come to her room above a bar in El Paso. She heard three soft raps. She opened the door to see him tall and large and blond. His uniform was too small. Army. "You Ellie Bee, ma'am?"

He was back from the war and due to get out in two weeks. She pleasured him and, she couldn't help remembering, he pleasured her, so that when he came back again and again and again every day for four days she was surprised to find herself looking forward to his coming.

No one had ever been like him, strong and decisive, yet kind. And he didn't consider her a whore, but treated her every bit like a lady. Something in her went back to the old bar in Harlan, where the miners would hold her on their laps and sing to her and be like so many good fathers to her. He was like them and somehow more, so that when he asked her to marry him she said yes and was never sorry.

He had a small ranch left him by his aunt who had reared him, and he put it in hock to buy two thousand acres more. He raised whiteface and there they were happy.

He never referred to her past and she never brought it up. He satisfied her daily hunger, and she his. A year later Enola was born, and as the child grew up, so much like her father, Bobby would set her down in front of him and together they'd ride his old gray all over the ranch.

Ellie could remember now seeing them ride in after a day on

73

the range: the blonde child, hair flying in the wind like golden flame, holding on to Bobby for dear life. Screaming and laughing. Her voice in the distance like Christmas bells. Ellie was almost jealous, but Bobby had enough goodness and love for them both. "And ten more kids," he'd say laughing.

When Enola was thirteen they put the land in hock again and this time bought five thousand acres. Not much by local standards, but times had been good and Bobby was confident.

Then the drought came and the grass dried up on the ground and Bobby paid a premium for hay. Then hay became really scarce and they burned the spines off the cactus and fed the cattle cactus. Bobby was still hopeful all through the first tough year. But sometime during the second year Ellie began to see the lines of worry on him. He became thin and his smile waned.

But the banker had assured him that if he'd just pay the interest on his note they'd be satisfied till times got better. That was all that made life possible for Bobby Vinson in those days.

And then a week before the bank failed the banker came to call. Ellie saw him coming up the road, a speeding cloud of dust behind a shiny gray Packard. He was a fat man, short and balding; he wore a gray suit and a gray Stetson. "He's not hurting any," Ellie thought as he waddled up to the porch.

His message was brief and pointed. The bank was in trouble and would have to assume ownership of the Vinson ranch. It would have to be sold. "Sold!" she screamed. "You said if we'd just keep up the interest till times picked up."

"I'm dreadfully sorry, ma'am," and she could see he really was.

"Is there any other way?" she asked. "Is there any other possible way we could hold on a while longer?" She was studying the man and was sharply aware of his approval of her. As a banker he must be a good judge of horseflesh. And he knows a good piece of ass when he sees it, she thought, and was surprised at thinking again so suddenly in the old way.

"Perhaps we could make a trade, Mr. Buchanan."

"What do you mean?"

"Me for the ranch." He turned red, visibly red. And he loosened his tie and sputtered.

"I don't know exactly what you mean?"

"I just mean, Mr. Buchanan, that you and I could work out a deal to make it possible for us to keep the ranch and for you to have something in return."

"Like what, Mrs. Vinson?" He was trying to smile now, but couldn't.

"Like I just *said*, me for the ranch. It's fairly simple."

"Can't. Not my bank. Not mine alone. Couldn't write it off. Not just like that." He fidgeted. He wished he could write it off. Goddamn, what a bitch this was. What a goddamn woman!

She stood in front of him. His face was on the level of her breasts as she began unbuttoning her dress. His eyes were glued to her fingers walking down the front, tripping regularly over a button, leaving it undone, the dress hanging open.

"Then what about the original promise?" she asked, looking into his eyes. Smiling into his eyes. Hers half-closed, lustfully searching, promising pleasures he hadn't known in years.

"You mean just pay the interest? You mean that?"

"That's right." She said, stepping out of the dress. His gaze was unashamed. Then he looked at her face again. "You're a beautiful woman." His voice cracked. She pulled her slip off over her head. She wore no bra and only her panties remained.

"Not just this once, you mean, Mrs. Vinson."

You little shit, she thought. But she knew she had him. She'd done it.

"You come once a month," she said as she touched the front of his trousers with the back of her hand. He took her hand and stroked himself with it, harder.

"Once a week," he countered.

"Two weeks," she said, unbuttoning his trousers.

"Two weeks," he breathed. And, as the little fat man mounted her she couldn't help feeling good about it. Remembering it later she thought, "Any woman would have done the same thing, or should have."

When the bank went under, the banker, Buchanan, was dispossessed except for some houses and a used-car lot across the tracks, and Bobby Vinson was divested of everything but his wife and

75

daughter, the paper against his land and cattle having been sold to an Eastern land company.

"By law we've the right to take possession," they told Bobby when two agents came out to the ranch. Bobby's usually ruddy features were ashen.

"Then at least let me stay on to run the ranch," he begged. They agreed.

Ellie knew it was all they could do. Bobby had declared he'd never pick peaches in California.

But Enola watched in helpless disbelief as her world withered up with the ranch. It hadn't seemed so bad that the grass was gone and the well was dry. She didn't mind doing without new clothes and a saddle she'd been promised. But then the laugh went out of her daddy and the shine on her mother's face turned into cold, taut fear.

"I'm going to sell the stock," Bobby announced one night after Enola had gone to bed. Ellie stiffened.

"You can't, Bobby. It's not ours anymore, Bobby." She stopped darning and looked at him. He wouldn't look at her. He stared out the window into the black, still night. She saw the first of the gray in his full shock of blond hair.

"They *are* our cattle, Ellie. They're my cattle. Mine."

"You'll get caught." Listen to me, Bobby, she screamed inside. They'll catch you and . . .

"Goddamn bastards won't catch me, Bee. I'll sell only half. I'll truck 'em over into New Mexico and sell 'em. They'll be slaughtered and gone before anybody can trace them."

So he did. He cut the fence wire and ran the old truck in. Loaded them up. Three trips into Hobbs.

And they caught him. There was a trial, and at the end of it during the sentencing Bobby wept silently, bent forward, broken and heaving. And before they came to take him away he exploded, bellowing and swinging, cursing and kicking. He broke tables and shattered chairs. Someone finally slowed him down by a blow with a chair leg, and four men carried him, bound and trussed, through a side door, then down to the basement into a waiting cell.

76

Enola cried herself to sleep that night and Ellie sat with her on the edge of her bed, wiping the child's face with a damp cloth and trying to choke back the hurt and bitterness welling up in her.

Ellie drove the old truck into town the next morning and went to the county jail to see Bobby. A deputy led her back into the jail and down a flight of stairs into the basement block of cells. Bobby was lying on a metal shelf that served as a bed. The deputy rattled the iron door and stepped back behind Ellie and stood there waiting and watching as Bobby pulled himself up. He sat on the edge of the shelf and slowly turned his head. He saw Ellie and his eyes filled. He lowered his head again then. His hair seemed white. His shoulders drooped. She gripped the bars and fought back a scream that tore at her guts and retched within her. She clenched her teeth. She could not trust herself to speak.

"Where's Enola?" His voice was weak and raspy, his throat raw.

"Not now, Bobby, not like this. I didn't want her to see you now."

He still looked at the floor. "They're takin' me to Huntsville. Ten years. Twenty-one head. Ten years. Twenty-one head . . . Ten goddamn years . . ." The rasp became a whisper. "Ten years . . ." He didn't look up or indicate in any way that he knew that Ellie was leaving, running out of the cell block up the stairs and out to the truck, where she gripped the door handle, lifted her face to the white-hot sky, and screamed, a long wail until her breath was gone. Then she sucked it in again and screamed again, and if there were gods to weep with her they wept in silence. By her own strength she held her shattered self together and weeping more softly she pulled herself up into the truck and drove home.

She slept soundly that night. The next morning she drove into town and went to see Mr. Buchanan.

"I'm sorry, Mrs. Vinson. I'm truly sorry about all of what has happened." He stood up and pushed his old straight-backed chair toward her.

"I can't sit down, Mr. Buchanan. I've come for business." He put the chair back under the cluttered desk.

77

"You needin' a car, Mrs. Vinson?"

"Bee, Mr. Buchanan, just call me Bee. And I need a car, that's right."

"They takin' your truck?" He looked out past the rows of dusty black used autos. Her old truck was a monster still breathing steam.

"Truck, house, land, everything."

"How, um, how you figurin' on paying for it, Mrs. Vinson, uh, Bee?"

He scratched the short yellow stubble under his sagging chin and looked at her with one eye.

"I thought maybe you could think of a way, Mr. Buchanan, some way."

He grinned, looked down swiftly then up again, appraising in a glance the soundness of the investment. "I got a cot in the side room, Bee." He started for it.

"Easy, Buchanan, right now let's find me a car."

They finally decided on an old Ford coupe. Not the oldest and not the newest on the lot, but it seemed the most sound. So they shook on it and he turned toward the shack. "Shall we, uh, fix up the papers, Bee?"

"Not so fast, Billy."

"Yes, ma'am." He grinned. His teeth were yellow.

"Bring it to the house in the morning, early. And, Billy," as she pulled up into the old truck.

"Yes, ma'am."

"Take a bath and clean your teeth. Every time you come to see me. You've let yourself go some since the bank failed."

"I will, Miz Vinson." He was visibly ashamed. And that was the way she got the old pickup and that was the way she got a house in town and just about everything else she needed. By taking her men out or meeting them at other places she managed to keep it from Enola for a time. Enola first learned of her mother's activities at school, and Ellie knew the day her daughter learned. It was in her face, in her voice—hurt, anger, disbelief, and even fear in a frightened, animal sort of way.

And there was no explaining. No way to.

Then came Charley Stipes, tough, brawling, good-looking foreman of one of the new corporation ranches. He was a good john for Ellie, plenty of money, new company truck, and fun, until he saw Enola and came to the house when Ellie was gone. He came bearing gifts and bore his great gift in to Enola and liberated her, and in so doing made it possible for her to see her mother through new eyes.

Then Stipes told someone else about Enola, and word sifted down to the high school boys, Enola's classmates: "Enola puts out." And she did, often and well, and enjoyed it while it was happening and hated herself afterward, and hated the looks the boys threw her way without shame, the grins, one to another, and the whispers and the motions they made after she passed them in a group.

She wanted her mother to learn about it and scold her so she could throw it back into her face and blame her for it. But, though Ellie learned in time, she never said a word to Enola. But they left Perryton soon after to go to Fairview, Oklahoma. Then there was Jonathan.

And, thinking of him only a few hours before beside her on this hopeful morning of the red sky, she smiled and touched herself where he had been.

She heard her mother's footsteps and she removed her hand just as Ellie walked into her room.

She sat down on the edge of the bed and brushed the yellow hair away from her child's face. "I heard Jonathan come in last night."

Enola froze, closed her eyes, then squeezed them. But somehow a tear pushed its way through and ran down her cheek, then another, and Ellie scooped the child into her arms and held her. "It's all right, baby. I know how you feel about him. How could I be angry? What could you ever do to make me angry, child?" She rocked her and stroked her face, and she felt two arms reach around her. For the first time since Perryton, mother and child held each other. The hurt flooded out of Enola as she wept in huge, quaking sobs and Ellie absorbed the hurt into herself. She would hold it there, then carry it away to dispose of it, little by little, in shallow breaths and short bitter prayers to nothing in particular.

79

And for the first time in two years they talked. "Tell me about him, baby." And she did until Ellie understood Enola's need for Jonathan, for someone, companionship, friendship, kindness, call it whatever. Enola was a soft, warm soul, vulnerable to hurt beyond most; a lot like Bobby, with the kind soul and willing hand, unbelieving that life is evil and people are, until it is too late.

"Why did you do it, mama?" Enola asked, pulling away and wiping her eyes.

"What, baby?" She knew what, but dreaded the facing of it, even the sound of it.

"The men, mama, why?" Mrs. Vinson, Ellie Bee Corrin, wiped her own eyes.

"It's what I was before I met your father. It's what I did when I was thirteen, baby, in my father's saloon. I ran away from home and worked in a house for four years. After that I went to El Paso and worked on my own. It's all I know. It's a way to make a living and it's not so bad to me. To others it is, I know, but not to me."

"But daddy!"

"He doesn't know."

"But he'll be out."

"No."

"What do you mean?"

"We got a letter I didn't show you, baby. Bobby's sick . . . he's not in prison anymore. He's in a state hospital in San Antonio."

"But . . ."

"There are no buts, baby, and no maybes. He is not expected to recover."

"Oh, mother!"

"Not expected to recover, they said, just like that, not expected to recover, period. Goddamn." She stood up and walked swiftly from the room. Enola bounded naked out of bed, caught the sleeve of her mother's housecoat.

"What are we going to do?"

Ellie stopped, turned and held the girl's face softly between her hands. "Baby," she said, weeping quietly, "there's nothing we can do."

She wiped her eyes. Enola disappeared and returned with a handkerchief, and Ellie blew her nose. "Now . . ." she said, resigned to life, "I have to get dressed and get the old jalopy over to Cleo Springs. Fred Bolusky's going to put on a set of tires today. Old ones are gone, soon be in shreds."

Enola wanted to ask, "How did you pay for them?" But instead she said, "I'll do it, mama. You stay home and rest and I'll take the car over. I can take my books and study while I wait."

"Think you can drive it over there and back in one piece? It gets pretty stubborn about starting sometimes."

"Just choke it good, you said."

Mrs. Vinson walked Enola to the old car and cranked it for her. It took three times but it finally hit, and above the clatter she yelled, "Let Fred crank it for you when you start back." Enola nodded and turned the belching, bucking old machine around in the yard, biting her lower lip in concentration. Ellie waved and stood watching her daughter being chased by a cloud of her own dust. The wind was rising; cold and gritty it flapped her housecoat open. She hugged it to her, frowned, and walked toward the house. The sky was less red now in the east. "It'll never rain again in this cursed, goddamn country. Never again." So she entered the old farmhouse to think again about what to do. It was always the same, what to do. She slammed the door shut behind her and sat heavily in the wornout chair in the living room, put her face in her hands, and wept. What to do. It was always that.

Jonathan had not wanted to leave Enola's bed, so he lay angrily on his own bed looking out over the barren fields through the naked trees on the creek. From his upstairs window he could see the Vinsons' house, and when he saw the old truck leave he rose already dressed and went downstairs.

Frank Hyde was sitting on the edge of Mary's bed, holding her thin hand in both his own, when Jonathan walked through the room without looking at either of them.

Frank rose and followed him out the door, speaking softly at the porch's edge. "Don't go away today, Jonathan. Your mother's had a bad night. I think . . . I think she'll go today, son." His eyes pleaded but the boy did not look at his eyes but only at the window beyond which his mother lay.

81

"The doctor's on his way over now, Jonathan."

"I won't be long."

Frank watched Jonathan hurrying across the burnt-out wheat, and he became aware for the first time that morning of the strangeness of the sky, and for the first time in two years he did not want it to rain, not without Mary. Not with Mary waiting these years to see it rain. Then he realized that what he saw in the distant north was not a rain front, but dirt, black Kansas dirt. Dust storm! Frank wheeled and yelled for Jonathan. Too late, the boy had disappeared down into the creek bed.

Fred Bolusky had seen the approaching storm and was locking up to go home as Enola drove up. He was fat and showed brown teeth as he spoke to her. "No more gas today, ma'am. I'm closed."

"Mama said you're supposed to put new tires on this car today, Mr. Bolusky."

He stepped a little closer and squinted at her, "You Bee's kid?" She nodded.

"She said she had a *little* girl." He turned his head quickly and spat. Tobacco juice tumbled through the air and splattered into a hundred little rolling balls of dust. He changed the wad to the other side of his jaw, squinted one eye, and looked back at Enola, appraising her. "You better stay at my house till this storm's over, child," He said. A trickle of brown drizzled down one side of his chin into the creases of his unshaven neck. Enola shuddered. She revved the engine and wheeled out of the driveway, barely missing the gas pump and scattering gravel and spraying the laughing Bolusky with a fine layer of red dust.

Her hands were shaking as she steered the vehicle back on the road toward Fairview. The storm was behind her and she didn't think about it as she drove.

Jonathan had not considered that it might have been Enola who took the car—she seldom drove it—so he let himself quietly in the back door and shed his heavy coat. He heard the sound of water being poured into the bathtub, and he smiled as he moved toward the bathroom, undoing his trousers as he went.

The bathroom door was open, and he could see the white outline of her buttocks in the darkened room as she bent over the tub preparing the bath. He brought himself hard up behind her, grabbing her and running his member savagely between her legs, and not until she screamed did he realize that this was not Enola.

She whirled and brought her right palm mightily across his face. The impact snapped his head to one side, and her nails raked into his temple, leaving raw, red paths.

He was temporarily stunned by the blow and surprised by the realization of his error, so that Ellie had time to get to the door and into the hallway before he wheeled and lunged for her. "Why not, by God? A whore's a whore." He caught her left leg with his hand, and she kicked her other foot swiftly into his belly, missing her mark by inches. He grabbed her waist and pulled her down to him. She slugged her fist into his groin and escaped into Enola's room, slamming the door behind her. He charged the door, crashed it open, and caught her trying to climb out the window. This time he twisted her arm and locked it painfully behind her. He was breathing heavily. "You dirty son-of-a-bitch," she cried. "You dirty son-of-a-bitch."

"Shut up," he breathed, putting pressure on her arm. She winced and he smiled. He reached his other arm around her and fondled her breasts, one then the other. Larger than Enola's. Then he pinched her nipple and she cried out again. He roared with laughter.

"Now we'll see how good you really are." He whirled her around and faced her and fell onto her. Enola's bed received them as he fought her legs apart. "See if you're as good as your reputation," he said. "See if you're good as your daughter." And he plunged into her. She was dry there and tight so it hurt her as he did it, and she pounded his head with her fists and cut into his back with her nails. He pinned her arms with his own and lay on her and in her, moving only slightly, slowly back and forth, regaining his breath and savoring the moment of his triumph. And then Ellie found his ear with her teeth and clamped down hard upon it. He screamed and tore loose, lifted himself and slapped her twice across the face, then doubled his fist and clubbed her head. Then, smiling again, he said, "You are a wildcat. Your daughter never gave me a ride like this." After he hit her he began to notice, to his satisfaction, that she was

83

becoming easier and a moistening happened around his member. As he increased the speed and depth of his penetrations she began almost imperceptibly to move with him and almost against her conscious will her body responded, and when he felt the spasms beginning within her he stopped and looked down into her bruised face. He smiled his all-knowing smile. "You love it, don't you?"

Her eyes opened cold and hard, "You started this, you animal son-of-a-bitch. Now finish it." And she pushed up toward him.

He laughed and began again at a slower pace, then faster until he felt her arms around him, and when she exploded her body arched up toward him, driving him deeper into her. "My God, my God," she gasped. He laughed and all the harder rode her to a higher peak of ecstasy than he'd ever reached before with Enola or in his wildest fantasies.

The sky was darkening and the fierce north wind threw cutting bits of sand into Enola's face as she stepped down from the truck and ran for the house, pulling her old coat tighter around herself. But Jonathan heard neither the wind nor the car nor Enola's entrance. It was her shattering scream that pierced his glory. He turned and faced her onslaught and withdrew himself from the struggling Ellie just long enough to meet Enola's approach with a bone-cracking backhand across her face. She screamed and flew backward, crumpling against the wall, and Jonathan once again inserted himself to finish his efforts. Enola shook her head and fought to stay conscious. Ellie screamed and fought in the iron grip of the now-coming Jonathan, who half-way through the spurtings brought it out and let it play a long white sticky trail on Ellie's belly. She wept.

Enola, afraid to come any closer, whimpered, "Why, why, Jonathan?"

And he said, "Whores are for fucking, and she loved it, your mother loved it! She loved every minute of it."

Then for the first time Enola saw her mother's face and saw the black bruise on the right side of her face and saw the blood around her mouth, and she turned toward the wall and vomited. Jonathan lifted himself off Ellie, and she sprang to her daughter and gathered her to her.

Jonathan walked past them as he left the room and said to the girl, who would not look at him, "Whores are for fucking, Enola. You should know that."

As he drew on his clothes he became aware of the wind's roar and the blackening of the sky. Rain! Goddamn it. He didn't want rain; he wanted the farm to die and loose him from it. Goddamn. But as he closed the door behind him he smiled as a wall of dirt hit him in the face. Now we'll have to go to California. Leave the goddamn farm and go to California.

Like a giant he walked through the wall of dirt, and the wind whipped his hair into a flame as he marched, feeling every bit the victor. He had found he could have what he wanted. He could take what he wanted. His hand went to his crotch and he squeezed himself there . . . affectionately.

Chapter

5

Frank returned to Mary's bedside, where he found her asleep again, apparently resting better after a bad night. He sat beside her, unaware of his own weariness and hunger, and he allowed memories long put away to tread as they would across the paths of his consciousness. How pretty she'd been in those first days, so clean and fresh and quick. What a change the years had forced. The lined face, cadaverous skull and mouth gaping in sleep; the stench, yes stench, of dying breath. She had been brave. Her religion, maybe, had helped her. He hadn't hindered her faith for a long time now, years; let her believe it. Maybe some people needed something. But that goddamn preacher convincing her she was healed, stupid, egocentric son-of-a-bitch. God damn. He rose to go to the kitchen.

"Frank," she whispered. He turned and sat back down, took her hand in his own and squeezed it. She did not squeeze his but lay there like a stick, cold and bony. "Frank, it's not long now."

His throat tightened and he fought back the hurt rising like a tide within him.

"I thought I was healed. I really did, Frank, but it's not to be." She paused and closed her eyes again. Frank thought she had dozed off again but she soon said, "So weak. Just no strength a'tall, and I felt so much better when Brother Tarler prayed."

"You were excited over hoping to get well, Mary; that made you feel better for a while, then you tired out again," he said lightly. His voice was strained and high.

"You never did believe he'd done it, did you, Frank?"

She saw him squeeze his eyes shut to trap the tears, but they sneaked out and with great effort she managed to grip his hand ever so slightly. "You're a good man, Frank. So good; you just question so much."

He said nothing. He was in control of himself again. And she was silent for a while. I must question, he thought, a god who'd make such a pitiful mess of things, then burn people for not believing. Son-of-a-bitch. The only thing that ever came between us was religion. And even now it's still there. Son-of-a-bitch.

"Where's Jonathan Alexander?"

"He'll be right back, Mary, said he'd be right back. Went to get a book or something from Enola."

"Take care of him, Frank. I've let him go too much, let him be unmindful too much."

Then she began to breathe in short, uneven breaths and tears crept out of her eyes, gray and cloudy. He bent to wipe them away and he kissed her face. "Hurtin' again, Mary?"

"Not much, Frank. It's gettin' dark out; what time is it?"

"It's nearly ten."

"Rain?" The excitement was evident.

"No, Mary, it's dust again, comin' from the north."

"Oh, my—"

"Could you take some broth, Mary, or something?"

"Yes, Frank. And fix yourself something." He patted her hand and stood and she added, "No, don't fix broth for me. Fix me an egg." He looked at her as if to question. She hadn't wanted an egg for so long. "Yes, one of Lucy's big brown eggs. Do it real soft and salt it a little. Sure will be good." She grinned and he smiled back at her. And then he went to fix her a big brown egg. Lucy's egg. He chuckled. Her favorite hen. Old red Lucy. He laughed again. God, he wished they could have another breakfast together, spend another springtime together. . . .

The wind struck the Hyde farm and the outside kitchen door shuddered, then flew open, blasting Frank with the black dust, topsoil dry and fine as powder. He put an arm across his face and bolted for the door, leaned against it and latched it. He looked out the kitchen window toward the barn. Tumbleweed and dead leaves and old newspapers, frayed and tearing, obscured his view.

87

He heard the barn door banging "whap, whap" against the side of the barn, a gray-black hulk against the darkening horizon.

There was almost no sky as he headed into the yard, bowing himself to the wind. The sky had turned to dirt no lighter than the earth. Now no horizon and no sun. In ten minutes it was as if someone had put a box over the land. Frank made his way toward the banging door and caught it just as it hit the barn wall, leaned against it, and held it while his fingers explored the latch, to find that it was broken, torn loose by the wind. He left the door and entered the barn, and his fingers found his hammer hanging in its place. Then from a jar on the beam he took a handful of large nails and nailed the door shut, pocketed the remaining nails, and turned back toward the house.

Mary would need him now, more than the barn or the house. As he struggled against the wind with one arm he guarded his face. This storm's worse than the other one. More wind. Darker, colder. A bolt of lightning struck something off to the west. Lightning generated by the billions of dust particles grinding against each other. Frank felt the hair stiffen on his arms and a chill pierced his gut. He heard a car door slam, muffled against the roar. To his left with the help of another bolt of lightning he could barely make out the old doctor, bag in hand, bent toward the porch.

The kitchen door had blown open again and the house was as cold as the outside; dust covered everything. He pushed the door shut and had the first nail started in it when Jonathan approached the step. Frank opened the door for him and, seeing him, the dust plastered in the deep scratches on his face, said, "My God, boy, what in hell happened to you?"

Jonathan grinned. "I hit a dead limb coming home."

Frank did not grin. It was not a scratch of that nature. He motioned toward the sink and said gruffly, "Well, get yourself washed up, mama's been askin' for you." And a tired voice behind them both said, "It's too late now, Frank; Mary's gone."

The door slammed open again. Frank just stood there and let the cold, dirty wind blow through him. He turned and slowly shut the door and leaned against it.

Jonathan followed the doctor back into the cold room where his mother lay. The bed was coated with dust and her face was. The doctor used the wet cloth he'd taken from the kitchen and washed the dust from her face.

Jonathan Alexander stood at the foot of her bed unbelieving until he could hold no longer the avalanche that was breaking loose within him, and for the first time in his life knew feeling for somebody else. A mighty racking sob escaped him as he fled to the stairs and to his room.

Dr. Herman sat with Frank all that day and night as the storm howled. Dust covered the floors and the furniture, and despite efforts to keep it out by hanging wet blankets and rugs over the windows it still came, an unwanted black presence to choke them and cover them.

They sat for a long time in the living room, silently suffering the statement of finality that the body of Mary Hyde presented in death, covered by the patchwork quilt, itself covered now by dust.

The lights went out in mid-afternoon and they moved to the kitchen. By the glow of a coal-oil lamp Frank fixed a pot of coffee for Doctor Herman, and the doctor scrambled himself some eggs and fried some bacon, and he ate, urging Frank to do so also. But Frank wouldn't eat as he sat staring out the blackened window through his own reflection and into the storm. While he sat, a truth broke through and touched his consciousness and then almost withdrew, elusive; with his mind he reached for it and shut everything else out and trapped the thought there and examined it inside and out and weighed the sense of it, and the sense of it made him warm and comforted as nothing else had in his life for months on end. After the doctor had returned from upstairs to offer Jonathan some coffee, Frank put the truth into words, and the words were to him like the light of day. When the old man came down the stairs again and sat himself down again, Frank said quietly against the storm, "You can't mess around with reality." The old man was aware Frank had said something and he turned toward Frank and said, "I'm sorry, Frank, I didn't get what you said," and he leaned toward him.

Frank said to him, "We've fucked up this country. We should have had sense enough, we farmers, to know you can take just so much out of the land without putting some back in. Our sin is not loving the land, our sin is fucking it. Sticking our plows into it and making it pregnant spring after spring and pulling its produce from it without any thought at all about how it came to be. And one day the land dies and the grass dies and the trees die. And the land just dries up and blows away, goes away. That's what's happening out there now.

"If we had really loved the land, our plows would have been caresses to the earth, and we would no more have abused the practice of farming than a man who really loves his wife would abuse the privilege of the bed." He was silent with this for a few minutes and Doctor Herman began to understand.

"The bank will take half my farm but I'll not continue farming the other half."

"What are you going to do, then?"

"I'm going away, leaving the land to rest, and when the rain comes again and the land is healed I'll come back, and when I put a plow to her this time I'll use good sense. The land is a woman."

"You can't just up and go pick peaches in California, Frank."

"Texas."

"Texas? What can you do in Texas?"

"Work. With my own two hands. In south Texas, on the border along the Rio Grande, is a valley where men are loving the land, where they water it like a garden and feed it like a child, and warm it in winter. The land is rich and there, doc, I can work . . . for somebody else."

"And Jonathan?"

"Jonathan too. We'll take the old truck and go. I'll sell the tractor and equipment and we'll have enough to go on awhile. I'm only forty-four, doc. I can work and Jonathan needs to, too. Jonathan too."

Doc was silent; they were all leaving, all the men and women who made up this country were leaving. Drying up and blowing away, lean in body and sick of soul, blowing downwind and blowing away.

"You can't mess around with reality, doc. What is, is. That's the

90

way things are. No amount of believing otherwise will bring the land back. No amount of faith will make that farm out there ready for seed in the spring."

"Mary believed. God, how she could believe. And that goddamn fool preacher. Preachers are the worst fuckers of all. They don't take their living by force; they take it by fraud. They scare the living daylights out of women and children, tellin' 'em about burning hells and judgment days and what all, and without a single goddamn shred of evidence for any of it they turn right around after scarin' 'em and tell 'em all about heaven. And if only they'll believe they can escape hell and get on to heaven. Damnedest fuckers of all, mind fuckers, mind cripplers. Not by force but by pure black fraud against women and children scared to death of death and life and everything else. They don't have a chance against the mind fuckers. Not a goddamn whisper of a chance. You know, Ben, you know what I'm sayin'?"

"I know."

"You can't mess around with reality, doc, but they do, the preachers do. They can't convince somebody that they're never going to die. Even they can't buck reality that far, so they convince them that death's not real, that it's not really death. And it isn't hard to convince people of that because they really want to be convinced. God, how they want to be convinced. And some need to be, I guess." He stopped and thought some more for a few seconds.

Doc set a cup of coffee in front of him. He lifted the cup, sipped it, and continued: "Some need the hope, I guess, but they wouldn't need it so much if they hadn't been preached at about hellfire and pitchforks as children and if they'd been taught the natural way of things.

"But when they are convinced that death's not real they sort of get the idea that this life isn't real either, that this is just a shadow. The real thing's comin' up. The big show's in the next world. So they live all their lives in the shadow, convinced that if they really enjoy this life they won't earn the next. So the church hooks 'em in. Hooks 'em in. Hooks 'em in.

"And one of the saddest parts of it all is that if you believe that crap you have to look at all unbelievers as outsiders, as fools, traitors to the cause, and obstacles to faith.

"Did you ever think of it that way, Ben?"

"A long time ago, Frank, so long ago I've put it all away. You should, too. Do you no good to mull over it like this. Make you sick at the world. Put it away and go on like I did. And don't look back, to hell with it."

The storm began to die after midnight, and by early morning the light of a cold moon showed the great heaps of dirt against the barn and the fences. The back door was impassable, a drift four feet high up against it. Dust had sifted through the cracks in the door frames, making little piles at all the doors.

When the sun came up, red and eerie, there were no morning sounds. The animals and chickens were silent. Frank stepped out the front door and stood on the porch. A slight breeze began already to rearrange the ripples in the sand. The broken carcass of a sparrow lay on the porch. Frank stooped slowly to pick it up. He looked at it, then leaned against the house; and, not for the bird, he cried.

He heard a car rattle across the cattle guard just inside his front gate. He looked up and saw the preacher and his wife. Mrs. Tarler was pointing at some of the more spectacular mountains of sand that had drifted along the fencerows and behind the outbuildings. The preacher was intent upon the wheel, maneuvering through the lesser drifts that crossed the road in long, thin lines. When he stopped the car Frank was standing ten feet away on the driver's side, and something about the way his face looked made the preacher reluctant to open his door. Instead he rolled his window down halfway, and as he spoke his breath frosted the window. "Good morning, Frank. We came as soon as we could. The storm and all. How . . . uh . . . how's Mary?" The preacher looked at doc's car. It was plain to see it'd been here all through the storm. The fenders on the wind side were scoured shiny from the sand.

"Don't get out, Preacher. No need for you here now."

The preacher studied Frank intently, red eyes, haggard face, and what was that in his hand? Frank flipped the bird toward the car. It landed on the hood and slid up against the windshield in front of Mrs. Tarler. She screamed, putting both arms over her face, and whispered, ashamed and afraid, "Let's go, Louis."

Then the doctor stepped out of the house and walked to the car. He leaned toward the window. "Mary died yesterday morning, reverend. Now, you'd better go. Frank's had an awful bad night."

The preacher nodded his head and shifted into reverse, then watched Frank as he turned and walked head down toward the porch, turned and sat down on it and stared silently at his own tracks in the sand. Then he looked up and saw again the dead bird on the car and looked at Mrs. Tarler and smiled.

The preacher looked at Doctor Herman. "Sometimes he's crazy. I'll swear. Sometimes I think that man is possessed of a demon."

Doc's voice was gruff; anger spilled into it, "Go on, just get out o' here." Then almost to himself he said as he turned, "You stupid goddamn fool."

The preacher started the car then stopped as Jonathan, crying uncontrollably, stepped out the door, off the porch, and ran toward the preacher's car. He opened the back door and stumbled in. Then the car crept backward over the wasteland and was gone.

Frank would have stayed away from the church during the funeral and made himself present only at the interment in the churchyard, but he reasoned that his absence would only lend support to the pity already felt and oft expressed by the church people toward Mary because of her husband. So he went to church to quietly watch the preacher commit verbal obscenities over her body.

The pigeons that lived in the eaves of the little country church left their nests when the people began to gather, and as Frank approached alone in his truck he noted their great circular flight with dry respect. Even the birds have got sense enough to leave before the fool starts his bellowing. But he did not laugh. He remembered long past when he had driven Mary and Jonathan to church here then sat outside in the truck reading Kant's *Pure Reason*, or trying to read, for when the preacher realized Frank was still out there he preached as loud as he could to get the word of God at him. The pigeons left that day too, Frank recalled, and had every Sunday since.

The preacher had no lack of audience the day they buried Mary

Hyde, and he had planned well for it. They had taken Jonathan home with them and Mrs. Tarler tried her best to comfort him; but he would not be comforted. "What can we do, Louis?" she asked. "The boy's grievin' more'n he can take."

"Let him be. God's talkin' to him. Let God bring him to his knees. We can't do God's own talkin' for him."

When it came to convicting souls of their sin and bringing them around to penitence Reverend Tarler believed in the legitimacy of any means at his disposal, and he was ready for Frank Hyde this time. "God has brought him low. He's been so proud in his wrongdoin'. Too proud. God took Mary so's he could get to Frank Hyde's crusty heart," he told his wife, and when she questioned this he said, "Mary told me herself she would gladly die, she said, 'if it would only bring Frank and Jonathan to Jesus.' She said it herself. You know yourself, Minnie, how she always prayed for the Lord to do his will with her."

So the preacher pondered his possibilities and thought of the glory of bringing such a hardened sinner to his knees. And he was prepared to do full justice to his high calling at the funeral of Mary Hyde.

The little church was already full when Frank arrived, and a crowd was gathering outside under a cold gray sky. Doctor Herman was standing on the steps awaiting him, and he and Frank entered silently, enduring the hurried whispers and craned necks that followed them to the front pew, where Jonathan sat alone, his head bowed, a few feet away from the plain gray casket at the altar rail. Frank sat beside Jonathan. The preacher sitting on the platform perusing his sermon notes saw with satisfaction that Frank put his arm around the boy's shoulder and his strong hand squeezed Jonathan's arm. The man is ready. God has brought him low. The Holy Spirit has tendered his heart.

When the preacher stood to deliver his sermon he was a man, some would later say, upon whom God had laid a great burden, for his hands shook and he felt within him that strange and trembling power that men feel who are about to deliver a blow for righteousness. He did, as always, stand at the pulpit with his head bowed and his eyes closed, clutching his Bible to his breast, praying briefly for the anointing of the Lord. When he did this there was not a whisper, not a titter, and mothers with small children fairly shuddered to think their own infants might, during this time, split the holy silence with some hungry wail. For it was well known that upon any disturbance this stern man of God would lift his fat hulk to full stature and would direct toward the unfortunate offender a pained expression of long-suffering mixed with a halfsmile designed to communicate that, while the infraction was unpardonable in the house of God, it would be kindly overlooked this time. All was quiet this morning. When the preacher finished his silent prayer he looked down upon a sober crowd. They had attended his funerals before.

"What I am going to say today," he began, "would be ill received by those who know naught of the Spirit's doings. For He has been heavily upon me, bearing down upon my consciousness. Today God's own finger is upon my back." He paused and traveled the faces of his congregation. "I can feel it," he said heavily, and they believed he did.

"I shall take as a text from the Word of God the most terrible words one could imagine to be spoken upon the untimely departure of a loved one. I read from Proverbs, chapter fifteen, verse twenty-five;

" 'The Lord will destroy the house of the proud.' "

He paused, laid down his Bible, gripped the sides of the dark old pulpit, and again scanned the faces to detect whom his text might have troubled. He did not examine the face of Frank Hyde, but he could have seen clearly the disgust heaped upon sorrow that Frank felt at that moment.

"When a man or a woman comes to God fully and completely and without hint of reservation," he paused, "he places himself absolutely in the hands of God. He belongs to God and is God's for God to do with as He pleases, as He in His infinite wisdom sees fit.

"In the hand of God lived our own Mary Hyde, in the hand of God, and as totally devoted to Him as anyone I have ever seen in thirty years in His work. And it was that devotion to God that caused her to become the most honored of His creatures, an instrument of His own design; a tool in the Master's own hand. And it was her desire to be used that brought to her so great a

95

suffering and finally death." The preacher closed his Bible and clutched it to his bosom and looked at his congregation and at Frank Hyde and Jonathan.

Frank sighed heavily. The doctor shifted his position. They both could see clearly now the tack being taken. Jonathan was receptive, guilt-torn, and malleable, and the preacher knew it.

"God works in mysterious ways His wonders to perform. And His ways are not our ways. So we cannot always see clearly what He is about. But in these times and during the long-running tragedy of this place," and his voice fairly boomed as he raised his arms and motioned to the windows and to the cold and lifeless landscape beyond, "in these times God has done almost all He could to mercifully bring a wayward people to their knees. Five years ago this land, this very land, was as green as the newest grass in spring. Its abundance surpassed that of any place on earth. Wheat, corn, cattle, and every good thing a people could want and more. But there was one thing that shouldn't have been here, one thing that carried in it the seeds of all the ruination you now suffer daily. That one thing was a sin, seemingly small in those days but a more terrible sin than ever any other. The most dangerous sin in the world, the sin of pride" and the windows rattled with the sound of his voice. Then he almost whispered, "The sin of pride. Pride."

He laid his Bible down again in the pulpit, then thumbed through it until he found what he wanted, looked up, then walked slowly away from his pulpit with his head bowed. He stopped at the altar rail, reached over and laid his right hand on Mary's casket and prayed: "Our Father, give us grace to accept this tragedy in a spirit of wisdom. Let us not cast aside this sacred sacrifice of Thy humble chosen. And give me strength this morning and fill me with spiritual power. Power to lead a people one last step to Thee. And help each of us in this house to search out the hidden sin of pride and slay it as a man would slay a viper in a sheepfold.

"Amen."

When he looked up and out over the church, the people saw a man weighted down. "I beg of you to listen carefully to me this morning, for I have never spoken under the Lord's anointing in

96

the same measure as I feel this morning. Nor have I ever been so called upon to direct the accusing finger of God's wrath as I feel today. And here before the remains of this, God's child . . ." He looked down upon the casket, squeezed shut his eyes, great tears rolled out of them; then he shook his head. "And here before this sweet sacrifice I dare not refuse to follow the leadings of the Spirit. I believe Mary Hyde would want me to be as direct as possible today, for it was for this that she chose to die."

Frank Hyde sat quietly, trembling with a mixture of unbelief and pure disgust. "Cruel," he thought but he showed nothing outwardly, and the preacher, standing again behind his pulpit, continued:

"When this land was blessed and our cupboards were plenteous and the banks were bustin' out with gold, did we give God the glory? Did people tithe their income? Did they even tithe their tithe? Did they go to church? Did they build a monument to God's goodness? Did they use their new-found riches to send the gospel around the world?

"No," he bellowed.

"No." He slapped his Bible on the pulpit. "No, no, no.

"To God's face we said 'No.' The people said 'No!' *You* said 'No'," and his finger roamed above the crowd and the people cringed.

"No, you bought more land and more cows and more tractors and built bigger barns and bigger banks!

"And standing between you and the light of God's love were your riches and your pride.

"Now right here in the Bible I find something about pride: 'Pride and arrogancy . . . do I hate,' saith the Lord God in Israel. And in sixteen five: 'Everyone that is proud in heart is an abomination to the Lord.'

"So the Lord took your riches away. To save you from pride, from your own sin. He just took it away.

"He caused the sun to shine hot and hard and he caused the rain to vanish. The very clouds were dry and the river gave up its cooling waters.

"It's all His, you know. It's all God's. He can take the rain away and bring it back. He can fill the river or dry it up. He can bring

97

thundershowers or dust storms. It's all His. He controls it, and to bring us to our senses He held back His favors to make us see that all our gain was God-got and not got by our own hand or our own wit. He took it away to bring us to our knees again.

"And it worked.

"This church has been full and flowing over for more than a year now. Men have begun worshiping God that never did before. Whole families have given themselves to Him, right here at our own mourners' bench. So you see, all that dust and dry out there are for good. But that's not good enough." The preacher stopped and roamed the faces in the crowd. "That's not good enough. When we *all* get back to God the rain will come and the crops will grow and the stock will fatten on the pastures. When we *all* come to God.

"This was Mary Hyde's task, her own mission, her own one purpose in life and death, to bring her family to Jesus."

A sister behind Frank whispered, "Help us, Jesus." Then another, "Help us, Jesus." Frank's face did not change; he continued to follow the preacher with his eyes, but Doctor Herman could see the strength in his sinewy wrist as he gripped the pew with his right hand.

A woman in back wept aloud. Somebody else blew his nose. The preacher moved back down behind the casket. "When Mary learned she had a dread disease she sent for me and asked me to pray for her family. Not for herself, for her family. And she told me that she would gladly ask the Lord to take her away if it would only bring her family to God." Jonathan sobbed openly, deeply. Frank gave the boy his handkerchief and then glared at the preacher, sought contact with his eyes, but the preacher would not look at him.

"And Mary Hyde considered all of us to be her family. Her brothers and sisters in Christ, and as He died to save us so she died to bring us closer to Him, to serve as an example of humility and grace." He returned to his pulpit, motioned his wife to go to the piano, where she began playing softly "Jesus Is All I Need." He spoke again.

"I believe Mary would have wanted me to do this today, to

98

open the mourners' bench to anyone who wants to rededicate his around the altar rail, and reaffirm your place in God's graces, do so now. Do it now. Come. Come!"

Jonathan Hyde was the first to kneel there at the foot of his mother's coffin. Then they came; almost the whole church, shaken by death and fear, came forward and crowded around, kneeling at the altar, and at the front pews, and in the aisle.

Frank stood and the doctor with him, and as the preacher watched in disbelief, they made their way tiredly around and over the weeping, wailing bodies, and left the church. They went to the grave and stood beside it and waited.

The people soon came pouring out of the church, and they stood outside waiting for the casket to exit, borne by six elders, down the stone steps and through the parting crowd. They put her in the ground then; the preacher read his words and the people slowly went away in old trucks and wagons and on foot. But Frank stayed, and the doctor, beside the grave as an old man and a young man put the dirt in, the old one pausing now and then to rest, and the young one stopping to light a cigarette, which he smoked to its end then flipped into the grave, almost filled now, then retrieved it when he realized what he'd done, apologized: "I'm sorry, Frank," and ground it into the dust with his heel.

Jonathan stood by the church with the preacher. The preacher was talking to him but Frank could not hear what he said as he watched the workers round off the top of the grave. They gathered up their shovels and from behind a tree took a pick and a file and a jug of something, and they left.

Frank felt a hand on his shoulder. He turned his head and faced the preacher. "Frank, Jonathan is going home with you now. He's just given his heart to God. Mary would be pleased with him."

Frank shook the meaty hand off his shoulder, turned, and started to walk away, then he stopped, whirled, and drove his fist into the preacher's soft paunch, and when the preacher, gasping in pain and shock, grabbed his middle, Frank's right hand smashed his jaw, lifted him off the ground and dropped him on the dry, hard earth. He crawled away from Frank, slithered frantically away.

He lay in the dust on his side holding his gut, rocking back and forth in pain. He tried to spit but could not, his jaw slack and dripping red.

Frank was sorry then, and turning away and walking swiftly toward his truck, he cried aloud and the great groans that escaped him were for Mary and Jonathan and for the preacher and for a damnfool God.

PART II

Chapter

6

There is something in the living that wants to be near the bones of its dead, something inherent that makes dear even the stinking remains of those most loved in life. Perhaps it is because the living think the dead would have wanted to rest in proximity to their homes in life, near the living; so the patriarch Jacob, dying in Egypt, commanded his sons to remember, when they returned to Canaan, to carry his bones home with them.

Or maybe it comes from a strong hope that those bones aren't really dead, and like Ezekiel one foresees those old bones dancing back to life to share again the joys known together, before the rude knife severed the cord and sent one into blackness, leaving the other to run grasping after hope like a drowning man grasping at straws. Would it were so. Would that the dead could live again.

But Frank Hyde could leave Mary's grave and go away because there was none of Ezekiel in him. Jonathan could leave because he believed the preacher that his mother wasn't really dead and, as the preacher said, would watch over him, be with him. And Jonathan could leave because he hated the farm and because of Enola; that was finished. So he and Frank boarded up the house and loaded the hand tools and Frank's books into the truck. Doctor Herman came out to see them off. Frank spoke to him about Enola and Mrs. Vinson while Jonathan was in the barn.

"Go see the Vinson woman, doc. I think Jonathan did something over there that day he came home all scratched up. He hasn't made a move to go back, and before it happened he was spending all his time over there."

"You think he hurt the girl?"

"No, not so much that. I want you to do something for them. Tell Mrs. Vinson if things get tough she's welcome to move in over here. Jonathan told me months ago that they lost their ranch over in Perryton and that her husband was sent to prison trying to get it back."

The doctor was thoughtful, trying to decide whether to tell Frank about Mrs. Vinson, but Frank knew. "I know what she's doing, Ben. It doesn't matter. The house is empty. I won't need it for a long time, and a house lives longer if somebody's living in it."

Doc Herman motioned toward the house. "Then why'd you board it up?"

"Because Mrs. Vinson might be too proud to accept."

But she wasn't. She didn't indicate to the doctor one way or the other. But as soon as he left she began packing. Her rent was due for the next month and she'd had to pay with money here, no flesh barter. And the Hyde house was nice, plenty of room, dishes, furniture, and she could afford a phone, good business. A plan took immediate shape, a large beautiful house, no more trips to Enid.

So Ellie Vinson and Enola moved in, and the house became known near and far as "Ellie Bee's," and she used it as it was until times got better. She entertained rich and poor, and as the years rolled by and she made enough money she carpeted the house and bought red velvet drapes and got new furniture. When the well started yielding more water she hired a gardener, and she had a lawn and roses and flowers. At Ellie Bee's were the best girls with the sweetest favors men ever paid for. And the best and sweetest of them all was the madam's daughter.

Frank and Jonathan had driven all night, both unable to sleep, Frank, grief-ridden, angry, cursing whatever God there should have been but wasn't and, Frank knew, would never be, kicking himself unmercifully for being too weak of mind to understand the meaning of it all. It made no sense without some kind of higher reason, that's true, some kind of God, some benevolence somewhere in the universe, but the gods of men made no sense either, fiends, tormentors of the weak, tormentors of the good, silent at evil. Ah, to be able to believe, to have such naïve faith as accepts a good God and the dead living again. What comfort. What peace to know, even to hope, that our loved will live and we will see them again. My God, what joy! But for Frank the knowledge that the book which offered hope was the same that imposed the madness of hell was too wicked for a genuinely good man to accept. Words formed his feeling for him, came to him and solidified his hurt, gave order to his broken thoughts as the old truck ground its way out of the ruins of their lives and toward hope.

Words . . .

They who by the thought of death and molding dry to dust ten thousand years are driven not to faith are driven all at least
    to Hope
    in something else
    beyond the grave.
Something more than coffin's cramped confining?
Shredded time unwoven satin tickling day-old growth of bearded upper lip untrembling?

"Are driven all at least to Hope." But Frank found it hard to hope.

But as for me I cannot bend my brain and press it down to lie at quiet, accepting peace within a box of silent faith in some Great God's Grand Plan to resurrect the dead and make things right for all the hurt, the savage acts, the early dead, the misery, the midnight wondering where the twisted minds, the souls of broken hearts are now.
Damn!
I cannot bend my brain
I will not bend my brain
I cannot mend my brain in places bruised by harsh reality unending tragedy.

I cannot.
Not for comfort's sake.
Not for peace.
Not for God.

The words lent him courage to continue. A man can be proud of his integrity. "I will not bow down."

And Jonathan couldn't sleep the night of the journey because his nuts ached. It had been over a week since that day at Enola's and he hadn't touched himself, a phantom of guilt hovering over him day and night, the preacher's words digging into his tortured mind. When he closed his eyes and dozed, his member, oblivious of mourning, rose forth and he dreamed, the same dream every time he closed his eyes. Naked, standing behind Enola, white and nude bending over the bathtub in the darkened room. There was that glorious second when he swiftly and expertly glided himself into her. She fought and then he saw that she wasn't Enola. She wasn't Mrs. Vinson. She was his mother. And the angry voice of the preacher kept saying, "You did this to her. You did this to her...."

Frank's hands guided the vehicle across the great King Ranch. Shallow patches of fog drifted across the road and the truck shot through them unconcerned. Frank watched the whirling ghosts chase their path briefly then rush back to fill the hole they'd made. The eastern sky gradually turned from black to deep royal blue and then to pale green. Distant purple clouds sent pink radiants into the waking sky.

Frank had first learned of the Rio Grande Valley of Texas from Army buddies in France. Some of them had been stationed in Texas prior to shipping out and several of them had planned to return after the war. A few had served under Pershing against the border raids by bandits like Pancho Villa.

The valley, not a valley at all actually, but a kind of delta, a strip of the most fertile and best-watered land in the world, forty miles wide and over a hundred miles long, stretched luxuriantly from the Gulf of Mexico up the great Rio Grande to Fort Ringgold.

There was oil there and gas, but the valley's most valuable

106

resource was its dirt, for ages growing nothing but cactus and grass and scrub mesquite, flooded almost annually by the silt-bearing waters of the Rio Grande, gathered by a thousand streams from the hills of New Mexico, Colorado, and even Wyoming. The first farmers found a rich brown land and a river. So they built great canals, criss-crossed the new land, hundreds of miles of life-giving man-made rivers. The valley floor was green with two and three crops a year, a virtual garden, the "Magic Valley," its people called it, for almost any crop imaginable would thrive.

Visitors and newcomers from the north had to drive across two hundred miles of often dry, near-barren ranchland, and when they entered the valley it was like stepping out of a desert into a greenhouse. One becomes aware, especially in winter, of the dramatic change in the color of the landscape, from dry winter brown to a warm emerald green. Then, in the distance—palm trees, great Washingtonians, stately, sixty, seventy feet tall, thousands of them ramrod straight, bearded giants, tropical wonders standing erect over the roads and along the edges of fields of carrots, onions, beets, tomatoes, turnips, and on and on and even in winter, for the frost seldom kills this far south.

And where the fields aren't filled with vegetables or cotton or miles of some golden grain there is the citrus, deep evergreen foliage, tons of oranges, grapefruit, the delightful tangerine, and the giant ponderosa lemon.

Jonathan sprawled out, leaning against the door, his head against the window, eyes closed. When Frank spied the first palms, distant sentinels on the valley's northern edges, he looked at them a few minutes then said, "We're going into the valley now, Jonathan."

"I'm not asleep," he said, straightening up. And they entered the Rio Grande Valley in the soft light of dawn. The earth had been brown and gray the night before, but now they drove into a world of greens. They passed a field of cabbage almost a mile across, the heads gray-green against the deep brown earth. And when they neared the first orange grove Frank slowed the truck, pulled to the shoulder, and stopped. They walked into the trees and examined the golden fruit. Jonathan plucked off two choice

107

ones and put them into his jacket pockets, then took another and began to peel it. Frank chose a large one and did the same. The aroma was sweet and fresh.

Jonathan unzipped his jacket and threw it over his shoulder as he walked back toward the truck. The orange was good. The weather was warm. The country was beautiful. But farms. Always farms. He cranked up, walked around to the driver's side, opened the door and pulled himself in. Frank stood beside the truck and removed his own sweater before getting in. "Where to?" Jonathan asked as he pulled out onto the highway.

"You tired?" Frank asked.

"Nope."

"I mean sleepy. You want to get some sleep before we look around some?"

"You?" the boy glanced aside at his father, whose eyes were exploring the landscape.

"No. Let's look around some, then find an old Army buddy of mine. Maybe he can head us toward something constructive." He watched the boy as he expertly shifted into second gear, then high, his eyes on the road, his mind far away. Where? His son was a constant trouble to Frank and had been since he was old enough to walk. Frank had wanted a son, and when Jonathan was born Frank felt that a part of himself had been reborn, a young Frank born of a union with the woman he'd chosen, tempered by her tenderness and her goodness, a son to love and romp with, to teach to shoot and ride and farm and fight. A mind to mold as his father had molded him. Someone of kindred spirit, more even than Mary, to share ideas with. That was what he'd wanted in Jonathan.

Then came the war, and before the baby could say a complete sentence Frank was in the trenches in France. Damn the war! For when he returned from fighting the Kaiser his son was not his own and maybe never would be. But there was hope. If any good came out of losing Mary, maybe it would be in the act of throwing father and son together.

But Jonathan had no such sentiments toward his father and never had had. Returning from the war as he had done, long gone and dearly missed, meant returning also to Mary's bed, thereby very abruptly removing Jonathan from it and jolting him immediately from the position of most important sharer of his mother's every breathing moment to what amounted to exile, a bed of his own in a room of his own—outcast. The child never quite forgave either of them. He would go with his father to Texas, for the ride. And if there was something there to interest him he could bend himself to fit for a time into his father's good graces. He could feel even now, with an uncanny sense of another's needs, his father reaching out for him, and with an uncanny ability to charm his prey he turned to his father and said, "It's really great down here, isn't it, dad?"

Perfect. Frank Hyde smiled at his son for the first time in nearly a year. And Jonathan smiled back.

Almost anyone in Hidalgo County, it turned out, could have told them where to find Jedediah Strunk, who, not at all to Frank's surprise, had gotten himself elected constable of the little town of Hidalgo and had made himself famous by chasing thieves and bandits all the way into old Mexico and bringing them back, in various states of life, for trial. He had been shot, several times, stabbed, and slashed open by drunken machete wielders, but he had survived. Jed Strunk was a giant, two heads taller than even Jonathan. His eyes were gray and they fairly twinkled as he threw his arms around Frank. "Franklin Pierce Hyde! What in the devil's hell you doin' down here? Thought you was an Okie through and through!" He turned to Jonathan. "This that kid I heard so much about?" As he shook Jonathan's hand the boy assessed the big man's raw strength and his athletic control of it.

Frank said, "Jed Strunk, this is my boy, Jonathan."

"Jonathan Alexander. Hell, I ought to of know'd you way yore paw raved on about you in the war." Jonathan's eyes went to Frank, a hint of surprise in them. "Gonna outgrow the old man some, ain't he, Frank?" Jed motioned toward a chair in the corner. "Sit down, son." Jonathan sat and Jed rolled his slat-back chair around his cluttered desk and pushed it toward Frank. "Well, what's up?"

So Frank explained the situation in Oklahoma and told him

109

about Mary. Jed sensed the hurting in him as he talked about Mary, quietly and reluctantly. His own wife had left him years ago, and he'd never gotten over the pain of it. He steered Frank away from his misery. "Ain't no goddamn depression down here. You come to the best country in the world." He spoke sincerely. "You lose your land up there, Frank?"

"Nope, able to keep most of it. But it won't grow wheat without water."

"Well, old buddy, you might's well climb into that buggy and go back up there and sell the whole blamed mess 'cause once you get a taste of this green valley you ain't a-wantin' to never leave." He squinted one gray eye when he made a point and butted his head forward, his graying hair splayed across his forehead.

Frank smiled, remembering Jed telling his whoppers in camp. He would make a believer out of anybody. "From what I've seen of it you're probably right."

"So now you're lookin' for a job."

"Right again."

Jed turned his head toward the door behind him and yelled, "Elizondo!" A skinny brown-skinned man popped into view. He wore a bedraggled uniform, a thin mustache, and a silver star. He had plainly been sleeping. "Elizondo, this is Mr. Hyde. I'm going to hire him on as deputy!"

Elizondo eyed Frank with suspicion bordering on instant dislike. "But, Meester Strunk, I am already your deputy." He said it quietly as if painfully explaining something very difficult to a child.

"Well, I need two deputies." Elizondo's face brightened and he reached over to shake Frank's hand. "Very happy to meet you, Mr. Hyde."

Frank stood up, "None of your goddamned shenanigans, Jed. I'm a farmer and I'm going to do farm work."

"Easiest job in the world, Frank," Jed asserted. "Sit on your lazy ass most o' the time."

"And the rest of the time you get your fool head shot off. Nope, not for me." And he grinned at Jed. "I'm a coward pure dee, Jed. I've got good sense to boot."

Jonathan wanted his father to take it, wanted him to *be*

110

something. A goddamn dirt-eatin' farmer. Shit. He eyed with admiration the heavy six-gun on Jed's hip.

"Well, you'll have a hell of a time makin' a livin' as a farmhand." Jed really wanted Frank with him. "Damn wetbacks'll work for nigh nothin', sun up, sun down seven days a week year 'round."

"Got to be somethin', Jed. I can wait on it a little spell. Get Jonathan in school and look around a bit."

"Hell, Frank, why not? You an' me'd have a hell of a time."

Frank was patient. He loved this big bear of a man. It has been said that men who drink together come to know each other and that men who go whoring together become closer than brothers. It is not so true. Men who kill together and stand together in death are nearer in soul than men can otherwise be. And how could he say to this man, in front of Jonathan and Elizondo, that he was ill of soul and only the land could heal him, not bullets and knives and opening wounds closed long ago.

His eyes pleaded and somehow Jedediah understood. Frank had always been a little strange, a little away at times. But he was real, by God, as solid as they come.

Elizondo asked, "Meester Jed, what about Mrs. Ortega?"

"Goddamnit, Lupe, why don't you mind your own business?" Then good-naturedly. "Why don't you go in there and lock yourself up and go back to sleep?"

"But I wasn't sleeping! I was cleaning the cells."

"And you got a little tired after last night, huh, Lupito?" He winked.

"Jus' a leetle tired maybe," and he disappeared, grinning, into the back of the building.

"Who is Mrs. Ortega?"

"What Mrs. Ortega?" Jed answered dumbstruck.

"Would she have any relationship to Jimmy Ortega?"

Jonathan asked, "Who is Jimmy Ortega?"

Jed looked at Frank incredulously. Then to Jonathan, "You really don't know?"

"I didn't tell him anything about the war, Jed. When I got home I hung it up for good."

"Just like that?"

"Jed, goddamnit, just like that."

"It hurt that much?"

"It's not that, Jed. I just never wanted to talk about it."

"I know. I remember. You always were quiet. Thinkin' all the time. Always carryin' a knapsack o' books. Damnfool professor." He slapped Frank on the back and looked at Jonathan, "Come on, son, we'll go see Ellen Ortega."

"Elizondo!" Jed bellowed. A clanking of cell doors. The officer appeared. "Lupe, I'll be out at Ortegas'. Hold down the fort." Jed placed his dirty Stetson jauntily on his head.

Elizondo immediately pulled the chair around behind the desk, sat down, placed his booted feet one over the other, and leaned back very officiously. Jed took a big cigar out of his shirt pocket, placed it in Elizondo's mouth and lit it for him, striking the match expertly with his thumbnail. "Now, your excellency, if you'll excuse us we'll get the hell out of your hair."

Elizondo extracted the cigar, blew a perfect ring of smoke, placed the cigar into the ring with one hand, and very deftly pulled it through with the other. He pursed his lips, the performer pleased with himself. "You are excused, Meester Sheriff. As you can see, I am bery beezy." Frank laughed out loud.

Outside Jed informed them, "Don't let that silly little clown fool you none. He's funnier'n hell but in a mean situation he's colder'n a witch's tit."

"Could have easily fooled me," Frank admitted.

"Nope. Uglier'n shit on a sharp stick. Only trouble is he spends half his time in Reynosa with the *putas* and can't stay awake on duty.

"What's a *puta*?" Jonathan asked.

"They ain't for you, boy. You don't even need to know about 'em." Jed grinned wickedly at Frank and Frank silently agreed. Hell yes, he thought, don't tell him about the goddamn Mexican whores.

Jonathan rode with Jed and Frank followed them in his truck. Frank was uneasy about meeting Mrs. Ortega and her children.

"Jimmy Ortega was the man that saved your paw and me's life in France," Jed explained to Jonathan. "Got killed doin' it."

Jonathan looked at Jed questioningly.

112

"His widow and her two kids still run the farm down here on the river. Damn good farm too."

"How'd it happen?" Jonathan wanted to know.

Jed pushed his hat to the back of his head and slowed the car. "We was runnin' from the Germans. They'd broke through and tore hell out of us and somehow eight of us got out of it and was high-tailin' it out o' there, me and your paw and Jimmy and five other guys, two of 'em Frenchies. Well, we blundered right into a whole mess of 'em and they might' near wiped us out. Got the two French fellers and three Americans right off. They surprised us with grenades, then started pickin' us off. Got me in the neck with shrapnel." He pulled back his shirt collar and showed the traces of an ugly white tear in the side of his neck. Jonathan was transfixed. "Then I got hit right in the ass." He chuckled. "Ain't gonna show you that'n."

"Did Dad get shot?"

"Nope. Not a scratch. Jimmy did, though, took a lick on the head. We thought he was dead. I wasn't out. I was still layin' there shootin' at the bastards."

"What'd Dad do?"

"He picked me up like I was a day-old calf and just walked off with me into the trees away from 'em."

"While they were still shootin'?"

"Shootin' like a son-of-a-bitch. But they missed us. Surprised 'em so. Him just walkin' out with me like that."

"They chase you?"

"Yep, but not far. Frank's a slick one sometimes. He carried me about fifty yards and set me right down in the damn mud. Then he took a Luger out of my belt, one I'd took off a dead German officer, and he took his rifle and headed back toward where we come from. Surprised hell out of 'em. I crawled up some so's I could see. He met 'em about fifty feet from where I was layin'. Must of been eight or nine of 'em that I could see. They didn't have anywhere to go and he wiped 'em out. Ever last one of 'em. Killed the last two with his bare hands. Broke one of 'em's nuts with his rifle butt and then chopped him in the neck with the side of his hand." Jed chopped the steering wheel and Jonathan winced. "And he broke the other'n's neck. Was over in half a minute. Said he learned how to do it from the Japanese when he was a kid travelin'. Damnedest thing."

"And nothin' happened to him?" Jonathan remembered hitting his father in the barn.

"Nope, and he didn't say a damn word. Just walked back and picked me up and headed out." Jed slowed the car and turned into a driveway. On either side were orange trees. "These have all been picked but there's still some on 'em." Jed pointed toward the sparsely fruited trees. "They have a lot of citrus but their main thing is cotton."

"What happened to Jimmy?" Jonathan asked, ignoring the citrus.

"Well, he come back there, unbeknownst to either of us. Frank was totin' me like a sack of feed, me beggin' him to put me down. Bleeding bad, but he just kept on sloshin' through that goddamn muck. . . . Then he came to a hill and climbin' up it he slipped and both of us flew ass over elbows, me cussin' bloody murder, loud enough for 'em to hear all over France, and within five minutes, before your daddy could get his breath back, two of 'em showed up."

"Germans?"

"Yep, 'n they had the drop on us. Frank had left his rifle. He had the Luger in his belt, but didn't have time to use it. They found it, though, when they searched us. Made one of 'em madder'n hell to see that German pistol."

"Were you scared?"

"Hell, yes, I was, but I was hurtin' more'n scared."

"Was dad scared?"

"Never asked him. He had more reason to be scared than I did anyway."

"Why's that?"

" 'Cause he could understand their consarned jabberin'. Next thing I knowed they made us both kneel down and they put that Luger at my head and a rifle to Frank's. He knew they was aimin' to kill us even before that, but there was nothin' either one of us could of done."

"Then what?"

"Damnedest thing. Jimmy Ortega came struttin' up the path

114

behind 'em like he was goin' to a Sunday-school picnic, except he had a machine gun with him, picked it up somewhere back there. When he saw what was about to happen he just hollered at 'em, 'Hey,' he said. That was all. They took their guns off us and when they did Jimmy dropped 'em where they stood."

"Saved your life."

Jed stopped the car in front of the Ortega house, adjusted his hat. "That's when Jimmy got it. The damn fool took off his helmet and bowed to us, grinning at us, and when he straightened back up a bullet went through his head. Never knew where it come from. He pitched forward in the mud and Frank run over to him. He was dead, though, and I passed out."

"Dad carry you all the way back?"

"That's what they told me, all two hundred forty pounds of me. I woke up thirteen days later in a hospital."

"He get a medal?"

"Got a lot of 'em but he wouldn't even take 'em. Said the one's deserved 'em was dead and he wasn't dead yet. He was strange like that sometimes. Damnedest thing. I was tellin' a chaplain, a priest, once in the hospital what had happened. Frank was there when I told him. The priest crossed himself, turned to Frank, and said, 'God was certainly with you that day.' Frank didn't bat an eye. You know what he said?"

"What'd he say?"

"He said to that priest, 'Bullshit!' "

Chapter

7

When Jed introduced Frank and Jonathan to Ellen Ortega Frank sensed for a fleeting second the delicate presence of a cloud between them, then it was gone. "Jimmy spoke of you often in his letters, Mr. Hyde, but he called you Francisco." Her smile was sincere, and at the memory of Jimmy's name for him he knew what it was, the cloud between them, a shadow over the past, an unwelcome exposure to graves long ago grassed over, like an unwillingness to visit your father's grave, not because you didn't love him, but because you did.

Fifteen years after her husband's death she was still a pretty woman, but there was in her face evidence of too long grieving, the full, well-shaped lips pressed more closely, it seemed to Frank, than they should be, and there were early lines on her forehead and at the corners of her mouth. Her hair, though, was still as black as night, and her eyes were full of light, quick and intelligent. There was a sadness about her which Frank was certain was not self-pity; rather it was caused by a very real sense of loss and gave her the widow's advantage of quiet resolve to accomplish alone what most women would consider absolutely beyond them.

Frank wanted to say to her, "Ellen Ortega, because of your husband I feel that you are no stranger to me, and I will tell you that I am no stranger to grief." But he did not. It was a thing to feel and not a thing to say. So he said, "You have a beautiful place here." And he wanted to add, "It is as wonderful as Jimmy told me it was." But he didn't say that either, and it seemed to him that she understood without his talking about it that he was a man who felt deeply, and he appreciated that about her.

She prepared sandwiches and coffee for a late lunch. "I haven't eaten yet," she said. "We are without a foreman right now and I've been seeing to the last of the grapefruit." While they ate they talked about farming in the valley and how good it was; and Jed mentioned Frank's troubles and his farm in Oklahoma. "I have heard how terrible it is up there, Mr. Hyde, how many have lost their farms."

"Oh, we've still got the place. There's just no water."

"So," Jed cut in, "he up and come to the valley like me and Jimmy tried to get him to fifteen years ago."

"Well, we thought we'd see what it was like down here. See if we could learn something about your way of farming." Frank didn't want to ask her for the job, feeling that it would seem he might be taking advantage of a relationship. But Jed did it for him.

"Walked into my office lookin' for a job." Frank hadn't wanted him to say that, but Jed was still Jed. "Told him I had one right there, Deputy Sheriff of Hidalgo. He come at the exact right time for it."

She was visibly concerned. "You are going to take it, Mr. Hyde?"

"Why, Ellen," Jed continued, "you sound disappointed. Why shouldn't he take it?"

She blushed and Frank rescued her, "You're right, Mrs. Ortega, it's not for me. I still want to farm."

"So farm you will." She rose and began clearing the table. "I need a foreman and you need a job. That will certainly be better than you chasing drunks and me picking grapefruit."

Jed grinned a mile. He winked at Jonathan and Ellen caught him. "Jed, I think you had this whole thing all planned out, didn't you?"

"You can know I did, Miss Ellen. You can just know I did."

Jed returned to town and Ellen showed them the foreman's house, a four-room frame structure not far from the big house. "This was our house when we were first married. It was Jimmy's

117

parents' home until they built the big house. When they passed away a few years ago I moved into theirs and gave this to the foreman."

"What happened to your foreman, Mrs. Ortega?" Frank asked as he heaved his box of books out of the truck.

"He went back to Mexico." She followed him into the house. He set the box on a table. "He was a good man, wife and four children. Saved every penny they could get their hands on. When they left he had enough to go back across and buy a little farm of his own. Things are different there. He got a nice little farm for a thousand dollars."

"Things are fast getting different here, too." He said, remembering Oklahoma. "I know a whole lot of folks would sell out for a thousand dollars cash, if they could keep from giving it all back to the bank."

"Yes, we are fortunate here, Mr. Hyde. Come, I'll show you what I mean." She led them around behind the big house, where, at the edge of the orange grove, they got into her pickup, a late-model Ford. Jonathan hopped into the back. "You have a fine-looking son, Mr. Hyde," she said when they were alone in the cab, "but he doesn't look at all like you."

Frank laughed at that. She was at first puzzled by his laughter, then realized what she'd said. "Oh, I didn't mean it like that." Frank noticed her cheeks had colored immediately.

"I know. He takes after his mother's people. Big red giants, almost all of them, except his mother, she's . . . she was smaller and somehow not red-headed." He was silent then, and she was, as they entered the orange grove. The Ford wound its way back under the canopy of the dark green trees. Moments like these, Frank thought, the quiet, beautiful moments, bring the hurt back. The moments you share. How she would have loved this place, this green place.

Jonathan in the back reached up and grabbed a ripe orange from a passing limb, settled down against the cab, and began to peel it. His nails bit into the bright skin, and he was immediately surrounded by its tart, clean aroma. He was tired and he leaned his head back against the cab and watched the limbs and sky patches swim by. His thoughts turned to Enola. The ache he'd felt earlier was worse now, screaming for relief. He closed his eyes and there was Enola in the water, legs around him, working him into her. There was Enola soft and eager, wet and wonderful in her bed. And then there was Enola crying and vomiting. And her mother, mother whore, pushing up toward him, bruised eye blackening, begging with her body for him to finish it. And all the guilt and remorse and sense of loss of the past week were swept away by a red flood of desire.

The orange was cool against his fevered lips as the truck bounced out of the grove and stopped.

Jonathan looked up. They had stopped on the bank of a river, and what they saw there surprised even Frank. He had always thought of the Rio Grande as a great river, but here in the center of a sandy bed a quarter mile wide was a tiny stream meandering like a small snake in a broad sandy roadbed, turning here and there as lazy whim would have it.

"So that's the mighty Rio Grande," Frank commented, stepping as near as he dared to the edge of the clay embankment thirty feet above the river bed. "It's hardly more'n a trickle. A man could step over it and not even stretch."

Jonathan remarked with a slight tone of sarcasm, for this was his father's river, his idea, his land, and his damn river, "It isn't much of a river."

"Not now," Ellen defended, "but in three months you wait. When the snow melts in the mountains and the spring rains come. That little trickle will grow to be a mile wide sometimes, spreading out of its banks."

"That's why this valley is so rich." Frank turned to Jonathan. "These farms are not really Texas farms; they are Colorado and New Mexico and beyond, washed into the river and dumped here to make a garden in Texas."

Ellen examined Frank's face appreciatively as she turned back toward the truck. "C'mon. I'll show you the rest of the place and then it'll be time for the kids to be home from school."

Not many people considered Lucinda Ortega pretty. She had her father's height and a strong, well-shaped body, legs long and firm, noticed appreciatively by Jonathan, who had hoped for

119

more in Ellen's daughter than what he saw before him; but beneath a plain child's face were the large upturned breasts of a woman. He smiled at her and his father was pleased when he said warmly, "I'm pleased to meet you, Lucinda." She could scarcely meet his eyes, so painfully aware was she of her uncomeliness. Being the unbeautiful child of the beautiful Ellen had confirmed in her mind her own feminine mediocrity.

"And this," Ellen continued, "is Ricardo." He was considerably smaller than his sister and a little younger. Frank guessed he was fifteen, it being nearly sixteen years since Jimmy went to the war. Jimmy had never seen his boy, but he would have been pleased with him, Frank thought as he shook the lad's hand. "You must be about fifteen by now, Ricardo."

"Rick," he corrected, asserting a manly authority over the right to his own name, smiling brightly as he did so, innately confident of being well accepted. He was of slighter build than his sister, but a load of books under his left arm indicated that he was the studious one. Jonathan disliked him immediately, and hated the easy smile and the way the boy's dark brown eyes fairly sparkled as he invited Jonathan to come help him feed his rabbits. Jonathan followed him reluctantly, deciding whether he would tolerate this pipsqueak.

They came to the rabbit hutches behind the barn and Rick asked over his shoulder, "You like rabbits?"

"I hate rabbits."

Rick opened one of the hutches and lifted out a great white buck, hugged it to him, and turned to Jonathan. "How can you hate a rabbit?"

Jonathan reached out and took the animal from Ricardo. There was none of the younger boy's tenderness in the way Jonathan held him. "I once crucified a rabbit." He captured the boy's eyes with his own and held them as he demonstrated, "Like this," and he spread the rabbit's two forelegs wide apart. The animal's hind feet kicked wildly in the air. Rick reached out quickly, clutched the struggling beast in his own hands. Jonathan released it, turned, and walked away into the grove. Rick hugged the animal to himself and made soft promises that there was nothing to fear, but he was afraid; and he was sorry Jonathan had come to his home.

Jonathan walked alone through the trees for a long time until he came to the river. He walked along the winding river for a while, and then he sat down on the bank and watched a skinny old Mexican man leading a donkey and cart out onto the riverbed toward the meandering stream. When the old man reached the water he allowed the little burro to drink while he took a tin bucket from the cart and began filling a large wooden barrel standing in the cart. He worked slowly and spoke to his beast as he worked, quietly lamenting that he was a peasant, complaining that he was born on the wrong side of the river. He didn't blame his parents or theirs; he didn't blame his government or himself or even his ill-risen stars. He blamed the river. "Why could not the Rio run a little more to the south, burro, and then I would have been born on the right side of her." He sometimes spoke to the Rio herself, always berating her. But every evening he came down to her and every evening she gave of herself freely.

And when the burro pulled the heavy cart across the sand and up the bank the old man gave the water to his corn and tomatoes and peppers. And to his pigs he gave very grudgingly, for they would drink it all without leaving him a little bit. Then he would have to make another trip and again he would berate the river as he took this time only the bucket for enough water to boil as the authorities had taught him, to kill the little beasties in it. Only he didn't boil the water anymore since the day he dropped a large red ant into the hot water before it boiled. The ant died and the old man decided it was enough just to get the water hot enough to kill the ant, for as anyone can tell you the red ant is the strongest of the little ones, and if he could not live in the hot water then the water was safe. It was in the nature of the authorities, the old one reflected, to be pompous, to overdo, to tax two pesos when one was enough, to drive in a huge black car when a small black car would be enough. To cause the peons to boil the water when it was evident to any fool that if the water was hot enough to kill the large red ant, strong as he was, the water was hot enough.

And so for years the old man had not boiled the water, and he had bragged to his neighbors that he was not one to be fooled by the authorities. He had not boiled the water and was not dead. And he would strike his lean, hard stomach with his old fist and beam with pride. But he did not even think to tell them that he seldom drank the water; he drank mostly tequila and sometimes wine when he could get it, and when he used the water at all it was to make his frijoles.

Jonathan and the old man heard the laughter at the same time, and Jonathan watched the old man smile as he looked toward the next bend in the river. He stopped filling the barrel, dropped the bucket, and walked toward the bank, then made his way slowly up it.

Jonathan listened carefully; something in the sound held him enchanted. It was the laughter of women, several, coming from downriver. He jumped forward off the bank, with one great leap, startling the donkey, which almost turned over the old cart. The old man looked back to see what was the matter with his beast, and when he saw the burro stop again he grinned at Jonathan and motioned him to come up the bank. He put a finger to his lips for silence. Jonathan followed, not knowing exactly what to expect.

The old man bent low in the tall grass and motioned the boy to do the same. They crept forward, the old man clucking gleefully, until they came to the edge of the bank where the winding river had turned south again. The old Mexican stopped and peered through the grass to the river bed below. Jonathan moved up beside him and parted the grass to look, and below, in a pool formed by the swirling river currents, were seven women, all of them naked, laughing, and throwing water on each other. Jonathan caught his breath and felt his groin tighten. The old man watched him and laughed approvingly at the youngster. Jonathan looked at the old man but did not laugh with him or even smile. There was something filthy, it seemed to Jonathan, about an old man watching women from the cover of tall grass.

But the women did not think so. They heard the old one laugh and knew he was there so they shouted at him, "Hey, viejo!" And in Spanish they asked him, "Does the old worm still live, old man?" And one of the girls, a large fat one, crawled up out of the water and walked a few steps toward the bank, her arms outstretched, shaking her huge breasts tauntingly before him, laughing, laughing. And, when they would say again, "Well, old man, does the worm still live?" he would smile a gummy smile, nod his head for them, and behind the cover of the grass would rub the place where the worm once lived.

Then Jonathan stood up, tall above the blowing grass, and held the women transfixed with his eyes. The laughing stopped. Jonathan just stared, feeling his hunger deepen. Then he walked forward and slid down the bank toward the fat one, never taking his eyes off her.

There was in her eyes a moment of almost fear, of uncertainty, but she stood there awaiting him with a half smile on her face. "You want to fock?" she asked. Jonathan smiled hard, his blue eyes dancing with measured delight.

"You bet!"

"Six bits," she said, turning her head to her girl friends, who giggled.

"Two bits," Jonathan said.

"Four bits," she countered, and the girls giggled louder.

Jonathan reached out and cupped her left breast in his right hand, then took her nipple between his fingers and rubbed it. She smiled as it hardened. He said quietly so the others would not hear, "I have no money ..." She slapped his hand away and started to turn, but he caught her arm and brought her around to him again. "I have no money with me, but if you like I will bring you a fat rabbit."

She studied him. "When?" she asked.

"When we finish. I'll go across, get the rabbit, and bring him back to you."

Again her eyes pierced his and years of handling men told her what to do. "Bring the animal and then you fock." She turned and he watched her gross buttocks riding back to the water.

Before he turned away he saw a girl he hadn't seen before. She must have been behind the others. Blonde and small, fair-skinned, and avoiding his gaze. He walked toward her and she retreated. He stood on the edge of the pool and examined her. She

123

ducked under the waist-deep muddy water and effortlessly glided away from him, her white shape barely visible in the brownish water. Then she stood up with her back to him and stepped up on the sand and walked toward the bank, head held high. Jonathan watched her with pleasure as she ascended the bank and disappeared behind the grass.

The fat one spoke. "She is the Princess, *americano,* and she doesn't like to be stared at. Now go get your *coneho* and I fock your ass." The others laughed aloud. Jonathan grinned.

"Where will you be?" he asked as he turned to go.

"In the last house on the street, up there." She pointed in the direction the blonde girl had gone. The fat one said, "Don't worry about the Princess. She won't fock you."

"Why not?"

"You don't have enough rabbits." The others laughed and four of them ducked the fat one under the water.

The red-light district in Reynosa, Mexico, in the thirties was little more than a shanty town located on a narrow peninsula which was actually a sharp bend in the river. There was a canal cut into the upper neck of the peninsula so that the only way whores' town, or Boys' Town as it came to be called, could be conveniently entered was by a bridge across the canal. This in effect isolated Boys' Town from the respectable part of Reynosa and allowed the authorities at the little bridge control over who came in. They kept women out except for the *putas,* the whores, and allowed only men to pass.

But Jonathan didn't enter the district via the legal bridge over the canal; he came from the other end, hopping over the river stream and climbing the clay bluff above the spot where the girls had bathed.

He entered the village of pleasures from the dark end, walking out of the evening shadows carrying a white rabbit in his large left hand.

The town consisted mainly of one long street with several short ones running off it, alleys actually. On each side of the long street was a row of small frame houses, simple one-room shanties. Jonathan walked past some with doors open and saw single beds, some of straw and corn shucks laid on rope webbing attached to rough wooden frames. There was the smell of corn tortillas in the air and coal-oil fumes from lamps and small cookstoves, and wax candles burning, lofting sweet airs to the multitude of saints watching over this place.

At the bridge end of this long street were several *cantinas* already hopping this early in the evening, filled with noisy youths drinking beer and tequila. Some of them warming up to the pleasures of the evening, but most of them drinking up enough courage to walk down the long street and select a fat hole into which he would stick his timid prick for two minutes, sense a faint titillation for four or five seconds, pay an American quarter dollar for the privilege, then go back to work tomorrow morning and boast to his fellows how he rode that bitch to heaven.

A band started up in one of the *cantinas*. The raucous, brassy music seemed to be a signal to the girls, who appeared in their doorways in varying states of dress, none very pretty that Jonathan could see, all being either too fat or too skinny, faces painted almost obscenely in oranges, reds, and pinks, their hard eyes following him and the few others, some coming for an early fuck before heading home. He thought then of the Princess and looked around for her. She was not to be seen. His eye caught the face of one of the bathers. She recognized him and called, "Hey, gringo, you want to fock?" He looked away from her and moved on toward the end of the long street where the fat one would be waiting. "Why don' you fock the rabbit, gringo?" and all the whores laughed.

He stood in the open doorway of the last wooden shanty on the long block. The music from next door was wilder and louder now, almost shutting out the sounds of the street, filling with drunken, boisterous men and drunken boys trying hard to be men. She sat on the bed, her weight heavy on it. When she saw him and stood up and motioned him to enter, the bed fairly groaned in relief. She said something in Spanish that he did not understand, so he stood there with the rabbit, now struggling to free itself from the strong hand that held it.

She motioned to the rabbit and said something else he didn't understand and couldn't hear well because of the rabbit, so he

125

held it out before her and began to squeeze it around the neck. Its eyes and his were on her, the rabbit's wild pink and pleading, and his dark and carefully savoring the fearful effect of the beast's slow death upon her.

She crossed herself and murmured something else and he grinned and tossed the lifeless body onto a small table which held a fluttering candle and a wash basin and a pitcher.

He kicked the door shut, unbuckled his belt, kicked off his boots, and let his pants drop to the hard dirt floor. She stepped forward, afraid to almost, but knowing that with this type one did what one had to do as quickly and as well as possible under the circumstances. She unbuttoned his shirt and helped it off him; with one hand she removed her dress and worked at the clasp of her bra, and with the other she cupped his testicles and squeezed them gently. When the bra was undone, and his hands were running freely over her body and into her pants, she felt his staff stiffen and felt the grand pulse within it.

She pulled him toward the table and poured some water from the pitcher into the small basin. From a drawer under the table she took a nigh-used-up bar of soap and washed his dick, working especially well around the head of it, knowing as she did it that this one was ready. This one carried a full load and would deliver without much coaxing.

Upon her in a short moment, he poured himself within her, and for the first time in weeks was at peace, and when thoughts of his mother or the preacher moved into his mental vision, he simply pushed his now softening prick in deeper and felt the extreme pleasure of it and forgot.

Chapter

8

There were moments when Frank almost couldn't bear the loss of Mary and the memory of her suffering, but the long farm hours, the ache in his back, the rich black dirt on his hands helped drive the brunt of hurt a little farther back into the darker recesses of his mind, allowing it painful dominance only when he encountered a new joy, such as the Texas springtime with its wildflowers, perhaps the most glorious in the world, and the soft spring rains. It was the first rain, the first for Frank in over two and a half years, that revealed to him how far away he was from healing. It came in the night, the rain. The smell of it woke him in the early-morning darkness a half hour before the first drops. He rose quickly and stepped out in the night chill. The sky was yet unclouded, the stars hanging low, the air still, but in the southwest, over the Gulf of Mexico eighty miles away, the sky lit up from time to time with the streaking fire of the first spring storm.

Frank went back in and dressed, pulling on his jacket, hitherto unneeded, then he went outside again, and as he walked into the trees toward the river, his eyes fixed on the towering thunderheads, he was stricken with the most sickening sense of loss he'd yet experienced. Here he was alive and well and waiting for the life of the land to wash down over him and bless him, awaiting the farmer's god, and Mary dead. He allowed himself to bear full focus on it as he walked through the trees and felt the breeze stirring, smelled the ozone-laden air. And in full realization of her death, irrevocable, dead one month, four weeks in the grave, a cheap gray box. Goddamn. Push it away! Push it away! The wind increased, blowing his jacket open; it was cold; he didn't care. He stood on the bank of the river and the great bolts of lightning struck around him and lit his haggard face. The first cold drops struck him and washed down his face, and then the deluge hit him. The deafening crack of thunder like nearby cannon vibrated his insides, and in the wind and the noise and the driving rain he stood on the bank of the ancient river, lifted up his head, opened his mouth, and out of him came the horrible animal cry of grief, the ageless, barbaric, almost inhuman groan of those whom death has cursed and left behind. And, if there were gods to hear Frank Hyde's hopeless cry that night of the first rain, they were gods of silence. And if they wept with him that night he knew nothing of it.

Ellen Ortega became immediately aware of the rare quality of her new foreman. She was pleased with him in so many ways she began almost without knowing it to limit her time in his presence. After years of being alone, of guarding her emotions, of stifling her once fully vented femininity, she feared to confront herself with even the possibility of an escape for the woman imprisoned within her. There had been no one since Jimmy who even remotely appealed to her as a prospective companion. Men were aplenty, and eager, as she learned very soon after Jimmy's death, but none with even the slightest traces of the qualities that had drawn her to abandon so entirely to Jimmy Ortega.

There was Jed Strunk, who let her know early on that he was interested, but she was not, and told him so, as kindly as she knew how, and he very respectfully kept his distance, for which she was grateful. He was a valued friend, his kindness and confidence were surely needed at times, and he came to visit from time to time, but he was not, as she very softly explained to him, the marrying kind, and he knew she was right. He was too wild and rough and prone some to wandering, and he knew it. But he would have married her if she had been willing.

In her new foreman there was something . . . She was poignantly aware of his present suffering and she knew from long experience that only time would dull the blade of hurt. Work would help, but she also knew that long after time and toil had taken the fine edge off the pain, merciless memory could turn the knife to its point and gouge again upon the least provocation. It had happened to her, often, and it happened one day when she had taken dinner to Frank in the fields.

He had worked for over a week in early February, plowing, getting the land ready for cotton. Day and night he was either on a tractor or seeing to it that other workers were plowing steadily in the fields. He slept little. He was tired but didn't feel it. He felt only joy to be in the dirt again. He seldom stopped to prepare himself a decent meal. Jonathan had been eating with Ellen and the kids, but Frank would fry up two chickens in his own little kitchen, throw three or four pieces into a paper sack along with a jar of water and head back for the fields. So one day at noon, with the kids at school, she made sandwiches and potato salad and deviled eggs, put a small crock of hot coffee into a pasteboard box and drove out to feed him.

He was standing on the back of the tractor behind the driver. He was watching the plowshares turn the earth, lost on the rich, clean smell of it and imagining the whole field, over a half mile across, green with the new leaf of spring cotton. The tractor halted abruptly, Frank looked around and the driver, a small brown-skinned man whose face was a perpetual smile, smiled now and motioned toward the river. The pickup was speeding toward them, bouncing joyfully along the turn now. Frank could just make out Ellen's form behind the wheel. He grinned at Emilio as he jumped off the tractor. "Emilio, *la señora* drives like Jehu."

He walked over to the pickup. "Hop in," she said smiling.

He did, saw the box of things in the rear. He instantly perceived that it was his recent neglect of himself and Jonathan in favor of the plowing that had burdened her with the necessity of feeding him. As the truck bounced over the ruts and holes of the turn row he became aware of her driving. "Like a man's driving," he thought, "strong, firm, letting the wheels take the road in their own stride, not jerking and constantly braking. But even at a speed dangerous for the average driver she read the oncoming trail and instinctively corrected for it." She was not aware that he was watching her, or that her driving was extraordinary, and

129

when she felt somehow as a woman does that she was being admired she gripped the wheel tightly, and unknowingly she blushed.

"You're a good driver, Mrs. Ortega."

"So are you, Mr. Hyde."

"How would you know that?" he asked. She slowed to a crawl, barely clearing the lower branches of a huge mesquite shading one corner of the field, then turned onto a grassy meadow shadowed sparsely by mesquite and ebony and hackberry. Beneath the largest ebony on a small knoll overlooking the river she stopped.

"I know that you are a good driver because I have seen you on the tractors," she replied, "day and night." He chuckled, got out, lifted the box out of the back, and set it down. He walked over to the edge of the river and surveyed its surprising growth, turned back to her when the food was spread. "It's turned into quite a river," he said as he sat down, his back against the tree.

"The little rain we got with all that thunder and lightning wouldn't have raised it much, but that storm moved on upriver; that helped. But the snows are melting in New Mexico and in the mountains north. The river will be like that, and more even, all spring." She handed him a sandwich. He bit a huge hunk from it.

"You were hungry," she said. "I knew you weren't eating right."

"You didn't have to do this, Mrs. Ortega. I don't know if I should thank you or spank you." He grinned. There it was. The openness. The honesty in him, the tender human kind of quality that made her uncomfortable around him, because a person like that gets inside you . . . is in a strange way contagious. So reminiscent of Jimmy. "Thank you or spank you." Pleased at the gesture and at the same time peeved because he felt he was being a burden. Such a man in the presence of a woman long alone, she pondered, requires a decision. . . .

After the sandwiches and the small talk he helped her put the stuff away. She drove the truck up close to the river's edge and they watched for a moment the swirling, surging currents. He watched her now watching it.

"It's almost frightening, isn't it, Mr. Hyde, the violence of it, its

130

wildness. Look, there's a tree in it, there." She pointed toward the far bank. He saw it bobbing and weaving, disappearing beneath the dark surface, then quickly coming up again fifty feet downstream, turning and thrashing like the antlers of a wounded stag.

"That's why I love it so much," she said, "the river. It's almost a living thing. . . ."

"It isn't alive," he said bluntly.

"What?" she asked, surprised.

"The river doesn't live. It is just there. A ditch worn into the earth by water that rushed to a lower plane without knowing why it is doing it or that it is doing it. The water has no mind, the river has no mind, it is not a friend or an enemy, it is simply there, a fact of existence."

"What are you saying?" she asked him softly, almost hurt by his words.

"What do you mean?"

He too, surprised at himself, smiled rather sheepishly, slumped back in the seat, "I'm sorry, Mrs. Ortega. What I mean is that I also sometimes have ached to tear open the ground and lovingly plant seed and watch it grow, being fed and watered by just such a river, and I have caught myself at times referring to the river poetically as 'my brother the river.' But in my mind I know that when the chips are down, Mrs. Ortega, a man is alone on the earth, and if he gets in the way of nature he is no more a brother to it than that tree was to the river that sucked it off its banks and drowned it. And yet," he looked again at the river and then at her and he smiled weakly, "and yet sometimes I love the river and, like the trees, I take my sustenance from it, one way or the other."

"But nature does not give back life it has fed upon; that's what you mean." She followed him in his thought.

"That's what I mean. It doesn't give it back. Man can find strength only in himself. I can come to the river and enjoy looking at it or I can cut into the earth with a plow and think upon it, but I cannot delude myself that I am brother to the river or husband to Mother Earth. My real strength, in the end, and my own joy and pride must be in the knowledge that I am fit to stand in the wind and not be blown down, to live through tragedy and maintain my dignity, to starve and not steal, to lose battles and

131

fight harder. If a man finds peace, ever, it is in himself."

When she looked at him there were tears in her eyes. "Jimmy said you were a serious man, but you are more than that, Mr. Hyde. You are a teacher. I have for many years felt what you are saying, but I couldn't say it." She wiped her eyes on her sleeve. "I couldn't have explained what I feel about life, but you have said it for me. If it is your books that have made you that way, you must allow me to read them."

By the time they reached Emilio and the tractor, Ellen Ortega had made her decision.

"Frank, tonight you will eat with me. And tomorrow and when you are working in the fields I will bring you a lunch."

He paused as he opened the door. "You don't need to do this for us, Mrs. Ortega."

"I know, Mr. Hyde. Maybe that is why I want to do it."

Chapter

9

There was ample cause, in Frank's view, for his feelings of relief regarding Jonathan. No battle had ensued over getting him back into school to finish his last semester, and the boy was apparently getting along nicely with Lucy and Rick, with whom he walked to the school bus each morning and from the bus in the afternoon, except for those days when after school he noticed Jed Strunk's car at the sheriff's office. Then he would walk over there and Jed would entertain him with war stories and tales of his south-of-the-border pursuits of bandits. Rick was forbidden to stay after school at Jed's, his mother feeling that a sheriff's office was no place for a boy to be for hours on end, but Frank thought Jonathan could only gain by being attracted to a man of Jed's caliber.

On those afternoons that Jonathan stayed in town, Rick found great pleasure in following Frank around the farm. There soon developed a close bond between the two. "Did you say, Mr. Hyde, that the fall of the Roman Empire was caused by decay from within and not from attackers from the north?" His eyes sparkled. He knew the answer but loved to hear Frank explain, and often he could get an entirely new idea from Frank Hyde, and that was not altogether true of his teachers.

"Why did the missions in early Texas enslave the Indians?" the boy asked one day while he and Frank were driving a barrel of gas out to a tractor.

"Did they?"

"Did they?" the boy countered.

"Yes."

"Why?"

"Because the Indians sometimes didn't want to stay at the mission and work in the fields. Sometimes some of them would run away and return to hunting and living like they had before." Frank glanced sideways at the boy, who was looking out the window at a cottontail speeding across the turn row out of a field of new spring turnips.

"So." The boy grinned.

"So what?" Frank asked.

"So, if the Indians wanted to be what they always had been, it should be all right. Right?"

"Wrong," Frank answered. "At least wrong to the priests and soldiers."

"What do you mean?" Rick was intent.

"I mean the priests had a job to do, right?"

"Right," Rick answered.

"What was their job?"

"You tell me."

"To convert the Indians."

"Right. And the soldiers' job?"

"To . . ." The boy thought. "To protect the priests."

"Right. So?"

"So if the Indians were running loose and free like wild Indians they weren't being converted, so there's another reason for the soldiers, correct?"

"What is that?" Frank asked, smiling.

"To keep the Indians locked up at night and at work in the daytime."

"I think you've got the picture." They stopped the truck, and Emilio, waiting there, hopped into the back and handed the gas hose to Rick, who put the nozzle into the tractor's tank. While Emilio pumped gas Rick pumped Frank.

"But there is a deeper question, Mr. Hyde."

Frank looked at him quizzically. It surprised him that a boy of his age should be concerned with curious problems of deeper

134

questions. And he sensed the boy was about to lead him into something. He listened.

"The more important concern to historians, it seems to me, should be whether the priests and soldiers had the right to force the Indians to convert to Christianity, Mr. Hyde. Don't you think?"

"I think you've got something there, boy. Where'd you come up with that deep question?"

"Just hit me one day. Bothered me some about the Indians being locked in at night."

"That's a bad thing."

"So I asked Father Tim about it."

"Who's Father Tim?" Frank asked.

"The priest. You'll meet him. He comes over all the time to see the workers' families."

"And what did Father Tim say when you asked him?"

"He didn't, at first. I could tell he didn't want to answer it. Then he said to me, 'The priests had the right because the soldiers had the guns.'"

"Well, I'll be damned," Frank replied. "Priest with brains. Damned rare." Rick grinned.

Emilio stopped pumping. Rick handed the nozzle up to him. To Frank, Emilio said, "Father Tim is one good priest."

"Not like Father Horrigan," Rick announced, "not strict."

Emilio laughed, pointed a finger at Rick: "And that is one bad leetle *hombre*. Too many brains get you into bad trouble, my friend."

Rick answered, "Father Horrigan doesn't know I have a brain, so no trouble for me. I ask him the safe questions: 'Who is Father Aristotle?' I ask him. You should hear his answers, Mr. Hyde." The boy climbed into the truck beside Frank; Emilio cranked the tractor and went back to work. "But to Father Timothy Morgan I ask questions like I ask you."

"To test us?" Frank grinned.

"To learn," he answered; then, "And to test."

Jonathan was rather pleased with his own situation and with himself. Rick had said nothing about the loss of the rabbit,

135

although it was certain that he knew who took it. So Jonathan reasoned that the boy feared him and would do nothing and say nothing about it.

School was no problem to him, and so far on the farm he had gotten by with working only as much as he wanted, which was just enough to pay for his visits to Boys' Town. These were becoming more numerous since he'd met the Princess and, because of her, more expensive. But she was worth it.

The second time he had gone across the river it had been necessary for him to wait till late when his father was in bed; he slipped out of his own bedroom window and disappeared into the orange grove next to the house. Twenty minutes later he was in Boys' Town asking for the Princess. Everyone knew where she was, in the *cantina*, but there was no way he could see her tonight, they assured him, because she was with a big shot from Reynosa and would be busy all night. "But," one of the girls told him, "you can fock with me."

But he went to the *cantina* anyway. She was there and she was indeed on the sloping lap of a fat-bellied big shot who was drunk and was feeling between her legs, under her skirt with one hand, and with the other was trying to get into her blouse. His face was nuzzled into her breasts and she was plainly not enjoying it.

Jonathan ordered a beer as one of the few Spanish words he knew was *cerveza*, and sat by himself at the bar and watched the fat man and the Princess.

He had never drunk beer before. It had been over four hours since he'd eaten supper. So in twenty minutes he was dizzy and disoriented, and when the fat man finally did manage to open her blouse and began sucking noisily at one white breast Jonathan stood up and walked over to their table. She was clearly struggling with him now but could not move. She was sitting on the only spot where she really could have hurt him. But to fight harder or to hurt him would have been an invitation to bring his goons down upon her and the whole place, so she quit struggling and allowed him to push her onto the table, where he stood unsteadily over her now, took his penis out and prepared to mount her on the table. He did not know that Jonathan was behind him and Jonathan did not know that three of the fat

136

man's young henchmen were coming up fast behind him.

Jonathan hit the fat one on the side of the face with a quick, hard right, and about the time he heard the Princess scream he felt a sharp pain in the back of his head. He didn't know what happened next.

One of the men stepped over him with a knife, leaned down and held it at his throat. The man looked up at his boss, just now beginning to focus on the full import of the situation. When he saw the knife at the boy's throat he shook his head, "No, Sancho. He's *americano*. Trouble."

When Jonathan again saw light he was in the arms of the woman he'd fucked the other night.

"Hey, *tigre*. Why you wanta get killed?"

So it was plump Rosa again that night and no Princess, but the next night the Princess was available and on that night she orchestrated upon him pleasures of such intensity that memory of them in the days to come were sufficient to drive him immediately into an almost madness of hunger, as they were, of course, designed to do.

He returned again and again, and once when his father asked him where he'd been he responded respectfully, "Down on the river. Just walkin', thinkin'." That was a good answer to give to Frank Hyde; it satisfied him and reinforced his earlier judgment that the boy was finally coming to himself. Jonathan knew that's the effect his answer would have on his father, and he smiled to himself as he entered his room.

Then the river rose and Jonathan couldn't get to the Princess. After a week it hadn't subsided. It had actually grown, more gorged with the angry brown water than before. After two weeks had passed he decided to cross the international bridge, but after asking a schoolboy he changed his mind. "The border guards will mention to Sheriff Strunk you crossed over and he'll give you hell about catching crabs or some damn thing. Wait till the river goes down."

"When'll that be?"

"In the summer."

So Jonathan began to get ideas about the daughters of the farm workers, some of whom went to school with him, but his schoolboy advisor said, "You fuck one o' them girls and you've had it. Sooner or later her old man's gonna find out about it or you'll knock her up and Big Saenz will have your balls." Big Saenz was the largest of the laborers, by far the coldest toward Jonathan, and well known to carry a knife in his boot.

So that left only Lucinda Ortega. She liked him, he could tell, and he was certain he could have her, but there were his father and Ellen. Too close. But as the weeks wore on she became more attractive, and the sight of her strong young body beneath the light summer dresses . . . He decided to move in, just in case. He carried her books, talked to her at school, was nice to her at home. And he made up to Rick, just in case.

But it was not until the Sunday of that year's first baseball game at the Ortega farm that he decided to initiate a campaign which would undoubtedly place him very happily between the handsome legs of Lucinda Ortega.

Every year on the afternoon of the first Sunday after planting, it was time for the *beisbol*. As if by magic old mitts appeared, along with a few old bats held together by black tape and wood screws and hope. And someone had a baseball, rarely new and sometimes in pretty ragged shape, but still a baseball. And as if by magic people showed up on the flat pasture near the highway on the Ortega Farm, where there was an old backstop made of railroad ties and chicken wire.

An old man with more chicken wire patched the holes left last year, and while he worked, amply advised by other old men who were all experts on this, the young men warmed up for the game.

People came for miles around until there were several hundred lining the base paths and foul lines. Old cars showed up loaded with laborers from neighboring farms. There were beer and tequila and buckets of tamales for sale. Children with old baseballs with no covers or ripe oranges or young green grapefruit played their own little baseball game across the road or behind the backstop or under the grownups' feet. "Hey, José, second base, second base!"

"Look José, Baby Ruth, Baby Ruth! José, José! Look!"

Then the other team came from Relampago, a small farming center on the old Military Highway downriver. They had a bus.

138

Nobody knows where they got it and no one from the Ortega farm even thought to ask. But they had a bus. Some bus. It had one fender on the front, no lights, one side of the windshield was missing, the tires were so thin the cords were showing, the body had rusted through in forty places and there were no seats in it, but, goddamnit, Relampago had a bus!

And while the people at the ball diamond warmed up and fixed the backstop and drank *cerveza* and ate good hot tamales they also and at the same time watched for Relampago. You could see two miles across the fields and down the Military Highway so that you heard the bus about the same time you saw it. When it presented itself, a distant popping sound, the people all got quiet and peered over one another toward the road, and if anybody didn't get quiet he'd be bombarded by a hundred quick hisses. Then a roar went up and the warmer-uppers hit a couple more fast ones and cleared the field for the Relampagos.

The whole town came on the bus and they kept pouring out of it, front and rear, long after it had stopped. When at long last it was emptied its driver put it painfully into gear and headed for the Ortega tractor barn, where Emilio would fill its tank as he had done for over twenty years and would do for twenty more. By the time Emilio and the bus driver came popping back, the game was starting. They had just enough time to park the bus and scramble for perches on its top before the umpire yelled,

"Play *bol!*"

Lucinda and Ricardo sat with Jonathan on the green hood of the John Deere, a demonstration, Jonathan felt, of how well he'd maneuvered himself into her affections and back into Rick's good graces. Lucinda had braved a new hair style for the day of the game, letting it fall freely over her shoulders in black shiny cascades, freeing it for the first time in years from the band that had pulled it straight back and held it in a single shock, which she sometimes tortured into one long pigtail.

"You should always wear your hair like that, Lucy," Jonathan assured her. "Looks good like that." He knew she would blush when he said it and she did, a fact which Ricky also noticed.

"Lucinda's blushing," he laughed.

"Ricky! Why don't you go sit with Mother?" She immediately

knew it was the wrong thing to say to Ricky, but it was too late.

"So you can be alone with Jonathan?" he retorted. "You're a silly girl." He slid off the tractor and entered a game of keep-away that a group of boys were playing with an old overripe grapefruit.

Ellen had watched the development of her daughter's relationship with Jonathan and was not altogether displeased with it, although she did suffer the normal misgivings of a mother seeing her daughter fall in love. Actually it was some relief to see her blossoming out now; other than Lucinda herself only she knew what tribulation the girl had endured during the last year. Father Timothy Morgan had arrived in Hidalgo about a year ago, and if ever a girl had been stricken it was Lucinda.

Of all the Ortegas, only Lucinda was genuinely religious. Ricardo read too much and asked too many questions to take anything as nebulous as faith very seriously and Ellen had been embittered upon the death of her husband and attended mass rather spottily. Only Lucinda, quiet and serious-minded, attended church with any regularity and with sincerity. She had, even before Timothy Morgan arrived, seriously considered giving herself to the church, but when he came, tall and dark and quiet, she fell in love as deeply as a girl of sixteen possibly could, which is considerable. And only Ellen saw it. The girl would not go to confession if there was any chance that he would be attending the confessional. She was absolutely silent and tensed if he came into her presence for any reason whatever, and if he spoke to her she reddened perceptibly and struggled to maintain presence of mind enough to answer sensibly, which was not always possible. So, with the church and Timothy Morgan the latest things in her life, it was only natural for her to decide upon the convent; she could never have Father Tim. Then came Jonathan Hyde.

He was, at first, rather distant to her, and she attributed that to her lack of beauty, her "plainness," as she told herself. But then he became quite friendly and spent more and more of his time with her, so that she began to believe just a little bit what her mother had told her: "You are not plain. It is simply that you have a different kind of beauty, child, you are what men would call a handsome girl. And anyway men don't marry girls for their

140

looks, not smart men or good men."

"But daddy . . ."

"When Jimmy Ortega met me I was chopping cotton. I was dressed in overalls and had a huge straw hat on. He fell in love with me that day, dressed like that. And he always said he liked me better like that, dressed for work, than in the finest dress I had."

"But you are beautiful, mama, in whatever you wear."

Ellen stood up and walked to the mirror in her room, looked at herself a moment. "Come here, Lucinda." Lucinda stood by her mother. "Now watch." Ellen gathered her own full head of hair in her right hand and pulled it back, tight, like Lucinda's and held it there. "Now, baby, notice anything?"

"It's amazing." She stared at her mother and saw not Ellen standing beside her but another Lucinda, a little older, features a little more finely drawn perhaps, but another Lucinda still.

"Now watch." Ellen took her own lipstick and lightly traced Lucy's almost smiling lips. "Careful to keep it slightly thinner than your lips, makes your mouth even smaller." Then swiftly she took down her daughter's hair and brushed it out and over her shoulders, all the while watching Lucy's face as the girl witnessed her own transformation. "There now. Now what do you see?"

"Mother! I'm almost pretty. I am. I am pretty. Am I?" She turned her face toward Ellen, who kissed her forehead.

"You've always been pretty, baby, but I thought you knew it and just weren't interested yet."

But she was too shy to make the change immediately. She waited until Jonathan showed interest in her and even then she only changed her hair. In her shyness she was reluctant to use the lipstick just yet. But now she would.

But it wasn't until he saw how Lucy looked at Father Tim that Jonathan made his decision.

Timothy Morgan came late for the game. He had once played with the Ortega team but had been chastised for it by Father Horrigan, who felt that a priest should be separate and somewhat aloof. Timothy disagreed but didn't say so and made it a point after that, when he went to the games, to arrive late, reducing the opportunities for Emilio or Saenz to pressure him into playing. They had heard some way that Father Tim was forbidden to play and wouldn't have urged him to, but Tim didn't know that.

He was tall and lanky, had dark hair and dark eyes, eyes deep set and softly brooding, "troubled eyes" it seemed to Frank upon first meeting him. His grip was firm as they shook hands. The young priest said, "You're the scholar I've been hearing so much about."

Frank turned toward Rick, who had just bounded into the pickup bed, and smiled at him, "Been tellin' our secrets, boy?"

"Yep." The boy grinned, then turned to survey the action on the field. Saenz had blasted a triple, tried to stretch it and was out at home after a bone-crunching collision. The crowd was furious.

"They play for keeps here, Mr. Hyde," Father Tim said as he pulled himself up on the cab to sit with Frank and Ellen.

"Men always play harder than boys," Frank offered.

"Boys play for fun," Tim said.

"Men play for glory," Frank added.

And Ellen said, "To prove they are men."

"Touché," Frank looked at Timothy. "She's the philosopher. . . ."

"So that's where Ricardo gets it." Tim smiled approvingly and Frank noticed the darkness was gone from his face, replaced by boyish light.

After the game Frank and Tim sat on the Ortega porch alone, Ricky called away by his mother: "Let them talk and get acquainted. They are alike in many ways." Rick agreed, but still wanted to be near them, to listen, so he retired as quietly as possible to his room over the porch and listened. He could hear their voices, but couldn't make out their words. "Damn." So he went to find Lucy and Jonathan, but they were nowhere to be found.

"Can you imagine that kid at his age reading Gibbon and Mill?" Timothy asked.

"He not only reads it," Frank added, "he has a pretty fair grasp of what's being said."

"I wish I'd been so inclined as a child," Timothy confessed.

"And I," Frank admitted.

"You weren't?"

"When I was his age the biggest thing in my life was raisin' a whiteface bull for the county fair. I didn't get really interested in books till I was nineteen or twenty."

"Rick said you didn't go to college. Traveled around the world instead."

"That's when I learned about books and ideas. And I didn't learn it like the schools teach."

"I hope not." The priest's voice was strong when he said that and Frank noted that the darkness was back in the young man's face.

When he was gone Ellen asked Frank, "Do you like him?"

"Yes, I do. Serious youngster."

She sat on the porch steps watching the sunset. "I think he's got troubles." She looked back toward Frank.

"Troubles? What kind of troubles."

"Head troubles. With his faith," she said.

"Religion? You'd think a priest would have no troubles with faith, the way they're trained. But you know I'll bet the best of them are fairly tortured at times trying to balance some of the tomfoolery they're supposed to swallow."

"And he's the best of them," she announced.

"What about you, Ellen?"

"What about me?"

"Religion. You don't seem to put much stock in it, seems to me," he stated quietly.

"I did at one time. Then one day I just didn't believe it anymore."

"Any of it?"

"Any of it, except God. I think there's a God. That's all."

"Why do you think that?" he asked carefully.

"Because I'm afraid not to."

Chapter
10

Jonathan Hyde was the most beautiful thing that had ever happened to Lucinda Ortega.

The day after the game she not only wore her new hair style, she had added lipstick as well. Jonathan was pleased, and to reward her he held her hand for a few minutes while they waited for the school bus. This affected her deeply, but affected him far more than she would have guessed. Had she been better versed in the way of the flesh she might have seen visible evidence, but in her innocence it never occurred to her even to look.

He had learned from Enola that a girl needs to talk, needs to feel close to a boy before she can even begin to feel right about having sex with him. He had learned that to get what he wanted he had to talk about what she wanted and say all the right things, and say the wrong things only often enough to plant the idea firmly in her tortured little head.

The change in Lucinda's physical appearance made her, to Jonathan at least, infinitely more desirable, especially since the river showed no indications of subsiding.

They were not allowed to sit next to each other in class; the seating was arranged alphabetically. But they saw each other between classes. During lunch Jonathan forewent the daily bullshit sessions with the boys, choosing to spend his time with Lucinda, "the new Lucinda" as he liked to call her and as she liked to be called.

He did not go to the sheriff's office after school anymore. He went home with Lucinda, and often they would walk the two miles to the farm rather than take the bus. Sometimes Ricky would walk along with them or run on ahead. "Ricky, why don't you take the bus?" she asked one day after school.

"Why don't you take the bus?" he countered, grinning. "You just want to be alone with Jonathan. Right?"

"Right," Jonathan stated. His voice was a little sharper than it should have been, causing Lucy to turn to him to examine his face. He grinned at her and said more mildly, "Right," which eased her noticeably.

Ricky did not want to risk the loss of Jonathan's favor and chose a move designed to keep the peace. He rode the bus.

As they were walking, she asked, "Why did you not want Ricky with us?"

He slowed, turned toward her, and said softly, "I think you know the answer to that as well as I do."

"Why?" she repeated.

"Because," he took her hand in his as they walked slowly along together, "because I wanted to be with *you* today, not Ricky."

"Does it matter?" she asked.

"What do you mean, does it matter?"

He spoke a little sharply. "Of course it matters. A guy wants to be with his girl, not with his girl's little brother." He knew what effect this would have, so he didn't even look at her. He felt her hand tighten in his, then he looked; she was blushing. Damn, she blushes a lot!

Father Tim began visiting the Ortega farm more often. If his superior had known about it and if he had known the reasons for it, he would have put a stop to it as quickly as he had ended Timothy's participation in the Sunday baseball. For Timothy visited the Ortega farm to talk with Frank Hyde. They talked about ideas and they talked about books, and if anything was harmful to the ecclesiastical balance of a young priest, according to Father Horrigan, it would be the unsettling influence of books and ideas, especially those of men like Frank Hyde.

Tim had first come into contact with the study of philosophy while in seminary, and there he first encountered questions which appeared to reveal inconsistencies within the framework of his lifelong faith. He was reading Immanuel Kant's *Critique of Pure Reason* when he came upon Kant's arguments against the church's age-old proofs for the existence of God. He read spellbound, and his insides quivered as he considered the implications of this man's ideas upon his life. How could he have failed to see these thoughts years ago? But, as a true believer, he closed Kant in the middle and went to confession and admitted his foundations were shaken.

"Tell me, my son, about the problems you are having with your faith," the old priest said softly and kindly.

Tim told him of his troubles. The old man smiled, "My boy, you have been classically duped by the devil himself." He chuckled.

"I don't understand." The boy was puzzled, but the old priest's attitude gave him hope.

"You did not read all of Kant. You read only so far as to become confused, then you quit. What if you had read only enough of the Bible to learn of Saul of Tarsus persecuting the followers of Jesus? You would have walked away believing Saul to be one of the most despicable of men. The same with Kant. Kant was a pious man, a believer himself, but he set out in his works to establish the firmest possible foundation for man's knowledge, and in his writings he sought to demonstrate how man might know of the existence of God. In his perceptive manner he showed that all the classical proofs for the existence of God could be logically refuted, and there you threw up your hands and quit the field.

"It is no wonder," he continued, "that the thinker discovered that man's proof could be refuted.

"They are 'man's proofs.' Don't you see? Man's proofs," he repeated. "Man's proofs can be refuted by man's logic because proofs are designed by men to gird up a weak faith. But what, my son, about God's proof?" Tim listened intently, holding his hands tightly together. Holding on to himself as if it were for the life of his faith.

"God's proof?" he questioned.

"Of course, God's proof," he thundered, laughing. "Read Kant all the way through and you will find the greatest champion for

God and faith and selfless living in all of modern times."

"What, what does he say?"

"Timothy, when you are tempted to sin, what do you feel within you?" the old priest asked, beaming.

"That I shouldn't," the boy admitted.

"And what is that feeling? Where does it come from?"

The young man smiled.

"You see what is meant by 'God's proof'? You feel God within as a moral guide. If your faith was affected by arguments against man's proofs, it shows that your faith was in man's proofs, not in God himself."

"I understand," Timothy admitted, feeling remorse already for having doubted.

"You must allow that inward tug of the hand of God to guide you, and as He guides you, know that He is."

"I will, Father." The young man was relieved, yet ashamed at the same moment.

"Kant says, 'There must be a God, else what would be the moral governor of the Universe?' You see, my son, without God all would be chaos."

"I understand. Thank you, father." And he went his way rejoicing. He read no more philosophy for a while. But he was troubled somewhat by something else. It seemed to him that the professors knew of his troubles, for he felt them watching him, some doubting, some reaching out ever to assist him. He was never again assigned difficult philosophical topics for reading or study, and from time to time the old priest fell into step beside him and inquired of the state of his soul, to which he always replied as affirmatively as possible. If doubts arose he pushed them down. He tried hard to reconcile his own thoughts with those of the fathers, and when it was especially difficult to do this he learned the habit of assigning the fault to himself, to his own human weakness, to his own sin.

Yet his troubles returned, time and again; and because he feared the church's opprobrium, and later the strong hand of Father Horrigan, he kept them to himself and suffered alone. No one knew the fine young priest had doubts.

It was Father Horrigan, stern, hawk-faced elder ecclesiastic, who caused Timothy Morgan to bring the full focus of his mentality onto the problems of belief. It concerned the doctrine of hell.

"Father Morgan," Horrigan confronted him one morning, "I have taken the liberty of examining the topics of your sermons for your first year here."

"Yes, Father Horrigan?"

"And I find one serious lack in their content."

"Yes."

"You have not, in a year's time, concerned yourself even once with one of the most important doctrines of the Church. Do you know whereof I speak?"

"No, father." Timothy did know, but to admit to this would be to admit too much.

"Do you mean to tell me that you can study and pray and prepare sermons for a year, and not even touch upon eternal punishment?" The young man was silent. "And, even when the church has called for this topic as the subject of our labors, I have discovered that you chose to go to something else." Timothy was still silent. He was faintly aware of his dislike for the subject at hand but had always decided that something else was more necessary at the time. And now he found himself more seriously concerned with it. Why did I flee it? Why do I now feel such an aversion to preaching it?

"You do *believe* in hell, don't you?" the old man asked sharply.

"Of course, father. I can't explain the omission without proper reflection upon it. I think it was because something else always seemed more . . ."

"*Seemed?*" the old priest screeched. "Seemed? Who are you to judge?"

"I will do better in the future, father." Timothy promised.

"You will do better next Sunday, and I will be here to hear."

"Yes, father."

Purgatory I can take, he thought, for the most wicked of men. I can emotionally survive the thought of darkness and aloneness, but I can't handle hell. So where is faith now that I need it?

148

Where is that magic faith that solves everybody's problems? Why didn't I dig into this years before? Why did I come this far without getting this settled? Fool. Fool. Fool.

But he did as he was bidden to do, and apparently the old priest approved because he never said any more to Timothy about it. If only he knew.

Questions of his own faith occupied him day and night. In the day he studied and in the night he prayed for deliverance from the fear he felt coming round him. He took every tenet of faith and labored over each one, and found for each one reasons why he should not believe. Why had he not seen this as a child? Why had he not examined these things more thoroughly in seminary? Fear. I would have had to face them and say, "I do not believe." Family, friends, church.

God. Why am I not afraid to admit this to God? Because I don't believe in Him? But I do. I have all my life. But do I?

It was in this state of mind that he met Frank Hyde the day of the ballgame, and it was this which later caused him to ask Frank if he could see his books.

It was a silly thing, he felt, to ask a man to show you his books, but to Frank it was not silly. It was as natural and as pleasing to him as if someone had asked him how the cotton was doing. He showed him the books gladly. He brought two boxes of them from Oklahoma, and now had them in his bedroom in several stacks. "I've got more," he told Tim, "But I left them in Fairview, not knowing how long I'd be down here."

"These are great, though." Tim took one from the shelf. It was the philosophy of Hume. He leafed through it and noticed it was filled with notes—the margins, the fly leaves, all the white spaces filled with notes and comments. And in the back was a thick bulge of folded writing paper also covered with notes written in a crisp, angular hand. He felt a warmth from the books, not a mystical thing, the warmth, but a comfortable feeling inside himself as he held the books of a man who loved them enough to spend hours with them. He picked them up one by one, Gibbon, Josephus, Havelock Ellis, Freud, Adler, Herodotus, Voltaire, Paine, Jefferson, and on and on.

"I have some really rare ones at home." Frank beamed. "A first-

149

edition Victor Hugo, *The Man Who Laughs*, bought in Arles for a dollar."

"Arles, France?"

"Yep. Got a signed copy of Voltaire's *Candide*, and an edition by Philidor on chess variations."

"You play chess?" Tim asked, clearly incredulous.

"Does that surprise you?"

"It shouldn't, should it?" he stated. "It's just that I meet so few here who do."

Frank Hyde and Timothy Morgan got along beautifully and were to spend a great deal of time together in the next few months discussing philosophies and writers; and occasionally, when there was time, they played chess. Timothy Morgan was a very skillful chess player and just as skillfully worked their conversations around to the topics he needed help on in his quest for truth. But, just as Frank usually knew what the young priest was up to when he transposed a chess opening easily into the Dragon variation of the Sicilian, he understood the meaning of the man's burning interest in the questions of the ages. "Frank, have you studied Kant as much as you have Hume?" Tim asked in passing one evening as they played chess in Frank's small house.

"More," Frank replied. "Much more." He opened a drawer in a cabinet behind him and took out a box, put the box on the table and opened it. He lifted out a thick stack of papers covered front and back with writing. "These are the notes of my running battle with Professor Kant."

Timothy laughed.

"I had struggled halfway through the *Critique* when I realized that Kant was not just another run-of-the-mill philosopher. It seemed to me that the fellow was the culmination of nearly eighteen hundred years of Christian thought. He logicized religion."

"That he did, or tried to."

"Then I just sat down and wrote out for myself what it all meant in terms of life and freedom and philosophical thought since he wrote it."

"And what did you decide?" Timothy took the box reverently and read the first page.

The thought of Immanuel Kant was the culmination of eighteen hundred years of Christianity. He put into philosophical terms the teachings of the church. As Paul synthesized early Christianity with Plato to make the religion of Jesus acceptable to the Greeks and Romans, and as Thomas Aquinas synthesized Christianity with Aristotle to make Churchianity seem logical to a then doubting world, so did Kant make religion palatable by making it seem philosophically acceptable. He logicized religion and was thereby the single most destructive force in the recorded history of ideas. He gave the educational and governmental institutions the tool they needed to enslave millions of minds. That tool was the idea that man has a duty to God, to the state, to society, to everybody but himself. He advocated the absolute abnegation of the self, a total sacrifice of the individual to society through the state.

"You know," Timothy spoke, "that's exactly what an old priest said to me over five years ago. He said that Kant was the greatest champion for faith in God and selfless living."

"To him that was good and to you that was good, then, but now you are having second thoughts."

"How do you know that?" Tim queried.

"If you weren't, you would have challenged my ideas about Kant." Frank smiled. "Right?"

"Yeah, I guess you're right," Timothy admitted. He sat down on the edge of the bed. His shoulders slumped. "I'm some priest, huh?"

"You'll never make a good priest until you do one thing."

"What's that?" Tim looked up at Frank, who placed the Kant back on the dresser.

"Stop thinking. Stop asking questions. Believe Kant. Believe that your duty is to your superiors. Let them think for you. Cease to be an individual, become a nonperson; own nothing, want nothing, do nothing for yourself. Be a sacrificial goat."

Tim was quietly astonished that he was speaking of these

151

things with an outsider, but he asked quietly, "You think then I'd be happy?"

"If you could do it. But I don't believe you can."

"Why not?"

"Because when they processed you for the priesthood they failed to scrape out all your brain. Somewhere back down the line you didn't submit. You kept a little bit of yourself for yourself, and now that self wants the forefront. It wants control. *You* want control."

"You sound like you've thought a lot about it."

"I have."

"Why?"

"Because the question of who owns my mind is the most important question in the world to me."

"Who does? Who does own it?" Timothy asked quietly.

"I do."

Chapter

11

Ricky Ortega first saw the boat as he sat on the river bank and watched the watery world flow by. It was just a small rowboat. It was blue. He saw it first when it was nearly a half mile upstream coming around a slow bend. There was no one in it. It pitched and turned this way and that, and bobbed about. It held him transfixed. Come close, just close enough, he thought. And, as if it heard, it did. The currents swept it in toward the bank not twenty yards out. He ran away from the river, then turned and charged at full run toward the edge of the bank. He saw the blue to the right of him as he cut into the water. He surfaced and saw that the boat was already past him. He turned and kicked toward it, laughing with delight. He knew he could catch it now. He kicked all the harder, gliding with the rushing water. He reached up and caught the boat with both hands and kicked toward shore. "Starboard," he thought, "leeward?" and he laughed again.

He told no one. If anyone should learn about it, he was certain it would then not be long until his mother would know, and she would make him give it up. He was too young and the river was too big. He put the boat in the water the day after he caught it, and he almost didn't get back to shore, so strong were the currents downstream near the bridge. He managed, but barely, to get close enough to the bank to grab a willow branch. Then he was two hours walking it a half mile back upstream, letting out all the rope he had, then guiding it around fallen trees and fallen banks and damnable prickly pear.

So he hid the boat and let it sit, with plans to use it in the main canal when school was out. But he never put his boat in the canal because Jonathan Hyde showed him something he'd never seen before, something across the river.

Frank Hyde took more time for himself after the cotton got tall enough to weed. He checked from time to time with Emilio to see whether the small army of weeders, wetbacks armed with heavy hoes, were staying ahead of the swiftly upshooting hogweeds and other miseries. "If there were no weeders," he told Ellen, "I do believe this entire valley would become a jungle inside a short month."

Ellen saw more of him during the day. She often had him for lunch, which she served on the porch. There would have been too much talk among the workers if Señora Ortega had entertained such a handsome fellow as Señor Hyde inside her home without the children's being present. After lunch they would sometimes just sit, sometimes talking, often not. He would read some days and make notes on his reading. When he did this she was eager to know what he was reading and what he thought about it.

"Here, read this paragraph, and you'll see what I mean." He handed her the open volume and she began to read it, "No, here," he pointed with his pencil. "Start here." And she would read it and then they would talk about it. He was often amazed at her ability to grasp difficult passages in even his most complex volumes. One day, after she had asked an alarming series of penetrating questions about a certain passage from John Locke on the subject of Christian faith, he was so surprised that he said without thinking, "You really *do* understand that stuff, don't you!" He knew it was a mistake the moment he said it, for a blush spread across her face.

"Of course I do. Did you think I didn't?" The thought of it infuriated her. She shut the book, put it on the table, and turned toward the door. He caught her by the hand and turned her to him. There were tears in her eyes. "Did you really think I'm so stupid?" she asked. A slight smile was appearing at the corners of her trembling mouth. She was beginning to be ashamed that she had shown so much feeling, but at the same time she was amused

154

at herself for jumping so quickly. He saw the smile and smiled himself.

"It's not that, Ellen. It's just that you don't meet many women you can talk to about these things, or men either, for that matter." He squeezed her hand. "I'm sorry. I'm pretty stupid sometimes."

"And I act like a schoolgirl."

"You had every right," he assured her. "I was wrong." He released her hand and turned toward the steps. "Guess I'd better check on Emilio." Halfway down he stopped and asked playfully, "Mrs. Ortega, do you also play chess?"

"No," she said, laughing, "but someday I'll let you teach me." And, when he was gone, she said, "When we are old."

Ricky was on his way to the boat late one afternoon carrying a small can of paint and a brush. The oars in the boat were old and beat up and barren of paint. Ricky would keep his prize shipshape.

But before he reached the boat, while walking up a trail which climbed the canal bank, he spotted Jonathan. The older boy was lounging in the fork of a tree high above the ground. He was barely visible through the thick foliage, but Rick could make him out clearly enough leaning back against a limb. Rick whistled. The foliage moved, and Jonathan looked down and swore. "What the hell *you* want?" he demanded.

"Whatcha doin' up there?" Rick wondered if Jonathan could see his boat.

"Watchin' the river."

"See anything?"

"Damn right."

"What?"

Jonathan thought a moment then called down, "Come on up and see for yourself."

Rick hid the paint and brush in the tall grass by the canal and ran toward the tree. In a few minutes he reached the limb. He was out of breath from the climbing. Jonathan moved over for him and Rick settled into a comfortable perch and looked down. He was high above the river. Good. He could not see his boat. "What do you see?" he asked Jonathan, who had produced a pair

155

of old binoculars and was looking downriver with them. "Where'd you get those?" he asked. "Binoculars, wow!"

"Field glasses. They were Jed's. They're not as good as binoculars, but he didn't need 'em since he got some new ones, real binoculars." He handed them to Rick, who quickly put them to his eyes and looked toward the bridge.

"You can really see Reynosa with these. Great, boy."

"That's not what I was lookin' at," Jonathan confided. He took the glasses back and aimed them directly across the river. And then Rick saw them. The whores. White nude figures bathing and playing in the Mexican canal.

"They used to swim in the river," Jonathan told him as he watched through his glasses. "But since it rose, the canal, bein' cut off like it is now, still's the only place clean enough. Wanna look?"

Rick reached for the glasses, but Jonathan held back, "One thing," he said.

"What?"

"A question."

"So?"

"You shouldn't look at 'em unless you're old enough."

"What's old enough?" Rick asked, breathing hard.

"Old enough to jack off," Jonathan announced to the youngster.

"Masturbate," Rick stated.

"What?"

"It's not 'jack off,' it's masturbate, the proper term, and I'm old enough." He took the field glasses. Jonathan let him, surprised.

"Where'd you get that 'masturbate' shit?"

"Father Tim. I asked him if it was wrong." He said matter-of-factly, as he studied the live panorama of bouncing, shining flesh across the river.

"You asked a goddamned priest if jackin' off was wrong?" He laughed. "You stupid shit. You knew what he'd say."

"He said it's okay in moderation when it is necessary." Rick smiled. "I knew he'd be sensible about it."

"Then he does it," Jonathan accused.

"Of course he does. He can't get married."

"He told you that?"

"No, stupid, but I know it. He'd have to; he's made just like we are."

"No shit." Jonathan was irked that this punk knew so much about everything any time he brought anything up. "Bet you never saw anything like that," he said, motioning toward the girls.

"You're right, but only two are really pretty." He handed the glasses back to Jonathan.

"You son of a bitch. You've never seen a naked woman before and you know it." He stared at the kid.

"Yes I have."

"Who?"

"My mother and my sister."

"Really?" Rick had him, and to impress his big adversary he told him how it was, how he'd sneaked looks when he was supposed to be asleep and how once he'd walked into the bathroom without knocking on purpose and had seen Lucinda standing up in the tub.

"And once I even peeked through the keyhole when my mother was taking a bath." The thought of it sent them both into a fever.

Jonathan handed Rick the glasses and with new respect said, "See the blonde? Off by herself layin' down? With her legs spread out?"

"Yes."

"She's really hot stuff."

"She sure is." He was held to the patch of hair a boy of his age dreams of seeing.

"Is she as good as Enola?" Jonathan asked.

"Who's Enola?"

"I mean Lucinda. Is she as good naked as Lucinda?"

"Her breasts aren't as large." He studied the small breasts. "No, they're not as big as Lucinda's."

"That's cause she's layin' down."

"Nope, now she's gettin' up and they're still not." He handed the glasses back to Jonathan, who watched the Princess pull on her dress. When she left, the others did too, following her down the path toward their shacks to receive their two-bit suitors.

"You ever fuck a girl?" Jonathan looked into the boy's eyes. "I'll know if you're lyin'."

"Nope. You?"

"Plenty."

"Not Lucinda," Ricky said quickly, and was relieved when Jonathan admitted not.

"In Oklahoma. A whore lived near us, I fucked her," he stated, "and her daughter, lots of times."

"Frank know?"

"Hell, no. Why should I tell him?"

"No reason."

"You want me to tell you about it?" Jonathan asked.

"Sure." So Jonathan told the boy all the succulent facts and even added a few things and especially embellished his own irresistibility when women learned he was so large. And he could not resist telling Rick about the Princess.

"And her." He motioned toward Boys' Town.

"Who?"

"Her. The blonde. They call her the Princess."

"You did it to her?" Rick asked incredulously.

"Plenty of times. Two, three times a week before this goddamn river fucked up everything."

"How'd you get over there?"

"I just jumped across the damned trickle of water, walked over there, plunked down seventy-five cents. She took off her clothes and let me have it."

"Damn," Rick breathed.

"And when the river goes down I'm goin' back and get myself fucked good and proper," Jonathan affirmed.

"We don't have to wait until the river goes down," Rick said thoughtfully.

"What?"

"I said, we don't have to wait for the damned river." And he showed Jonathan his boat.

Timothy came to the farm more often, ostensibly to play chess, but his real motive revealed itself in the long periods between chess moves when Timothy insisted upon pumping Frank for everything he knew about this subject or that, and invariably the matter of greatest import turned out to be related to religion.

"Frank, why don't you believe that the church is God's representative on earth?"

"Because the church says it is and nothing else or nobody else or even God himself has ever told me that; and when I consider the possible motive behind their saying that they have the 'keys to the kingdom,' so to speak, I am brought to doubt their sincerity."

"What motives?"

"Money, power, political and personal control over people's lives."

"But for good purpose."

"That's what I'm talking about, purpose. You asked me why I don't believe that the church is God's representative on earth. You can't be serious."

"I am serious."

"Do you believe it?"

Tim's right hand went to his collar and a smile crossed his face. "I am a priest."

Frank looked at Timothy and wondered how long the young man could go on believing. "I do not believe that the church is God's representative on earth because I know too much about church history. I presume you are talking about the Catholic Church, and not about one of the hundreds of other groups who also claim to be God's chosen few."

"The Catholic Church."

"I do not believe it because to believe that what the early Popes did to Europe, and what the Crusaders did to the Jews and Turks, and what the Catholics did to the Indians, and what the Catholics and Protestants did to each other, to believe that all that was done by God's representative would be to believe that God is an ogre."

Timothy Morgan was silent.

159

"Aren't you going to refute that statement?"

"No."

"You can, you know."

"How?"

"Simply by saying that when the church does good it is being the representative of God and when it does bad it is being the representative of the devil." Frank smiled at his own invention.

"And then you would answer."

"What?"

"That as an institution it cannot be trusted not to misuse its powers."

"Right."

"But, Frank, don't you think it has done more good than bad, I mean in the long run?"

"No."

"Why?"

"Because it tries to ban independent thought. It attempts to make people, by fear or fraud or force, believe as they are told. By teaching children that they have to believe what they are told, they cripple them for life, they make their necks soft for the yoke of government. Check your history. Have you read Gibbon?"

"No."

"Josephus?"

"No."

"Polybius?"

"No."

"Well, read 'em."

"I will."

"Something else you should think about."

"What's that?"

"When you study world history, consider a correlation between the church's times of greatest power and the world's periods of deepest darkness and then try to determine what measures the church used to control thought during those times. Remember the Inquisition?"

"Yes."

"Well, also study the lives of Bruno and Galileo. Try to find out

160

why Pope Innocent III had Arnaud kill twenty thousand heretics at Béziers in 1209. Read St. Bernard's letter to the Crusaders assuring them that Christ is glorified by the death of unbelievers in a Holy War."

"You sound like you've really dug into this."

"I have."

"Why?"

"Because when I was young I had to figure out which church to join, which one was right. To do that correctly, it seemed to me then, was to examine all of them. Damned waste of time, mostly, but it gave me something to do, I guess."

"You don't believe in any of them?"

"Nope."

"God?"

"Nope."

Tim was silent for a long time staring out over the fields. Then he asked, "Then what do you believe in?"

Frank smiled and tears welled up in his eyes. "I believe in life. In sunshine and rain, children and wheat and cotton and men's minds unfettered by faith or fear."

Tim repeated, "Unfettered by faith or fear."

"The two are related, you know, faith and fear."

"How?"

"They are brothers."

The boys did not wait for the river to recede but went instead, that very night, to the village of whores. Jonathan knew Rick well. He understood perfectly how the boy's mind worked and he correctly assumed that the younger boy was afire with the first flame of youth. He was like a young bull, no reasoning, no direction, just blind desire. So Jonathan supplied him the direction and overpowered his reason with tales all that day, tales of his own exploits. And he told him about the pleasures of Boys' Town. Before Rick knew it, he and Jonathan were in the little boat pitching and bobbing dangerously on the swift river. By last faint light of day they entered Boys' Town. Jonathan stopped at the shack of the most beautiful *puta* he knew besides the Princess.

161

"Felicia, this is Ricardo Ortega. Fuck him well." Then he continued down the street to the first shack, and there he enjoyed the Princess.

It is enough to say that Ricardo completed, in manly fashion, the task he came to do. Felicia later told Jonathan that his little, still-growing prick had stood bravely and spewed forth violently, even though its young owner was visibly scared to death. And, although Rick suffered initial pangs of guilt the rest of that night, he awoke the next morning with sufficient tool to make the trip, and would have immediately had Jonathan not advised him it was best to wait until dark.

The two became fast friends. Rick saw less of Frank; and Jonathan seldom stopped by the sheriff's office. They painted the boat and patched a couple of slow leaks and sat for hours relating their exploits in the whores' beds.

Jonathan told him about the Princess, about how tight she was and how wonderfully warm she was on cool nights; and how marvelously wet and dripping with desire she was for him. But Jonathan would not allow Rick to have her.

Chapter

12

Lucinda Ortega had become in many ways as beautiful as her mother. Her perpetually pensive expression had almost vanished under Jonathan's gentlemanly attentions. He had very studiously discerned her emotional needs. He knew that she wanted to hear about herself. And he knew how to make her laugh.

Jonathan was to Lucinda as he had been to Enola, a very special person, a tall, handsome creature easy to be with, easy to talk to. Before long he had explored every nook and cranny of her soul, knew every high and every low place, the glorious peaks and the shadowed valleys. She even told him about her secret love for Father Timothy, which she insisted was dead even before Jonathan came. Jonathan knew, of course, that this was not true, and that if she only knew it she loved Timothy still. But for a time she was in Jonathan's spell, which cast a soft warm glow upon her spirits, so that it did not seem wrong to her when they progressed from holding hands to tender embraces and tender kisses made warmer and gradually hungrier by the long hours spent together at school and before school and after. She was aware of the deeper needs developing in her, and it seemed normal and even desirable to discuss them.

"Lucy, there is something I feel I should talk to you about." They were alone in the kitchen.

"What, Jonathan?"

"Well, it's kind of hard to talk about."

"We can talk about anything, Jonathan." She became quite bold.

"Anything?" he smiled.

"You dirty boy," she teased him. "Yes, anything you want to talk about is all right with me" she assured him.

"Well, it's about Enola."

"Enola? What about her?"

"Well, she was, uh, different than you in some ways."

"How do you mean?" She leaned forward and he reached across the table and took her hand.

"Well, she was just different, one way." He hesitated, feigned embarrassment, and continued. "She was different sexually."

"How?"

"She didn't think it was wrong to go to bed with a boy."

"Really?" She was visibly shocked and her face reddened immediately. Then she thought. "Jonathan, did you? . . . I mean did she ask you to . . ."

"She asked, many times."

"But you didn't."

"No."

"I'm glad you didn't."

"So am I, now." He looked into her eyes and smiled and held her hand tighter and was silent. And she was quiet for a moment, until . . .

"I wanted to terribly at times but . . ."

"It was best you didn't, Jonathan."

"I know, now. I didn't really love her, Lucy. It would have made it different if I had loved her."

And Lucinda thought, "Like with us."

"She did it with other boys, though. She told me that."

"I'll bet that hurt you."

"It did, but she didn't do it while I was going with her. I know that. That's what I wanted to talk to you about." He looked at her again to be certain where he was. "She explained to me something I never knew before about girls."

"What on earth?"

"That, you know, where a boy and a girl like each other a lot

164

and kiss all the time they get all excited. Boys too. The girl gets a really nervous feeling, you know, down there," and his eyes flicked downward, indicating where he meant, "and sometimes it's even so bad she can't sleep." He questioned her with his eyes.

"I know."

He smiled wanly. "So she told me that there was something she did at night that made her feel better and made the feeling go away."

"What was it?"

"Maybe I shouldn't be telling you this. . . ."

"You can tell me, Jonathan. You are more to me than just a friend now. You can talk to me."

"Well, I don't want to cause you to feel like that unless you can do something."

"What did she do, Jonathan? *Tell* me," she urged.

"Well, she rubbed herself down there for a few minutes and the feeling went away and she wasn't uneasy anymore."

"Oh."

"See, I told you I shouldn't have mentioned it."

"No, you should have."

"Well, if I shouldn't have, I'm sorry."

"Don't be silly." She stood and came around the table. "I have felt like that, lots of times."

"Like right now?" He touched her face and smiled. Her face was warm and flushed.

"Yes, talking about it makes it stronger. It makes me feel all quivery."

"Me too," he admitted. "Sometimes . . . sometimes . . . I don't know if I should tell you."

"Tell me."

"Sometimes it's the same with me. Like with you and Enola. I mean sometimes mine gets to feeling like that. Even so bad sometimes it hurts, aches there, and . . ."

"Go on," she said. "When will you learn? You can tell me anything." And then softly, "I want to know everything about you, Jonathan, no matter what it is."

"Well, sometimes I do that to myself what she did, what she

taught me." They were both silent for a while after that. He could feel her breathing deepen and he felt heat coming out of her body.

Later she revealed, "I knew about that, Jonathan, that touching it makes it feel better."

"Have you already done it?" he asked, surprised.

"Not really. I just did a little. I guess I was a little afraid."

"Afraid? Of what?"

"Well, you know, that it's wrong and all. When we were little we were told not to touch it or play with it."

"I know, me too."

"So I guess I just thought about that and wouldn't let myself touch it."

"Me, too, for a long time, until Enola explained something to me."

"What?"

"That we were little kids when they told us about that. How would you like to have a little boy or girl who went around playing with himself, especially when company comes?"

She laughed.

"They told us not to when we were kids and just forgot to tell us any different."

"That makes sense." She wanted it to make sense.

"And as far as it being wrong, now consider that your body develops somewhere around fourteen and you don't get married until you're what, twenty? twenty-one? Are we supposed to live in agony for six or seven years? That's why I just don't feel bad about doin' it."

"I see what you mean."

"Besides," he said as he hugged her strongly to him and pulled her down to his lap, "besides, it's fun." He grinned and she blushed.

When Father Timothy Morgan returned to his room after speaking with Frank Hyde he always made notes on Frank's responses to his questions, and he wrote down any new thoughts which might have occurred to him while talking with Frank. He wrote his notes in a small notebook which he hid beneath the

166

mattress of his bed. He felt guilty doing it and cursed himself for feeling so. "Am I a child that I cannot think? Cannot faith sustain examination? If it cannot," he told himself one day, "then so much the worse for faith." It seemed to Tim that Frank's reasoning was insurmountable in whatever area they discussed.

"Did you do it?" he asked as they walked toward the road to catch the bus.

"Yes."

"Did you feel bad? After, I mean."

"A little."

"Well, don't."

"I won't."

"It felt good, didn't it?"

"Yes."

After school, when the bus pulled away from them at the long Ortega driveway, Jonathan and Lucy walked hand in hand so slowly that Rick and the others went on ahead of them. When they were out of sight Jonathan turned toward the baseball field and they walked across it, entered the orange grove, and walked through it slowly until they reached the main canal.

"I want to show you my secret place," he confided.

"Your secret place?"

"I need a place all my own I can go to and be alone."

She was moved. Her heart beat quickly. She said nothing.

"I wanted you to see it and know where it is." He led her up to the canal bank through the chest-high Johnson's grass and toward a huge corona vine wreathed in its small brilliant pink blossoms. The area was alive with the hum of bees. He stopped at the vine and pulled back a part of it, and she saw that behind the vine was a small secret room in the vines. He entered and was bathed in the purest green light shining as if from the living leaves themselves. Her white dress was yellow green with it. And there was the constant soft voice of bees. Jonathan turned and faced her and smiled, and opened his arms to her. She leaned into him and felt the uncontrollable hunger of the lonely with a friend finally, the unloved with lover found. He kissed her softly and she kissed him back. He felt her tears warm on his face and

167

they lay back together on the spring grass. He stroked her face and neck, and he kissed her eyes. His hand pressed downward and found her firm breast. She moved toward him and felt him hard against her and knew the pounding of her own heart and his. His fingers discovered the opening in her dress and started in toward her breast and then retreated. "Should I, Lucy?"

"Oh yes, Jonathan. I love you so much, Jonathan." So his fingers opened the buttons to her soul and his mouth found her virgin breasts. He pulled her dress up and ran his hand up her legs and pressed the warm place there and in a moment when he entered her and she cried out from the pain of it he smiled. And just before he planted his seed within her, without care or conscience, he smiled again.

That night in her bed she wept. In fitful sleep were dreams of a man upon her and it was good, but she awoke in the dream and waves of guilt shuddered over her. When she slept again the man was upon her again, but his face was not the proud confident visage of Jonathan Hyde. The man upon her bore the kind and thoughtful countenance of Father Tim. And when she awoke again there was amidst the guilt a kind of bewilderment, for she was certain it was Jonathan Hyde she loved, and why was there guilt in love?

She went with him the next day to their green place and she told him about the guilt, but not about the dream.

"It is natural to feel guilty," he explained, "when all your life you've been taught it's wrong. But, Lucy baby, tell me how could anything so beautiful be wrong? Tell me. How can love be wrong?"

"Do you still love me, Jonathan?"

"I still love you, Lucinda."

Ricardo became addicted to Felicia. She was a slight, laughing girl. He became jealous when he thought of her with men even though he knew that it was what she did.

Jonathan still preferred the Princess, but offered to trade one night when Rick told him how good Felicia was. "But the Princess will suck you for two bits more," Jonathan coaxed him.

"So?" Rick countered. "Felicia does it for nothing extra."

"For nothing?"

"Because she loves me."

Lucinda waged a desperate warfare with guilt, whose powerful force at times she managed to evade almost completely. But she did not know of its subtle ability to work havoc beneath the surface. She changed again, from the happy, carefree child she had become upon first loving Jonathan, to a quiet, fearful person with a dried-up smile. This was partly aggravated by a gradual suspicion that Jonathan was changing toward her. She still went with him to the green place, but it was not the same as before. He was often not kind and loving and listening, and she was no longer innocent. He admitted to her that she was an expert lover, but he also revealed that she was not, in fact, his first. He told her the truth about Enola and gave a slightly expurgated version of his afternoon with Mrs. Vinson. But he assured her that she was the last and would ever remain so.

Ricky, knowing Jonathan better than anyone else on the Ortega farm, became suspicious of Jonathan and his sister. He saw her change and knew what was going on. One day he followed them to their place, and listened. That night he confronted Jonathan with it.

"I know about you and Lucy."

"What do you mean?"

"I know you've been fucking her."

"You're crazy."

"I saw you. At the canal."

"You go to hell."

"Does she know about the Princess?"

"You go to hell."

"What if she finds out? What if I tell her?"

Jonathan was silent as he considered the threat. Then spoke, "If you tell her I will kill you." And the way he said it, Rick believed him.

About a month before school was out Lucinda began to suspect that she was pregnant. She told no one, not even Jonathan, but pressed him hard for an understanding between them. In all of his "I love you's" and "forevers" he had never been specific. She had taken for granted that they would one day be married, and often she would mention matters such as "how our home is going to be," travel together, and even children. And when she talked like this he would smile and hug her to him, and she took this to be an expression of assent.

"Jonathan, we haven't talked specifically," she said one day on their way home from their green place, "about what we are going to do after we graduate."

"I thought you were going to college," he said quickly.

"Well, I was till I met you." Her voice was weak and tremulous.

"What do I have to do with it?" he asked. She stopped and held his arm and turned him around to face her. She was crying now.

"Jonathan, I *love* you."

He looked away. She touched his cheek and turned his face back down toward her. "I *love* you and have given myself to you, Jonathan, *completely*. Doesn't that count for something?"

"To tell you the honest truth, Lucinda, you were never as good in the grass as Enola." She doubled over and grabbed her stomach, cried out from the pain there, and turned away.

"I'm going to the house," he said.

Rick found his sister at dusk standing dangerously near the river bank, looking down into the swirling brown water and crying. Her eyes were red and her face was wet and puffy.

"Lucinda!" he called. She turned and began to walk away. He darted after her, caught her arm. "What's the matter, Lucy?"

"Nothing anybody can do anything about now," she said.

"You havin' trouble with Jonathan?" he asked. She nodded her head and wiped at her eyes with her sleeve.

"You're better off without him, Lucy."

"But I love him."

"You get to know him better, sister, then you won't love him; you'll hate his guts."

She did not go again with him to their place. Nor would she allow him to touch her intimately. She held his hand and walked

170

with him and tried several times to talk to him, but when he realized that she would not play his game any longer, he moved quickly away and spent more time with the Princess.

Then Lucinda told him.

It was Saturday and he and Rick were in the field irrigating. She brought them sack lunches. Lucy sat with Jonathan while he ate. When he had finished she said, "Jonathan, it's time we faced facts about us."

"I already have, baby. We are finished; there isn't any 'we.'" He stood up and turned to go.

"We are going to have a baby."

He stopped and turned back slowly. His gray eyes were cold and hard. "You're a goddamn liar." He started toward her slowly.

"It's true."

"You're lying. You'd say anything to get me, you sniveling little whore." He stopped in front of her, took her shoulders in his hands, lifted her up and began to shake her. Rick came running toward them brandishing a hoe and screaming at Jonathan. "Don't you touch her! Turn her loose! Damn you, Jonathan!" He swung the hoe at Jonathan's head. Jonathan saw it just in time. He ducked, threw Lucy to the ground, and kicked Rick in the middle. The smaller boy grabbed his belly and fell, writhing and gasping for breath. Lucy ran to him.

Jonathan picked up the hoe and walked toward them. She covered Rick. "Leave him alone."

"I'm just leaving the mosquito his hoe. Hey, mosquito, your stupid sister tried to make me think she's pregnant."

Rick asked, "Is it true?" Lucinda looked at Jonathan, then at Rick.

"No," she said quietly.

"You see?" Jonathan said. "Your whore sister is also a liar." He laughed and walked away.

"Lucinda," Rick demanded, "is it true?"

"Yes," she said. He held his weeping sister to him and felt very much a man to protect her and comfort her, but when he turned to watch Jonathan Hyde walk into the oranges he felt only fear and hate. He shivered against the body of his sister.

171

A few days later Jonathan was walking into town after school. The sheriff's car approached him and slowed to a stop. "Hop in," Jed called. Jonathan did. "Wanta make a couple o' bucks?" Jed asked.

"What doin'?"

"Workin', what else?" Jed studied the boy carefully.

"What kind of workin'?"

"Puttin' up a tent for an old preacher. I'm goin' over there now."

"Okay, what the hell?"

The Reverend Mervel Horner was a little bit of a man with no hair on his head except what protruded obscenely from his nostrils and ears. He was thin and red and wrinkled, and his eyes were slits, slightly slanted. His general appearance led one to believe that his ears should be pointed, but when one examined them they were not actually.

"We usually don't have to pay for the tent raising," he said, "but we're not in holiness country now. No sir, we are smack in the middle of the devil's country. Catholics, these people." He squinted his eyes at Jonathan. "You be Catholic, boy?"

"No sir." Jonathan smiled his ready smile, his easy one.

"Then what be ye?"

"Methodist, sir, I was born a Methodist, sir."

"What brand?"

"I don't know, Oklahoma Methodist, I guess." The man squinted further; Jonathan could not tell whether it was meant to be a grin or a grimace.

"No, son," he answered kindly. "What I mean to ask is, are you of the holiness Methodists?"

"I'm not sure."

"Have you been saved?"

"Yes sir."

"When?" The grin-grimace again.

"When I was six."

"Were you sanctified?"

"I don't know what that means," Jonathan answered, turning

172

to Jed, who simply shrugged his shoulders and looked uncomfortable.

"Well, then," the little man said slowly, "if you don't know what sanctification is and you were saved at six, then I'd say you were due for an overhaul job. Wouldn't you say?"

"Yes sir."

Jonathan helped lift the tent, but was told to return the next evening to collect his dollar. As he was leaving, the preacher Horner stopped him. "How'd you like a permanent job?" He grimaced.

"Doin'?"

"Liftin' that tent and lowerin' it and drivin' the truck."

"You mean it?"

"Yes. How old are you?"

"Eighteen."

"School?"

"Be out in two weeks."

"Good, be back here tomorrow night and every night after that and help out with the usherin' and offerin'. You got folks?"

"Just my dad."

"Well, bring him too."

"Nope, I can't bring him."

"Why not?"

"He don't believe in God or nothin'. He won't go to church."

"Never?"

"He'd likely kill me if he knows I'm goin' away with you."

"You a Christian, boy?"

"Yessir."

"Then don't worry about it. I suspect the Lord knows all about it."

"Yessir. I suspect he does." Jonathan smiled.

He would not tell his father about his arrangements with the preacher. When the time came he would just leave, "Then to hell with this shit hole," he thought.

But he could not resist the temptation to tell Rick.

"Two more weeks and I'm done with this shit hole," he told the boy as they waited for the bus. Lucy had stayed home. Rick was surprised when Jonathan waited with him. Since the day in

173

the field he had steered clear of Jonathan as much as possible. So had Lucy. And Jonathan was happy to be done with them. But he couldn't resist holding himself up to Rick just one more time.

"What do you mean?" Rick asked, not looking at him.

"I mean I've got a payin' job somewhere."

"Doin' what?"

"Truck driver."

"Who for?"

"Somebody."

"Big deal."

"No, really. You know that preacher's truck?"

"The red one?" Rick asked.

"That's her. I gotta drive that and carry that tent for the preacher. All over the United States."

"So."

"Soon's school's out we're headin' for California. How about that?"

Rick turned to him slowly. "Does that preacher know you're leavin' Lucy with your baby in her?"

In a split second Jonathan's right hand had gripped Rick's lower jaw and his strong fingers were pressing in. Rick was silent, but his eyes reddened and tears from the pain flowed down his cheeks and onto Jonathan's hand. "Your sister is lying. Your whore sister is lying, you little son-of-a-bitch!" He squeezed as hard as he could and Rick winced with the pain. When he let go Rick rubbed his jaw and began to cry softly.

When he gained control again he said, "You won't go with that preacher, Jonathan."

"What's that, mosquito?"

"I said, 'You won't go with that preacher.' " His face was dark and his jaw was set.

The bus stopped and Jonathan had to let him go, but as he watched the boy he thought, "What if the little shit does go mouthing to the goddamn preacher?" A darkness came over him and he began to feel the same trembling feeling he'd had before the fight with Billy Risedale.

That afternoon he confronted Rick at the rabbit hutches. Rick was carrying a sack of feed, going from hutch to hutch, feeding.

"Hurry up," Jonathan commanded. "We're going across."

"Not me."

"Yes, you, goddamnit."

"I don't want to go."

"Since when?"

"Not with you."

Jonathan stepped close to the boy and reached for his jaw, but Rick quickly shoved the heavy sack of feed at him and darted toward the house. Jonathan side-stepped and started after him. In a few long strides he had him. He knocked the smaller boy to the ground and pounced on him, looking this way and that to be certain no one was watching. Then he slapped Rick and held him by the back of the shirt and growled at him, "I want to go see the Princess and I don't want you out of my sight going to that goddamn old preacher, so the safest place for me to have you is across that damned river so you can't get back before I do. Savvy, Mex?"

Rick still said nothing. Jonathan's free hand went to the boy's testicles and he began to squeeze. Rick cried out and his hands pulled at Jonathan's but Jonathan squeezed tighter. "Yes," Rick said. Jonathan released him and slapped his face.

Rick rolled over and grabbed his balls and cried softly. "I won't tell the preacher, I swear it."

"You're goin' with me to the Princess. Get up."

"I won't tell your goddamn preacher friend. I want you to go with him."

"You're a lyin' meskin son-of-a-bitch. Now get up!" He lifted Rick to his feet and shoved him in the direction of the river. "I might even let you watch me and the Princess." He laughed. "Do you good."

When they reached the boat Jonathan made Rick pull it by himself out from under its covering of brush and vines. Then he held the bow rope and made Rick get in first. When he shoved off and stepped into the boat Rick saw something in Jonathan's face, in his eyes, that caused Rick's bowels to churn. A smile covered half Jonathan's face, a fierce darkness masked the other, as he lifted his eyes to meet Rick's.

Rick began paddling madly for the bank, but Jonathan had the

175

other oar in his hand and he struck it at Rick's hands, causing him to release his oar to the river. He grabbed for it, but it was already gone from him. He turned to face Jonathan, who was now moving toward him slowly. His eyes were cold and unsmiling, though his lips smiled. One bank of the river passed behind Jonathan's head, then the other as the boat turned around in the powerful currents.

"Jonathan," Rick spoke softly, unbelieving, "what's the matter with you?" Jonathan kept crawling slowly inch by inch, watching the fear in the boy's face.

"Jonathan!" he cried. "What are you trying to do?" Jonathan only smiled. When he reached the boy he stopped in front of him and reached into his pocket. He took out a large Barlow knife and began slowly to open it, savoring the fear on Rick's face. Then Rick jumped into the river, and it was a few seconds before Jonathan realized that his prey had escaped him.

Rick came to the surface and saw the boat bearing down upon him. He dived again and when he came up again the boat was between him and the bank. The swift water tugged at him. It was hard to keep headed one way. He did not see the knife when it came and the blunt butt of its handle caught him on the shoulder. His arm stiffened and he tried to swim without it, but could not in the turbulent river, so he let the river carry him. He saw the boat lunge toward him and even heard Jonathan grunt as he flung the oar down at his head, missing by inches. He went under again in the blackness of the dirty water and stayed down as long as he could. His head began to hurt from holding his breath. His shoulder began to ache and burn and he wondered if the knife had actually cut into him. When he came up again he was near a log, which he grabbed with relief, and he laughed and then he began to cry. When he last saw Jonathan he was holding on to a willow branch and trying to pull the boat back to the bank. Jonathan turned to watch as Rick slipped away from him into the gullet of the damned river. He cursed and pulled the boat around the tree and toward the bank.

Free of Jonathan, Rick had time to assess what had happened. It was clear to him that Jonathan had slipped a cog somewhere and that he had intended to kill him. For what? Because I might tell

176

the preacher? Doesn't make sense to kill somebody for that.

Holding on to the drifting limb with his left hand, he flexed his right arm. The bad pain had subsided, leaving it sore and stiffening. He turned and looked back. The boat was no longer visible. His eyes scanned the south bank of the river, then the north. No one.

He held the log and kicked for the left bank, looking up from time to time to watch for Jonathan. The log moved slowly toward the shore, and then a swirling current would throw them back toward the middle. He kicked mightily, but could not get it over. Have to leave it. He kicked away from the log and fought the brown water for his life. He felt it surge and knew fear again and fought harder. His breathing was deeper and fitful, and his lungs began to hurt down deep. He made progress. Lost it. Then made some more. Then some more. Just a little more. He reached up to grab at a willow branch. Missed. He got the next one. Broke in his hand. The next branch was dead mesquite. It shouldn't have held him but it did. He lay for a moment in the water, getting his breath, knowing he couldn't take long. Jonathan would be coming. Damn, he's crazy, he thought.

He reached for the next limb closer to the bank, caught it and pulled to the next and then felt bottom with his feet. He pulled up quietly and crawled quickly up the bank. He peered over the top carefully. Nobody.

He slid part way back down the bank, sat down and took off a shoe and poured the water out of it. He started to put it back on and thought, "I'm faster barefoot and I might have to get back into the river if Jonathan comes after me." He smiled. He wasn't afraid of the river and he knew Jonathan was not that good a swimmer. Jonathan Alexander the Great is scared of the water. He laughed quietly to himself and pulled off the other shoe and placed them both on the bank high enough to keep them safe. Then, feeling mildly exhilarated at having outfoxed his pursuer, he scampered back up the bank and charged out on the river path, running as fast as he could.

He did not see who it was that stepped out of the bushes and onto the path in front of him, but he knew who it was and whose steel fist struck his thin gut with the force of a sledge which lifted

177

his small body into the air and out over the river. He fell slowly through the feathery blackness and tried to breathe, but the water filled him up and he was one with it. After a struggling moment he was not aware of the darkness or the river above him or the burning pain in his gut.

Early in the morning of the next day the searchers found his shoes. Two days later an old woman fifty miles downriver saw him floating in the river. The body was taken from the water near Brownsville; late that night they brought him home.

Lucinda was in hysterics. Ellen was unbelieving until she saw him for herself, and then she was strangely calm, remembering that day long ago when she got the government's black-bordered letter.

Father Timothy came and spoke to Lucinda. She was quiet for a while and when she was quiet she began to think and thinking brought about in her head horrible suspicions that simply could not be. Then the doctor came and gave her something and she gave in to it and sank back into the guilty sleep the troubled living know.

There was nothing Frank could do but be there, nothing he could say or even wanted to say. When Ellen saw the boy's body Frank was near her. She turned to him and leaned against him and tried to breathe deeply and control herself. He put his arms around her and tried, unsuccessfully, to hold back his own tears.

Jonathan revealed to them that Ricky had gotten a boat from the river. Jed Strunk reasoned that the boy must have lost the rope or discovered the boat missing and run after it and dived in for it and drowned.

"But his shoes were wet," Frank said.

"That's what I can't understand about it," Jed said.

"He could have fallen from the boat, made it to the bank, taken off his shoes, then gone back after the boat," Jonathan offered.

Lucinda caught herself looking at Jonathan. He met her accusing eyes with his own steel gray, and she looked away and tried not to think.

At the funeral Jonathan wept with the rest of them, pleased with himself that he could do so, thinking all through it, "Too bad the little shit got in my way. He was damn likable at times but too bad he had to poke his nose in."

As they left the cemetery Jonathan couldn't keep from smiling as he thought of himself driving that big truck, sitting tall in that big truck, pulling away from the farm and his father and Lucinda. "Goddamn that pregnant bitch Lucinda," he thought. "She caused the whole goddamn thing."

Chapter

13

The morning that school was out Jonathan left town driving the big truck loaded with the tent and the chairs and the pulpit. They had loaded up the night before. The little preacher and his large wife were waiting in their car outside the school. They drove him to the preacher's truck and followed him out of town and east toward Brownsville for their next revival meeting.

The reverend was especially proud that the boy hadn't even mentioned money. He said to his wife, "That boy's not like most people. He's no money grubber. He's grown up under an ungodly father and he wants a chance to spread his wings spiritually." So the preacher brought up the subject of money when Jonathan was packing the chairs.

"Son, you still haven't asked the most important question about this job."

Jonathan turned to him and said seriously, "I'm not interested in money."

"Now that's good, but what are you interested in?" The reverend squinted, intent upon this new brand of creature who didn't care about money.

"Reverend, I'm going to be honest with you and tell you something I've never told a living soul." He put the load of chairs on the truck and spoke softly. "When I was a little boy I felt God's hand on me in a strange way. Every time I'd go to church with my mother I'd feel a little voice inside saying, 'Jonathan Alexander Hyde, you're my boy. You will preach the gospel and bring souls to me.'" Jonathan paused, looked away, then continued,

"And you know, my mother knew about it without my tellin' her and on her deathbed she . . ." his voice broke, "she . . ."

"Now you don't have to talk about it, son. You just go on with those chairs. We'll talk tomorrow." The little man was touched and he laid a hand on the boy's shoulder.

"Nope, I'm okay. It's just that she's only been gone since winter. It's still . . . it's still hard to think about it, but she said to me, she held my hand and said, 'Jonathan, the Master's touched you and you're special.' That's what she said. And then just before she died she said, 'You serve Jesus, Jonathan. You do just like he wants. You serve Jesus.' " The preacher was wiping his eyes with his sleeve. "And, reverend, that's why the money don't interest me. I want to drive this truck and go around with you. I want to learn somethin' from you. I want to learn preachin'."

The reverend stood there for a moment. A minister lives for that one soul of souls who will follow him into the pulpit, one who will win many souls and for whom celestial credit is due. In his heart Mervel Horner knew that this strapping youth was the one upon whom his mantle would fall. He knelt in the grass beside the truck and began to pray: "Father, thou hast blessed my life beyond compare to this day, and on this day thou hast revealed to me the culminate blessing of them all, an Elijah for my mantle, Thy mantle." And Jonathan smiled as the little believer prayed, but beneath the smile he began to see a way, a way for himself, and it pleased him.

That night he walked openly across the Reynosa bridge and down into Boys' Town and took his last pleasures with the Princess. He didn't say goodbye to her or even to his father. He didn't leave a note. "Good enough for him," he thought. And the next day after school he was gone.

Frank Hyde sat alone in his little house, a book open in his lap, unread since dark and little read before. His thoughts were gray as are the thoughts at times of men who refuse to believe in angels. Faith, he thought, is not a matter of choice. If it were and a man could find real comfort in it any man would choose to believe. But he would want to believe what he wanted to believe. I would want to believe that Ricky didn't hurt when he drowned,

181

that Mary isn't really dead, that Jimmy Ortega is alive and well and farming cotton in the happy hunting ground. And I would want to believe that somewhere down the road somebody would teach Jonathan goodness. If I could believe like that I would make it rain in Oklahoma.

But the truth is a man has no choice. He has to believe what he sees. He is a coward otherwise. Gird up your nuts and weather the storm and earn the right to enjoy the rainbow because you did not despair in the storm.

When he thought like that and stood straight in times of trouble it always strengthened him and gave him courage to wait for morning, gave him need to see and touch and smell and taste the morning. A man who thinks about how wonderful his heaven is gets himself into a pretty low opinion of the here and now. Which ain't half bad if you stay out of the river or don't get cancer or have sense enough to keep away from wars. Not half bad. He closed the book in his lap and gripped it and put his hand's strength onto it. He smiled and stood up, confident the storm had passed and they could get back to the cotton and the hay, the beans and baseball, the books and the laughing again.

And then he heard Ellen's voice at his door. "Frank?" There in her voice was the storm again. The jagged edge of hurt was buried in it.

"Yes, Ellen?" He walked to the door and opened it. Her hand took his. Hers was cold and trembling. "What's the matter?"

"You shouldn't sit in the dark, Frank. It is not good for a man to sit alone in the dark." He stepped back and pulled the light string and turned and saw her eyes were red and her face was drained of color. "Turn it off." He pulled the string again and the light fled from the room. She opened the door and went out again. He followed her out and they walked to the porch of the big house and sat there quietly until Ellen said, "Lucinda is pregnant."

Frank stood, walked toward the porch rail, and gripped it. He stared at the ground below.

"So this is why he pulled out so quick." He spoke to Ellen behind him. "If the boy were here right now, Ellen, I think I could kill him."

"How do you know it was Jonathan?" she asked.

"It was Jonathan," he said quietly. "She was sweet on him. I thought he was growing up. I thought he really cared about her."

Ellen came to his side. "That's not all there is to it, Frank. . . . There's more."

"More?" He looked at her. The light from the living room revealed the tempest within her. She was crying. "What else, Ellen?"

"Lucy . . . She thinks Jonathan killed Ricardo."

Frank froze. His mind revolted. He knew Jonathan was a destroyer but . . .

"She says Ricky told her Jonathan had threatened him if he told she was pregnant.

"He was going to tell that damned preacher on Jonathan so Jonathan wouldn't get the job. Rick wanted Jonathan to marry Lucinda."

Frank sat down heavily and put his head in his hands. "It doesn't make sense," he said.

"Does anything?"

"Where is Lucy?" he asked.

"She's packing. I'm taking her to San Antonio."

"What's in San Antonio?"

"My father. He'll understand and take care of her."

"I'm calling Jed, Ellen. I want him to talk to Lucy and then go with me to find Jonathan."

"No."

"No?"

"She's been through too much already. No more."

"But Jonathan. . . !"

"I don't care about him. Just keep him away from my daughter!"

The truth ate into his gut like worms at work in a dead thing. Jonathan had done this thing. He was capable of it. Frank's eyes filled with hot, angry tears. His fists clenched. No god to blame, only himself for not knowing long ago what could turn a little boy into a beast and finding that thing and killing it. Son-of-a-*bitch* what was it! Then I won't talk to Lucy about it. I'll get Jed and go on. He turned and started down the steps.

"Frank." He didn't turn around to her, but only stopped and waited. "Yes?" he said.

"When you find him and talk to him, no matter what you find out I don't want Lucy hurt anymore."

"I know, Ellen."

"Even if you think he's guilty of killing Ricky there's no way to prove it. The court would put her through too much."

"But I've got to find out about my boy. After what he's done to Lucy I've got to know if he's a killer on top of that."

"What good will it do?"

"I need to know."

He went into the dark house, put some of his books in one box and his clothes in another, and left in the dark of night. As he drove through the fields toward town the cotton crop was a pale blue-white with the rising moon, only a blurred ghost of what he'd hoped for.

Jed Strunk was filing reports in his office when Frank arrived. The deputy was asleep in a cell. He awoke when Frank closed the door and lay awake, listening.

"Jed, do you know where Jonathan and the preacher went?"

"I think they's headed for Brownsville, Frank. What you up to this late?"

"Lucy thinks Jonathan killed Ricky." He sat heavily on the couch. Jed stopped his filing.

"What?"

"Lucy," he repeated, "she says Jonathan killed Ricky. And I think she might be right."

Jed was silent. He eyed Frank with one eye squinted shut. He closed the file drawer and sat down on the couch beside Frank. "Now you just tell me what the hell you're sayin'." So Frank told him in a low, quavering voice. He seemed to Jed like a man dragging an ugly hook across the bottom of a black lake, and the lake was Frank's own soul.

"So I want you to go with me."

"I'll go with you, but it won't do any good, Frank."

"Why not?"

"On account of Lucy didn't see it happen and ain't no way Jonathan's gonna own up to it. And anyway her bein' pregnant with his baby'd sorta give any good lawyer ideas she had an axe to grind against Jonathan. Better let it be, Frank, better for you and Ellen *and* Lucy, better all around."

"Better for Ricky?" Frank asked bitterly.

"Be past midnight 'fore we could get there," Jed said.

"Then we'd better be goin'."

They took Jed's car and drove in silence.

They found the tent on the Military Highway, just outside of Brownsville. Jed coasted to a stop near the tent, reached for his flashlight and got out. Frank followed. Jed played the light over the area. The big truck was parked behind the tent. He saw an electric box on a rickety pole near the truck. As he reached for the switch he saw out of the corner of his eye a dark figure lunging toward him. He reeled and lashed out at it with his open palm. The figure crumpled. He switched on the light. Jonathan Hyde was just getting to his knees, wiping blood from his nose.

"What the hell you tryin' to do, boy? Goddamn!"

"Thought you was thieves," he groaned.

"Thieves?"

"I sleep out here in the tent and watch the equipment. Part of my job." Frank knelt down and wiped the blood from the boy's face with his handkerchief.

"Here. Put your finger right there." Jed placed Jonathan's finger on the bridge of his nose. "Hold your head over like this so the bleedin' will stop." He showed him how. Jonathan did and soon the bleeding subsided.

"You all right, now?" Jed asked.

"Yes." He wiped his nose on his sleeve. "What are you doin' down here?"

"We came to talk, Jonathan," Frank said. Jed saw the love in this man's eyes and felt the pain there.

"Talk? In the middle of the night?"

"Look, Jed. Is there someplace to get some coffee around here?" Frank asked.

"Not this late. There's some bars open, but ain't no coffee in 'em, Frank."

"I've got some in my truck," Jonathan said.

Jonathan stood up and walked toward the truck, where he

185

found a fruit jar full of lukewarm coffee. They all drank. Then Jed spoke.

"Son, reason we came over here this time o' night is there's some talk in Hidalgo that you know more about Ricky's drownin' 'n you told." Jonathan turned his back to them and walked to the truck. He put his hands against the truck and leaned toward it for the longest moment. Jed glanced at Frank. Frank awaited the boy's explanation.

In time Jonathan turned to them. His eyes were moist. Even in the dim light the two men could see they were reddened. "It's true," he blurted out. His fist closing and opening. He stepped back and leaned his back against it and he stared at the bare light bulb near the tent entrance. "It's true, but I just couldn't tell anybody. It's one of the reasons I had to go." He looked at his father, pleaded for understanding with his eyes. Then he looked at the ground. "See, Lucy's pregnant." He glanced at Jed then down again. "I, uh, I thought she loved me. . . . I really thought she honestly did care about me. We talked about when we'd get out of school and get married and have a life of our own and all. Hell! I thought she meant it so we, uh . . . well, we . . . then she came up pregnant and she turned into a different person. She hated me. Didn't want me around. Didn't want to talk to me ever." He turned and sat down on the truck's runningboard. "Then Rick found out."

"How?" Jed asked, curtly.

"I don't know." He tossed a glance toward Jed. "But he put pressure on us to tell and get married and she didn't want to."

"Why?" Frank asked, softly.

"He said it was wrong for her to have a baby and not be ma—"

"No. Lucy. Why didn't she want to?"

"I don't know."

"Okay, Jonathan, now what about Ricky's death?"

"I . . . I, uh, don't want to say."

"Why? Say what?" Frank said.

"It won't do anybody any good now. Least of all Ricky."

"It didn't just happen accidental, did it, son?" Jed suggested.

Jonathan cast a surprised glance at Jed. "How'd you know

about that?" Jed said nothing. The boy looked at Frank. "How?" Frank was silent.

"Did she confess?" he asked guardedly.

"Not exactly," Jed offered.

"She didn't mean to," Jonathan whispered. "It was a mistake." He paused, then sat down heavily on the runningboard again. "Oh, she was mad, okay, but she didn't mean it to happen like that."

"Tell me about it, Jonathan," the sheriff asked.

"We were down by the river...."

"Who was?" Jed asked.

"The three of us. We were arguin'. I was tryin' to get Lucy to change her mind about us and she got mad and shoved me. Ricky was behind me and was pushed over the bank. That was it." He put his face in his hands.

"Son, why didn't you tell us that before now?" Jed asked.

"Lucy didn't want to. She felt it was her fault. And she didn't want anyone to find out about her bein' pregnant and all. Hell, I don't know."

"The shoes." Jed spoke. His thin slit eyes fixed upon the boy's steel-gray eyes as he glanced up. He searched in vain for fear, for sign of deceit. Nothing.

"That was earlier. He got 'em wet at the canal. We just put 'em there to dry out."

"Why there?" Frank asked.

"So nobody'd wander by and pick 'em up."

Frank and Jed looked at each other. Jed just shrugged his shoulders. Frank said, "Wait for me in the car, Jed. I'll be right along." Jed turned and walked into the darkness back to his car.

Frank looked at his son a long time before he spoke. Then softly, "Jonathan, you killed that boy because he was going to tell that preacher what kind of person you are. And you made Lucy think you thought a lot of her just so you could use her. I want you to know that there are people who know it and I want you to know one other thing. I want you to know why you do what you do...."

"You can't prove any of that," he said. There was, it seemed to

Frank, the slightest smile on the boy's face.

"No," Frank admitted.

"So now tell me what makes me so wicked." He allowed the smile to show itself, to show Frank Hyde there was no fear of him.

"Somewhere way back you decided that no one else matters. I should have known that that day you hurt that poor rabbit."

"You shut up about that!" he barked. "Goddamn you."

"You hurt that animal with no thought of it," Frank continued. "And you used that Vinson child and even Mrs. Vinson at the same moment your mother was dying."

"You shut up. Get away from me. All you've ever been to me is a damned bother," he attacked.

"Yes, I suppose you would see it just like that."

"There's no hell," the boy said quietly.

"What?"

"I said, 'There's no hell,'" he repeated. "You said there's no hell, so why should I worry what I do?"

"Yes, there is."

"What?"

"I said, yes, there is a hell, you're makin' your own. Everybody makes his own. You don't start noticin' it till late. Then all those people you've hurt and used start showin' up in your sleep. And one day when you need somebody the most, nobody'll be there because you shit on everybody."

"I don't need anybody."

"You needed that preacher. Bad enough to kill Ricky for it."

"The preacher needed me," he blurted, his eyes hard.

"You're not even denying it."

"There's no hell and no God so why shouldn't I take whatever I'm big enough to?"

"Because when you hurt people weaker than you, and steal from them, you place yourself outside decent humanity."

"Bullshit."

"You are denying the value of law and fairness and simple human decency. You are fair prey to every thief and murderer you ever see. You can claim no rights but your own animal strength, and someday somebody stronger than you and just as

188

stupid will hurt you and you will lie on your back and whimper, 'Unfair, unfair.' "

"Bullshit."

"But you'll have no help because you've already thrown that out: fairness, right, decency, all gone. That's what 'outlaw' means. You'll go through life without love or respect or anything earned without cheating for it."

"Bullshit, old man."

"You're a parasite, Jonathan."

"You're full o' shit . . ." and Frank's fist licked out like a felling axe and caught the grinning Jonathan squarely on the point of his nose. Frank had thrown wildly at him in rage and was actually sorry when he saw the boy's nose begin to bleed again. Jonathan straightened up, wiped his nose, saw the blood on his hand, and grinned wickedly at his father.

"Do it again," he said. Blood curled around the corner of his lip and down his chin. It dropped onto his white shirt. Frank's eyes filled. His throat choked. "Go on, father. Hit me again. It's your duty to remove me from 'decent humanity,' isn't it? If I'm all that bad. Isn't it your duty?"

"No," Frank whispered as Jed came up behind him. "That's what I've been trying to tell you. I have no right, nor do you. That is why we have law, to keep big men from beating up on little ones."

"Then you've utterly failed, haven't you?" Jonathan said, as he wiped his face again.

"Yes, yes, I have," he whispered and he turned quietly and walked heavily, wearily into the dark toward the car.

After a long silence Jed spoke as he drove, "He's lyin', Frank."

"I know," he groaned.

"Lucy just doesn't fit what he was sayin'."

"I know. Anyway he didn't deny it when I accused him."

"There's no proof, though, Frank. If I had a hair of evidence I'da brought him with us."

"Goddamnit, Jedediah, what in hell is it makes him think he can kill and hurt like that? What the hell did I do wrong?"

Jed didn't answer.

"Do you know what he said back there? He said there's no God and no hell so why can't he take what he wants? That's what he said. That makes me wonder. It's my fault that way I guess. He knows I didn't believe his mother's religion."

Jed looked at him, slowed the car. "You know I recommended him to help that preacher raise that tent?" Frank said nothing.

"Well, just the other day the preacher came over to the office. Wanted to know what kind of boy Jonathan was. Hell, I told him he was a good boy, hard-workin'. That's all he ever showed me. Then the preacher said something."

"What? What'd he say?" Frank asked.

"Said Jonathan was gonna be a preacher. Said he was the most spiritual boy he'd ever knowed. Loved him like his own, he said."

Frank thought about that. "You know, when he was just a little boy he told people he was going to be a preacher. Mary really pushed that and the preacher at Fairview did too. Looks like they won out."

As he lay on his pallet bed of old quilts on the platform in the tent, Jonathan began to feel again the strange power that had come upon him the day his mother died and which came upon him more often now in the meetings, a slowly, yet unmistakably crescending presence of a power greater than himself which seemed to enter him and which he became. He felt then that the Spirit of God had entered him and that he was in some strange way some part of that God himself. In those moments there was nothing else and nobody mattered except Jonathan Hyde and his Spirit power. And when the thing had gone and he lay alone fearful and breathing heavily he knew his father was wrong; there was a God and there was a hell and he was indeed justified in doing whatever His Spirit moved him in its strange way to do. When he thought a little more about that, his justification, he closed his eyes, and as peacefully as only babes and the good and the supremely wicked, he slept.

It was easier on Ellen that Lucy seemed to be accepting her pregnancy well, if not actually, then at least outwardly, with much care for her mother's feelings. Because of this, preparing for the trip to grandfather's was much less a task than it might have been. Lucy only objected once, weakly, but with sound reason.

"There's really no sense in going so soon, mother." She was not at all eager to explain all this to that kindly old man.

"Yes, there is a reason," Ellen said. She sat watching Lucy sort through her clothes.

"Well, nobody'll know for another two months, then it would just be like I'd just gone off to college."

"No. In a few days now there will be talk. Frank went to Jed, so Jed knows. If Jed knows there's too much chance of that worthless deputy knowing."

Lucy paused. "Then everybody'll know it. Oh, mother!" Her hands went to her face. The shame burned hot on her. She tossed her dresses on the bed, then knelt there and placed her head on her mother's lap and cried. Love for her daughter and rage and hate for Jonathan Hyde choked her throat so that it was a long moment before she could speak.

"Child do not be ashamed for the child. There is no doubt in my mind that it was begun in a moment of your own purest, sweetest love and there is no wrong, no sin in love. You loved him and trusted him and he betrayed you. Your only error was just that, a mistake. You were too young and too dear and too damned trusting, but the child is pure, Lucinda, and you will love him just as much as I love you."

"And Ricky," Lucy thought. "As you have loved Ricky." And the tears came then for both of them. When they subsided Lucy hugged her mother to her and said to her, "You are so good, mama. I love you so much."

"I know, honey."

"Mama?"

"Yes?"

"I hope it's a boy."

"Me too, child. A little, wonderful little boy. Me too." And for the first time in weeks there began to be a smile working into her pain.

Before they left Hidalgo for their drive to grandfather's Ellen stopped by the sheriff's office. Jed's car was there. She walked into the office. The little deputy sat at Jed's desk. He rose quickly

191

and called out, "Sheriff!! There is a visitor to see you!" He moved around the desk and pushed a chair forward, motioning for her to sit down.

"No, thanks, I can't stay but a moment."

Jed appeared from behind the big barred door. He was unshaven and his hair was mussed. He didn't look much worse, she thought, than he did when he was fixed up Sunday-go-meetin'.

"Hello, Ellen. I didn't go home this mornin'. Got in too late," he said, reaching for his hat on his desk. He put his hat on and his hand came down over his face, feeling the two days' stubble. "I look like hell, Ellen. You shouldn't come callin' so damned early, girl." He smiled. "Coffee?"

"No thanks, Jed. Where is Frank?"

A look of discovery appeared on his grizzly face. "I told him you'd be up here first thing after him. He wouldn't listen, Ellen. He was hellbent for leather to get outa here."

"I know," she said.

"I talked him into gettin' some breakfast . . . "

"How long has he been gone?"

" 'Bout an hour, I'd say."

"Back to Oklahoma?"

"Fer a spell, he said. Then mebbe California or Oregon or who knows?"

Ellen turned to go. "Ellen," he said. "Just a minute." He turned to the deputy, "Elizondo, take my car down to Toadie's and get him to fill 'er up and change the oil."

The little man scurried out.

"Ellen, Frank didn't want to go. I could tell. But he's sorry as hell about what's happened."

"I know he is, Jed, but . . ."

"He just feels he's to blame."

"I know he does. Did you find Jonathan?"

"Yes, Lucy was right, Ellen. He did it, but there's no way to get it on him. No way, and he ain't about to confess."

She turned again for the door. "Ellen, Elizondo overheard Frank tell me about it last night." He saw her back freeze. "He even went out to the farm and questioned Emilio."

192

She whirled around. "Anyone else?"

"He says not."

"If it's just Emilio it's not so bad. He wouldn't spread it around like some of the others. Jed?"

"Yes?"

"Will you go . . . ?"

"Already on my way. I'll see if Emilio talked to anyone else and tell him that it was all a mistake and to keep his mouth shut.

"Ellen, look, I know Frank's headed north. All I've got to do is call some of the boys up around Alice to just sort of, uh, detain him a little? You're goin' through Alice aren't you?" he grinned.

She smiled. "That would be nice," she said.

In the car, Lucy said, "Why did Frank want to leave?"

"He didn't."

"Well, then, why *did* he?"

"Because he is a man of principle. He feels he's partly to blame and he's sick over it. He won't be comfortable where he doesn't think he's wanted."

"Is he?" Lucy asked.

"What?"

"Wanted. Is he wanted?"

Ellen slowed the car and looked at Lucy. Her emotions were very much on the surface these days, and through the mist she whispered, "Yes, honey, yes he is . . . very much."

Lucy reached over and took her mother's hand off the wheel and held it in hers for a long time. Then she said, "He'll be waiting in Alice, mother, you'll see; and if you don't talk him into coming back home I'm going right over to him and tell him you love him. I'll do it, too."

"Does it show? That much, I mean?"

"It does."

"He's a wonderful man."

"He sure is. He's what I thought Jonathan was. Jonathan must have learned from Frank how to be kind and good, and he could be that. He was so wonderful, mother, at first. Then he began to change and he turned into someone I didn't know, mean and little. I was a perfect idiot."

193

"You let your heart do your thinking and your heart was not made for thinking."

Frank was indeed sitting in his old truck at the police station in Alice. A half smile crept slowly over his face when he saw Ellen walking toward him, and she knew it was because he appreciated the ingenuity of their using the police to delay him.

Lucy watched them as they talked and dreamed of how it might have been. How if Timothy had not been a priest. How if Jonathan had been as he seemed to be. How even if Ricky had not died. But wishing made nothing different. Reverie ended, she sat in silence and waited for her mother.

When Ellen returned and started the car Lucy saw that her hands were trembling. "Mother, you're shaking!"

"I know."

"Is he coming back?"

"Yes."

"Did you tell him?"

"I told him I wanted him to come back. That I really wanted him to; that I needed him to."

"You didn't tell him . . . ?"

"He knows."

"But . . ."

"No buts," Ellen broke in. "He knows."

"But you have to *tell* him."

"At the right time. Listen, honey, I'm going to leave you at papa's, then head right back. Do you mind so much?"

"Do I mind! I wouldn't have it any other way."

Frank walked alone in the orange grove behind his little house. The freshly plowed dirt between the trees smelled good to him. The stars were low and brilliant. The evening warm and quiet. How deceptive, he thought, is nature. The beauty and serenity of life on a quiet evening. Enough, perhaps, to attribute it all to the kind benevolence of a superior wisdom. Until one hears the stillness shattered by the last desperate shriek of a field mouse feeling the amoral claws of an unremorseful owl simply doing what comes natural to him. Natural. Nature. How wonderful for the owl. How inexpressibly horrible for the mouse. How does the mouse feel about God and goodness and wisdom and justice. God's creation? The mouse, taking his life from simple grains, corn and roots, the owl taking his life from a living, thinking, feeling thing. Jonathan and Ricky. Nothing can be as beautiful as nature on its good days. He thought of Ricky and the cotton and the baseball. Or as ugly as nature on its horrible days. Like the day Jonathan Hyde decided to feed on others and learned to kill things in the night.

He heard Ellen's car and he started back toward the house. She was knocking softly on the door of his darkened house when he walked into the yard. "Ellen."

She whirled to face him. He assured her. "It's just me," he said.

"Just you. When I didn't see your truck I thought you'd gone away again."

"Nothing in Oklahoma. I drove the truck around to the side to unload my junk."

"I'm glad you came home, Frank," she said as he took her hand.

"Do you know why I came back?"

"Yes."

"And you?"

"Yes."

He held her hand in his hands and turned her face up to his. He kissed her forehead and drew her to him. "You are one wonderful woman." Her arms tightened around him. "I was afraid I'd never see you again," he said.

"You were wrong to leave," she whispered.

"I know." He kissed her then, on her cheek and then her lips, and she was softness to him. He tasted the salt of her tears and wiped her cheeks softly with his fingers.

Chapter
14

Father Timothy Morgan stood before the desk of his superior. Father Horrigan's visage revealed a state of nearly uncontrollable fury. "You were directed," his voice was tremulous, "by the wisdom of the church to further your own state of grace, to strengthen your faith, and to assist in the work of the parish. Were you not?"

"That is how I understood it," Timothy said. What new madness has come upon this old man? he thought.

Then the old priest stood up and turned to the file cabinet behind him, unlocked it, and took a small notebook from it. Tim recognized his own signature on its front cover and knew then what angered the old priest.

"Is this yours?"

"It is and you have no right to it."

"Right? Right? Who is talking about right? The man who writes in a book . . ." He opened the notebook, turned its pages and found a passage he had already marked with a red pencil. " 'So it seems,' " he read, " 'when one studies the unembellished history of the church, reconstructs the formulation of its primary doctrines, examines the motives of its chief leaders, that the honor of its purpose, the veracity of its scriptures, even the very existence of its prime deity is suspect!' What is meant here, Timothy, by prime deity? Are you suggesting that the church has more than one God?"

Tim didn't answer. Instead he just stood there, tears brimming in his eyes. His last hope for the church and his place in it was lost. The things he needed to be able to stay within it were kindness and understanding by its father priests, the old ones, who had undoubtedly been through the fires of doubt before and had come out of it strong and full of faith. But this old fool of a man screams and rants like a fruit peddler from whom a child has stolen an apple.

"Well, speak! You appear so eager to write blasphemies in your secret little book! Speak!"

"There are those critics who suggest that Christianity is possibly polytheistic, with its prayers to the saints, the importance given to the Blessed Mother, and the terrible power attributed to Satan himself. Even the angels are given superhuman attributes and are godlike in that respect." He spoke directly and slowly, staring into the eyes of the incredulous old man before him. "And even the church's insistence upon the doctrine of the trinity suggests, at least to outsiders, a theistic pluralism of sorts."

"Blasphemy!"

"To you, perhaps, but to one whose mind is still his own it is fair grounds for thought."

"Thought?" the old one barked. "You are not supposed to think, only to believe, to have faith. The thinking was done two thousand years ago and the church has prospered upon it for these twenty centuries, and you challenge that edifice?"

"I have not challenged. I have only questioned."

"A question is a challenge. God is not obliged to answer questions. You are a young fool who believes his own twisted mind more than the accumulated spiritual wisdom of the saints."

"I'll take my book, now, father, if you don't mind."

"You will not. This is to be sent along with my report to those who will decide what is to be done with you."

"Nothing will be done with me, father. No more. Not with me or to me or even for me. I value my mind above yours, the Archbishop's, the Pope's, and all the saint's and you will not take it from me."

"You are a young fool."

"Maybe, but I am my own fool."

He leaned over the desk and took his notebook in his left hand. The old man would not yield it, held on to it, and tried to pull it away. Tim's right hand gripped the old priest's wrist and squeezed like a vise until the book was released. Timothy leafed through it to see no pages were missing, then turned to leave.

"Where are you going?"

"I will be gone in fifteen minutes. Where I am going is none of your business."

Timothy gathered up his clothing and the few books he wanted, put them in a pasteboard box, and started walking toward the Ortega farm. He was aware of the old priest's eyes on his back, and he had a sudden angry urge to reach down and pick up a handful of rocks and hurl them back at the ignorant old man, who had not an ounce of human kindness in him. But he did not. How foolish they think I am. Am I? He remembered his father, how badly he'd wanted his son to be a priest. Now what will he think? The old fear of disappointing his father made his stomach feel queasy, and yet he walked on. I'm really doing it. I'm getting free! They don't own me anymore. They can't make me believe what I can't believe or shame me for not believing it. If there is really a God somewhere he would understand that, being free. Not the church's God; not old make-'em-all-bow-down Jehovah-God, or burn in the fire. Not that God. And he walked on and the more he walked the better he felt about it. He didn't have to bend himself to someone else's mold. No more. Never again. No more.

Frank, from his tractor, saw the tall dark figure turn off the highway and start down the lane past the ball diamond toward the farm. It's Timothy. He finished the row he was plowing, then drove the machine out of the field and toward Timothy, who set the box down when he saw the tractor coming.

"You walk all the way from town?"

"Yep," he said, grinning.

"Climb up. Just in time for supper, I reckon." Frank took the box aboard.

"You did it, didn't you?" They hadn't talked about Timothy's leaving the church, but Frank had suspected he might.

"I did it." He pulled himself up behind Frank.

"Sooner than I expected, too." The young man laughed. "Father Horrigan found my notebook full of unspeakable blasphemies."

"Found it?"

"He was nosing around my room, I guess. Anyway he was going to report it and send it away to the Bishop and that'd mean I'd be sent away to some monastery, who knows where . . . for rehabilitation. Like a shoe to the cobbler for resoling."

"Do you know what you're doing?" Frank asked as he put the tractor into gear.

"For the first time in my life."

At supper Ellen asked Timothy to stay with them as long as he wanted, offering him a job if he wanted that, too. He accepted both. "But I don't know for how long. Have to think things out. Where's Lucinda?"

"She's visiting her grandfather near San Antonio," Ellen answered. "We're going to run up there in the morning."

"Oh." Tim continued eating. Quietly, thinking. Then, "Mrs. Ortega, this might seem inappropriate, but there's something I should say before I accept too much of your hospitality and all. But . . . well . . . I have never met a finer girl than Lucy and . . ."

"Now what?" Ellen thought. "What has he heard? What does he know?" Then to Tim she said, "And what, Timothy?"

"Well, it's just that I wanted you to know that I have feelings for her, that's all." His face turned red.

"Oh," she said.

Frank said nothing. He watched Ellen.

"I simply mean, Mrs. Ortega, that I have often thought that, if I were not a priest, if I were free, Lucinda is the girl I'd most . . ."

"Oh my God!" Ellen cried. Her hands went to her face. Frank was up in a second and put his arm around her.

"I . . . I'm sorry, what . . ." Tim was crushed. "Mrs. Ortega, what . . . ?"

"No, Tim. It's not you. It's something else. Frank, you tell him. All of it. He has to know."

Frank and Tim went to the porch and Frank went over the whole thing. Jonathan and Ricky, the trip to Brownsville with Jed

199

to talk to Jonathan, the pregnancy, all of it.

When he had finished Tim sat silent for a moment then stood up.

"Frank, this must be awful tough on you."

"Lots tougher on everybody else. Think of how Ellen must feel about it, and Lucy, and even Jonathan."

"I'd hate to live with that if I were Jonathan."

Frank said nothing. So Tim told him, "I still want to go with you to see her, Frank. This doesn't change anything with me. I just hope it won't make it harder on her."

"It will." Frank said. "You know, I don't think anyone has ever told you. . . . She really was crazy about you a few months back."

Tim moved toward Frank again and sat down on the steps beside him. "You mean it, Frank?"

"She told her mother she was crazy mad in love with you."

Tim smiled.

"That's why she wanted to join a goddamn convent when she got out of school."

"Are you kidding me? No, you wouldn't about a thing like that."

Lucy's grandfather loved his goats as other men love horses or dogs or their children, and he smelled a little bit of goat and didn't even know it. His goats had names like Ruby or Maria or Gregorio. Lucy learned the names of all the goats and thought it wonderful that each one knew its name and would respond to it. It made her love the old man even more because he was kind to the goats. Only those unfortunate kids who were going to be turned into *cabrito*, goat meat, did he not name. "Because if I name them I will not kill them, so I will not name them." But sometimes a young one is born that is something special; he is so beautiful or so ugly or he follows the old grandfather around. Then he gets a name and he doesn't even have sense enough to know that he is lucky, but he is lucky. That is why Ruby and Gregorio and Maria are not just memories of some fine barbecue. It is because they are the lucky ones.

At first the knowledge of Jonathan's seed within her was a sickening thing. Lucy thought of it at first as some disgusting mass of phlegm he had beguiled her into receiving under the guise of love. And when she thought of it she shuddered and felt sick and wanted to scream. Then after a few days reason returned unexplainedly and ruled that the child would be, like all babies, beautiful and soft and full of warm, sucking needs, and she would be a mother to it as Ellen had been to her.

Naked before the mirror every morning, she looked for the changes that would soon come. Her hands pressed her flat belly and her breasts. She tried to imagine how she'd look, but couldn't, though she knew how she'd feel about it, and tried to ready herself for it.

She was in the kitchen preparing supper when they arrived. Grandfather, on the porch waiting for them, saw the dust long before they got to the house. He shouted to her, "They're here, Lucinda!"

She was taking a roast out of the oven, so she yelled back, "All right, grandfather." She heard the car pull into the yard as she carried the platter to the table, already set and waiting. She set it down and when she looked up, there standing in the doorway on the other side of the table was Father Tim, smiling at her.

"Father," she gasped. "What . . ."

"Not 'father,' Lucinda, not anymore." He wore a khaki shirt and denim jeans. His black dress shoes were out of place.

"I don't understand . . ." she said. Fear crowded into hope and almost smothered it. Ellen came in then, leaving Frank and grandfather talking in the front yard. The look on her mother's face wasn't worry anymore or fear or pain of any sort. It was the peace she found in her mother's eyes that gave her grounds for a semblance of peace herself.

"Hello, mother," she said, softly as she hugged Ellen. Then she turned to Tim, looked at him, then back to Ellen. "Mother, I still don't understand."

"Come with me," Tim said, taking her hand, "I'll explain."

When they were out the back door Tim said, "I want to talk to you, Lucy." She was trembling, but her mother was happy. Why?

201

They walked to the goat shed and beyond, and when they came to some rocks he stopped and sat down on one and she did too, trying not to let it show that she was puzzled almost out of her mind. He knew the uncertainty she was experiencing, so he didn't make her talk.

He spoke softly.

"You are troubled now, Lucinda, because you don't know what is going on. It is very simple. I am no longer a priest. To explain why is as simple as saying I no longer believe what priests have to believe, but I don't want to trouble you with that. We have plenty of time to talk about that. . . ."

"We have *plenty of time?* 'We?' " Lucinda asked.

"The important thing is that being no longer a priest I am free to do what I want and I am going to tell you what it is; and if you do not feel the same way, I want you to tell me honestly, and I will forget it." He looked at her and wished there were an easy way.

He stood up and turned around and looked back at the goat shed and beyond to the little house, then he turned around and said. "Lucy, priests are men. At least they are at first until they allow the man to drain out somewhere over the years and then they become dried up old things like old maids that have been passed by. But when they are young they still dream, in guilt and in pain always, but they still picture in their minds a girl, the perfect girl they would love to love, if only they could. They think about her far too much and they know it is useless and only harmful, but the man inside isn't dead yet. Sometimes she is the wife of someone in the congregation; but the priest still loves her in his heart, even though he knows it is wrong. Sometimes she is a teacher in the school or a clerk in the town. And the greatest torture is when she comes to the priest to confess. At least you spared me that, Lucy. . . ."

"Oh!" she gasped and her hands flew to her face. He went to her quickly and wanted to touch her, but did not. Her sobs shook him and his own eyes filled. He knelt by her and laid a trembling hand on her brown hair. She looked up, her eyes red, and between racking breaths she said, "No, no, no."

202

It was what he'd expected. This was hell on her, so he tried to make it easy. "I know about the other, Lucy." She stiffened beneath his hand and the crying stopped. She wished she were dead. The shame was a clawing beast within her. Hell would be much better than his knowing. "I know about it, Lucy, and it doesn't matter. It doesn't matter!"

She looked up at him then and he saw the color drain out of her cheeks; saw the beautiful dark eyes cloud over with doubt. She almost whispered, "Is it because of this that you came? Because you pity me and want to save my shame?" He saw the pride in her as it set her face.

"It is not because of shame, Lucinda, or because of pity. I think it is because of . . . because of love, I think, although I have had so little experience in that."

She did not know what it was or how it happened, but it was as if she were a child again and every Christmas wish and birthday dream had come true. The doll, the purse, the bike, and now this dream, this impossible happening. The dark thing within her slipped away and hope found a foothold. This was why her mother had smiled so.

"I am not asking you to commit yourself now or even to tell me how you feel about me. All I ask is that you let me come to see you, and that we have a chance to talk and get to . . ."

She couldn't help laughing and crying at the same time. Her hands went out to his and held them tight to her, and she was nodding her head yes, and crying and saying, "Yes, yes." And she wanted to say, "Is it really happening? Are you really here?" but all she could say when she looked up and saw the goats playing on the rocks around them was "That's Gregorio." And they both laughed.

Sheriff Jed Strunk married them two weeks later on a Sunday, and there was a feast in the yard for all the hands and the friends; and afterward there was a baseball game.

Timothy played in some of the game while Frank and Ellen and Lucy sat on the hood of the tractor and watched and talked.

"Lucy, I know grandfather wants you and Tim to go to San

Antonio and live with him, but you don't have to do that," Ellen said as they watched the game.

"What do you mean, mama?" Lucy asked.

"You and Tim can have the 'little house' if you want it. Frank is moving in with me," she smiled, "just as soon as we're married."

PART III

Chapter
15

A very strange thing began to happen inside Jonathan Hyde. He began to believe that he actually was God's servant, and because he was strong and knew how to maneuver people, souls, then he would be God's special servant. And he began to be just a little bit sorry about Ricky, and often tried to pray about that, but he became more and more convinced that Rick had been an enemy of God in trying to prevent Jonathan's joining the preacher. So Rick was dead and Jonathan was alive and Jonathan tried to even things up by promising God he'd do anything he wanted. That made him feel better, and he thought God felt better about it too, because it didn't trouble him anymore except occasionally in a dream, which he never seemed to remember the next morning anyway. If he had done anything wrong, he told the Lord, he was sorry about it and wouldn't do anything else unless he'd talked to God about it. And if that didn't satisfy his God then Jonathan never heard about it. He began to be further encouraged about his own state of grace when he started reading the Old Testament. He learned what God's prophets and judges had done, how many people they had killed, women and babies even, because they got in the way of God's will. And God commanded it! He slept a bit better after that, but he never told Reverend Horner or Mrs. Horner about Ricky. No, he didn't think even they were close enough to God to understand about that.

Jonathan learned much from Brother Horner about religion and especially about the art of the revival and the moving of souls. "Poor people," he said, "take to religion better than rich people, and we're right in the middle of a depression. Most everybody's poor. When they's poor they lookin' to get the Lord's help. When they's rich, or just got plenty, they don't need Him till they get sick. Then when they's sick everybody comes runnin' to you, especially if you're a healer. I haven't ever been really a healer, not really one, but now a good healer, he gets crowds now, I'll tell you, and offerin's. Nobody gets the offerin's a good healer gets, a really good one, that is."

And he taught Jonathan how to get more money out of crowds. "Get 'em to singin', happy songs, glad snappy songs. Then get 'em to stand up and clap they hands. Get 'em to move, to feel religion. Takes their minds off their troubles and makes 'em turn loose of their money. Then there's special offerin's. A special offerin' is when you ask 'em to help with a particular need like new tires for the truck, or an overhaul job on the motor, or a new piano. They give better if it's *for* somethin', doncha know, somethin' special. And sometimes you can get a group that's a little better off to make a special offerin' to carry a revival to a poor community hard hit. If you're gettin' above average offerin's in a new town, you know they aren't as bad hit as others. There's when you get 'em to make special offerin's to help take God's word to some poor place, doncha know."

So Jonathan listened to him and stored away all he learned as they traveled from town to town, working their way up into the heart of Texas, then across Louisiana and into the Deep South. And he watched the reverend as he ran his services. He learned to tell as well as the reverend the rise and fall of emotion in a congregation, and he began to be able to estimate just how much money they could squeeze out of each crowd. "The Gospel moves on gold," Horner was fond of saying, "and it should, for gold is God's, ever bit of it, and someday He's gonna gather it all up and pave heaven's streets with it, and you won't need it in hell." That always got a good offering, that one did. Jonathan stored that one away, too.

The little old evangelist made Jonathan read the Bible through from cover to cover. "That's one thing you'll have to do before you start preachin', son. Nothin' worse in the Kingdom of God than a preacher that doesn't know his Bible."

"And memorize!" Mrs. Horner urged. "Memorize, memorize!" She gave him a list of the more important verses. "You look those up and put 'em to memory, Jonathan boy. They'll put you in good stead when you stand before the flock of God."

"She's right," Reverend Horner said, "Nothin' makes people believe in a preacher any more'n if he can stand up there and spout off verse after verse, whole chapters sometimes, without once lookin' in the Book."

"Remember Brother Nelson in Pacific Grove?" she said, "He could quote the whole Gospel of John word for word without a miss. I heard him do it once, in prayer meeting. He was testifying and got blessed nigh to pieces, started quotin' John and just wouldn't set down. Old Sister Neely got so happy she took to shoutin'. 'Glory, glory,' she'd say over and over. And little Mother Harmon, she took to runnin' up and down the aisles a-cryin' and wavin' her hankie. What a prayer meetin' we had that night all because Brother Nelson quoted John." She looked wistfully back into that night's place in her memory. "Old Brother Nelson's dead now," she said sadly.

"Yes, gone to be with Jesus," she assured them. So Jonathan began reading and memorizing.

Sister Sarah Horner was a very large woman. She made three, maybe four, of her husband. She was a real help to him and an important member of their team. She led the singing in the meetings and did considerable praying. "She's the best prayer of any woman I ever heard. Prays better'n most any man can." And she liked to pray, indeed she loved to be called on to pray during the revival meetings. She'd start out soft, with a little girl's voice, slowly twining its way through the tent, around and around the people one by one and around the chair legs and the pulpit and the mourners' bench and the three tent poles, and then she'd take hold and start to cry her prayers, and if she was standing up she'd bang the back of the chair in front of her, and if she was kneeling down she'd pound the seat of the chair she knelt at until, almost hoarse and out of breath, she'd raise her arms and cry out, "Oh Lord, we supplicate thee! Oh Lord, we supplicate thee!" And those souls given fully to the spirit would truly feel closer to the

Lord, and those that weren't would either be laughing or scared half to death. She loved to pray, but she didn't much like to lead the singing, not because she didn't have the voice for it—she did—but because she liked to play the piano better. She loved to play the piano even more than pray, so when Jonathan came with them she began listening to see if he could sing, and when she saw he could, a plan began to work itself out and she went to work on him.

"Jonathan," she said to him when they stopped for lunch on their trip from Brownsville to Corpus Christi, "I've been listening to you and you've got a wonderful singin' voice."

"I do?"

"You truly do, a gift from God if I know anything at all. Have you ever led singin' at all?"

"No, ma'am."

"Well, you'll be great at it. I'll show you some things about it when we get to Corpus. My, how the Lord works."

So Jonathan stood in the pulpit, hymnal in hand, and boomed out the words to the old songs. Sarah loved it. Tears poured down her face as she sat in the front row and watched the boy take hold. The little preacher took note of it and knew immediately what she was after. He smiled and kept it to himself, but when he asked for the offering that first night he asked for a special offering, a piano offering, and on the eighth night they had money enough. The next night Sarah had her piano; and the people who came to meetin' had to sing double loud just to hear themselves sing, for Sarah banged her heart out on that piano.

There were big crowds at tent meetings in those days. The little preacher was right; people do tend to wax religious in hard times. Indeed, many preachers welcome depressions and catastrophes as some generals welcome war, offering plates at ready arms. Some even get rich.

They came into town and raised the tent on a vacant lot, preferably one donated for the purpose by a businessman or farmer eager to lend a hand to the good Lord. Donated labor often even raised the tent. Even the sawdust on the ground was given to them, or there was no sawdust.

The people came from miles around in creaky old wagons and

sputtering old trucks. There were tobacco-chewing, work-hardened men and baby-toting women and children by the dozens. Some came hungry and all came soul hungry, searching for some solace for the ails of a sick economy and a thirsty earth. They turned to religion as they turned to Roosevelt, anything or anybody with a promise; and if anything thrives on promises it is religion.

Those were the days of the mourners' bench, a low, flat bench in front of the pulpit placed there for sinners to come to and kneel at and there mourn and weep for their sins and beg God's forgiveness. Jonathan soon learned that it was around the mourners' bench that the entire meeting was structured. Every song, every sermon, every word uttered was either to pull in a good offering or to draw a worthy catch of souls down there "praying through" at the mourners' bench. The plain wood bench became an altar upon which men and women and children offered their souls to God. Many a wallet and purse were offered to God there and sanctified there, and carloads of tobacco and not a few whiskey flasks were confiscated there in the Lord's name and poured out in the sawdust.

So preachers learned to get people to the mourners' bench any way they could. The numbers of souls he got down there on their knees were his crown in heaven; they were his reputation on earth. And the number of souls a preacher got to the "altar" decided whether he preached Christ or went back to working somewhere or looking for work. So Jonathan learned. He listened to Mrs. Horner when she told him, "Smile when you lead the singing and sing loud and lively except during altar call, then don't smile, look sad like all those people out there are slipping away into hell. They are. And sing soft then, firm and soft."

He learned too how different sermons seemed to draw larger altar calls. Reverend Horner taught him: "Hellfire almost always gets 'em, scares 'em. They need to be scared. Doin' 'em a favor to scare 'em. Most people'd never bother at all about religion if they wasn't scared of dyin' and goin' to hell." But some were drawn more by love sermons, not many, but some. "Love messages seems to get to them that's already Christians, them that need to be sanctified. You gotta preach to 'em to just offer themselves

211

body and soul to God and He'll come in and burn out all the selfishness and littleness and natural orneriness we's all born with."

The reverend let Jonathan sit up on the platform some nights during the sermon so he could learn, by studying the faces in the crowd, who was feeling conviction for his sins. "You just might want to go down into the aisles and talk to someone personal and invite him to the altar," Horner said. Jonathan watched the people closely and began to be able to tell just which ones would break down and give in to the spirit and come down and "pray through to victory."

"Those are the ones you preach to. You can tell who they are. Sometimes you'll have to look 'em right in the eye whilst you're preachin'! They'll be dead certain somebody told you their own little sins. It'll scare the daylights out of 'em, then God'll get His hooks into 'em and not let go." These were the things Jonathan learned from Mervel and Sarah Horner.

But one thing troubled Jonathan. His state of grace was not always as steady as he allowed the Horners to believe, for no sooner had he gotten his body and soul all devoted to God and put his mind in the proper spiritual attitude than his old friend pecker began to announce his hungry presence and the most reverent thought of God became the most irreverent flashback of Enola or the Princess or the pure-little-girl whiteness of the virgin body of Lucinda Ortega. There was no denying it for long. The ghostly figure of Mrs. Vinson bent over her bath or standing naked in the open doorway, firm, full breasts beckoning, taunting. And he'd sin again with his hands and have to beg forgiveness again and again, and over and over he'd climb the prayer ladder to the high place of favor in the Lord, and each time he'd promise God and himself that he'd not fall again. He'd pray for special strength and was assured he had it. Then he'd get a swift glimpse of a passing ankle or a breast straining at its dress and he'd be in a flash the same male rutter he always was. He hated himself for it and denounced himself to God and began again, and again, and again.

The long nights under the tent bedded down alone behind the pulpit were torturous hours for him. In those times he would wonder whether he should keep on trying, wonder whether by some chance his father might have been right about religion. But if so, why was he, Jonathan, so gifted? And he was. No doubt about that. And why had everything worked out the way it had? No. This was his cross to bear, his own personal mountain to climb. Reverend Horner said he was God's man and God would do great things through him. Besides he could not imagine himself doing farm work, for his father or anybody else, anywhere. And if he could later get his own tent . . . Brother Horner had a fine car and enough money to eat at fancy restaurants and stay in hotels. A good night's offering sometimes was more than a week's wages for a workingman when there was work. And if he could be a healer . . .

He opted for religion and fought a holding action with his pecker.

He had been with Brother Horner almost a year when he preached his first sermon. Two months before that he met Cerese. Cerese could make a man forget religion.

It was spring in Alabama. Jonathan slowed and turned in to a truckstop. Reverend Horner had given him full rein with the moving after three moves. He trusted Jonathan with the truck, so he and Mrs. Horner went on in the car to make arrangements for newspaper coverage and radio announcements for the next meeting. He pulled up to the gas island, got the tank filled, parked the truck on the lot and walked back to the café and ordered a hamburger. There were seven or eight drivers sitting at the counter and several people in booths. As Jonathan waited he noticed one driver in particular, a young blond man, short and rather well built. He noticed him only because he was sitting with a girl whose face was the most exciting he'd ever seen, exciting probably because of the total abandonment to pure sensuality in its expression. She was beautiful. Her hair was darkest brown, almost black, long and windblown. Her skin was so fair as to reveal the faint blue shadow of veins beneath the surface. Her nose was slightly too long and her mouth somehow too wide. But when she smiled it was real and then you could see;

213

it was in her eyes, dark with long black lashes. No hate in them, no hurt, and when she looked at somebody she did not look at his nose or his chin; she looked at his eyes, right into him. She got to a man that way and let him know by that that she was open. There was nothing closed about her, nothing. And she said that with her eyes and with her face.

Jonathan's hamburger came and the girl and the blond friend got up and left. He watched her through the plate-glass window and wished there were no sign painted on the window so he could see all of her. All he could tell was that she was thin, wore a red sweater, didn't have big tits, and her plaid skirt was too short.

His hamburger didn't have onion on it, but he didn't raise hell about it because he was still thinking about the girl and trying to decide whether to jerk off or pray. He tried praying and all he could see in his mind's eye was those dark eyes and he wanted her. But she was gone.

The hamburger was flat and he left half of it on the counter, gulped down the coffee, and left. The nervous weight of desire cramped his lower belly. He wanted to get in the truck as fast as he could and pull over somewhere out in the country and feel the spilling of the stuff that most troubled him and most pleasured him. He gave no thought to God or the Reverend Horner or anything but his vision of the dark-eyed girl.

When he pulled himself up into the truck she was sitting there beside him, her feet on a small tin suitcase.

"You didn't take long to finish that hamburger," she said. Her voice was deep and clear. The accent Southern, unhurried. She was very carefully applying lipstick, and it seemed to Jonathan that she was smiling slightly. He stared at her, trying to find a spiritual reason for her being there. It is in the nature of religious people to find God's will in everything that happens. It is easier for the old Christians to see the crystal-clear plan of God in the most unreasonable of circumstances, especially the unreasonable circumstances. It is not so easy for the young.

Two possibilities came to Jonathan's mind as he started the truck: she had been sent either to test him or to reward him. He did not think, after hearing Reverend Horner expound for hours

214

on God's abhorrence of sex and especially sex out of wedlock, that his God was apt to send along this kind of reward. Besides, God is not often known to reward with physical pleasure, so liable was it to draw one's attentions away from God himself. In such case, he reasoned, he should throw her out, which he did not because of a third possible reason for her being here; maybe God sent her to get spiritual guidance from him, Jonathan Hyde, minister to be.

And besides, even if she had been sent to tempt him, it would be the easy way to simply kick her out. How could she tempt him if she were not here with him? He remembered her look in the café and was certain that a woman who looked into a man's eyes like that was just asking for it.

"What are you doing here?" he asked without looking at her as he ground into second gear.

"I need a ride to Florida," she said. He hadn't considered that possibility. She removed her shoes and pulled her feet up under her. She let the shoes drop one by one on the old tin suitcase, then reached down and arranged them neatly, side by side.

"Why couldn't you just ask?" He glanced at her. She seemed self-assured as she looked away and out the window into the pines rushing by. "Besides, how'd you know I was heading for Florida?"

She looked at him. "I saw you pull in. If you'd been goin' the left fork you'd've parked on the other side headed that way. You just come right over to the edge of the road and headed it out the way you'd go to Florida."

He didn't say anything for a while, but was aware of her touching him all over with her eyes. Her skirt was too short and the way she was sitting showed her thighs, naked white against the brown truck seat and her plaid skirt.

"What's your name?" she asked.

"Jonathan."

"Jonathan. Mine's Cerese."

"Cerese. That's a pretty name. Who was that you were with?"

"You mean that guy at the truck stop? Just a driver. Picked me up in New Orleans."

Jonathan looked at her again. She was very small but very well

215

put together. "Did you just hop in his truck, too?"

"Nope. I just do this sometimes." She smiled. Her mouth was set a little crooked when she smiled. She kind of pulled it down on one side or up on the other, but it was a genuine smile. Then he looked at her eyes, rather into them and into her again, for she was open and was speaking to him with her eyes.

"Why'd you pick my truck?"

"I almost didn't."

"Why?"

"Because of the sign on the sides. I thought you might be a preacher or somethin'. But, if you were, you wouldn't have looked at me like that in the café. And I saw you watching me. Right?"

"Where you from?"

"Los Angeles."

"California?"

"That's right."

"Why'd you leave California? I heard it's great out there. We're headin' that way after Florida."

"It's not as great as all that. Girls can't make a decent dollar anymore what with all the free stuff and all. Good houses all doin' poorly. Too many poor girls from Oklahoma and Arkansas and Kansas walkin' the streets." She watched for his reaction. She always liked to see how men reacted to what she was. She knew they suspected, but they didn't expect her to tell them just like that. But Jonathan said nothing. Was expressionless.

"So that's why I'm going to Florida. Girl friend in the business went down there Christmas and just loved it. Lots of rich people down there. A good girl can do pretty good, she says."

"Are you good?"

"How do you mean?" she said, sliding over toward him.

"You know what I mean, a good whore." He looked at her again and she laughed out loud.

"Whore!" she said. "That's good. I like a guy that can look a girl in the eye and say that. Shows he knows what he wants. Say it again."

"Whore," he said and looked at her again.

"Feels good to say it, doesn't it? Whore. It feels good to be able

216

to say it to yourself, too, and know it's true and not be ashamed of it."

"You're not ashamed of it?"

"Not a damn bit. I used to be, though. I started when I was eighteen. I loved it, but I hated myself. I did it for a while, then quit because I couldn't stand the thought of what I was, but I couldn't stop. I love it. I truly do, so I started back. Then I met a woman who'd hustled for thirty years. She was fifty but she looked thirty or even less than that fixed up. Know what she told me? 'Cerese, baby, hustlin' don't make you old if you love it. You get old from the boozin' and chain smokin' and not sleepin' well and hatin' yourself, mostly hatin' yourself.' So I stopped hatin' myself for it. She made sense. 'You are what you are, baby,' she'd say. 'Fish like to swim, birds like to fly. I'll ride a wild cock to beddy bye!' So I started enjoying myself, believe me."

'Why, uh, why didn't you just find a good man and get married?"

"Two reasons. Not too many men want a wife who's had a thousand strange dicks stuck in her. And not many men could stand up to fucking me twice a day for forty years."

"I could." When he looked at her he wasn't smiling.

"You're dead serious," she said.

"How about three times a day?" He smiled and the ache began again. She put her arm across his shoulders and softly scratched her nails down the back of his neck. He shivered and felt the slow pulsations as his cock strained against his jeans. He wiped his palms on his pants and slipped his right hand under her skirt. "You weren't kidding, were you?" he asked.

"Does it feel like I was kidding?" She raised her skirt and removed her panties in one smooth motion, then lay down on the seat with her head on his leg. He pulled the plaid skirt up to her waist and cupped his palm over the blue-black bush, running one finger into it slowly. She put both hands above her head and unbuttoned his jeans and worked him out and into her hands. "Nice," she said when she felt it.

"No kidding, three times a day?"

"At least," he breathed.

He stopped the truck. They opened the back door and crawled

217

in on top of the tent, then pulled the door almost shut so that just a crack of light shone upon them. In a half a minute, finished, he lay heavily upon her, sweating, both of them breathing hard.

He began to experience the self-loathing that comes after moral failure. He, Jonathan Hyde, who could do anything, had determined not to give in to his flesh, and he had failed. Again. How would he ever withstand temptation in his own body? Fucking is as natural as breathing. Maybe it isn't wrong. But it is. "Thou shalt not commit adultery!" How could a man be a preacher who could not control his own sinful passion? How indeed?

He would pray again and God would forgive him again as he had always, but how to stay pure, how to turn off the powerful urge to spew one's seed to kingdom come?

"Cerese, will you marry me?"

"If you were serious about that three-times-a-day business I will."

"I'm not kidding, Cerese."

"I'm not either, Jonathan."

"You'll have to take up religion and follow me and this tent all over the country."

"You're layin' on top of a whore in the back of a truck and you're tellin' me I've got to get religion?"

He rolled off her and laid his arm across his eyes to keep out the shaft of sunlight. "This might sound silly, Cerese, but I think I'd better tell you."

"Tell me what?" She lifted his now limp pecker and let it fall. Did it again and smiled as it began to squirm back to life.

"For almost a year now I've been drivin' for this preacher, liftin' this tent, helpin' with the services, leadin' singin', and he's teachin' me about preachin'."

"You're a preacher?"

"Nope. Not yet, but I will be, soon. I've been workin' on my first sermon. I hope to preach it in Tallahassee."

"So what's so silly about that?"

"It's not that," he said. "It's that for all this time I've had a terrible problem stayin' right with God."

"Women?" She smiled.

218

"I promised God I'd stay pure, and I just haven't been able to do it. Up and down, up and down."

"Sounds like a frustrating existence. Where'd you find the women if you're traveling with this preacher all the time?"

"I didn't really. I just couldn't keep 'em out of mind."

"You mean you jerked off? For a solid year?"

He nodded his head.

"Oh, brother. You mean I'm the first piece you've had in a year?"

"That's the truth."

"Well, then I'd say you've done pretty good. How much tail did you get before you took up religion?"

"Plenty."

"How plenty?"

"I knew this whore in Mexico, the Princess, her name was."

"The Princess, imagine that." She chuckled.

"Then there was this Mexican girl in Hidalgo and a girl and her mother in Oklahoma."

"A girl and her ma. You were fuckin' both of 'em?"

"Yes." He couldn't help the pride he felt.

"Well, anyway you needn't feel like the wickedest thing in the world if I'm the first in a year," she said.

"That's what I'm tryin' to say, Cerese. I think maybe, now don't laugh at this, I think maybe God sent you along."

"Me?" she asked. "God doesn't even know I exist."

"Don't say that. He does know. He knows everything and everybody and everything about everybody."

She was silent.

"So when I saw you in that café, and later in the truck, I couldn't figure out why God let me be tempted like that, knowin' how I am and all. You know, Cerese, I think God knew I needed a wife and he knew you needed a husband to match your own need." He looked at her. She was looking out into the shaft of light and crying. She felt for his hand, found it, squeezed it.

"Jonathan, when I said back there that I loved being a whore I lied. It is true that I like to have sex. I do like to fuck, but sometimes the men are real bastards, and dirty. It isn't a good life

219

at all, but I've just got to have sex a lot. I'm just made that way."

He sat up and pulled her into his arms. "God made you that way," he said to her, "for me."

"So let's do it again, shall we?"

"Nope, he said, "not now. Not until after the wedding, till after we're married."

She was still for a moment when he said that, thinking. Then she said, "Jonathan, if you are ever cruel to me, even once, I'll get up and walk right out of your life and you'll never see me again."

He looked at her strangely. A shaft of light ran down across her face and across one breast; the nipple was firm and hard.

"And the cruelest thing I can think of is to tell me you won't fuck me till we're married."

He didn't say anything.

"If you really believe God sent me to you why don't you take advantage of it?" She was scratching him just under his balls and watching him grow. He began to appreciate what God had done for him.

Chapter

16

He dropped her off at a tourist court on the west side of Tallahassee not far from where the tent would be. Then he went on to find the preacher.

Cerese came to him in the tent that night, and in his bed they discussed how best to introduce her to the Horners. The simplest way, it seemed, was for Cerese just to come to the revival every night, and they would make it seem as if Jonathan had just taken a fancy to her. She was not prepared for what she found there; the singing, the emotion, the convicting words of Reverend Horner's sermon, all seemed directed right at her. The preacher's eyes seemed to look right through her. It frightened her, and she did not return that night or the next night to Jonathan's bed.

But on the third night Horner preached on hell, and told how God loves all sinners and would save them from their sins, wash them and make them new. Something gripped her insides, and when eight or ten people went forward to the mourners' bench that night, she was with them, praying for her soul's salvation, getting God's grace on her.

While she prayed, Mrs. Horner came and knelt by her and put her arm around her shoulders and prayed with her and for her. When she lifted up her head Jonathan saw a different Cerese. There was no sensuality in her face, sweetness and beauty, yes, but the sensual hunger was replaced for the moment, at least, by a kind of joy, a relief from the preacher's convicting words. She looked up toward Jonathan and smiled, and he smiled, but slowly; and then wondered why he wasn't happy about it. He wasn't certain whether he liked Cerese like that.

Cerese came to him later, but for talk and not for sex.

Mrs. Horner introduced her to Jonathan the next night and they talked awhile as Mrs. Horner watched approvingly. When Cerese had gone Mrs. Horner told Jonathan, "She's such a nice girl, Jonathan, don't you think?"

"Yes ma'am, she is a nice girl."

"So sweet."

"Yes, ma'am, she is."

The next night after the services they talked longer, and later Mrs. Horner told Mervel, "I think Jonathan kind of likes that little Cerese." So Mrs. Horner planned a picnic for Saturday and arranged for Jonathan to invite Cerese. Afterward, at the picnic in the city park, while Mr. and Mrs. Horner dozed in the warm spring sun, Jonathan and Cerese walked hand in hand and talked until they walked into the trees and bushes, where they pressed together. She prayed for strength to ward off her own revived need.

"It's so hard to wait, Jonathan. How much longer?"

"We'll be here another three or four weeks. I'll break the news to them next week and we'll be married the week after that."

"I'm glad we're waiting," she said. "It just seems right. It isn't easy, though."

"Want me to do you?" he asked.

She shook her head.

"No," she said, "let's wait."

So they waited.

Reverend Horner was not difficult to convince that Jonathan should marry Cerese and Cerese should travel with them. Jonathan confided in Mrs. Horner regarding his feeling for Cerese. Mrs. Horner was ecstatic: "Mervel, you know how you've dreamed of having somebody to carry on your work." It was true, he wouldn't be able to carry the load much longer. Somebody would soon have to share in the preaching and later take over entirely. "And Cerese is a fine girl, a fine girl, and she cares about Jonathan, you can see it in her eyes. She cares about him."

"That's true," Horner admitted, "and he'll have to have a wife. A strong boy like that'll soon need a woman."

222

"When'll you let 'im preach first?"

"Gainesville," he said, "or Ocala."

"Good," she said. And to herself she thought, "The sooner the better."

Before the wedding, which took place in the revival tent on the last night at Tallahassee, Mrs. Horner talked to Jonathan. "Jonathan, it won't do for Mervel to know I'm telling you this, but you should know."

"Yes, ma'am."

"He isn't well, Jonathan."

"I know, Mrs. Horner. I can tell sometimes when there's a bad strain on him and all."

"Well then, you knew. I worried so about tellin'."

"No need to worry."

"Well then, you know he sort of has you in mind to carry on the work."

"Yes, ma'am, I supposed that. In fact things he's said led me to think he had that in his heart."

"You're such a good boy, Jonathan. We feel toward you like our own. Mervel so wanted a boy of his own, but we just weren't blessed that way. You've come along at the right time, too."

"Yes, ma'am."

"That's why I wanted to talk to you about all this. I wanted you to know in your heart that this is what you feel called to, tent meetings, and that Cerese will be happy in it, too."

"Yes, ma'am, she will. We've prayed about it." That was the thing to say.

Jonathan Hyde's first sermon blessed the Reverend Mervel Horner more than he'd allowed his tired heart to hope for. Jonathan stood above the congregation and peered out over them. They were the kinds of people he'd hated in Oklahoma and in Texas, mostly farmers with their simple faiths and errant habits, small-time clerks, laborers, service-station attendants still smelling of gas and oil, and the unemployed. Always the jobless and the hungry come to get God on their side. He looked down on them and wondered why God worried with them, but was satisfied that God wanted their souls, too.

Jonathan surprised even himself with the ease with which the good words poured forth. "God," he said, "is in the heaven-building business. Here, let me read to you what the Bible says about God's business, about what God is doing these days: 'I go now to prepare a place for you.'

"Now that verse is about heaven, but I'm going to preach about hell, for hell is the more likely home for most of you here, and you should be prepared for it before you get there. I mean you should at least be told what you're getting into so that when you get there you won't have any room at all to complain about your sorry state.

"Then why did I read a text about heaven?" He paused and looked out over the crowded tent.

An old sister sitting next to the aisle about halfway down said a loud "Amen, preacher." That "Amen" made Jonathan feel good.

"I read this text to get it fixed in your mind that Jesus himself is right now building heaven. He's up there getting things ready for his flock, the few of them there be, while most of you are getting ready to go someplace else.

"It's like a bride workin' a long time on her wedding dress and gettin' all ready for the wedding, gets to the church only to find out her man up and decided not to come. All that work and gettin' ready for nothin'.

"You goin' to hell when heaven's all ready for you is like lettin' your mother fix a huge Sunday dinner and you not even gettin' out of bed for it." A chuckle tittered across the congregation.

"Silly, isn't it?" He paused, then roared, "But not half as silly as you comin' to a church a thousand times actin' like you're all dressed up for heaven, but knowing full well when the roll is called you won't even be there. You'll be someplace else. Where?

"You *know* where! Burning and suffering and screaming in hell. And for what? What is it that stands between you and your God? What is it that is keeping you right now from the full grace of God?

"I think we can find out." He paused, pulled a large white handkerchief from his pocket and wiped his face with it. He'd seen a preacher do that once. He looked out over the crowd again and this time looked into their eyes, especially the ones who looked the most uncomfortable. Then he repeated, "I think we can find out what it is that will keep you out of heaven and put you in hell. Let's see if we can.

"Something is standing between you and God, something you are not willing to put on the altar. Now I'm going to ask God to put that sin on your mind right now, to remind you of it right now, tonight, what it is that's endangering your soul.

"Now everybody close your eyes while God puts it on you, while he puts that sin in front of you. Everybody now, close your eyes. Right now. Close 'em. That's right. Now let's be quiet a moment while God works in us." For a few seconds a hush settled down over the people in the big tent, then Jonathan said clearly and firmly, "What are you thinking about right now? What's on your mind? That's it. That's what God's warning you about. That's what is sending you to hell. That sin right there. God wouldn't fool you. He wouldn't story to you. He's showing you what you're gonna think about for eternity in hell. You'll think about it in hell because you'll remember this night when God warned you.

"Now I'm through. I'm going down to this altar and kneel down and ask God to touch you heavy. I'm not going to beg you, but if you want to get right with God you come and kneel and ask God to forgive you whatever it is that'll keep you out of heaven and send you to hell." He left the pulpit and knelt at the mourners' bench. He was only there for a moment when he heard them coming and felt them fall heavily upon the bench and heard their weeping and praying, some groaning in despair. He heard an "Amen" behind him and knew it was Brother Horner. Mrs. Horner began playing softly "I Need Thee Every Hour" on the piano.

When he looked up Cerese was beside him, praying. On the other side of her and to his right the altar was filled, young people and old, farmers and shopkeepers. He knew then without a doubt that he was God's man, that God was pleased with him now, and once again he began to feel that strange power moving through him. Yes, he was now a man of God in whom God worked. He felt good about it.

225

Jonathan and Cerese lived in the tent the first few months of their marriage. Both of them were pleased with their little arrangement and congratulated themselves mutually upon pulling it off. They hadn't lied to the Horners, not really. Cerese had explained to Mrs. Horner that she was on her way to Miami to find work, "Office work if I can," she had said, "but I can work as a waitress if I have to." That was the closest she had come to storying.

Cerese was unlike any girl he'd known. He could lead the others around, fool them with words; not Cerese. He sensed this immediately, so he didn't even try. Cerese was strong. She brought to his life a balance that made it possible for him to concentrate on his godliness.

It was his godliness that caused Cerese the first slight tremors of uncertainty about him.

"Godliness," explained Brother Horner, "is nothing more than a man concentrating on the attributes of God, love, and wisdom. Think of God, put him on your mind all the time, pray much, be open to Him always, and you will become Godly; you will become Godlike."

"God has another attribute," Jonathan told him.

"What is it?"

"Anger."

"Yes, that's right, but you must remember that His anger is directed always toward the sin and never toward the sinner. He is a God of love."

But it seemed to Jonathan that God was also angry at the sinner; otherwise, why send him to hell? So anger and hell became important themes in Jonathan's preaching. He soon knew of every Biblical reference to God's anger and the way he vented his wrath upon his erring people. He told these tales with enthusiasm from his pulpit. "The wrath of God" became his battle cry, and he scared the wits out of small children and weak-minded women. Reverend Horner was mildly disturbed over the severity of the young man's sermons, but their success, as evidenced by greater and greater numbers at the mourners' bench, was unquestionable and served to uphold his earlier high opinion of Jonathan.

226

Cerese loved him. She hadn't intended to, at first, but she grew more fond of him each time he came to her bed and each passing day that he was kind to her. He had proved man enough to give her what her body craved, and the preacher in him had not yet decided that such craving was sinful, or that it hindered the growth of godliness and should be supplanted by prayer and supplication.

She had not yet revealed to him that there was much about religion that she did not subscribe to and did not understand. It was enough that God had made it possible for her to have Jonathan, and forgiveness, and still have ready access to complete physical gratification. It would be stupid to question such a setup, so she did not.

Cerese became pregnant and gave birth to a girl, whom Jonathan called Angela. "Angel. She is, too, and will be." The child was beautiful: dark hair, large searching gray eyes, and a soft little voice which Jonathan said was more like singing than crying. When she cried in the night he was up in an instant. Cerese marveled at him. "The child is a part of me," he told Cerese. "She is me, my flesh and blood and bone."

"And mine," she corrected.

"Yes," he said, but it seemed to him that the child was so much more his than hers, though he didn't say it.

When Angela was two Mervel Horner died and left the tent and trucks to Jonathan, provided Jonathan would send half his offerings to Mrs. Horner, who would go back to Ohio. This he agreed to do and did for a year and a half, until his popularity as a hell screamer filled his slate and his coffers; then he began to send her only a little more than he usually had and let her believe it was half. It was only fair, he thought, because the offerings had grown so much and it was due to him, his preaching, and nothing else; besides the old woman only needed so much anyway. When she died he was relieved of even that burden, and he bought a new truck and a fine car and paid cash for them both. It seemed to him that all of this was simply God's way of saying, "Thank you, Jonathan Hyde."

Wherever he went crowds gathered. Soon the tent was too small, so he began renting city auditoriums. Then he bought a larger tent, a huge white one with three poles, and hired a crew to travel with him. He hired a booking agent and a professional singer and a pianist.

One night during an especially effective altar call as two thousand people sang "Almost Persuaded," he felt that electric presence running through his body and he commanded the sick and ailing to come forward. As they came he put his hands upon them, and some later swore they'd felt the power and from that moment were healed. In this manner was Jonathan Hyde made a healer. He gave God all the credit, but kept much of the glory. He put the largely expanded revenues in the bank and took all this to be another sign that God was pleased.

Angela Hyde was a joy to the God-ridden life of her father. Her dark hair became long and black and wavy. Her skin was milk pure like Cerese's and her eyes a steel gray. She had a clear bell-like quality in her voice, and when she was four years old they discovered that she knew by heart the words to most of the songs they sang in the revival meetings. Jonathan dressed her in a long white gown and made her sing solos during the song service. It frightened her to have to do it but she did it for her father. She loved his deep, rich voice and his kind blue eyes; and she looked forward to the penny he always pressed secretly into her hand each time she sang.

He added her name to the posters and included her in all the news releases. Cerese wasn't so sure that it was a good thing for the child.

Angela was still a tiny girl when war broke out. Wars are almost as good for religion as depressions. The preaching business boomed. Jonathan's stern God was using a man called Hitler to bring the world to its knees; so the war was a good thing for Jonathan and his kind, though they seldom admitted it, even to themselves.

Ultimately it was Jonathan's God that came between him and Cerese. The healing part of his services gradually became more and more important and, he said, more and more taxing upon him. It took strength out of him, he said, to heal, and he must be pure and as close to God as a saint to draw God's power through him. They had been married eleven years, the child was ten, when he decided that the sex act made him less pure and drew strength away from him and away from those whom he would touch for God.

Before that time Cerese had enjoyed as much of him as she wanted. Her slightest hunger had been filled. She had only to make a breast visible to him or brush the back of her fingers across the front of his pants to bring the hot flame of desire over him. Little then stood in the way of their lovemaking. But now he began to exert will power over his natural drives, and their beddings were reduced to half. He prayed for strength and promised God he'd abstain, and he did as long as he possibly could; and then his wild and hungry animal thrusts were done too soon to bring any help to her own need.

She became aware of a wildness in his eyes and sometimes she saw his hand shake almost imperceptibly. She knew that it was simply the intensity of the force within him. She wanted to take him in her arms and comfort him and open herself to him and coax him to spill his power into her and be done with it, but he would not yield.

He slept little and prayed much.

Before the child had come and while she was still a toddler Cerese had gotten a special thrill from dressing and undressing in front of him, watching him turn on to her lithe, graceful body. She especially enjoyed standing nude in front of a mirror while brushing her hair as he lay on the bed watching.

So she resorted to that again. He lay on the bed fully clothed, resting before leaving for the tent.

Cerese came out of the bathroom naked, dripping wet except for her hair, which was under a towel, turbanlike. She walked to the mirror, removed the towel, and began drying herself.

"Go back in the bathroom," he commanded.

"It's all steamy. It'll ruin my hair."

"What if Angela comes in here?"

"So? She won't see any more'n she already has. Besides she's asleep."

"Well, I've got to go, anyway."

"Why?"

"Why? To pray. To prepare for the services." He sat up and

started to put on his shoes. She walked over to him and put a foot on the bed beside him and opened herself to him.

"All this is silly, you know," she said as she continued drying.

"All what?"

"All this holy, holy act. You know God doesn't mean for a man to give up fucking his wife." He didn't like her to use that word. She hadn't in years. He jerked his head up to face her.

"Why are you acting like this?"

"Because I'm dying for a fuck, Jonathan. My cunt is aching for it, honey; it's been a week, a whole week. I can't take it much longer."

"Pray," he said.

"Why? What's so wrong about a man fucking his own wife?" she cried. He was silent for a moment, gleaming pride for his ability to sit unmoved not twelve inches from her cunt.

Then he said slowly, looking right into her eyes, "I am the Lord's vessel, Cerese. I must abstain from carnality, from it in any form. I must be pure. I must not enjoy the flesh. I must cut it off and fling it away from me."

"You're mad," she said. His eyes were like fire. "I've watched you get so filled up with self-importance that you think you are God Almighty Himself."

"I am filled with God," he said. "I am filled with God, and in that sense, my child, in that sense, inasmuch as I am totally usable to Him I am one with God. God and I are one. In that sense it is true." The thought thrilled him and he stood up and walked away from her. "That is what I will preach tonight," he said to himself, "how we are one with God when we are a vessel pure and filled with the Spirit of God." And he did, and a hundred or more souls came forward and begged to be filled, cried to become one with God. When they in their honesty and sincerity offered themselves completely to their great and fearful God, a great feeling of relief surged through them, flooding them with electrifying emotion. Such a thrill, a glory to have finally done it, to have finally, once and for eternity, cast aside self-love and every vestige of the carnal mind. To them in their childlike faith that emotion was God filling them and empowering them.

A man shouted for pure joy. A woman screamed. An old saint in a flour-sack dress began running up and down the aisle waving a white handkerchief like a victory flag, shouting, "Glory be to Jesus, oh, glory, glory, glory!"

The Reverend Jonathan Alexander Hyde presided over the glory and tucked that sermon away in his mind. He would use it again.

Cerese received no blessing. She was not absolutely certain that Jonathan was not right. Perhaps God had spoken to him. He had some kind of power, no doubt about that. She'd seen too much to doubt it. Maybe like Samson his strength was special and could be drained away from him. Could she stand not to have him? Could she bear for long the suffering her body was going through right now looking up there at him and knowing he was burning for her. Why did it have to be this way? What was it with the Reverend Jonathan Alexander Hyde?

In bed he didn't sleep. He kept running the sermon over and over in his mind. It amazed him, always, after such a sermon, that he was capable of forming such thoughts, putting together such phrases, moving souls. Surely God was in him. But he burned still.

Cerese lay there beside him, wanting him, wanting to talk with him, to try to understand what it was that was making him this way. The heat in her was intense. It wasn't easy, this self-denial, and she didn't like it a damn bit. She touched herself and wanted to rub it, needed to do it, but dared not. She touched his chest with her hand. He didn't move, nothing, no signal, nothing at all. But was this silence a signal? She breathed deeply, hoping. Her hand explored his chest, then moved down. She passed his flat, hard stomach. He breathed deeply, but still did not move. Her hand grasped his cock. Hard. She worked it out of his shorts and moved herself over him and mounted the horn swiftly and expertly. She began slowly but could not stand the pleasure, the pain of it, so she finished it wildly, and as she came, wet and wonderful, she wept and hugged his chest. In a moment she sat up again and began again, to finish him off. She felt his huge hands under her thighs. He lifted her off him and pushed her to

231

the bed beside him. "But, Jonathan, you! You need it now."

"No," he said. "I no longer need it."

"But, Jonathan."

"Go to sleep." He turned his back to her and slept. He didn't hear her crying. Nor would he have cared much if he had. She was becoming quite a burden for him with her hungers and her needs. She hadn't grown as he had, nor would she. She didn't even want to. That was something: she didn't even want to.

They grew further apart. Jonathan gave Cerese just enough of himself to keep her hoping, but never enough really to satisfy her. She still loved him and thought he might come through this and want her as before. Cerese resorted to the comforts of her own hand, in the shower or the tub, whatever was available in the hotels, which were in themselves becoming more and more a drag on her sanity. She lay long in the water, keeping it as hot as she could stand it. She brought herself to satisfaction as many times as it took to drain her physical want completely. Her emotional needs were still unsatisfied, however, but he seldom touched her and almost never talked as they had before. She needed that; she needed the kind consideration of just someone good and caring to talk to. It had been a long time since Jonathan had been considerate and caring. He talked only to his God and for Him, except when it came to Angela. He talked to Angela and filled her full of his God. He loved her for the way she followed him and so eagerly sought to please him and his God.

Cerese lost interest in Jonathan's God. At first she prayed to Him and begged Him to release Jonathan to her, but He did not listen. Then she prayed for relief from her own body's bondage. Still He did not hear. She tried to give herself totally to Him, but it did not change Jonathan toward her, and it did not change her body, so she lay in her hot baths by day and slept by her cold man by night. God had done nothing for her.

Cerese was sitting alone at the counter in the hotel coffeeshop in New Orleans. She was alone because Jonathan was speaking to the local ministerial alliance, a task he hated because in his view, and God's, the local ministers were always too lax, all of them, on their sinful parishioners. "You don't preach enough on the essentials!" he harangued them. "You never preach anymore on the subject of female dress, on lipstick and rouge, on jewelry and the whorish dying of hair. All these things, if neglected by the local ministry, will creep in like an insidious plague, fill the women with pride and the men with lust. Now how can you expect to have a Godly community and a Godlike church if the women are proud hussies and the men are prowling, lustful beasts? The proper state of the Christian female is that of quiet submission and the male that of sincere and practiced abstinence from the pleasures of the flesh." It was the same sermon each time, and Cerese was embarrassed by it and simply stopped going with him. When she had gone to the meetings and he had come to the part about male abstinence, she felt all eyes were upon her beauty, as they were, and she felt that every person there was wondering how Jonathan Alexander Hyde could manage practiced abstinence from that, and they were. It seemed to her that her holy husband would be pleased to have her stand and testify that, indeed, the good reverend had not touched her in fourteen days and that only at her insistence and only out of pity for her, so that it was, in fact, an expression of Christian charity and not an act of bestial lust. But he did not go that far, and she did not give him another chance. This is why she sat alone in the Jung Hotel coffeeshop in New Orleans. The child was with her tutor, diagramming silly sentences. Cerese was trying to decide what could be done to salvage her "fucked-up life," or rather her *un*fucked-up life when a voice at her side brought her back into the world. "Ma'am, will you pass me that sugar, please?"

He sat to her left. He was blond, with blue eyes crinkled at the corners, laugh lines. He took the sugar, "Thank you, ma'am," set it down, and added cream to his coffee, but no sugar. He tasted his coffee, smiled at her, and said, "Just right. Thanks."

"You didn't use the sugar."

"I know." He smiled again; the crinkles spread.

"Are you flirting with me?" she asked, trying not to smile.

"Yes, ma'am."

"Good," she said, "I think that's just what I need."

"I know."

233

"How do you know that?" she asked, turning toward him.

"You were down here yesterday looking just as sad and lonely as you were a minute ago."

"Where did I sit?"

"Right over there." He pointed toward a booth in the corner.

"How did you see my face?"

"In that mirror," he said. She turned. Sure enough.

"Who are you?" she asked.

"Blair Anderson. Andy for short."

"Andy. Why do you trouble yourself with my troubles?" she asked.

"No reason," he said. "Nothing better to do, I guess." He laughed.

"Well, thanks a lot."

"I didn't mean it like that."

"I know."

"Look," he said. "If you're all by yourself I've got the whole afternoon free."

"What are you proposing?" Her voice betrayed her lack of calm and she knew it. That bothered her even more.

"Well, I really meant I'd take you through the Quarter, see the artists at work, have a beer, maybe ride the streetcar out to Audubon Park. That's all I meant, but I'm open for anything really, anything you are." And then he smiled again and she smiled back.

The French Quarter is a night place. In the afternoon it is just stirring awake. The burlesque houses, the jazz halls, the beer joints were only now opening their doors, not for business, but to let in the fresh air and draw out the musty, tobacco-laden air from the previous night's bash.

The moment Cerese had agreed to go with this strange, happy man she began to be afraid, not of him but of herself. It was no easy thing after these many years of absolute devotion to one man to commit herself to an afternoon with a stranger. But it was easier than she'd imagined.

They entered a small dark bar and found a little round table. "Want to take off your sweater?" She didn't. He ordered a beer, she coffee.

234

"You don't live around here," she said, half a question.

"No, I'm from Oregon originally. Just got out of the Army and wanted to see a little of the country before settling down."

"Good idea. No sense going too soon to the salt mines."

"No, ma'am, no salt mines for me."

"Then what?" she asked. An old Negro was sweeping up. He was wrinkled and stooped over. He sprinkled an oily red compound on the rough wood floor and then swept it up section by section. He hummed something slowly under his breath as he worked.

"Gonna start my own photography business." Andy smiled. "Gonna shoot weddings and babies for a living, then play around some on the side."

"I'll bet you'll be good at it. Kids won't be able to resist you."

"One smile and they're all mine." He laughed. The old man swept closer, noticed them.

"How'd do, Mr. Andy," he said.

"Okey doke, Mr. Shine. You?" Andy returned.

"Cain' complain. Cain' complain." He swept on.

"I shot him two days ago. Got a whole roll on him. Can't wait to develop it." He looked at her. His eye swept over her. He touched her chin and turned her face slightly away from him.

"You really are beautiful, you know," he said. "I would enjoy doing you."

She smiled and tears came. She tried to laugh, but it wasn't very good.

"Now what the hell's the matter?" So she told him as briefly as she could and without showing self-pity.

"Sounds like a real son-of-a-bitch, if you ask me," he said. "If you don't mind my sayin' so."

"He's not really, not always. Sometimes he can be nice," she said, smiling, "like old times, but that's rare anymore. He's so caught up. It's just not the same as before when we met."

"When you say it's just not the same, you mean he doesn't even sleep with you anymore?" he asked. She blushed and he said, "I'm sorry, I had no right to ask that. Look, if you're finished with your coffee let's go ride the streetcar."

"No," she said, "I'd better go back now."

235

"Really?" He grimaced. "I'm just getting to know you."

"Yes. I have to go back now."

"Okay," he said softly. "I understand." He paid and they walked back. They didn't talk until they neared the hotel, then she said,

"I'd better go the rest of the way alone."

"Okay," he said. "Tomorrow?"

"No. No, I don't think so."

"Look," he said as he turned to go, "I'm in 1530 if you need someone to talk to."

"Will you be here long?" she asked.

He looked at her eyes, "I don't know," he said.

He went to the revival that night and sat in the row behind Cerese and just to her right. He watched her. She didn't know he was there. He studied the service as only one emotionally unattached to it can do. He saw how the song leader used words and music to create just the precise mood. You start out by singing songs praising God and His wonderful universe, then about His bleeding son and His saving grace. Then you take an offering and then you sing some more, and when the people put their voices together in song they become closer to each other in spirit. By agreeing to songs and singing they give almost unconscious consent to the order of things and consent to the words of the songs which describe them as sinful wretches, filthy worms of the dust worthy only of the fires of hell. Consenting to this low indictment in song prepares their unperceptive mentalities for the practiced art of the chief hustler of souls, the preacher himself. When the preacher then told them of this Jesus so bereft and broken on the cross for their own sins, they were willing to do anything, give anything for forgiveness from a now angry God.

Andy hated the sermon and loved the sermon giver's wife. He sat and watched her and felt sorry for her and for her little daughter beside her, raven-haired beauties both of them. He wanted to photograph them together, nude and with their black hair loose and hanging down. He looked at the preacher, his craggy, sculpted face, the red hair and the hard gray eyes. Handsome, in a way, but hard. "Biblical," he thought, then

236

thought it strange and then not so strange that the man seemed biblical. He was that, a fiery prophet. He would shoot the reverend too, and he would do him as a prophet of God, and he would do the daughter and Cerese.

The next day as Jonathan Hyde sat in his hotel room reading his Bible and preparing a new sermon there was a knock on his door. He opened the door and faced a blond, kind-faced man, slightly shorter than himself.

"Reverend Hyde?" he asked.

"Yes, what do you want?"

"I'm Blair Anderson, photographer. I attended your meeting last night and decided that I wanted to photograph you."

"I don't understand," he said.

"May I come in?" Andy asked. The preacher stepped back from the door and Andy followed him inside. The preacher returned to the table and sat down and began writing. Andy sat down too and said nothing, only watched the big man writing. Reverend Hyde looked up at him. "Well?" he said. "Tell me what you want." And he continued to write.

"I am a photographer. I want to do a picture story on you and your team, including your family of course, if you have one, for *Life* Magazine.

He stopped writing and looked up. "You write for *Life?*"

"No. I'm not a writer. I take pictures. The story will be done by Brad Goodrich. He writes for them. We've collaborated on two other things."

"What things?"

"One on the reconstruction of Germany, focusing on the war's effect on the German family. The other on what was left of a Jewish family migrating from Dachau to Palestine."

"You went to the Holy Land to do that?" he asked.

"Yes, I went with them. I was in the Army with the division that liberated Dachau. I got to know this family and asked to do a story on them for the Armed Forces News Agency, got lucky, and was given permission to do it. Later I sold some pictures to *Life* and Brad did a story."

"Golgotha," Hyde said. "Tell me about Golgotha."

So Andy spoke with him for an hour, describing the sights he

237

saw and photographed in Palestine. When Cerese came in with Angela, Andy was still sitting there talking with Hyde. "This is Mr. Anderson, Cerese. He's doing a story on us for *Life* Magazine."

"How do you do, Mr. Anderson? This is our daughter, Angela."

"Hello, Angela. Did anyone ever tell you you look like your mother?" Andy asked.

"Lots of times," she answered and smiled. She was pleased with that. Her mother was the most beautiful person in the world. She only hoped she looked like her.

"Would you like some coffee, Mr. Anderson?"

"That would be nice," he said and she left the room. She felt she should be angry with him for coming, but could not bring herself to be.

She could not help trembling when she placed his coffee before him. He noticed it and felt a twinge of guilt for surprising her. She was beautiful, but her clothes were atrocious, colorless, and so plain. But her face, classic. And her body. What a fool was the Reverend Jonathan Hyde.

" 'Jonathan Alexander Hyde,' I'll call it," he told them, " 'An American Ezekiel.' " And the Reverend Hyde smiled quietly.

He started shooting that night. He got numerous shots of Hyde in the pulpit, his eyes hard, his great hand holding a Bible aloft, his mouth open and screaming, "Repent! Repent! Repent!"

He got a beautiful shot of the child dressed in her white robe, her angel hair streaming down her shoulders. Sweetness.

And Cerese. She would not smile, or could not in the tent.

Later he asked Hyde, "Reverend, I would like to get some shots of Angela and Mrs. Hyde in their daily routine, the child with her teacher, Mrs. Hyde shopping. Stuff like that."

"Good," he responded. "Tomorrow. I'll speak to Mrs. Hyde."

"Will you be able to be there? To get the whole family in, you know," Andy asked.

"Unfortunately not, Mr. Anderson. I have to speak to a school group tomorrow afternoon and I'll be down here all morning preparing for that, praying and filling with the Spirit."

"Ain't you something," Andy thought. But he said, "See you tomorrow night, then."

238

He reported early to the Hyde suite, accompanied Angela to her tutor's room, and shot six pictures of the child and the old teacher bending over a book, then went back to Cerese.

When she opened the door for him she asked, "Why are you doing this?"

"Are you angry?"

"No."

"You should be."

"I know, but I'm not. Now why?"

"You wouldn't understand," he said.

"Try me."

"You have some coffee?"

"Yes."

They sat at the table across from each other and he told her, "I'm not really sure why, Cerese. I'm a photographer I guess that's a start. Part of it, anyway. I can sell the pictures to *Life*. The writer I know has heard of your husband. I called him and he said to send him the stuff. But that's not all of it either."

She was silent, watching him.

"The rest of it is you," he continued. "I've known a dozen women in the world with beauty in your class. A dozen, no more. For a cameraman that's just too much to take. More than the preacher thing I wanted to shoot you."

"That's it?"

"Yes, almost."

"Almost?"

"And I like you."

She was quiet for a moment. Then "I'm in a hell of a shape. I was afraid you were a low type just after me, then I was afraid you weren't." She smiled.

"I've been so fouled up lately."

"I wish I could help you."

"You can shoot me," she said, smiling. "That'll give me a boost."

He hesitated for a moment, wanted to say, "I can do more than that," but said instead, "Then let's shoot."

She was a natural. She knew she was beautiful and said it with

239

every motion, every gesture. "Your clothes are atrocious," Andy told her.

"I know," she said, "but if I wore what I like my husband would kill me."

"Look, let's buy you some stuff."

"What do you mean?"

"I mean let's go across the street and I'll buy you some decent up-to-date things with short sleeves and a decent neckline. Something with some color, no more blues and grays and blacks."

"I can't do that," she said.

"Why in hell not?"

"It just wouldn't be proper."

"Fuck proper," he said; then, "I'm sorry."

"No, say what you want. It's good for you. I used to myself."

"Why not anymore?" he asked.

"You know."

"Say it," he urged.

"What?"

"Fuck. C'mon say it. How long has it been since you said it?"

"You're an absolute idiot." She laughed.

"I know it. Say it."

"No."

"Say it. For me."

"No."

"Why?"

"Fuck," she said softly.

"Again." He laughed.

"Fuck," she said louder. "Fuck."

They both laughed. Then he said, "Let's go get some clothes."

"Fuck clothes," she said. And as his camera clicked she began to undress, and when she was completely naked she asked him, "What would you do if Jonathan came in?"

"Probably get the shit kicked out of me. Wouldn't be the first time. What would you do?"

"I don't know," she said. A pained look came over her. She picked up her clothes and said to him, "Go away."

"Why?" he set his camera on the floor and moved toward her. She held her clothes over her body and turned away from him.

240

He touched her shoulder and pulled her back around to him. "I'm sorry," he said quietly. "I didn't want to hurt you. You're all messed up right now; I just wanted to help you unwind."

"I know . . . just go," she said quietly, breathing heavily.

"You think I'm a bastard," he said. Her face jerked up to his and her eyes opened.

"No," she said, "you're the most refreshing thing that's happened to me in years. That's the trouble. I don't know if I can handle that."

"You can," he said. He turned her around fully facing him, took her clothes away from her, and threw them away, pulled her in to him and kissed her mouth. She didn't resist. "Cerese, I know what you're going through. I've known you three days and already I know what a fool your husband must be. No man in his right mind could . . ."

"Go," she said, and he did.

At two o'clock his phone rang. "Yes?"

"Andy?"

"Cerese?"

"Can I come up?"

"Of course you can. The door is open."

Three minutes later she was standing outside his door. She stood there a full minute without knocking until it opened and he smiled quietly and stepped back. She was embarrassed and her face turned red. "You know what I came for."

"Whatever."

She took off her clothes and lay on the already messed-up bed. She was crying as he entered her, softly. He kissed her and tasted the bitterness of tears. He lifted his face and saw the crying turn in a moment to a soft smile. "Uh, that's so good. God, how I need that."

An hour later she lay exhausted on his heaving chest. "Andy?"

"Yes, ma'am."

"Thank you."

"Thank *you*."

"Do you know how long it's been since I've had it like that?" she asked.

"Do you know how long it's been since I've had it like that?" He chuckled.

She looked at him, "How long?"

"Never," he said. "Nobody has ever pulled it out of me like that. Never."

"That's good," she said and they both slept.

She came to his room the next morning and the next, then again in the afternoon. On Saturday afternoon they met in the little bar in the French Quarter. They sat in a corner. He was drinking bourbon, she coffee.

"What next, Cerese?"

"Don't spoil it, Andy."

"We've got to talk about it."

"No, we don't."

"You're scheduled for Denver in three weeks."

"How'd you know that?"

"And you're through here next Thursday. I just asked Jonathan. You can't stay with that damnfool preacher," he said.

"I have to."

"Why? Angela?"

"Of course, Angela."

"Next time you get a chance you take a good long look at Angela, Cerese, and ask yourself just how much influence you have over her life and the way she is growing up."

Silence.

"You'd have to get her completely away from that monster and all his goddamn religion to do anything at all with her or for her."

"What do you mean?"

"Well just *look* at her. She's not a normal child. She's beautiful and brilliant, talented, but her little mind is so goddamn warped she doesn't even know what's real."

"Andy!" she protested.

"I'm sorry, Cerese. She is going to be one fucked-up female," he said. "What does she want to do with her life?"

"She wants to be a missionary," Cerese said quietly.

"There. You look at some of those little missionary girls, dried-up little white-faced biddies, no life and no blood . . ."

242

"Okay," she said. "I know. But what can *I* do?"

"Not a goddamn thing. Not now. You should have gathered her up and run like crazy years ago."

"I know."

"Now you can only save yourself." He ordered another drink, threw it down in three quick gulps. "Baby, I'm leaving."

"Leaving?" Her eyes were frightened.

"Tomorrow. I'm flying to Seattle and I want you to go with me."

She reached down for her purse. There was no handkerchief in it. "Here." He handed her a napkin. She wiped her eyes.

"You know why I married him?" she asked. "Because he was good and kind. He loved me and he was good in bed. That's right. I married him because he could fuck like a stud bull three, four times a day. That's really all I wanted. What does that make me?"

"You're being too hard on yourself, Cerese."

"Oh no," she said, "I know what I am. I'm a goddamn whore, Andy. There's one thing I've got to have and if I don't get it I'm a wreck. What does that make me?" Her beautiful face was red and set hard.

"Cerese, you just shut your mouth a goddamn minute and let me tell you what you are," he said. "You're a normal woman. Sure you like to fuck. So do I. So did two dozen other girls I've shacked up with from Johannesburg to Tokyo in the last twenty years. You also like to eat and work and play and talk. You knock fucking because your goddamned righteous husband and two thousand years of fanatics tell you it's nasty. To hell with him! You won't be gone ten days, Cerese, and he'll find something to stick it in." He ordered another drink.

"You get off your own back about that, girl. That's stupid. You want to fuck, then fuck. To hell with religion. It's all a pile of shit in the sky anyway, every damn bit of it."

"Why are you doing a story for *Life*, then?"

"You just wait till you see it," he said. "Just wait." He shot down his drink, paid the bill, and they left.

"Are you going to the room with me?" he asked.

"Yes." She smiled.

243

When they were done he said, "Look, Cerese, I'm leaving early in the morning. I love you."

"Don't say that," she said.

"It's true. You're one fucked-up broad, but I love you. You're good. You haven't given yourself a chance."

"Don't," she said.

"I'll be in Seattle. If you want to come, come. We'll get married the day you get there. Bring Angela if you can, and if you can't, come anyway. She's in love with her father and you simply can't help her." He got up and put on his pants. He took two hundred dollars out of his wallet and put it in her purse. "It'll be hard for you to get money if you leave him," he said. "You'll need that even if you don't come to Seattle." He put on his shoes, shirt, and jacket. "I'll be at this address," he said. He handed her a small piece of paper, squeezed her hand, kissed her on the face, and left.

That night with Jonathan Hyde in bed beside her was one of the worst of her life. She had loved him and believed he had loved her, but it was apparent to her now that he was so bent on becoming "God's man" that he would never look at her again, at least not as before.

Her mind raced nervously. She was frustrated at every point. Even her daughter was no longer her own, had grown distant. What to do? Andy was real. If he said he loved her he meant it. But did she love him? Was it only physical? How to know? Would it last? He must want me, she thought; he could have about anybody he crooked his finger toward. And he smiles a lot. He's happy. She wanted him, physically. She wanted him in her and she wanted his arms around her. She wanted him to tease her and smile at her over a breakfast table. Was that love? Married twelve years and still didn't know what love was? Had it been Jonathan's cock then? No, he was different then; he showed interest in her and was kind. Not like now.

Her body burned. She had thought many times since Jonathan had begun this craziness that she would just go back to the old life, but she really didn't want that either. There was a greal deal to be said for tenderness and kindness and the kind of closeness that comes from a one-to-one relationship. But that was gone now. She touched herself and moved her hand into the hot wetness. It wasn't as satisfying this way, but what else did she have? She touched Jonathan with her other hand, found his prick, soft. She took it out of his shorts and worked it with her fingers as she did herself. In a moment it was a hard, pulsing beast. She heard his breath deepen as she pumped him faster and faster. She came and he did too. She wiped her hand on the sheet and lay back, breathing hard, considerably relieved. Why did he make her do this?

His voice was a chill in the night. "Have you no pride, woman?" The light flicked on and he sat up in bed. He turned to her and placed both hands on her face and squeezed hard. "You will never do that again. You are a whore, woman, and God will find you guilty of whoredom." His voice was deep and slow and angry. He removed one hand and struck her fiercely on the face with his closed fist. She screamed and sank back, stunned.

Angela sat upright in bed, then ran to her parents' bedroom. "I heard something," she said.

"It was nothing, probably," Jonathan told her. "I'll check. Go back to bed, Angel." And she did.

When the child was gone Cerese said to him, "You are mad, Jonathan. You're mean and evil."

"You will sleep in another room henceforth, woman. I'll not be troubled again by your lust."

"You enjoyed it, you son-of-a-bitch, and you know it." She half smiled at him and half glared.

"Shut up," he ordered, "and leave my bed."

She did. She dressed quickly; her face was red and hurt. Her eye was swelling. She went to the lobby and phoned Andy's room. No answer. She went to the desk. The night man informed her that Mr. Anderson had checked out hours ago.

She registered in another room and went up and went to bed. She did not sleep. Her eye hurt too much.

In the morning she phoned Angela's tutor and asked her to send the child to her when she came in. She ordered coffee and was drinking it when the child knocked on her door.

"Mother! Your face! Your eye!"

"It's all right, Angel." She closed the door and they sat down.

The child touched her mother's face softly. "How did this happen?" she asked. "Last night?"

Cerese did not know how to tell Angela that her father was a bastard. She said nothing.

"Mother, did father do this? Was it you who screamed?" Then a funny look came over her.

"What is it?" Cerese asked.

"We've been praying for you, mother," she said, and she took on an air of superiority.

"Who has, child? What do you mean?"

"Mrs. Baggett and I. Father asked me to pray for you and Mrs. Baggett is helping me."

"Why did your father do that, Angel?"

"Because he said you were still of the flesh."

"And what did he mean by that?"

"I'm not sure, but I think I know."

"What?"

"Remember Judith Hartso?"

"Reverend Hartso's daughter? Yes, I know her."

"Well, when we were there Judith told me all about the flesh and how it is weak and what men and women do who are still uncommitted to the Holy Spirit. And how some women who are sinful still do it."

"Do what, Angela?" It seemed incredible. Cerese wanted to know what this was and why.

"You know, mother. How you get babies. That." She was near tears.

"Who told you about that?"

"Judith."

"And how did she know?"

"She's twelve."

"That doesn't mean anything, dear."

"She saw her mother and father."

"When they were doing it?"

"Yes."

"Is that what you mean by 'of the flesh'?"

"Partly, yes. You are supposed to do it only when you're to have a baby. They had a little baby after that."

"I see. And me? Did your father tell you that about me?"

"No. He just asked me to pray for you because you were still of the flesh. Mrs. Baggett said you were a woman of the world, that she could tell you didn't have the Spirit, and that we should pray for you."

Cerese was silent for a while. Her eyes misted over. She hadn't realized how far away from these people she had come and from her own sweet child. "Angela, you are so young. There are some things you don't understand now and won't for many years. But you must understand one thing. I love you very much and I am not evil and I am not bad. And think about this too, child. When you came into our room last night what did your father say?"

"That nothing had happened."

"Was that the truth?"

The child did not answer.

"Answer me, Angela."

"I don't know."

"You will one day. I just hope it doesn't hurt too much when you do."

The child stood to go.

"Don't go just yet, Angel. I want to talk to you a minute."

"Mrs. Baggett is waiting for me. She said don't be long."

"I know, child. I won't be." She poured herself another cup of coffee. "Sit down, Angela. I want to tell you something very important." The child did sit down, but in a chair across the room.

"I am going away, Angela." The girl looked at her mother. Her lips were quivering ever so slightly and her eyes were afraid.

"Someday I hope you will understand. Maybe you never will." Cerese was crying now and her bruise hurt terribly. "I am going to always keep in touch with you and will always be ready to come to you if you need me. Or if you want to come to me I'll send you the ticket the very day you call. I'll send you a phone number and an address when I get settled, love. Come here." Angela ran to her. Cerese hugged her and they both cried.

"Why, mother?" she cried.

"Because your father doesn't love me anymore and he doesn't need me anymore. One day you'll understand that."

247

"He's not bad!" she screamed. "He's good. He's my father and he's good." She wept deeply after that. Cerese held her and spoke softly and kindly to her.

Sometime later after the child was calmed she stood, straightened her dress, and simply walked out of the room.

She did not tell Jonathan she was leaving and she didn't leave a note. She flew to Seattle and took a cab to Andy's address. It was winter there. Small patches of white snow on brown grassy lawns and dirty brown snow in slushy strips on side streets set her to shivering, but she wasn't sure if the shivering was from the cold or from a case of nerves.

Andy was in his car backing out of the driveway when she arrived. He saw the cab and stopped. She got out and opened her purse to pay the driver and Andy realized who it was. He opened his car door and got out slowly. "Well, I'll be goddamned!" He laughed out loud and took the small suitcase from her. "Baby, I didn't think you'd do it." he said.

"Glad?" she asked, still uncertain.

He stopped and pulled her to him. "If you hadn't come I was comin' after you," he said. "Climb in," he told her as he tossed her bag in the back. "We've got to go shoot a wedding."

When Hyde realized she had left him, he left the hotel and headed for the French Quarter. He knew the whores solicited there and thought that to be the most logical place for her to find a man. "A man is what she's after. I'll catch her at it, I will," he thought.

He walked for four hours all over the Quarter. He walked into every bar and strip joint and looked at every face. She was nowhere. In Iberville near the river at midnight a black whore approached him. She was skinny and old and had brown, rotten teeth. Hyde shoved her off the curb. She fell into the street and rained foul curses upon him as he strode on without looking back.

In a small, dark alley bar he spotted a slim, blackhaired girl sitting alone at a corner table. He was sure he'd caught her. He walked to her and sat down and then realized he was mistaken.

"Well, lookee here," she cooed. She was young and hard looking. He got up without saying anything. She was up in a flash beside him, holding his arm. He stopped. She reached for the front of his pants and gripped the bulge she felt there. "Look, baby," she said softly, "I can fix that thing. Here, feel this." She took his hand and moved it downward. He didn't resist. She had on a full skirt. It gave way nicely as she dragged his fingers across her cunt. "How 'bout that, huh?" She pulled him along with her toward the back. He didn't resist.

In a dark alley she knelt and extracted her prey's root, and while he leaned against a cold brick wall she did marvelous things to him with her mouth until she felt the spasms heighten, then she substituted a handful of toilet paper for her mouth and patted him and cooed to him and squeezed his balls, while he poured his sperm into her tissued palm.

He returned to her the next night and the next night and every night until the New Orleans meeting was over, and then he repented and swore never to do it again.

The story in *Life* did not mention Cerese and didn't include a single shot of the evangelist's wife. The photos of Hyde, though, were to his liking although they were not intended to be. They showed him to be the wild-eyed hell screamer that Andy had seen. One shot caught him in the pulpit, Bible held high in the air, one hand formed into a fist. Light glinted from his eyes and his mouth was agape, with white teeth flashing. Anybody could see his resemblance to a madman, but to Jonathan Hyde the pictures showed a man of God in earnest; his preachments were given credence by his fire-breathing countenance.

Angel was shown to be the sweet child that she was, however used by the fanatic that was her father.

It was from this magazine story that Hyde presumed the truth about Cerese and Blair Anderson. No matter. It was good not having her watching him, always watching him. Now there was only the child.

He began to look for a place to settle, a church and a home. He would pastor the church during the winter and hold revivals in the summer. Mrs. Baggett could take care of Angela and the Reverend Hyde could be free. He thought of the whore in the alley and was so thankful that he had a forgiving God.

PART IV

Chapter

17

The boy stood for a long time looking into the gallery on North St. Mary's Street. The owner remarked to his wife, "He's out there again, Louise." Louise appeared from the back room. She was a slight, graying lady with a perpetual smile.

"This is the third time this week."

"Fourth. He was by this morning."

The child was small, thin, about ten. His hair was black, and the darkest busiest eyes sped over the canvas on display, a sea painting of a ship in a storm. The ship, a three-masted schooner stripped for weather, was fighting for its life near a gray, rocky coast. The crew could be seen readying lifeboats.

"He loves that painting," Louise said. The child stood a half hour then seemed to become aware of himself. He walked slowly away from the window then broke into a full run and was gone.

He was back the next day and the next. It was April in San Antonio; the spring rains hadn't yet spent themselves. On Saturday morning it rained off and on, sometimes just misting, then growing to a downpour for a few minutes, then suddenly stopping. A new painting was out. A work depicting a little girl and a dog. She was laughing and pushing the little dog away. The animal had the hem of her dress in his teeth and was tugging on it. It was a warm, carefully done work. The girl was blue-eyed with braided blond hair. The dog was of undetermined breed, white with brown and black spots. It was misting when the boy first saw the painting. When Louise noticed him standing out there it was raining hard, yet he stood there still, his nose white against the cold glass. Louise was at the door in an instant. "Young man, you get in here out of that rain!"

He turned slowly, then looked down at his clothes. He started to bolt away, but the little woman held his arm like a vise. He felt himself being propelled along behind her into the gallery itself. "Charles!" She called when they were back inside. "Bring me a towel!" A surprised Charles came out of the back room, saw the boy soaking wet, then went back to get a towel.

"You come back here, Shorty, and we'll get you into something dry." The lad obeyed. He walked toward the back room, surveying all the beautiful treasures hanging on the walls.

Charles closed the back-room door and commanded the boy to get out of his clothes. He did so slowly, his eyes fixed on the easel and the unfinished painting sitting toward the back of the room near a large window. There was the smell of oil paint and turpentine in the room and the man smelled of them too. The boy looked at the man again in a new light. Were all those pictures the work of this man's hands? He looked at the hands as they struck a match to light a little gas stove. There were smudges of red and brown paint on them and on the front of his light green gownlike shirt.

"Here." The man took off his smock and tossed it to the boy. "Put this on and stand by the fire till you get warm." He opened the door. "Okay, Louise. All clear."

He had the painter's smock on and was standing at the easel when Louise came in. Charles had turned a stool upside down in front of the fire and had hung the wet clothes on the legs.

"Child, what is your name?" she asked.

"Rick," he said, hardly turning from his view of the canvas.

"It speaks," Charles said. Rick smiled.

"Did you paint all those?" he asked.

"Not all," he said. "About half."

"The one in the window?"

"No. That's a Mueller. I'm Herter. Here, I'll show you." He took the boy into the gallery and pointed out his work and that of others. "You see here's my signature, C. Herter. I did all these on this wall." He motioned toward the wall and the child turned to examine the works of this man whose painter's coat he wore, all covered with reds and browns and smelling of turpentine and oil.

They were beautiful, all Texas landscapes depicting the rolling Texas hill country covered with bluebonnets and sage and spotted here and there with a cactus or a small, sturdy oak. In some there were barns and fences and a few Herefords grazing near a trickling stream. There were windmills and old wagons. One had a cowboy on a tired old horse, and in one had been painted the ghost of a longhorn haunting the broad Texas plains. The child looked from the paintings to the face of the man whose hands had made them. He smiled.

"Do you like them?" Charles asked.

"Yes," and turned again to admire them; something in him ached, the same deep hurt that had brought him to the window of the pictures.

"Do you paint?" the man asked.

"I have some watercolors and some pencils. I mostly just draw," he answered quietly.

"You'll have to bring some by and let me see your work," Charles said. A strange look came over the boy's face and he ran to the back room again and grabbed his pants. From a hip pocket he pulled out a soggy thick handful of papers. He opened them carefully, unfolding each one tenderly and spreading it out before the fire. Charles watched the child spellbound. They were pencil drawings of remarkable maturity. One was the ship picture that was displayed in the window last week. It was well done, with shadings and tones in blacks and grays that Charles knew bespoke hours of painstaking care. It wasn't large, done on common school paper with arithmetic on the reverse side. Charles picked it up carefully and looked at it a long time. On the arithmetic side was the child's name: *Richard Morgan, Roosevelt School.*

"Louise!" Charles called. When she came he handed her the drawing and turned and went to his canvas and began to paint. She looked at it a moment, then examined the others.

"Rick," she said, "will you show me how you draw?"

He picked up his pants again and took out a stubby school pencil, looked around the room, then said, "I don't have any paper."

She got him a pad. He sat on the floor in front of the fire and began to draw. It was the little girl and the dog in the big painting in the window. He worked for half an hour seemingly oblivious of anyone else in the room. Then he handed it to her. She took it to Charles, strangely silent behind his canvas, and handed it to him. He looked at it a moment and his eyes filled.

"Louise, I was thirty years old before I could do that."

"Rick, come here." Louise called. He came away from his drawing slowly, reluctantly. "How old are you?"

"Ten years old," he answered, eying Charles's quick hand at work.

"Where do you live?"

"San Pedro Street," he said without looking at her.

"How long have you been drawing?" she asked.

"Since I was a little boy," he answered, "long time."

"Rick," Charles broke in, "why do you draw?"

"Because it's fun," he said. "I like it."

Charles smiled, "Touché."

"Touché." The boy grinned.

"What do you want to be when you grow up?" Louise asked him.

"Even before I grow up," he said, "I want to do that." He pointed at Charles's canvas.

"So you will."

And it was thus that Rick became a painter. It would have been his father's desire that he become a baseball player or some kind of athlete, for the boy was quick and strong and could have done well at that. Such a desire was understandable, for Timothy Morgan had become a high school coach after he returned from the war. Lucinda would have wanted her son to be a doctor; that was the logical choice for a boy with brains as far as she could see, for she had herself become a nurse and would have wanted to be a doctor if things had been different. But neither mother nor father nor grandmother nor grandfather would have stood for a minute in the way of this boy and his love for painting, so eager was he and so promising.

The Herters visited Timothy and Lucinda Morgan in their home and offered to give the boy lessons in painting.

"He'll pick it up fast, I'm sure. In a couple of years he'll be good enough to start selling his work."

"He's that good?" Timothy asked. Rick had been excused for the moment.

"He will be," Charles assured them.

He came every day after school and on weekends he worked at home. His school lessons suffered at first, but after a good long talk with Charles he buckled down and there were no more C's on his report card.

Mr. Herter was a big man and he towered over his diminutive protégé as he stood over the boy's easel and advised him: "That's not quite right yet, Rico."

"What, C. Herter?"

The tree. The tree is too green, Rico. Where did you get that green, boy?" Rick picked up a tube and showed it to Charles.

"From here."

"Permanent Green Light?"

"Yes. That's a helluva green, huh, C. Herter?" He grinned.

C. Herter grinned back. "Don't say that when Louise is present, kiddo. She'll throw us both out."

"Okay," he said, grinning.

"Now about the green."

"I know, mix it myself."

"Blues and yellows," Charles began. . . .

"And ochers and umbers," Rick continued.

"And reds for graying. Right, foulmouth?"

"Right, C. Herter."

"Why did you use that awful green when you knew better?" Charles asked.

"To try something."

"What?"

"Something."

"It didn't work."

"I know," Rick said as he began to scrape out the entire tree. "You are a hard man, C. Herter."

"And don't you forget it, kid."

When school was out they headed for the countryside every day for a month, sketching. They sat for hours side by side, sketching cloud formations, trees, barns, everything.

"Not so much detail, Rick," Charles would tell him. "These are just studies."

"Hokay, Mr. C. Herter, just lazy, easy studies, just shapes and shadows, right?"

"Right."

Then they took their paint boxes along and they made small color sketches, quick, to catch the light and the shadows.

"We'll put these away to work from this winter. Then we worry with detail and texture. Now we create, then we polish."

"You are a hard man, C. Herter."

"Don't you forget it, kid."

Sometimes on Sunday they went to amateur art shows around the city, and Rick began to become aware of how good he was. "I can do better than that," he said.

"Of course you can. You should. Do you know why?"

"Why?"

"Think about it," Charles told him. And the boy was quiet as they walked among the displays.

Later he said, "You are right."

"What do you mean?"

"I should be better. I would be unhappy if I could only paint as well as that."

"Don't you think those people are unhappy with what they have done?"

"Yes, but maybe that is the best they can do," Rick said.

"Then that is the sad part," Charles added, "that that is their limit. That is the best they can do and they will never get any better."

"I feel sorry for them."

"So do I," Charles said. "Never brag on yourself, son. If you are better your work will show it far better than your mouth."

"I'm sorry, Charles. You are right."

"Of course I am, kid, and don't ever forget it. You want some ice cream?"

"You damn betcha, C. Herter," he said, grinning. "Only this time I pay."

"You've got a foul mouth, punkin. This time you pay. I'll take a double dip."

Charles taught him for two years before he decided to show the boy's work to the public. Even his parents hadn't seen his later stuff.

"We'll surprise 'em," Charles said. "Don't show 'em any of these. They'll see 'em at the show."

"When?" Rick asked.

"In May."

"That's next month."

"That's right."

"I'm scared," the boy said.

"Why?"

"Just scared."

"Good."

The night before the show they moved all the other paintings off the walls and put up Rick's. Louise noticed the boy's hands shaking as he leveled a large landscape. She put an arm around him, "What's the matter, son?"

"Nothing really."

"You're worried about tomorrow."

"Yes, ma'am." She could see he was near tears.

"Why?"

"What if they don't like them?"

"So?" she shrugged. "What difference would that make? You know they are good. I know it, and if Charles didn't think they were good he'd never let you show them, right, Charles?"

"Right, kid. Look, I'm going to teach you something very important about the art world right now. Okay?"

"Okay."

"Some people will say unkind things about your work. The better you are the more you can expect them to try to find something wrong with you, and they'll take the one thing that's not like they think it oughta be and they'll knock hell out of it. Some of them will do it honestly and some will do it out of pure meanness or out of envy. Every once in a while you'll run into somebody who'll see something in your work even you never

259

saw, a weakness, a flaw, and if you've got any sense you'll listen and experiment and learn. But most of these yahoos don't know their elbows from their asses. . . ."

"Charles!" Louise jumped.

"Sorry, Louise, but it's true, Rick, and you'll just have to take their damned snotnosed remarks and go on your way. Okay?"

"Okay."

"There's another side to it, Charles," Louise put in. "Most people who see your work won't know a thing about art, but they'll tell you how wonderful it is. Don't let that swell your head. At twelve years old no one is as good as he's going to be. You've got a lot of time and a lot of work ahead of you."

"I know."

"See you do, punkin." Charles told him, "Now what kind of prices you want for this junk?"

"Prices?" Rick asked.

"Sure. You're not going to give it away are you?"

"Damn!" he blurted, then looked at Louise and covered his mouth.

"Charles," she said, "see where your language has gone."

"The kid has ruined me," he said. "Right, kid?"

"Right, C. Herter," he said. "You price this stuff. I'm going home." He turned to leave.

"Seven o'clock, Rick!" Louise called to him.

The Herters hadn't arrived at six-thirty so Rick opened up. He couldn't believe the prices Charles had put on his stuff. One hundred dollars, fifty dollars, eighty-five dollars, two hundred? "Damn," he said as he surveyed his work. "We won't sell nothin', not a damn thing."

Out of twenty-two paintings they sold twelve. The most expensive ones went first. Charles did not introduce Rick until most of the crowd had seen the work. Only a few knew the stuff was done by a boy. He said later, "I didn't want to sway them. If they'd known they couldn't have viewed objectively. As it was most of the stuff went before they knew."

The summer he was fourteen they painted the sea. They camped out on Boca Chica, a clean stretch of beach near the mouth of the Rio Grande. They got up early to catch first light and they were painting when the sun went down behind them. They drew seagulls and crabs and boats and distant ships at sea. They would swim in the pounding surf and study the action of the waves from the surface. Charles taught Rick how to stand dead still in the face of a huge breaking wave and watch it until the very split second it crashed down on top of them. The water was always changing color, from a gray muddy brown one day to a green or a gray blue the next.

They studied the sand and the wind patterns in it. Sometimes they'd find where the wind or water had moved the surface of the sand away from an old wine bottle or a Civil War button or a rusty gun frame, and they'd paint those things.

When they opened their seascape show they showed their stuff together, and Charles's work just barely outsold Rick's.

The summer he was fifteen Rick and Charles went to Mexico, to Monterrey, and painted the peasants in the hills and mountains. They painted goats and bears and wild asses in the Hausteca Canyon and the waterfalls just south of the city. But Rick liked the people and he spent most of his time just sketching them, the old ones especially, with the tired lines in their faces and the shadows in their eyes. He loved the people.

Charles would not show with Rick this time. "Remember the amateurs, the ones you said should be unhappy because that was the best they could ever paint?"

"Yes."

"I am fifty and I am as good as I am ever going to be. You are thirteen and already better than I. I am happy for you and sad for me."

"That's not true."

"It is true. I will always be in the minor leagues. That's all right. I would not want to be anything but an artist. But you. You will soon be in the big leagues and one day the best of the best if you do not get spoiled. That is why we can't show together. I am too vain, that is why." He looked away toward a large painting of a Mexican boy leading seven goats through a mountain pass.

261

"That is a helluva painting, kid; not a great painting, not yet, but a helluva painting still."

"You're a good man, C. Herter." The boy's voice cracked.

"Your voice is changing, punkin. You're growing up. Good thing you don't paint with your voice."

"Good thing."

Chapter

18

When Rick was sixteen Charles went to Lucinda and Timothy and told them it was time for the boy to begin life sketches.

"Naked?" Lucinda questioned.

"Yes. It is the only way an artist can really learn."

"But he's only sixteen."

"I know, and just barely that, but he's more mature than most kids his age," Charles said.

"He can learn a lot more than just art," Lucy said. "Tim?"

"Who will model for him?" Timothy asked.

"Professional models, good decent ladies who model fashions for advertising agencies right here in San Antonio. Rick will pay them out of his earnings. The men will be whoever I can get at the time. If we had an art school here he could just enroll to get his life studies. There's the University, but they won't take him. He's too young for that, they say."

"Is he?" Tim asked.

"No. He's just right. He needs a constant challenge. He learns everything so damned fast."

"Okay," Tim said. "Go ahead."

"Timothy!" Lucy protested.

"Honey, he's not your little boy anymore." Tim smiled at her. "Time he had some fun anyway. Go ahead, Charles."

"I cannot until Mrs. Morgan is also in agreement. He is only sixteen. I can see her point, too."

"Right," Tim said. "Lucy?"

"You're right," she said. "I'm being silly and old-fashioned. If that is what he wants then it is best to go ahead." She smiled at Timothy. "Might do the little devil some good."

"Not too much, I hope," Charles admitted.

It was fun, but Rick never admitted to Charles or anyone else how much fun it was to sketch a live model in the altogether not six feet away from him. At first it was difficult to keep his mind on his work. He found himself spending too much time working over certain more troublesome areas. Charles noticed and said, "Kid, you've got the breasts right. Go on to something else."

"What?"

"I said the tits are okay, kid. Do the arms. You need work on the arms."

"You're a hard man, C. Herter," and the model would giggle and wink at Rick.

They didn't have a public showing of his first batch of nudes because it might have been troubling to Charles's clientele to face the fact of a sixteen-year-old's painting a live nude like that. The community just wasn't ready for that, he told Rick.

"They don't know asses from elbows," Rick reminded him.

"Elbows from asses," Charles corrected.

"Right."

Rick Morgan often amused himself at school during especially boring classes by sketching the girls in the class without any clothes on. After several life-studies classes he began to be aware that he could look at a girl and determine exactly what she looked like without her clothes; teachers too. He had a sketchbook filled with every female in all his classes. They were all shapes and sizes. Great fun. He told no one what he was doing, not even Charles. The prettiest ones he did over and over in the most alluring poses.

But the most beautiful girl in the school wasn't in any of his classes. She was not in his classes, but he was aware of her and studied her at every opportunity.

One day he approached her in the hall. "Angela?"

She stopped, smiled at him, "Yes?"

"I'm Rick Morgan, Angela. Could I talk with you a minute?"

264

"Sure, Rick, but I've got a class this period."

"So lunch?" he asked.

"Sure, here?"

"In the lunchroom I'll save you a seat." And he turned and walked away. She watched him go. He was thin and small, but there was something about him.

She was afraid he would ask her for a date, something she always dreaded. It was hard for a sixteen-year-old to explain that she couldn't date and never had because her father wouldn't allow it.

He surprised her. "I want to paint you."

"Paint me?"

"Yes, and enter it in the State Fair Art Show," he explained.

"The State Fair, me?"

"Not you, the painting."

"What would it mean? I don't understand. You mean I would have to pose for you?" She blushed.

"You'd have to sit for me four or five times at various stages of the work, yes."

"I can't," she said and her eyes clouded.

"Why not?"

"I just can't."

"I'll pay you, Angela, and it won't take much time."

"Oh, it's not that, Rick. It's my father. He wouldn't like it and I can't do anything he doesn't want me to."

"I could ask him for you."

"Oh no, don't please."

"My dad could ask him."

"No, Rick," she said.

"Why?"

"Can you do it here at school, like during the lunch hour or just before school in the morning?"

"No. I need at least two hours four or five times. Look," he said, reaching for his notebook. "I did this last period." He handed her a sketch.

"This is me, Rick!" she exclaimed. "This is really me."

"It's yours," he said as he stood up. "See you around, Angela."

265

"But, Rick . . ." she said, looking up at him.

"Yes?"

"I'm sorry."

"It's okay. Don't worry about it." He smiled and walked away.

Angela Hyde loved her father and she knew he loved her. Otherwise why would he be so concerned? Since they had moved to San Antonio life had been more difficult for her. On the road doing the revivals she had been sheltered from "the world" as her father called it. He warned her of the temptations she would encounter when she started to the public schools, and he had been right. But it seemed that he was far too strict. He allowed no dating, no extracurricular activities, no sports. And she obeyed. Her life was one devoted to God and entirely to God.

"When you were born, Angel, and just old enough to be out, I took you to church, my own old tent, you remember, and there before God I laid you down on that altar and offered you to God, to his service. And you heed that when the temptations come." And so she did.

She still sang in her father's church and she traveled with him occasionally during the summer to sing for his revivals. He had her cut a record, "Angel Airs," and sold it on his trips. She sang on radio and television now and then when local religious programs asked her. Her life was devoted to God and religion and her father. She had no time for anything else.

Rick sat on the steps of the school and watched her come up the walk. She moved with a natural grace free of the feigned lilt of many of the school-yard beauties imitating the latest Hollywood sex symbol. She saw him and smiled. "Good morning, Rick."

"I want to show you something." He opened a huge portfolio and extracted a canvas and turned it toward her. "Like it?"

"You did it anyway, Rick. Oh, it's so pretty! But I look so sad! Why?" She turned to him.

"Because that's how I see you sometimes." He pulled out a dozen studies of her done in pencil and pen and ink. "See."

Most were sad and pensive views of a beautiful dark-haired girl reading, writing, eating, or just sitting.

"Am I really like this, Rick?" she asked quietly.

"Really. Something bothering you?"

"No. Look, Rick. It's not right."

"What?"

"The painting. It's just not me."

"Then sit for me," he insisted without smiling.

"I can't," and she turned and walked swiftly away.

"Shit," he said, half to himself, and put the painting back. It really wasn't her and he knew it, but he had thought seeing it would change her mind. "What *is* it with her?"

Rick hadn't taken art at school. It would have been a waste of time, but he knew the art teacher well. They had taken sketching trips together and Rick had been instrumental in arranging for some of the teacher's work to be shown at the Herter Gallery.

"Len, you know Angela Hyde?" he asked.

"Sure, what about her?" He was setting up his props for the next class.

"She's beautiful, right?"

"No doubt about that, Rico."

"So she won't sit for me."

"She can't. Her old man's a crazy preacher down on Bryan Street at that big church down there. He won't let her out of his sight. They wanted her for chorus here, but he said no."

"Why?"

"Scared she might do something sinful, I guess, I don't know." The bell rang and kids started coming in. Rick had to hurry to his class.

"That's a real crock," he said to Len as he left.

The next Sunday morning he was up early. He bathed and spruced up in his best clothes. On the way out he passed his father reading the Sunday paper on the front porch. "Hey, what's the big deal?"

"No big deal." He grinned. "Do I pass?"

"Pass. Where to?" he asked.

"You wouldn't believe it."

"Try me," Tim said.

"Church."

"Church?" He dropped the paper and looked at the boy quizzically. They had never taken the boy to church and had

267

endeavored as well as possible to explain to him why they were no longer churchgoers. Rick knew that Tim had been a priest and understood how he felt about religion. "No big deal," Rick had thought. "Makes sense." So he never went either.

"You chasin' a woman, kid?"

"Right."

"Do I know her?"

"I don't know, she's in school. Angela Hyde."

"Nope, don't know her. She's not in sports, right?" he asked.

"Nothin', she's not in nothin'," he said as he went down the steps. "Her old man's a preacher and he won't let her." And then he was gone, leaving Tim stunned.

"Hyde? A preacher." Frank had told Timothy of Jonathan's endeavor and Tim had seen the *Life* spread several years ago. Could it be? He dropped the paper and went to the phone, picked up the book and leafed through it. " 'Hyde, Rev. Jonathan A.' That's it, Alexander." He made a note of the address then returned to his paper. At twelve o'clock he was parked in the front of the church. The people began filing out fifteen minutes later. Rick saw the car and ran toward it. "What are you doin' here?" he asked. "Feelin' sorry for me?"

"No, just drivin' back from school; forgot my gradebook. Thought I'd pick you up."

"How'd you know where I'd be?"

"Magic." He grinned. He started the car, then looked again toward the church. Yes, there he was, Jonathan Hyde. Graying already. And the girl, beautiful.

"That's her," Rick said.

"What?" Tim bolted back to reality.

"The girl, that's her, Angela."

"The dark-haired one?" he asked innocently.

"Right. Some chick, huh?"

"Some chick is right." He grinned as he pulled away. "You and her, you close?" he asked.

"Nope. Not my fault though. Her old man's. He is somethin' else. No more church for me. Bad. Bad. Bad. You really used to do that for a living?" he asked, incredulous.

"Something like that," he said. "Not that bad, though. That's why I got out. Just couldn't buy it anymore."

"Good. I can't buy it either. What's for dinner?"

"Worms and hair," Tim said seriously.

"Good, I'm starved."

Angela kissed her father on the cheek before he got in his car. "How long this trip, father?" she asked. "It always seems forever when you're not here."

"A month at least, honey. Maybe more. They like us in East Texas." And he was gone. That was one reason he had chosen Texas; his brand of religion was good there. And San Antonio had a large Mexican population, mostly Catholic, and he thought he could open a full gospel mission and pull them away from the priests in droves. He had started the mission in a small store building in the south part of town, but it was not pulling them away in droves. They didn't really trust the big, loud white man as he shouted that their priests were of Satan; and they thought that the little storefront mission was not a good trade for the huge stone cathedral just four blocks down the street. The reverend preached there anyway every Sunday afternoon and every Thursday night, and he kept praying that God would break through to the Mexicans down there and move them toward his truth.

His ministry was failing; he felt it. His sermons just didn't have the same old fire, not in his church, not in the mission, and especially not during the revivals he still held three or four times a year. The attendance figures for the church and the mission services were lower on the days he preached and higher when Brother Logan filled in during his absence. The old fire was gone. Was it just that these were the 1950s and people didn't have time for church, time for God, time for God's man? That was some of it, but the other was most of it, the old fire was gone. And he knew why.

It was being impressed more and more upon him when he tried to pray. A vision of his latest sinning would loom up before him and obstruct his soul's view of heaven. His prayers would

269

get enmeshed with the pleasures of the flesh and they would not fly away to deliver themselves on high before the throne of the Almighty.

"What to do?" he asked himself as he drove. He had asked it a hundred times. "What to do?" For a year he thought about it and tried to pray about it, but the visions of the sinful women he'd been with clouded up again before his eyes and moved his flesh to hunger more for sin than his soul hungered for God. And lately every time he asked, "What to do?" bits of Bible came to him: "If thine eye offend thee pluck it out!" But what did that mean? Was that the message of the Spirit?

"If thy right hand offend thee cut it off and cast it away, for it is better that thine eye and thine hand suffer the fires of hell than thine whole body." Again and again these words came to him. Every time he looked at a woman; every time he thought of finding relief for his hungering flesh. "What to do?" The answer was obvious. It frightened him and he tried to stop thinking about it; he could not.

In the years since Cerese had left him he had had many women and had suffered storms of recrimination after each one. "What to do? What to do? If thy testicles offend thee . . . Stop! Stop! Don't think about it. Pluck them out . . . Stop it! Stop! For it is better . . . No! No!" He'd seen his father do it to hogs and bulls in Oklahoma. . . . "Stop it!"

"It settles 'em down some. Gentles 'em. Does the same for a dog," he remembered his father saying. "It keeps 'em from prowling."

"Shut up!"

At night sometimes he felt the cold knife and he'd wake up in a sweat. "But what else?" He tried to abstain, but no use. He could not. He could go for weeks in the grips of moral agony, then in a flash he was headed for the Quarter in New Orleans, San Francisco's North Beach, that old house just outside Lawrence; wherever he was there were places he could get it, and having been there once insured that the next time he was in town he'd go there again.

He could not resist, so great was the promise of female flesh yielding under him. Yet, when it was done he felt the fires of hell, and sometimes he felt the knife. "Stop! Stop it! Think of the sermon tonight. Think of anything. Believe me, deliver me!"

"Rick?"

He looked up from his lunch. "Oh, hi, Angela. Sit down." He pulled a chair out for her.

"I can't sit down, Rick. I've got to go, but I just wanted to tell you I can sit for you now if you still want me to."

"Hey, that's terrific! Sure, I still want you to."

"Is it too late to enter it?" she asked.

"You mean the State Fair? Yeah, I already did another one for that. But I still want you, Angela. When can we start?"

"Today?" she asked.

"Right. After school?"

"Okay, where?" So he told her and she left. Only then did it occur to him to wonder why the change.

At home just after school she picked up a stack of music sheets and went to the church just across the parking lot. Mrs. Baggett would think she was just going to practice and wouldn't suspect a thing. Once in the church, however, she put the music in a pew and went out the back way into the alley, hurried out to the side street, and walked the ten blocks to the gallery on North St. Mary's.

"What kept you?" Rick asked, smiling. It was hard to smile when his work was being kept waiting, but for Angela he would smile. He wondered if Mona Lisa was always on time when she sat for Leonardo and if he was a patient man.

"I had a long walk from school home, then from there to here. Two miles, I'll bet." She laughed nervously as she looked around the room. Two unframed nudes leaned against the wall. She blushed and tried not to look at them. He was mounting a piece of canvas on stretcher strips and didn't notice that she'd seen the nudes. It never occurred to him to put them away.

He finished quickly and turned toward her: "Look, Angela, I really do appreciate you doing this."

"It's okay," she said. "I wanted to anyway."

"But your father . . ."

271

"Father's gone for a month. And I didn't tell Mrs. Baggett where I was going. She thinks I'm in the church practicing. It's not like lying, is it?" She asked for assurance, but down deep it "felt" like lying, in deed if not in word, and her sensitive conscience troubled her.

"He should let you do more, you know that?" Rick said as he placed a stool in the light of the large back-room window. "You know what my father always says?"

"What?"

His hand touched her back and he pressed her forward. "Just a little forward, Angela, that's it. Good. Now." He touched her cheek and gently turned her face away from the light. "There, that's just perfect." He stood back and studied her for a second, then placed his fingers softly under her chin and lifted her face ever so slightly. "God, you're beautiful," he said, and she blushed.

He returned to his canvas and began to sketch, carefully at first to catch the outlines, then swiftly and expertly to work in the exact locations of the parts of the face, the hands and arms.

"Rick?" she asked, being as still as possible in such a tiring position.

"Yes," he snapped.

"Your father, what were you going to tell me he always says?"

"Oh. He always says you've got to give a kid some rope so he'll be used to it and not hang himself with it later."

"What does that mean?" she asked, turning toward him.

"No! Don't look at me, Angela. There, that's it. Good." He began sketching again. "It means that you need to experience life now so you won't be overwhelmed by it later."

"My, you're a philosopher, too!" she quipped.

"Right," he said, smiling, "Vincent Van Aristotle."

"Your father's probably right. But my father is too, in a way." But Rick was lost in his work and did not answer.

An hour sped by. "Rick?"

"Yes?"

"I've got to go."

"Already?"

When she was gone he worked another hour, then went home.

At the supper table he told his father, "Guess who's sitting for me."

"Who?" he asked.

"Angela Hyde. How 'bout that?" He saw his father's eyes flick over to his mother's face. It seemed to him that she paled slightly.

"Who is Angela Hyde?" she asked, shoveling another batch of potatoes onto her son's plate. He was too little; she wanted him big and strong.

"The most beautiful girl I've ever tried to paint, that's who. And how I've tried. Her old man's a kook, won't let her do anything," he said, shoveling the potatoes into his busy mouth. He smiled at his father. "Some chick, huh, Dad?"

"Some chick. How'd you do it?"

"Her father's gone. On some kind of church doin's and she's sneaking off from the old Baggett that lives with them." He chuckled at his own joke.

That night he awoke just after going to sleep. He thought he heard his parents arguing. The glances across the table at supper had set his mind to wondering for a moment, as had his father's being outside the church that day, but he had promptly put it out of his mind and put into it the painting he was working on. But were they arguing?

He got out of bed and moved quickly into the hallway. At his parents' door he paused. They were quieter now, but he could just barely hear his mother, "Well, it troubles me, Timothy, that you knew he was seeing her and you didn't stop it."

"Lucy, I didn't want to stop it. You can't stop it even if you try."

"But he's crazy and dangerous and I don't want my son seeing his daughter. Good Lord, Tim, what if he found out about him?"

"About Hyde? He won't. Hyde won't let it go that far. Besides she's scared to death of him. She won't even let him know she knows a boy. He's saving her for Jesus," Tim said.

"Good God," Lucy said. "That poor child."

"Don't you worry, honey, our little painter just wants her on his canvas, not in his bed." He chuckled. Rick found himself blushing at that.

"How do you know he hasn't been messing around with some of those nudes he's been doing?" she asked.

"He would have told me," Tim assured her.

"Did you ask?"

"Yes," he said. "Now go to sleep."

Rick thought about it. So her old man *was* a kook. Was it the religion they didn't want him messed up in? That must be it. Damnfool preacher. That's why daddy was there waiting for me after church.

A few days later he told his father. "Dad, you and mom don't have to worry about me gettin' mixed up in Angel's religion."

"No?" he asked. "Who's worryin'?" He put aside the paper he was reading. Lucy wasn't home yet.

"I heard you and mom arguing about it the other night."

Tim was quiet for a moment. "What did you hear?"

"Not much. Just that mom was worried about me and Angela."

"Well, son, you know how mothers worry about their little boys."

"I know," he said, "but she shouldn't."

"Good."

"Dad, what is it that I shouldn't know about Mr. Hyde?"

"It's really nothing, son."

"You don't want to talk about it?"

"Okay, we'll talk about it."

Timothy Morgan didn't answer for a long moment. What do you tell the boy? What is right to tell him? How much can he take? Part of the truth? Which part? "Son," he said, "it's a bad deal and your mother shouldn't know I told you, okay?"

"Okay."

"You had an uncle, your mother's brother, younger by two years. He was drowned when he was just a kid. His name was Rick too, Ricardo, just like you. You look so much like him it's frightening sometimes."

"Nobody told me."

"It's just that nobody wants to talk about it."

"Why? I mean people die."

274

"Everybody thought Jonathan Hyde did it."

"Killed him?"

"Never proven."

"I don't understand. Who was Jonathan Hyde? I mean how'd he get into the picture back then?"

"Jonathan Hyde is Grandpa Frank Hyde's son." Bam! It took a few minutes for it all to soak in.

"Then, daddy, Angela Hyde is what to me, my cousin?"

"Only by marriage, son. Grandpa Hyde is not your real grandfather."

"Right. But I can still see mama not liking Hyde even if it was never proved he did it."

"Right, so let's not bother her with it."

"Okay, right."

Tim thought about it often afterward and each time decided he had done the only thing he could have. How do you tell your son whom you love that he's not your son, that he was instead fathered by a monster? How indeed.

Rick Morgan took a new interest in Angela Hyde. She was more a person to him, less an object to be studied, less a model with a beautiful face with facial planes and bone structure and skin texture. She was a maiden now, trapped as it were, in the clutches of a fiend who just happened to be her father.

And she sensed the change. He urged her to rest now and then as he worked. He introduced her to Mr. and Mrs. Herter. He walked her to the back of the church and waited while she dumped her books and grabbed her music. Then later he walked her to the church again. He began to see women in a new light too, not as models with only bodies and no faces or models with faces and no bodies, but as whole people with feelings and hurts, joys and needs. And he began to be aware of how fragile a thing a girl can be, how full of moods and silences and unspoken gestures. And how complex. And in all his learning he began to be aware of changes in himself. He wanted to talk to her and listen to her talk to him. He wished she would wait with him behind the church for just a moment more before going in. He wanted to touch her, to feel the skin on her face, to grip her waist with his arms. To . . . God what he wanted.

Angela too became aware of the reality of her father's warnings. "The world and its pleasures will corrupt. Enjoy the world and God will fade away from your vision. Take its pleasures, and prayer and devotion will seem like work instead of the soul's rejoicing." It had begun to happen. She had taken an interest in a boy, and already it seemed that he was more important than anything else, than *anyone* else. And it *was* hard to pray and read the scripture; it was more like work. It even scared her a little to walk through the big dark church on the way home. But he was *so* good. And he *was* cute. He was mannerly and so grownup. He'd never done anything even remotely wrong.

He took his time on the painting. He deliberately did more studies than he normally would have and he stopped working far earlier and began the slow walk home with her sooner than was absolutely necessary. Louise looked at Charles as Rick and Angela left the gallery one day and said, "What do you suppose is the matter with our young Rembrandt?"

"What indeed." Charles smiled.

It had been a month and the painting was not yet finished. Both of them wished they had another month.

"Father'll be home soon," she said as they walked slowly side by side. Rick wanted to hold her hand, had wanted to for weeks, but dared not. "I think I'd better not sit again, Rick. I mean after tomorrow."

"Okay," he said. "But . . ."

"But what, Rick?"

"I was going to say that I couldn't finish the painting with only one more, but that's not true."

"I know." She smiled. "At first you said just four or five sittings. I hate to say how wrong you were."

"Not wrong, Angel, just smart. Old Rick ain't no dummy." He reached for her hand and found it, and held it. He didn't look at her, nor she at him. "I . . . I could paint you from the beginning if I never saw you again." He looked away.

"Oh, Rick," she said, "could you really?"

"Of course." He looked at her now. Her face was red and her

eyes were misty. "I might get your nose on a little crooked and you might wind up with an extra ear. . . ."

"Oh, you." She laughed. Her father *wasn't* right. It was good what she had with Rick and he was good, so good. She squeezed his hand, then looked at him. It seemed to her that he was blushing. She knew she was, but she didn't care.

"Angela?"

"Yes?"

"School's out in three weeks."

"Oh, I know. I wanted it over so badly. It's such a drag. But . . ."

"But what?"

"Father says I must go away to a Christian school this summer and until I graduate. He never had the chance because of the depression and all. There's this Christian school in Nebraska that he . . ."

"Nebraska!"

"Yes."

"That's too far away, Angel. I'd never see you."

"That's sweet of you, Rick, but . . ."

"What?" he said. "But what?"

"But you'll have the painting." She tried to laugh but it just wasn't there.

He looked away, then thought. "How 'bout a Coke, Angel?"

"It's late," she protested.

"Won't take long." He tugged her arm and she followed. There was a drugstore a block away and they went there and sat in a booth.

"Two chocolate malts," he told the pimply-faced boy who waited on them.

"You said a Coke." She laughed.

"Big spender, I am." How do you say what you want. You joke around it. Why couldn't her father be like mine? Why?

Jonathan Hyde drove into the parsonage driveway. He sat for a few seconds then got out. He could hear Mrs. Baggett's radio. Some preacher was selling a "prayer cloth—blessed with tears shed at the very spot where Jesus died." He entered the house. "Mrs. Baggett?"

The old woman appeared. She was startled to see him. "You're early," she said.

"Where's Angela?"

They sat together for a half hour nursing the malts, saying little, just looking at each other.

"I have to go, Jonathan."

"So soon?"

"If Mrs. Baggett ever checks the church she'd know something's going on."

"Would she tell your father?"

"I don't think so. She thinks he's a little rough on me, so sometimes she's good about things. She's a good old woman, used to be my teacher when we were traveling with father. When my mother was with us."

"Where's your mother now?" he asked as they left the drugstore.

"In Seattle. She's married to a big photographer or something. He did a story on the revivals for *Life* when I was little."

"You ever see her?"

"No."

When they neared the church they slowed. Neither wanted to leave.

"Angela, I wanted to ask you . . ."

"Yes?"

"Could we ever date? I mean like other kids?"

"We just have three weeks and I could never get father's approval."

"Then this is it?"

"I guess so. We can still be together at school for a while," she said quietly, looking away.

"Be together!" He had heard it. She meant it. She really wanted to be with him.

"Angela?"

"Yes?"

"Look, Angel, there's something . . ."

"What is it, Rick?"

"I mean, look, Angela, I like you, a lot, I mean. You're not like just another girl. . . ."

"I know what you mean, Rick. That's how I feel about you."

"Really, Angela?" He squeezed her hand so hard it hurt, but she didn't mind. "Can I . . . can I kiss you, Angela?"

She was silent, trying to catch her breath. She had imagined what it would be like to be kissed, to be cared about, to be really cared about.

"It's okay, Angela. I understand if you're not supposed to." He released her hand and turned to go. "Tomorrow?" he asked. "I mean you'll sit tomorrow?"

"Rick, come with me," she said, and she reached out and took his hand and pulled him along with her toward the back of the church. The door was opened and they entered and walked down the steps into the basement. "Quiet," she said, "in case Mrs. Baggett comes over."

Then she turned to him.

He took both her hands and pulled her toward him. When she was near he placed a hand behind her head and drew her face to his. She was afraid and trembling. He kissed her softly on the forehead, then kissed her mouth easily and quickly, then looked at her. She was smiling sweetly. Her face was red and hot. She opened her arms and hugged him tightly to her. And then footsteps above them, heavy and quick, and Hyde's voice boomed out: "Angela! Angela!"

"Oh my God, Rick, run!" She pushed him away. "Run!"

"No."

"Run. Go. If he finds you here with me . . ." They heard him run down the stairs toward them. Rick darted behind the door just in time. The big man ran into the room.

"Angela!" He saw her. "Why didn't you answer me? What are you doing down here?" When the man's back was turned, Rick took the opportunity to sneak carefully out of his hiding place. He would have gone unnoticed had the stairs not creaked on his way up to the basement door.

Hyde turned and ran into the hallway and looked up just in time to see the dark figure of a young man push the door shut.

279

He ran up the stairs, threw open the door, and charged out into the alley, but Rick was gone.

Angela was crying when Hyde returned. "Come with me, girl." He half dragged her up the stairs and through the church. His face was red and his eyes were red and wild and his chin quivered. "You are a whore's daughter," he screamed, "but you'll not play your mother's part."

In the house he dragged her into her bedroom and threw her on the bed. She could not control her sobbing and could not answer him when he screamed, "Who was that?"

She wept the harder. She had always feared him, even her love for him had been a kind of fear, but he'd never spoken harshly to her or laid a hand on her in anger. He shook her and she cried. He slapped her face and she screamed and Mrs. Baggett appeared at the door. He shoved her away and slammed the door shut.

He turned to Angela and grabbed her face in a huge hand and squeezed. "Now you will tell me who it was this time. Tell me!" He slapped her hard across the mouth and went quickly to her bathroom and rummaged through a box under the sink, throwing things wildly out of it until he came upon a rubber hose. He dug deeper and found the hot water bottle and a long black syringe tip. He put water in the thing and returned to her. He put a hand in the neck of her dress and tore it open and pulled the dress piece by piece off her. She stared in wild-eyed horror as he pulled at her panties and ripped them, too, and flung them away. Then he spread her legs and inserted the syringe into her . . . "No. No. No," she whimpered.

"There is one thing you do not understand," he growled with a hoarse voice. "The male is a rutting beast and he will plant himself in any whore he can find, and you took him in the church, in God's own house. Did you lie down for him, Cerese, or did you give it to him standing up?" And she was Cerese to him, the body was the same and the face was the same and they were both whores. "You were a whore from the beginning. Whore! Whore! Whore!" And he slapped her again and again. She tried to wriggle free. She kicked and screamed and arched her body and tried to strike him with her fists. He fell on her and held her down. He placed his knee on the bottle and it emptied into her.

The white young body beneath him was Cerese, Cerese in the back of the truck, Cerese in the tent on the boards of the platform. She felt his hand go down between her legs and felt the syringe being pulled out of her and then she felt her legs being forced wide apart, and when she realized what huge thing was being forced into her she tried to scream, but something happened in her and everything turned black.

When it was done he went out to his car and took a small leather bag off the back seat and let himself into the church. He could not have seen the young man standing at the door of the house ringing the bell.

"Yes?" Mrs. Baggett answered the door.

"I want to see Angela," he said, opening the door himself and going in. "I'm the one her father saw her with. I wouldn't want him to punish her for being with me."

"You can't see her right now," she said.

"Angela!" he called, then turned to the old woman. "I want him to know that it wasn't her fault she wasn't home."

"Well, he's not here. I saw him go to the church. I was just going to check on Angie now. If it's all right with Reverend Hyde you can see her later, but I don't think it will be. He was terribly upset . . ." But Rick was already headed for the church. He thought Angela might be there, too. He could just hear the preacher bawling her out.

The front door of the church was locked and so was the side door. Rick went around back and let himself in at the same back door from whence he had just fled. He yelled out, "Reverend Hyde?" Nothing. "Angela?" No answer. He heard a noise, something clattering on the cement floor in the basement, and he crept carefully down the basement stairs. There was no one in the first two rooms he checked, but in a third, the furnace room, there was the Reverend Jonathan Hyde lying face down on the floor in a pool of dark red blood. A shaving kit was open beside him and a safety razor had been screwed open and was lying in the blood. He turned the man over. His testicles had been cut from his body. The man held the grisly, dripping things in one hand and a razor blade in the other.

He opened his eyes and looked up into the face of the boy

kneeling over him; he screamed, "No!" He crawled away and cringed against the wall. He held up his open hand to ward off this spirit that had so plagued his conscience for nearly twenty years. The blade fell to the floor. "Just let me die! Just leave me and let me die!"

Rick stood up. He had to get help.

"Here." The man thrust his left hand forward and opened it to show the ghastly part of himself he had plucked out. "This is the demon that was in me. It was the fault of these and your lying sister that you are dead."

Rick turned and ran out of the room and up the stairs. The man's crazed voice followed him, "It is better that these things be plucked out and cast into the fires of hell . . ." and Hyde lifted up his left arm and threw them away from himself. "Into the fires of hell," he said again as they landed on the cement and tumbled to a bloody stop against the base of the furnace.

Angela did not return to school, but arranged to take her final exams at home. Rick tried several times to see her but she wouldn't see him until the day she was to leave.

He came up the front steps and she was standing in the door. "Hello, Rick," she said from behind the screen.

"Hi, Angel," he said. "Can I come in?" The door opened for him and he saw the bruises on her face and knew for the first time that the man had beaten her.

"Your face, Angela. Your father?" he asked. She turned and walked to the couch and sat down. He sat beside her. "I don't want to talk about it," she said. "I only agreed to see you because you were so good to me and I wanted to tell you that I'm leaving."

"Leaving?"

"I'm going to visit my mother in Seattle. This afternoon."

"Oh," he said. "But you'll be back."

"No."

"Oh." He reached out for her hand. She jerked hers back.

"I'm sorry, Rick. You'd better go now."

"But, Angela . . ."

She got up and fled from the room. The sound of her crying

reached into him and caused a knot to form in his stomach. After a moment he turned around and left the Hyde house and walked slowly home, thinking to himself that if he could only follow her to Seattle . . . But it would never work. Not now.

And he wished with all his heart that he hadn't phoned for help, that he had simply let Jonathan Hyde die.

Chapter

19

Richard Morgan became a better painter during the summer between his junior and senior years. He became concerned about painting the man inside the man, the inner man. He abandoned his canvas of the beautiful Angela and painted the stunned, soul-sick child who was only a shadow of her former self.

He painted the girl's father as he stood in his pulpit haranguing his parishioners on the terrors of hell, and the preacher's face was the face of the fear-crazed man who clutched his severed manhood in his bloody hand.

He painted Timothy Morgan and captured the deep puzzlement, the intense concern that often spread across his visage even when he sat alone, simply thinking.

He did his grandfather at his chess board, smoking a pipe, his serious blue-gray eyes staring far off into some unnamed time, remembering.

He put in paint the fierce independence of his grandmother, Ellen, standing on the banks of her river, surveying its power, blessing it and cursing it with her eyes. There was his great-grandfather of the goats, only recently dead. His face was deep brown and weather-lined. He stood among the rocks and the goats, and he was smiling at the rocks and the goats, a good man and a peaceful man in a peaceful and simple time.

He painted Charles with his brushes and paints. He caught Louise at her prim best and painted her smiling quietly. And he did his mother at her most beautiful, a madonna with child. She wept when she saw it.

There was no longer any deep need in him to show his work and get praise for it. He knew it was good. He had learned that he was his own best critic, the only one that counted.

He learned something else that summer. A fashion model who had sat for him the year before came to him and commissioned a painting of her mother.

"Sure I can do it from the photos, Melissa, but it wouldn't be right. I mean *she* wouldn't be right."

"I don't get you, Ricko," she said, shaking her head to flip her flaming red hair over her shoulder. "You can paint anything from anything!"

"Sure. Like I said. I can paint her exactly like that picture right there," he motioned toward the photo on his stool, "and you'd have a copy of a photo for $200.00. If I painted something a little different from that it probably just wouldn't be like that. How does she laugh? Cry? How does she look when she's serious or sad? You have three photos of her smiling."

"So?"

"So that's why I need to meet her, to know her." He went back to work on the canvas before him.

"How much time would you need?" Melissa asked.

"Three days sketching her, two hours at a time, twice a day." he said.

"How about two days?"

"Two days. When can she come?"

"She can't. We have to go to her."

"Why?"

"She's sick, she can't travel. I go see her every other weekend."

"Where?"

"Uvalde."

Rick talked to his dad and then Tim convinced Lucinda. "He's growing up, mama. He's not our little boy anymore." She resisted a little at first, as always, then surrendered.

"Timmy, he'll soon be eighteen."

"I know, baby. I know."

Melissa had been a serious model when she sat for Rick the year before, and unlike most of the other girls she had taken a real interest in his work. Now this Friday night, sitting beside her

285

on a bus to Uvalde, he found her just as inquisitive about his work as before.

"The woman by the river, 'Ellen' you call it. That's really good," she said to him.

He sat by the window studying his own reflection in the mirror. He toyed with the idea of a self-portrait.

"Are you asleep?" Melissa touched his arm.

"Uh? Oh, no. Sorry, what were you saying?"

"I was saying I like the trend your work is taking."

"You mean the people?"

"Yes, the soul paintings."

"Soul paintings?"

"That's what I call them. They are, you know."

"That's good. I'll remember that when Louise sends out the invites for the fall show." He smiled at her. "Thanks."

"You're welcome, Tiger."

It bothered him a little when she called him that. It meant more than he was ready for. "What does that mean, Tiger?" He grinned at her.

"Pet name, Tiger. You really don't like it, do you, Tiger?"

"I don't know," he said. He looked back into himself. "Is this the one?" Every boy waits for *the* time, *the* one. He had seen her body, had studied it carefully and was moved by it to experiment, and had, influenced indirectly by Melissa and a dozen other girls, learned how to release the pent-up drive within him. He had done it himself, had enjoyed it and never once felt a moment's guilt. But he had long been aware of what pleasures such a girl could inflict upon just such an innocent, unassuming lad as he. . . . He smiled to himself in the window and made a decision.

He felt her hand on his arm again. He turned back to her. "Yes?"

"Rick, can I ask you a question?"

"Shoot."

"It's personal."

"I said shoot," he said, grinning. "I have no secrets from my matron."

"Matron?" she moved away in mock surprise.

"How old are you, Melissa?"

"None of your goddamn business, Tiger. Why do you want to know? Anyway, I'm the one who's asking the personal questions."

"So ask," he said. He knew how old she was, twenty-four. Her model's contract had her birth date on it. Charles insisted. He didn't want any minors' suits.

"Maybe I shouldn't be asking this, but if you are you won't care, and if you aren't you can just tell me so."

"Are what?"

"A homosexual."

"A what?" he asked, too loud. People turned around to look at them.

"Shh..." She ducked down in her seat. "Okay...I just thought I'd ask."

"Damn, Melissa, what even made you think it?"

"Because, Tiger," she snuggled up real close to him and looked him right in the eyes, "you haven't made a pass at me all night."

How do you tell a girl that you don't really know how to go about it? "Look, Melissa, I'm new at this sort of thing. I wanted to, a dozen times since we left, but..."

"You mean you've never..."

"That's right, mama. The little boy has never had the pleasure." He chuckled nervously. He wished his voice were deeper.

"You mean with all those naked bodies around? Maureen or Nancy? Francine, what about Francine? Didn't she..."

"She would have, I think. She acted like it. There just wasn't an opportunity."

"Opportunity?" She laughed. "For what? All you needed was ten minutes in the back room." She reached over and kissed him on the cheek. "How many girls have you kissed?"

"One" he said, "once."

"Look," she said, "there's no one in the back. Let's go back there." She got up and headed for the rear of the bus. Without hesitation he followed. His hands were sweaty and shaking. His mouth was dry. He wished he knew more about what to do.

Melissa taught him. In the back of the Uvalde bus she taught him. And he was grateful. She showed him how everything worked, let him try all the buttons manually. "How about all that?" she asked.

He didn't answer. She had him by the root and was making it very difficult for him to concentrate.

"Here," she said, leading his hand to her own need. So he rubbed her there with his deft and delighted fingers. He was fascinated by the little thing that grew up under his fingers. She began to gasp and he felt her belly arch and become rigid. She quivered a few times, then got very still. In a moment she snuggled closer to him and whispered, "You ready for yours?"

"Ready, hell," he said hoarsely, "I already did!"

"You did?"

"Hell, yes." She felt him. Sure enough he was fading fast.

"What'd you do with it?" she asked. He held up something white in the dark. She moved nearer, then giggled, "My panties. You shot your wad in my goddamn panties, holy shit."

"Sorry, mama," he said.

"Was it any good?"

"You were squeezing too hard," he told her, leaning back and breathing deeply.

"I don't know what I'm doing when I get excited," she said. "Can you do it again this soon?"

"In a minute," he said, feeling her breasts. "You almost killed the little feller."

But Uvalde came up before Rick did. They zipped everything back up and waited for the bus to reach the station. She draped her panties over the seat. "A little something for the driver," she said. "He missed all the fun."

They were met at the station by an old man whom Melissa introduced as their foreman. He shook Rick's hand. His grip was firm, even powerful. "You the painter gonna paint Miz Burns?" he asked as he helped Rick load their stuff into a twenty-five-year-old pickup truck.

Rick explained that he was the one. He was accustomed to people's being surprised at his youth. It no longer bothered him.

They drove a half hour south of town, then east on a gravel road for a while longer. It was a dark night and cloudy, so the

288

inside of the cab was pitch black. Melissa found his lap with her right hand and began to work her prey into another frenzy, using just two beautiful fingers. Just before the fireworks started he took her hand away. In a moment it was back, but just to feel, then just to hold it quietly while she talked to the old man for the rest of the way.

Melissa went to her mother's room while the old man showed Rick his room upstairs. He was in bed when she knocked, then peeked in. "You get settled okay?"

"Yep, your mother feelin' bad?"

"No, she's okay. Just tired. She'll be up before anybody else in the morning. You tired, Rick?"

"Not really, you?"

"Not really. Look, Rick, I'm right across the hall, if you want to come on over."

"Now?" He grinned. She sat down on his bed and put her hand on his cover in just the right place.

"You're ready right now, aren't you?"

He just grinned. She got up and left. He waited a few minutes and carefully crossed the hall and let himself into her room. It was dark. He kicked something and it went crashing across the room. She giggled. "What was that?" he whispered.

"That was a chair. What did you hit with it with?"

"I broke my foot."

"Good. I was worried."

He found the bed. She opened the covers and he crawled in. She was naked and warm and softer than he'd imagined. She showed him what was good and it was good.

"Don't go," she said, when they were done. "Just stay right here. I can cuddle right up like this and you can go to sleep with your hand right there. Good."

Chapter

20

At six o'clock Melissa's mother maneuvered her wheelchair to the foot of the stairs and with her cane, which was always hanging within her reach over the back of her chair, she began banging on the banister. "Lissy!" she yelled. "Breakfast." Then she just sat there until a few minutes later Melissa's tousled head peered out at her.

"Mornin', mama."

"Get your hair combed, girl, and let's eat breakfast."

"Okay, mama." She stepped across the hall and tapped lightly on Rick's door, then hurried back into her own room.

"You wait till I get downstairs, then when you hear me talking to mama you can go across the hall." She brushed his hair out of his face with her hand. "How are you this morning, lover?"

"Rarin' and at 'em as you say on the ranch." He yawned.

"You want a quickie?"

"What the hell's a quickie?" he asked.

"Here." She pulled back the covers and mounted him quickly. He was ready in an instant. She inserted him expertly and smiling at him the whole time she rode him to a small glory.

"That's a quickie." She laughed, breathing hard.

"Damn," he breathed.

Mrs. Forney had breakfast on the table when Rick got down. Mrs. Burns and Melissa were waiting for him. Melissa had already told her mother that the artist was young, but she wasn't expecting the boy who sat across from her.

"How old are you, son?" she asked.

"Seventeen, ma'am, almost eighteen."

"You'll be a big man, son. Mark my words. You aren't stunted. You'll start shootin' up directly, you wouldn't believe."

"I hope so, Mrs. Burns."

She had been old when Melissa was born and she looked older now than she was, but when she sat in her chair near the north window her face was proud and her eyes as alert as ever. "You know why she wants this thing painted, son?"

"No, ma'am," he said as he sketched quickly.

"She's afraid I'm gonna up and die. That's why." Then her eyes wandered away and she watched the cloud shadows play across the hills in the distance.

Melissa rode ahead of him slowly, guiding her horse down the steep trail. He followed carefully behind, wishing he had dismounted before they started down. At the bottom they both dismounted and let the horses graze on the new spring grass decorated by a profusion of the wild lupine, the colorful and hardy Texas bluebonnets. The Alta Frio River, cold and clear, cut its way slowly but inexorably deeper into the limestone bedrock. There was a grove of cedars growing down to the water's edge. She took off her boots and put her feet in the water. He sat cross-legged on a rock jutting out over the swiftly moving water. "Isn't that cold?"

"Freezing. There's a spring right up there." She pointed to a sheer wall of rock above them on the other side where a steady stream flowed out from crevices fifty feet above them and slithered noiselessly down the rock until it disappeared beneath the fallen boulders at the base of the wall.

"Like it?" she asked.

"Prettiest spot in the state, I'll bet," he said.

"I can show you others."

"No time," he said, "but I'd like to see more of this country."

"You can come back any time. I'll come with you."

"It's a deal," he said.

291

She sat a few minutes longer with her feet in the water then got up and sat beside him.

"I really enjoyed last night," she said.

"You did?"

"You?" she asked.

He smiled. "Thanks," he said, "I'll make it up to you."

"The hell you will," she said. "You don't owe me a *damn* thing."

"Oh yes I do. You're something special, Melissa. Lissy. That's what your mama calls you."

"She always has. Daddy did too. I like Melissa, though."

"I like Melissa, too," he said, "every bit of her."

"Every bit?" she asked.

"Every bit," he said.

"What best, artist?"

"I'm not sure." He grinned. "I'd have to see it all again to be real sure."

"Is that a proposition?"

"That's what it is." So they moved to the cedars.

She lay on their clothes on the grass. Her red hair flamed out against the bright green. Her white body caught the sun and warmed to it and took life from it and gave life to him.

"Tell me," she whispered as he lay atop her, moving slowly trying to keep control, "when you were sixteen and painting all us naked girls, did you want to fuck us?"

"Yes," he said. "Did you want to fuck me?"

"I've always liked you," she said. "You're different. But you seemed so young then."

"And now?" he stopped and lifted himself up and looked in her eyes.

"Not now," she said. "Now I know you are older. Older than eighteen. Don't stop," she urged him, wriggling her bottom. "It feels *so* good." So he continued and she moved with him and he was grateful.

They lay for a while longer exploring each other's bodies in silence. She touched him in ways and places he'd never been touched before. "You are some kind o' woman," he told her. "Why are you this way?"

292

"What way?" she said quickly. She got up on her elbows and looked at his face.

"I mean so free. You've got to be the most uninhibited person I've ever met." He looked into her green eyes and saw fire there. He smiled at her. "I like it," he said. "I like you. You're special. But you are different," he finished.

"This is my life I'm living and it's my body I live it in. I can do what I want. And who I want. If they want me to."

"Believe me, Melissa, I do," he told her.

"You don't know if you do or not," she said bluntly. "Right now you like me because I'm the first girl that ever let you stick your dick in. You wouldn't be worth a damn if you didn't, and because you like your friend pecker you like the girl that takes care of him. Right?"

He didn't say anything to that. Maybe she knew what she was talking about.

"Am I right?" she asked.

"Maybe so, Melissa," he said seriously, staring off at the horses. "But I want you to know that you are really someone special. Maybe it is my dick talking; but if it is my dick," he grinned, "the little fucker's got good taste."

"You're impossible," she said, pulling him down to her. He kissed her again and thought that she was wrong. She was a very special girl.

He spent a lot of time with her back in San Antonio. Often he'd skip sketching trips and go instead to her apartment on the river.

"You've got articulate fingers," she whispered, writhing slowly in response.

"That's not all." And he found a sweet red nipple with his mouth and played it with the very tip of his tongue. "How's that?" He stopped for a moment.

"Don't. Don't stop. Now, now." So he didn't. He liked to watch her when she came, the flush, the deep breathing, the little groan and the quivering flesh beneath him.

She lay naked in the sun, her legs open, her body arched slightly upward. Her hand was on her little button, caressing it slowly, deliberately. He stood above her, the hot sun glistening off his lean brown body. He had his cock in hand and was pumping it slowly. She grinned at him and he at her. " 'Bout ready?" he asked. "I am."

"Okay," she said, "Go!" So they both went faster. He saw her arch even more toward him, then her bottom began moving up and down in little fitful breaths. She squealed, "Oh, oh, oh."

He fired off into the air and watched it plummet into the dusty clumps of grass beside her. He collapsed on her, and entered her, and they began a slow dance of bodies.

"Dreadful, aren't we?" She asked.

And then the summer was gone.

His last year of school was a personal trial for Richard Morgan. Halfway into it he told Melissa, "I'm not going to college."

"Good," she said.

"Good?" He was surprised. "I expected you to raise hell and tell me it's for my own good."

"It's a crock," she said.

"You never said much about it."

"I took two years and dropped out. They wanted to make me take six more hours of literature and two more math courses and a course in music appreciation." She grimaced. "And the education courses were tommyrot, same damn crap taught by the dullest, most lifeless professors in school. So I thought, if these gray clods are the experts on teaching and their teaching is the poorest of the lot then I sure as hell don't need their expertise."

"My Grandfather Hyde didn't go to college," he said. "He just took off around the world. He'd see things during the day and read at night. Still reads."

"So don't go to school," she said. "You're going to paint anyway."

"I want to travel for three or four years," he said. "Paint and travel. And I want you to go with me."

She was quiet. She looked into his eyes, then away.

"I'm serious, Melissa, I want you to go with me. I love you and I want to marry you."

She was still silent. Huge tears sparkled in her gray-green eyes and a tiny smile changed the corners of her mouth. She reached for his hand and found it and held it in both her own.

"Why do you want to get married?" she asked him.

"Because I love you."

"So. What does that have to do with it?"

"Two people love each other, they usually get married."

"Not me." She looked back into his face. There was a resolute set to her jaw.

"Why?" he asked. "You mean never?"

"Is that so hard to understand? What happens when you get married?"

"What do you mean?"

"I mean when you get married you make a promise, right?"

"Sure. That's the whole idea of it."

"That's what's wrong," she said. "You promise that for the rest of your life you'll never, never, ever love any other man but your husband and you'll always live with him where he lives and go where he goes and do what he does, right?"

"Right, but . . ."

"The rest of your life!" she exclaimed. "How old are you?"

"You know, eighteen." He wished for all the world he was ten years older and knew what in hell she was talking about.

"Eighteen. Are you willing at eighteen to tie yourself to a woman for the rest of your life, knowing that either one of you might be a totally different person in just a few months?"

She was groping for a way to put it into words. "What it is is that you are selling your entire future for security now. You are eighteen. You are wonderful. But what and who are you going to be at twenty-five, at thirty, at forty? Will you be someone I can even like, let alone love and respect?"

"Are you saying I'm too young?"

"No, damn it. I'm saying I won't marry you or anyone else, not now, not ever."

He just sat there. She knew he hadn't understood. "Rick, why do you want to marry me? Why can't we just go on like we are?"

"Because I love you and I want to make you mine forever, not just for now." He thought that should have sounded good to her.

"That's what I mean. Did you hear what you said? You said, 'I want to make you mine forever.' *Make you mine.* Rick that means that my freedom to grow and to change is absolutely canceled, morally and even legally. Do you see what I mean?"

"It means that you don't love me as much as I love you."

"No it doesn't," she said. "Love has nothing to do with it. In fact, if you really love someone you don't want to put them in a cage of words and promises and binding legalities. You can't want someone to be with you simply because in a fit of passion she promised you till death do us part."

His face said, "What the hell is this!" His eyes told her he hadn't understood.

"Okay," he said. The weight of it was crushing. He had foreseen her laughing and crying and falling into his arms and promising forevers. But what was all this shit about freedom and . . .

And she saw that he was still a child. That all his drive and talent and personal kindness and his apparent maturity were only conditioning. He said what was expected of him; he worked hard and his painting showed it, but he hadn't lived enough yet. He didn't understand. He thought you married a woman and you owned her. . . .

"I was wrong, Rick, not to go into this sooner, but I thought you'd play around some. I thought once you got a taste of it you'd go hog wild. That you'd go on to school and we'd see each other now and then and . . ."

"Is that all it was to you?" Resentment was set like stone in his gray and petulant face. "You mean you *wanted* me to fuck around?"

"I wanted you to learn to love. I saw something in you I respected, a quality, call it a pursuit of quality. It's in you, in your work. When you latch onto something you hang in there. You want to own it, to control it. That's great, except you can't do it with people. You'll kill them. You'll destroy what you love in them."

"Okay."

"Okay what?" she asked.

296

"Just okay, if that's the way you want it."

"Think about it, Rick. Just think about it."

But he would not, not for a long time. He loved her and she didn't love him. That was enough to think about now.

Chapter

21

He finished his school year without seeing her. He had been hurt when Angela left, but he understood that. This he didn't. He thought about it a long time and couldn't make any sense of it. The only thing he could figure was that she wanted out and she'd gotten out, so okay, to hell with it. He'd wanted to say to hell with her but he couldn't bring himself to say it, not about Melissa, not Melissa.

A week before he left for Europe he was sitting in the public library making notes on the museums of France when he saw her on the sidewalk. He got up and walked to the window and watched her. She was alone and in a moment she was gone.

He had planned to be in England a month. He spent six and would have stayed longer, but he'd given himself three years and for some unseen reason he felt tied to that discipline. But France was another story. Everywhere he turned there was something beautiful and wonderful to see and to paint. He liked the people better than the English and he had loved the English. The French were a wilder, more open people; even their art seemed undisciplined and free. And the women.

He came close to losing his hurt over Melissa with the French girls. They loved him and he loved as many of them as possible. And he painted them.

He sent Charles most of his work and Charles framed it and sold it in his gallery or farmed it out to other galleries. He entered some of it in shows, the best of it, and won awards.

Much of his work was purchased in San Antonio and much of

that by a slender red-haired lady who never quibbled over the prices.

He thought he'd forgotten Melissa and didn't need her anymore until one day in Spain when he was finishing a painting of a woman sitting alone in a courtyard and he realized the woman bore a striking resemblance to Melissa.

A year in Spain, then six months in Portugal painting the people and the boats and the goats and the low stone houses and the grapes. It seemed to him that the world was made for him to paint.

He went to Rome and was there a year, then Athens for almost as long. Timothy and Lucinda flew to him in Athens and spent a month going over the old places there. He was tickled to see them. He wanted to ask if they knew anything about Melissa, then he remembered that they never had known about Melissa.

When Tim and Lucinda went back home he left Athens and moved on to Germany for a while and then back to England.

It was during this time, in the early sixties, that Vietnam became a real place to Americans.

Rick's American friends in England were opposed to the war almost to a man. But to Rick it was simply what it was to many other American boys who were eager, always pushing manhood. The drums, the flags, the love of glory.

They watched the reports on television. They saw the copters and the tanks, the little brown men, only boys themselves, parachuting into rice paddies. They saw little white staccato puffs of smoke coming from the jungle.

And millions of Americans saw themselves in uniform and imagined themselves as heroes, fearless and invincible. A few even saw themselves coming home in flag-draped coffins to worshiping families; fine words would be spoken, "ultimate sacrifice," "the last full measure of devotion," "the selfless gift for freedom." Those dreamers concocted visions of glory and they never felt the whump of steel entering flesh or smelled their own rotting limbs. They never, *never* caught a glimpse of themselves stumping around with one leg or blind or with half a stomach.

When their draft notices came, some of Rick's American friends

299

left, one by one, for Sweden, for Canada. Some went back home to hide in the cities, the communes. Some went to jail.

When Rick's notice came he quietly packed his belongings and flew to Texas. He went to his grandfather.

"I don't want to go, grandpa," he told him.

Frank Hyde was old now and gray. But his grip on life was as strong as it had been forty years before. He sat on the steps and listened. He seemed to listen even when no one was talking, and he waited a long time before answering. Rick had become a joy in his life. It was as if the other Rick had not died, so sharp and quick was he, and so full of life. He was the child Jonathan should have been and the only good thing to come out of Jonathan Hyde; and now he stood before a decision a man should never have to face.

"You don't want to go to war?" he asked, gazing out over green fields toward the river.

"No."

"Why?"

"It isn't because I'm afraid, grandpa. I am a little afraid, but that's not it."

"What is it, Son. Tell me why you don't want to go."

"Because it's all wrong. It's not what the government says it is, grandpa. We're not fighting for democracy or freedom this time. Diem is a dictator. I don't want to put my life on the line for him. Not for him."

The old man smiled. "That's selfish, Rick. You know that?" And he thought, "That's what one other Rick would have thought, too. That's how he would have thought."

"Of course it's selfish. So is breathing."

"It's the same thing, isn't it?"

"Same damn thing, grandpa. I can't let somebody else choose for me who I'm going to die for. Only I can choose that. When I let them tell me who to die for, I'm a slave and we're not supposed to be slaves here. Not supposed to be."

"Not supposed to be."

"Why doesn't the government say, 'We'll let the young men decide if they want to go fight to keep Diem in power?' They

300

have a right. Why don't they do it that way? Because they know the American people don't give a damn about Vietnam. They don't want to go so the government has to make them go. We are slaves." He looked at the old man.

"What are your alternatives?" the old man asked.

"Alternatives? Jail or run." Rick breathed.

"Pretty slim choice, son."

"I know."

"You decide. We'll help you all we can."

"What would you do in my situation, grandpa?"

"I wouldn't go to jail, son. I wouldn't go to jail."

Rick went out on the porch and listened for a long time to the night sounds. When the lights went off in the house he walked through the orange trees toward the river and he sat down on the bank of the river and listened to its slow, watery whisper. In the distance he could hear the noisy jukeboxes in Boys' Town across the water and occasionally an angry voice or the laughter of a whore at work.

Freedom. Those we empowered to guard it use the power to tax us and to fight their wars and to do wonders in the earth. They do some good, too, but the good is at the cost of freedom. Jail or war. Across the river to freedom, but not Mexico, they'd send me back.

In the morning at breakfast he told Ellen and Frank, "If an armed force were lined up across the river, grandpa, I would be out in the cottonfield with you ready to fight them off. I would be afraid, but I wouldn't run, I'd fight. But from this Vietnam thing I'm going to run."

Silence.

"It's wrong and I'm going to run."

Ellen was crying softly, she was an old woman now, straight and proud. "I wish Jimmy Ortega had run," she said, "from that war fifty years ago."

"That was a different war, Ellen. We were a different people in a different world." Frank said softly. "But I know what you mean."

"It wasn't a different war. Not to me, not to any woman. It is the same war and always the Americans, the God-almighty

301

Americans feel obligated to send their sons. Do we so love war that we rush to every fray in every little corner of the earth?"

"Not me, grandma."

"Good, Rick. I'm proud of you; and if you ever need anything . . ."

"I don't need anything, grandma. Just a place to hide."

Back in San Antonio his mother helped him pack and Timothy advised him. "Canada is best, Rick. Not so far away that we couldn't get up there now and then."

"There's someone I want to see before I go," he said. "I'll be back Tuesday."

She was weeding the rose garden when he walked up behind her. "Melissa."

She turned to him. She didn't recognize him at first, then "My God, Rick?"

He just grinned and opened his arms and she was in them in an instant, laughing. "My God, I can't believe it."

"It's me, baby, the tiger himself." He took her left hand, and examined it. "Married yet?"

She jerked her hand away. "Not yet, Rick, but you tempt me. My God, how beautiful you are." She turned and pulled him with her. "To hell with the roses," she said. "Let's go inside."

So began two of the finest days in his life, laughing and riding and loving. Days he would remember a thousand times before he saw her again.

"I didn't understand what you meant about being selfish until just recently. I didn't savvy what you meant about marriage, about freedom."

"What enlightened you?"

"I got drafted."

"Drafted? Rick! Shit." They were sitting at the dining-room table eating a sandwich.

"When do you have to go in?"

"I don't."

"What do you mean?"

"I mean I'm going to Canada."

"Canada?" Then she jumped up, for she had just remembered

302

Mrs. Forney was still in the kitchen. The old woman was standing at the stove stirring a pot of something. Melissa turned back, "I don't think she heard anything. She lost her son in Korea. She doesn't speak kindly of the peaceniks.... It'll take guts to fight the government."

"You can't fight 'em, Melissa," he said. "You have to hide from them."

"Canada, huh? I wonder if I'd like Canada. Can I go?"

"Would you, Melissa?"

"I don't know why I let you get away the last time."

"Six years," he said.

"I'm an old woman."

"You know I've always been a fool for older women."

At the airport they left Tim and Lucy at the gate and had started toward the plane when they heard a voice behind them, "Richard Morgan?" And they knew that Mrs. Forney had indeed been listening in the kitchen.

It came down to a choice between jail and the Army. Neither one made sense. Down deep he felt he should resist the Army and take the consequences, whatever they were, but prison scared hell out of him. Just the thought of five years in a cage, five years! He visualized queers and rednecks and some World War II hero just watching for a chance to put a knife between his ribs. So he compromised with his conscience. I'll go, he said, under protest, and I'll paint the war from a soldier's point of view, and I'll show the world what war is. They'll wish they never saw me. Down deep it seemed the right thing to do to just let them put him in jail, not to give in. But he said, "I'll just paint the goddamn war."

Chapter

22

The Reverend Jonathan Alexander Hyde spent a year in the state hospital at Austin. Early in his stay there Frank Hyde came to visit him and was advised not to disturb him. He came again and again and was allowed to see him from a window. Frank looked out on a plush green garden, where a tall, red-haired man sat alone. He had a large Bible under his arm. With his other hand he gestured and he preached to the trees and to the sky and to the passerby, who simply ignored him or stared at him strangely.

"That's all he ever does, Mr. Hyde," the attendant said.

Frank turned to him. "This is the first time I've seen him in too many years," he told her softly. Suddenly he was tired. "I'd better go now."

On the day Jonathan was released he refused to see his father. Frank got back in his pickup and drove slowly home.

Jonathan caught a bus to San Antonio, went to his bank, and, after drawing out every cent he'd saved, flew to Los Angeles. He found an old store in the slums and rented it and in a month he opened a church with ten souls present on the first Sunday. In six months there were a hundred. After the first year there were too many to meet in the little store, so he rented an abandoned church and it served for two more years.

With a membership of over a thousand people nearly three years after he left the hospital he broke ground for a new tabernacle. He began two small missions and they grew.

He was finally what he had wanted to be, God's man. He was

not born to satisfy his flesh. He worked from morning till into the night. He prayed and studied and visited the sick. And he preached. And when he preached it was with such conviction and total abandon that people were struck to their hearts. He knew their secret sins. They feared him and obeyed him and followed him step by step to his harsh brand of Jesus. "There is no room to compromise. You must belong all to God or all to hell. There is no middle ground." There were backsliders and he went to them in their homes and where they worked and he browbeat them back into submission to his Jesus. He made them believe in hell and they loved him.

Alone one morning eating breakfast he paused suddenly and stared for a long time at a spot on the wall in front of him, then he pushed his plate from him and got his black coat and walked out the door. By noon he was in Seattle. He looked up Blair Anderson in the phone book and directed a cab to his address. When he walked into Andy's shop Cerese was there alone. His eyes were cold. She said nothing, wishing that Andy were there.

"I came for my little girl."

So he *was* sick.

"She doesn't live here anymore, Jonathan." Her voice trembled.

"Do you fear me, woman?"

"No."

"You should fear God. Where is my little girl?"

"Angela is not a little girl, Jonathan. She's a grown woman and she doesn't live here anymore."

"Where does she live?"

"You mean you don't know?" she asked. "You haven't ever heard her? She's singing. You can't turn on the radio without hearing her. Angel. She's Angel now."

"I didn't know." He turned to go, then, "Where does she live?"

"Don't go to her, Jonathan. You'd only hurt her. She's never gotten over whatever it was that happened down there."

He half turned to her and his voice was like thunder. "Woman, where does she live?"

"Find her yourself, Jonathan. I'll not tell you."

He turned again for the door. "Wait," she said. She disappeared for a moment then returned and handed him a record and jacket. It said in flowing gold script, "Angel." There was a picture of her, a soft, dark-haired angel with petulant lips and seductive eyes.

"You have ruined her." He removed the record and slowly bent it double and dropped it on the floor. Then he ripped the jacket in four pieces and flung it from him.

"*I've* ruined her?" Cerese said, her voice a low guttural groan. "Did you know she was married?"

"She's married?" He looked up.

"Was, not is. Do you know why? She couldn't fuck, Jonathan. She couldn't bear to have her own husband inside her. If I had had any idea you'd done that to her I'd have killed you, Jonathan. I would have."

His face became blank, without care and concern. He simply walked out the door and was gone.

Angela did not want to see her father. But he came anyway, and when she opened the door she knew it would be him.

"Angela." He pushed the door open and entered her house.

She shut the door and turned to him. An insane fear ran through her like cold water. He turned back to her. "You must come back, child."

"No, father."

"You could do great things for God, now. With your singing how wonderful now to turn to him."

"No, father. Please go now."

He turned toward the open door leading to the patio and walked outside. He stood at the low rock wall and looked down into the Pacific and his eyes watered as he studied the jagged rocks. He turned toward her, his back to the ocean, a strange, hurt look on his face. She saw some fear, too, as he moved away from the wall. She backed away from him.

"A madness came over me, child. I can't explain it. Just don't let me stand between you and God."

"Go away, father, and don't bother me. I just can't take it."

He knelt down before her and began to pray. He wept and prayed and she backed away from him and went back into the house and locked the door and pulled the drapes. When he looked up and she was gone, he stood up and turned to the ocean and looked at the rocks for a long time; then he walked around the house and was gone.

She lay on the bed. A low, long groan came up out of the depths of an aged hurt she thought had eased. It hadn't. Her father had come, finally. After three years, and it was as bad as she'd imagined.

All that was in her until that day he found her with Rick had cried out for her father's God and for her father.

"I loved him, not as a child loves, but deeply, as a woman. I was glad when mama left. He was mine. How many times had I dreamed, how many times had I wished I was not my father's child, but my father's wife?"

In her child's mind it seemed to her that what had happened was just punishment for her sin, but Blair Anderson convinced her there was nothing to that, and it was over. Until she married.

Skip Pullen was a photographer friend of Andy's. He hired Angela as an assistant for the summer before she was to enter college. She never got to college; they fell in love and were married that October.

She was gloriously happy and only mildly concerned about the first night. He was a kind person, content to wait until after the wedding. Andy had explained her church background and he had understood perfectly. Fine. Until she began to scream when he entered her. They tried again the next morning. The same uncontrollable fear, and pain.

She saw a doctor. Nothing. Skip talked to Andy. Andy talked to Cerese. Cerese talked with Angela, or tried to. She could get only so far as to learn that Jonathan hadn't just had a "breakdown." He had raped her.

Psychiatrist. No success. Another. Frustration. At first there were only kindness and understanding between Skip and Angela, but the strain was there beneath the surface and it grew. Arguments. Tension. More frustration. Separation. Divorce.

Angela went to San Francisco and got a job as a barmaid in a lounge at a Howard Johnson's which featured a small combo and a singer.

Angela enjoyed working there and being alone. She enjoyed

the combo and the songs. She began to sing them at home; she wrote down all the words and learned them by heart. When the girl would introduce a new song Angela would learn that, too.

There was a large old downtown church near her apartment and one Sunday morning she dressed up and went. There was a peacefulness there. It was different from any church she'd ever known, quiet. No shouting, no weeping, no amens, and no altar call. There was a real choir. She felt safe there and she began to go each Sunday morning. It was a refuge, a haven.

One night the singer at the club didn't show. Nick, the organist and leader of the group, was furious. They found out that she had flown home. Her mother was ill.

The drummer, Harvey, said, "I told you we need a stand-in, Nick. Those things are going to happen."

"I can sing."

Nick turned around. "Angela?" He laughed. "You? Forget it, babe. It takes weeks to get this stuff."

"I can do it."

"Forget it," he barked. She turned away.

"Maybe we should see if she can," Harvey told him. "She's a beautiful girl."

"Man, she's the most beautiful and the coldest broad in the world. She couldn't warm up to this for nothin', man. Just forget it. We'll just play."

"She's not cold, Nick. She's just come through a divorce. She's been hurt some."

"How'd you know that? She never talks to anyone."

"She just never talks to you."

"Fuck you, Harvey, and cut the crap."

During the break Harvey asked her. "Can you really sing, Angela?"

"I used to sing."

"Where."

"In church."

Harvey chuckled. "We don't do 'Rock of Ages,' honey."

Her face froze. She turned away. He touched her shoulder. "Hey, kid. I didn't mean anything by that."

She smiled. "I can sing 'Rock of Ages' if you want, but I can do anything Liz does."

"Will you stay later?"

"Yes." '

So at three o'clock in the morning she sang for him. He played the organ for her and didn't say anything. He led her through the whole repertoire, and when they had done everything the group was into it was six in the morning and he just sat there for a moment when she finished the last song. She knew he liked it. She knew she sounded good.

"Have you got a pants suit?"

"Sure."

"Something really dressy?"

"Yes."

"Wear it tonight."

"What about Nick?"

"Leave him to me."

That night she sang in Liz's place. Cold chills ran down Nick's spine as she moved into "Summertime" and "Please Don't Go Away." Harvey grinned at him and shot him a finger behind the bass drum. He grinned back. The other guys in the group looked at each other. The crowd stopped talking and nobody left. Angela sang and felt something she'd never felt, something deep and warm and electric. After each song the crowd clapped harder. At intermission they simply stood up and cheered. The band stood up. Nick bowed to her.

She cried.

It was the beginning. Nick knew somebody who knew somebody and she got an audition; then they cut a single. It hit. Another and another. Then an album and the Carson show.

She dumped Nick. He wanted to play games and she wasn't playful. He turned into a real shitheel so she dumped him.

Harvey was older, forty, and good to her. He didn't push. They formed a new group with Harvey running the show. They did Vegas and Reno. She became a sex symbol and they played up to it. Pictures of her were almost nude; her act took on a vampish air. She learned the sexy moves and exuded a sensuality that moved men to fantasies unlimited. They called her Angel and she went to church every Sunday.

And she didn't fuck.

Harvey loved her from the beginning and protected her from all the hounds descending upon her every time she turned around. It was convenient for them to slip into the pretense that she and Harvey had a thing going and it was hands off for anybody else. It was easier that way. It was also easy for Harvey to slip into the delusion that there was something there. She was sweet to him and appreciative, but the first time he put his arm around her she stiffened slightly. She knew he was aware of it and wished she hadn't. She didn't the next time. In fact it was nice, good for a man to be there, and she liked him.

One night he kissed her and she kissed him back, but he took no liberties beyond that until he told her that he loved her and wanted a deeper relationship, even marriage if she would.

"Harvey, there is something wrong with me."

"I know, baby, you had a bad marriage and you never got over it, but . . ."

"That's not it, Harvey."

"What then?" he asked softly. "What is it? What's the trouble?"

"I can't have sex, Harvey. I can't do it."

"What do you mean, you can't?"

"I mean when I got married and Skip . . . on the first night I couldn't. My head's all fucked up."

"Holy Jesus, Angela."

But he continued to be good to her. He stopped seeing other girls. He hoped to hell something would work out. He kept hoping.

"Why don't you see a doctor again, Angela? No, it's not because I'm horny, which I am, but it's for you, kid. You need to get straightened out. Life's too short to pass up something as good as sex."

"It is good, isn't it?" she asked.

"Beats the hell out of card games."

"How good is it, Harvey, really?"

"Better'n anything, kid, no kiddin.' "

"What do you do for sex, Harvey? You don't see anybody anymore."

"I quit seeing girls when I fell in love with you, baby," he said quietly. "It just didn't seem right."

She started to cry, softly, "But don't you have needs?"

"Kid, I'm a whole bundle of 'em."

She was quiet for a while then, "I can't, Harvey."

"What?"

"No doctor, no marriage. Not you, not anybody. Never."

Chapter
23

The old woman had gotten caught in the crossfire of a firefight in a small village north of Danang. Rick didn't know whether she'd been hit by American bullets or Viet Cong, but she was hit and she lay twitching and coughing in the street, face down, her head twisted grotesquely. Her eyes were screaming.

Rick couldn't move. They were firing into the town from the jungle. He was pinned down alone. When the firing stopped because of the arrival of copter firepower he went out into the street and knelt down beside the old woman, dead now, and put his finger in the blood and dirt and sketched her small, still form on a sheet of newspaper. When he was done he picked up his M-16 and walked away. "My Mona Lisa," he thought. "My Christina, goddamn."

When he rejoined his group his lieutenant said, "Where in hell you *been?*"

"Got pinned down on the other side of town."

The officer saw the newspaper. "I told you no more of that shit, Morgan."

"Fuck you, Cistern." His name was Sesterman, but they called him Cistern. It fit his personality.

"You'll be in the book for that, Morgan."

"And you better watch your ass, lieutenant."

"Is that a threat?"

"That's what it is, kid. Just watch your goddamn yellow ass."

"You're supposed to be helpin' burn this town."

"Not me, kid. You burn it."

"That's an order!"

"Fuck you, Cistern. I'm not burnin' this goddamn pigsty."

On another day Rick and five other men were making their way back through the jungle toward their fire base when the man at point signaled quiet. Every man froze. Rick was in the rear and when the firing started and he saw the others cut down before him he left the trail and crawled through the dark growth and lay there breathing hard and listening. He heard them laughing and congratulating themselves. He lay till dark, scarcely moving. When night came he stayed where he was, waiting for the moon he knew would show at midnight. He dozed off twice but was startled awake by crawling things that he couldn't see. He remembered a dove his grandfather Hyde had shot while hunting whitewing in the valley. The bird went down, but they never found it. "He went into the bushes. He'll die there I guess, or somethin'll get him come night." The boy lay awake that night thinking about that little bird and all the things that might get him. He thought about that bird tonight and figured he'd been dead seventeen years and it hadn't mattered a damn bit. He wondered if in seventeen years it would mean a damn for anyone alive that four men had been chopped up on that trail.

Them and thirty-five thousand others and who's gonna give a good goddamn in seventeen years? Then what matters? To whom? Me.

Grandfather had said this war would be different if we were fighting to win it. "You can't contain a cancer, son. You have to cut it out with a knife or burn it out, and the idea that government's place is to redistribute wealth is a cancer. A government that is strong enough to redistribute wealth must be strong enough to first take it away. To give that kind of power to mere mortals is to insure that there will be more taking and keeping than redistribution. And even if there is redistribution the state has to have enough policemen to keep the producers producing. There's no way it can work."

So what am I here for? He was soaking wet in his own sweat but he didn't drink any water until a half hour before he was to break cover. How'd I ever get sucked into this?

The moon was high and it was barely light enough to make out

313

objects in front of him. At first morning light he dragged into the fire-base perimeter. By the time he realized something was wrong it was too late. The base had been taken. Five little brown men stood in the path before him, smiling. Their guns leveled on his navel. He simply dropped his rifle and raised his arms. One of his captors stepped forward and with the butt of his rifle cracked him across the eyes.

It was the pain he was first aware of, his head and his face, then his hands and feet. He realized immediately that he was being carried on a mountain trail and he was trussed up like a pig. His hands and feet were bound to a pole. At first he thought it was night. How in hell can these devils see? . . . And then he turned his head and peered this way and that, nothing.

Son of a bitch!

Am I blindfolded? He felt nothing but the pain, the throbbing. He opened and closed his eyelids, nothing there. Nothing there.

He began screaming and he tugged at the ropes tying him to the pole. They dropped him on the rocky path and one of them kicked him in the side and he passed out again.

He awoke to his own screaming and fevered babbling. "What now, grandfather? What now. Hell, hell, hell . . ." and then the blessed respite, the blackness within the blackness.

He lay on the ground half aware of people standing over him, children shooting mock guns at him. A soldier's boot was against his neck. He could feel the man sway as he warded off the curious onlookers.

He didn't know how long that went on. By and by he felt the boot pummeling his rib cage again, and he knew someone was untying the rope on his feet. They were shouting something at him, commands. Then a hand gripped the back of his shirt collar and pulled him to his feet and shoved him forward. He ran into something and fell again. They kicked him and cursed him and he got up and fell again. A voice from a few yards away. A question. The kicking stopped. Someone knelt down and touched his face. My God, the pain of it. The kicking started again, then a harsher command from the kneeling man. The kicking stopped. Curses from others standing near. More commands. Silence. Someone else kneeling. Softer hands this time, and water. A wet rag on his eyes, wiping softly, cleaning off the crusts of blood. The sound of the rag in a pan of water being squeezed out. The hands again. He wanted to open his mouth and bless this Samaritan but he knew he could not speak without crying out. A hand held his chin. Fingers opened his mouth. Aspirin? Something. Squeezing water into his mouth. Harsh commands from someone standing near. The kind hands jerked away. He felt himself being lifted again by his collar. On his feet. A rope around his neck this time and someone in front of him pulling him along with savage jerks. The crowd roars and laughs. He stumbles, falls, gets up again, then waves of nausea and again the blessed blackness within the blackness.

He was in a room with other Americans. One, a medic, sat beside him, and when Rick stirred he called, "Sergeant, he's coming around."

"How is it, Morgan?"

"I can't see, sergeant."

Silence.

"The others got it. I made it back but they surprised me at camp. Hit me across the head with a rifle butt."

The medic asked. "Can you see anything at all?"

"Nothing."

"Sometimes when you take a lick like that the blindness is temporary."

"What do you mean, temporary?"

"I'm not sure, Rick. I'm not a doctor and I don't know a damn thing about it, really. It's a shock-type thing, though. What you need is just to rest now. Much pain?"

"And then some. Are you Sieminski?"

"Yes."

"Where are we, Minski?"

"North. They'll probably move us again. I don't think we're across the DMZ yet."

When he awoke again the others were gone. "Minski?" Nothing.

"Minski! . . . Sieminski!"

Nothing.

Alone. Why'd they take the others?

A door opened.

"Who's there?" Silence. A hand on his arm, a rope. The man tied his hands and put another rope around his neck and said something and pulled. Rick lifted himself off the floor. Nausea. He stopped a moment and steadied himself. The pain came again in waves. He vomited. Curses from behind him. The rope tugged at him and he stumbled forward out of the hut. He felt the sun on his wounded face. Chickens cackling. The smell of dung and freshly turned soil. A motor bike in the distance.

They walked for a short way in the sunlight and then shadow. The sound of trees in the wind. Bird calls. The smells changed. The sweet dank odor of rotting leaves. The hot mustiness of jungle. The trail became uneven. He stumbled. Again. The rope pulled tight and cut off his wind. He flexed his neck muscles and gained breathing room, but the effort caused him to groan from the hurt in his head.

Chapter
24

A verbal command he couldn't understand stopped him and he felt something touch his hands. The ropes were cut. Something pressed his stomach. He reached for it and grabbed it. Shovel! Another command. Dig?

Slowly he stooped and began. Dread froze the muscles in his legs. Fear knotted his stomach. The pain in his face subsided and became of little import as his brain raced. He began to think of dying and then pushed that away. A blind man in a jungle? No chance. How far away was the soldier? He knew the man was behind him. Had he sat down? Then death began to crawl up and down his arms and legs. Breathe deeply. Work slowly. He gripped the shovel like a club and stood up. A command from behind. Still he stood, listening. A command again. He's sitting down! The voice continued cursing. That word again. Dig! So he stooped to dig, and when he heard the grass rustle again as the man sat, Rick whirled and swung the shovel at the spot where the man's head should have been.

Nothing.

Laughter.

Sickness in his gut.

Dig.

When it was enough the man stood and took the shovel and commanded again and put his hand on Rick's shoulder and turned him so that the American faced the hole in the ground.

Rick's heart raced and he wanted to scream out, but thought

317

also to stand still. He felt something small and hard against the base of his skull. Visions of Melissa riding nude, golden, laughing on a white horse.

He heard the click of a hammer cocking and he steadied himself and looked at the vision of the laughing girl on the white stallion.

When the explosion should have come, it didn't.

A voice. Another voice. A woman? Chattering. Then the soldier. Then the old woman. Then both together. What in hell?

Then Rick felt the rope again. His hands were being tied. The rope was looped over his head again and tightened down on his throat. I'm not going to die! The old woman pulled on the rope and Rick stepped out of his hole and followed her, the pain in his face returning with the realization that death had, for the moment, passed by. He heard the soldier calling something to the old woman and she grunted something back. They rounded a bend in the trail and started up the mountain.

They walked for hours before they stopped. Night had fallen. The night sounds had begun, the crickets and the short, shrill cry of bats. He ached and the long stumbling walk had nauseated him. His face began to throb again.

The old woman put a chain around his neck, said something to him, fastened the chain to a tree and left him.

His sleep was fearful and broken by the cold and by the damp ground, and none too soon the sun came and he felt it stinging his face. Sounds of children around him, laughing, sneering, moving closer.

He couldn't see the sticks they held or the stones, but he saw light! Light?

He sat up and touched his eyes.

Oh!

Easy. So tender.

And then he heard the first stones falling. One hit the tree and fell near him. The children screamed gleefully and moved closer and began to hit him. He put his arms over his face and turned his back to them and knelt at the base of the tree and began to cry.

They moved closer and screamed louder. One began hitting his back with a long stick. He whirled and his arm swept savagely around and struck two of them and knocked them away. His retaliation took them by surprise, but they backed up and began throwing stones again until they realized he was blind, and then they fell upon him, kicking and clawing and screaming.

The old woman spoke sharply, only once, and the children fled.

A bowl of rice, a cup of water.

Light! If I can see light I can see. When my face is well I'll see! I'll never paint children again. Not innocent children. In his mind he pictured a sweet child in a pink dress. She was smiling, but there was a touch of evil somewhere. Her eyes. Yes. That is where it will be, in her eyes. And in her hands. My God, I can see light!

When he had finished the rice and the water, the old woman laid him down on the ground and began to wash his face with a cloth. Then she put some foul-smelling oil on him. She gave special attention to his eyes, opening each one carefully and rubbing easily around it. He could see the shadow of her body.

She disappeared for a few minutes and then returned and undid the chain from around the tree and spoke to him and pulled on the chain. He stood up unsteadily and followed her.

They walked for a mile or more along a road and then she slowed and pulled him off to the left and walked a little further. Then she took off his chain. She put his hands on a long pole extended horizontally in the air. She gave it a push and it moved a little.

She spoke again the same word over and over. Then she pushed his back and then he pushed and her word changed and she laughed.

The pole turned easily as he stumbled around in a great circle. He heard her to his left rustling something, then heard her hacking away with a knife or an axe. The pole began to be harder to push and he smelled something sweet. Cane? A cane mill? I'm a goddamn mule? He slowed and a torrent of curses rained upon him. He pushed hard again and his old woman laughed again

319

and chattered while she fed the mill and rejoiced at her good fortune.

He pushed until his shoulder and back ached and he slowed again and stopped. An outburst of curses were flung toward him. Then he felt a cane beating his back. He started pushing again, and again the old woman laughed and went back to her work. He tired again and slowed down and the curses came again, but before she could get to him to beat him he stepped to the left where the pole was lower, leaned against it with his chest, put his iron-heavy arms over it, and let them rest. He pushed with his chest, and the old woman laughed with happiness and praised herself for being smart enough to buy such a smart American. Then she paused and thought about that and determined to keep a very close watch on him. Such a smart one could not be trusted.

When he fell it took her a long time to get him up. She tossed away the cane she was beating him with and picked up a switch and began stinging his back and his neck.

When he fell again this didn't work, so she began kicking him in the ribs and stomach. He struggled to his feet and began to swing wildly at her. She simply stepped back and cursed him from a safe distance until he fell again, and then she ventured forth carefully and aimed a foot at his nuts. "Ha!" she yelped and doubled over in laughter as he grabbed himself and groveled in the dirt, groaning and crying.

She shuffled over to the cane mill and picked up his chain, shuffled back and put it around his neck again, and began pulling. He got up slowly and began walking behind her.

In the morning when she brought his rice and water to his place under the tree he ate it greedily as she stood and watched. When she took the bowl and cup and turned to go he said to her, "Fuck you, grandma." She only chuckled and shuffled toward her shack.

He was stronger that day. She let him rest several times and even gave him something to eat. She only beat him once with the cane and that didn't hurt very much. It was worth the beating to get the rest.

That night when she got him home she put him in a cage made

of bamboo and brought him something to eat, rice again, and when he finished he said to her, "Fuck you, grandma." He slept better in his new home on a bamboo mat, and his face didn't hurt.

The light was brighter in the morning. He could barely make out broad masses of color, the sky and the road and the green of the cane and the rice as they walked to work.

He was wide awake early the next morning waiting for the sun because he was sure his vision would improve more and more. It didn't. It was the same every day after that. All day long he stared at the pole as he pushed it, searching in vain for some sign that his eyes would clear and he could see something definite. Nothing.

He suffered attacks of deep despair. "I could take it if I could see. Hell, if I could see I could get the hell away from here."

He often thought of Melissa and saw her almost always as the nude golden girl on the great white horse, but sometimes she was the quiet and confident friend with whom he could talk. Sometimes he did talk to her, and when grandma answered him he'd say, "Fuck you, grandma."

Sometimes Melissa would come to him in his sleep and would be his lover. They would romp and play in the cool Texas river, he would rest in the strength of her sweet arms as they held him, and he would smile in his sleep and groan.

He learned the way to work, and sometimes grandma would let him walk ahead of her. He tried to figure out what was along each side of the road, and sometimes during the long hours pushing on the mill pole he would reconstruct the route until he knew the area by heart.

He knew where the irrigation ditches were, and he knew where houses were, where children played, and where to expect the dogs. He learned every hole in the road, and he knew where the sand was soft and where it was packed hard.

Then he tired of thinking of the road and he began to think about the paintings he had done and the people he had painted. He remembered every mole and wrinkle and every expression of the people he knew and loved, his grandfather's friendly twinkle

321

when he asked hard questions he already knew the answers to. He strained to see his mother's kindness and could bear it only a short moment. Then he began to talk to them while he worked, and he didn't realize he was talking out loud until the old woman grunted and then he'd say, "Fuck you, grandma. Fuck you and yours, grandma, fuck you with this goddamn mill pole." He chuckled thinking about that, and she chuckled and cackled something and piled more cane into the mill.

Chapter

25

One day he heard bombing in the distance. Then off and on he'd hear jets swooshing overhead. One day there were helicopters, flying low. He stopped pushing and looked up, listening. Too far away. The old woman came running and slipped the chain over his head and left it on for several days after that. There were no more helicopters for a very long time.

One night he awoke and he could see. Outside his cage he saw Melissa sitting on a white horse. She was looking into the distance. She was troubled. His Grandfather Hyde sat on an orange crate reading some huge old book. Next to him sat his mother and Timothy Morgan. "Mother?" he spoke loudly. She looked up and smiled at him, then she turned her head away and he knew that she was crying.

Timothy said, "Hang in there, son."

"I'm okay, dad. I'm hanging in there. I hate it here though." And then he turned over and went back to sleep.

He didn't remember the dream the next morning when he awoke and didn't remember it until midmorning; then he stopped pushing and began to think about it, but the old woman started her cackle and started toward him. He resumed his labor and she went back to the mill. But he still thought about it and didn't push as fast. Grandma cursed him from afar. And he answered, "Fuck you, grandma."

One day Rick heard the sound of a stone or something hit the pole near his head. Then he heard giggling behind him. Then there were more stones. One hit him in the back. He knelt down and covered his head with his hands. When the pole stopped the old woman turned and saw what was going on. She charged the children and they scattered, shouting back the same curses she rained upon them. She turned and started back toward the mill. The children then moved bravely closer. Quick as a snake she whirled and caught one of them, a boy, who squealed and screamed as she happily beat the shit out of him.

When she grew tired and released him he ran toward the road, where he stood and cursed her soundly.

She simply stood there for a moment chuckling and cackling, and just before she went back to work she yelled after him, "Fuck you, grandma."

Rick's visitors were coming every night now. They sat on chairs and rocks and boxes and spoke to one another and to Rick, and Rick spoke back.

"Hang in there, kid."

"Okay, dad, thanks, dad."

Sometimes he heard his grandfather discussing philosophy with Karl Marx and Immanuel Kant and Jesus and Ayn Rand.

"Miss Rand, you are the only important thinker I ever read who doesn't lapse into the sin of faith."

"Faith is unreasonable," she said.

"True," Frank Hyde said.

"Faith is all the simple people have to fall back on though," Kant said. "Faith is necessary."

"Necessary for what?" Marx asked. He appeared angry.

"If the people didn't believe they would someday all be equal; they wouldn't follow you," Jesus said. "It is only faith that keeps them in chains."

Marx pursed his lips in thought and his eyebrows lifted in surprise and he began to think.

Frank Hyde chuckled as Marx thought. And it seemed to Rick that the ground trembled while the bearded old man thought how best to get the people to believe.

They came every night and argued. Sometimes Rick asked questions. Sometimes Melissa would ride up to the circle of visitors and sit behind them on her white horse and peer at the

324

blind and bearded man in the cage, and then she would ride off. The first time this happened Jesus looked at Frank Hyde and asked, "Who was the broad on the horse?"

"That's Melissa. She loves the kid."

"Oh," Jesus said. "I wish she loved me."

"She doesn't believe in you," Rick said.

"Oh. Too bad for her, kid. And too bad for you."

"Oh, fuck off, will you? Please."

"That's tellin' him, kid," Timothy said. "Hang in there, kid."

"Okay, dad."

There was a small canal running near the cane mill. Sometimes Rick would leave his pole and make his way toward it and there wash his face and arms. Sometimes he'd dunk his shaggy head in it and let the muddy water cool him. One day after he'd lost count of time, months after his arrival, the weather was extremely hot, and when he went to the water he let himself down into it completely. His bare toes gripped the clay bank and he stayed down in the water until the old woman came cackling fiercely, and then he climbed out. The water in his hair and clothes cooled him for over an hour, so he did it again and again, and the old woman simply marveled at such an American.

Then one day he was climbing out of the canal and his fingers dug into the clay bank for support. When he climbed out and went back to pushing the mill pole, he became aware that he had kept a handful of clay and he was kneading it with both hands while he moved the great pole with his chest. He worked the lump into a round ball and then into a square and then into a pyramid. Then he made an egg shape and punched into it a nose and punched eye sockets and pinched off a little of the clay from the bottom of the lump and formed little ears, and he made a mouth and chin and then he crushed it and did it again and again. That night before it was time to quit he went to the canal again, and this time he filled his pockets with clay and took the clay home with him and struggled into the night making heads and smashing them, learning, learning, learning, and laughing with the joy of it.

In the morning he broke the lump of clay and carried it in his

325

pockets back to the canal; when it was time to quit work again, he got some more clay and worked with that clay into the night. He worked until his hands were sore and then he slept. For the first time in months he slept in peace. He had forgotten the circle of spirits that night.

Then one night he wanted to do Melissa's face. He worked and struggled and punched and gouged and shaped the clay this way and that. A dozen times he tore it up and started again, but he couldn't make it work. He couldn't see her. His hands trembled and he choked. His eyes, wide open, searched the darkness. He tried, like the witch of Endor, to call for the sitters. "Grandfather, where are you? Where are your friends? Melissa?" he cried aloud.

"Goddamnit, where is everybody?" and he brought both fists down on the lump of clay and beat it faceless and began to scream over and over again, "Melissa! Melissa! Melissa!" until the old woman came cursing in the night and threw a bucket of water over him. He lay on the floor of the cage and cried until he slept, and in his sleep Melissa came to him and lay beside him and put her head on his shoulder, and they lay like that for hours. He had no need to open his tired eyes because he could see her there on the grassy slopes by the river.

His life went into the clay. From his fingers his life bled into the clay and the clay became life. It became his mother's face and then his father's. Grandfather Hyde grew out of the clay and then his grandmother. Then he began to do the faces he had painted and by and by he did Angela Hyde, and when he was done he sat in the night and remembered and he called for the sitters and showed them Angela and asked his mother what it was about Angela and Reverend Hyde he wasn't supposed to know. He asked his mother again and then she just vanished. He asked his father and Timothy just looked at Frank and then looked away. Frank didn't look away. He looked at the bust of Angela and smiled and said, "Remember. Just remember." So Rick sat remembering. He smashed the clay and worked it again, remembering. A face grew out of it. Jonathan Hyde. A satyr's face, grimacing and menacing. Screaming, eyes wild with fear, or hate?

He was back in that room, that basement room in the church. Jonathan Hyde was holding something in his hand, grisly, bloody. He was saying something. What? What was he saying? What? What?

He looked out to his grandfather. He wasn't there. Nobody was there, only Jonathan Hyde's screaming eyes. Rick ripped the satyr's face apart and it lay in pieces.

One night in his cage he asked his grandfather, "Why are we here?"

"What do you mean?" The old man shut the book he was reading and peered through the darkness, squinting slightly and leaning forward.

"I mean generally, why this? Why me? Why all this?"

"You mean other than the obvious, besides the fact that you happened to be in the wrong place at the wrong time? You mean is there a deeper purpose? Did some power, good or evil, place you here for some overriding purpose? Is that what you mean?"

"Yes, that's what I mean."

"You are here because you are a slave fighting against other slaves. You kill them and they kill you. The old woman bought you from that soldier and she owns you. That's why you are here.

"If there is any higher purpose or sensible reason for suffering, millions of people have died without knowing what it is.

"You are here because the old woman's ox died. If that ox hadn't died you'd be dead now, long since."

"Maybe I'd be better off."

"You'd never have learned how to make a face out of clay."

"Maybe that is the higher purpose."

"Maybe."

"No. You are right. I am here because that old woman's ox died." And that angered him. There was no God. No higher purpose. The government was a tyrant. The old woman who could have helped him had caged him and used him for an ox. That a man's life meant so little. He began to cry and the cry was a long, terrible moan from deep inside him. It was the cry of a man alone.

When the old woman came for him the next morning and handed him a bowl of rice soup he threw it in her face and refused to leave the cage. When she beat him with a cane he took the cane away from her and hit her with it as hard as he could.

327

She screamed and fell to the ground cursing him. He struck her again and again until she rolled free and ran away. She did not come for him that day or the next, and he sat outside the cage alone and hungry, but a victor. He knew that she could kill him any time, or have him killed, or simply watch him starve. I could leave, but where would I go?

On the third day he heard her in her hut chattering, chattering. Then he heard the chickens cackle as they scattered before her. Then he didn't hear her anymore until she was right on top of him and it was too late. She hit him on the side of the head with a shovel and he crumpled to the ground. When he awoke he was in his cage again and she was standing outside chuckling.

She fed him and he ate. The next morning they went to the mill. And again he did the ox's work.

As he turned the great mill pole he thought that the trouble with the whole world is that no one wants to turn his own mill pole.

Funny, that's what grandfather had said, something like it anyway, sitting on the front porch at the farm. Some people farm and others sit around waiting for the harvest so they can steal it.

In Russia it's all legal like. The thieves even took away the land and then "let" the farmers work it, and then took the produce in the name of social justice.

In America you work your ass off and the government takes half in taxes and another ten to twenty percent through inflating the currency. What's the damn difference? A slave by any other name.

He awoke to the sound of distant gunfire. The muffled whump, whump, whump of artillery fire both frightened him and gave him hope. He listened all that day and thought the battle was moving closer. The next day the sounds began earlier and they were closer. When he trudged down the road to the cane mill he tried not to hope that he might be rescued. He dared not. Then he heard the copters. They were distant, but he heard them before the old woman did. When she did she stopped for a moment and pulled Rick to the side of the road into the cane. The helicopters flew right over them and were gone. Then the old woman pulled him back onto the road and they went to work.

328

His heart beat wildly when he heard aircraft, jets, flying high overhead. He could barely stand it when he heard gunfire in the hills not far away.

Then he heard the copters again, coming back. Again he heard them before she did, and he waited until she did because then she scrambled for the rope and came to him with it and tried to put it around his neck. She never made it. He grabbed her hands and brought a knee up into her old belly. When she crumpled he picked her up and carried her to the canal and held her under the water. She was kicking and clawing; his wild blind eyes were wide with the horror of it. Then when she was still he let her slip down into the water, and he turned and ran to the road, screaming and waving his arms to the sky.

The kid in the doorway of the big ship saw the figure running down the road, and he opened fire. It is difficult to distinguish a tall man from a short man from an altitude of a thousand feet, but then the man fell, clutching at his back then his chest.

"My God!" the kid screamed. "Lieutenant!"

The ship set down a few feet from the man, now bloody and still, lying in the dust. Two men jumped out and picked him up and put him in, and the copter flew off while the door gunner, tears streaking down his face, protested to his unseeing, unhearing buddies, "Christ, I didn't know, how could I know?"

"Is he dead?" the pilot asked one of the men through his mike.

"Yes," the man replied.

So the pilot didn't hurry back to the base. It wasn't until they had set down and started to unload the body that someone noticed that the red foam on the man's chest was moving just a little, in and out.

Chapter

26

Angela Hyde had never forgotten Rick Morgan. Even when she became Angel, silky-voiced and sensuous, childlike, yet so apparently full of sexual hunger and pursued by countless men eager for her. All of them, absolutely every one of them, left her cold; she could not bring herself to allow any of them to advance beyond the most initial forms of acquaintance. Only one person in all her life, in all her memory, seemed to her now to be kind and good. Only he would have loved her with a true tenderness. Perhaps, she had thought at one time, perhaps he would even have loved her without wanting to use her body. She had thought that once, but had discarded that notion as she grew older. Men simply have to have it, her mother had told her; they just have to. So she thought of him in a different way after that. He was her lover and in her fantasies he would come to her out of a misty light, surrounded by an aura of goodness, and when he entered her it did not hurt. Once in a dream he entered her and she even got pleasure from it. Shortly after that Angel flew to San Antonio and visited Rick's parents and learned that he was missing in action. She also learned about Melissa and that he had loved Melissa and was planning to marry her. She determined to look at her problem in a different light.

She visited a doctor and with her help began to understand the significance of what Jonathan Hyde had done to her. She tried to convince herself that sexuality was a natural and fully desirable aspect of human nature, and little by little she succeeded to the point of experiencing for brief moments small but unmistakable pangs of desire.

She read about sex. Went to movies where the sex act was depicted in absolute detail. Listened in earnest when show people talked about their intimate relationships. One day when she felt a petite ripple of physical excitement between her thighs she touched herself and was rewarded with increased excitement that left her decidedly desirous, for the first time in her life. She ran a hot tub of water and lay in it and, for the first time ever, loved herself.

She was beginning to believe that perhaps there was some hope for a normal relationship, when one night on a television news program she saw him. He sat in a wheelchair. He was thin, emaciated; his eyes were bandaged. His mother and father and a beautiful red-haired woman stood beside him. After recovering from the initial shock of realizing that it was really he, she suddenly wished that she were that woman with him. She would give all she possessed to be standing there beside him. She would remain with him always and care for him and love him.

She listened carefully to the words of the newsman to see where it was that they were taking him. The next morning she made arrangements to go there herself. She would see him. At least she would see him and talk with him and then perhaps . . .

He sat in the sun in a wheelchair. A voice, velvety, quivering, penetrated the darkness, "Rick?"

"Yes?"

"It's Angela," the voice said.

"Angela?"

"Hyde."

"Yes, I know."

She stood for a moment not knowing what now to say. He was tall. She could tell that even as he sat in the chair. He was brown and strong. A smile spread across his face. He looked toward her. She could not see his eyes behind dark glasses. "How are you, Angela?" he asked. He lifted his hand toward her. She took it and held it.

331

"I'm okay," she said. "You?"

"Much better now." He squeezed her hand. "What's this I've been hearing about you?"

"Probably mostly P.R."

"You're famous," he said.

"So are you."

"Not for anything that matters."

"What *does* matter?"

"Someday I'll tell you," he said.

"When?"

"Any time."

"Will you come see me when you get out of here?"

"I will for sure," he promised. His smile was from deep down, real, warm. It went through her like electricity.

"Alone?"

"You mean will Melissa come too?" he asked.

"I shouldn't have said that," she apologized.

"Melissa and I are going to be married," he said.

"Oh."

"You didn't know?" No answer. He reached out. Then he heard her crying softly. "What's the matter?"

"It's nothing, really."

"You don't cry about nothing."

"I'm not crying."

"Sounded like it."

"No. I'm okay."

"Good, now let's talk about how you got to be so famous."

So they did. She pushed his chair into the shade after a while. She sat on the ground and leaned against a tree and watched him begin to fashion the ball of clay into what she thought might be a man, maybe an old man, and they talked.

Melissa came then and Rick introduced them, and Angela was surprised to find that she actually liked her. She could see Melissa loved Rick, took care of him.

When it was time for her to go, she invited them both to come see her.

"I'll take a rain check this time," Melissa said. "But Rick can go. He's got to go to the hospital in San Diego after they get him all healthied up here. I've got to go home for a week and take care of things. Then I'll get back for his operation."

"Operation?" Angela asked.

"My eyes," he said, "they think they can fix me."

Then she did cry. Melissa took her in her arms and held her. Rick was silent. He tried not to think about it, the operation, seeing again. Painting.

Before she left she asked him about the bust he was making. "Who is it?"

"Seem familiar?"

"Vaguely. Who?"

"Someday I'll tell you," he said.

"Tell me now."

"Now is not the time."

In the taxi on the way to the airport she remembered the old man with Rick on the telecast. His grandfather! Sure it was. Then why all the mystery?

It was a month later when she heard a rapping at her front door. She wondered why they hadn't used the doorbell.

Then just before she opened it she realized and cried out, "Rick!"

"Right," he said as she opened the door. "How'd you guess?"

"Oh, Rick! Come in here."

He turned and raised his cane to the taxi driver just now returning to his car. "Okay, Billy." The young man retrieved two suitcases and carried them across the lawn and up to the door. They stepped aside for him and he took them into the house. Rick paid him, then turned to Angela. "Angel, this is Bill Turney. He wanted me to get him your autograph."

"Yes, ma'am," he said. "I'd really be proud of that."

So she walked over to the stereo and got her latest record, signed the jacket quickly, and, smiling, handed it to him with a kiss on the cheek. He turned red, managed to mutter a passable thanks before he made his way out the door and toward the car. When he was halfway across the lawn Rick remembered something and called him back.

"Billy?"

"Yessir?" he turned and looked back.

"Come here," Rick called.

As the youngster approached, Rick thrust a twenty-dollar bill toward him. "You forgot my fare," he said.

"Oh, yes sir, thank you, sir." And then finally he was free and she threw her arms around him and hugged him.

"How are you?" she asked, laughing.

"Healthy as a bear." He looked down at her through dark glasses. He saw a faint dark blue where she was, brought his hands up to her face and touched her lightly with his fingers, "saw" her through his hands. She was very still, examining his face. "You are still so very beautiful," he said. "I will have to do you."

"Do me?"

"Sculpt you," he said.

"Oh. Damn." She laughed. "I thought I might be finally getting to you."

"You did that a long time ago, girl. When was it? Eleventh grade?"

"A hundred years ago."

She put his things in his bedroom and they talked, both of them, of things neither found all that interesting. But neither had the strength at the moment to speak the truth.

She cooked supper for him, a quick steak and potatoes. Afterwards they drank wine in the patio overlooking the Pacific and they talked of more nonsense until she said, "If you had your stuff with you, you could do me tonight."

"I brought it," he said.

"But no clay."

"Clay too," he said.

"Really!"

"Sure, it's all in that old suitcase."

"Fantastic!" she exclaimed. "Do you feel like it?"

"Never felt more like it." He laughed.

She left then and returned with the suitcase. "I should have known it had something in it. It weighs a ton!"

"Don't think an artist would travel without his tools, do you?"

He took it from her and opened it. His fingers examined the contents, removed the heavy, moist lump of clay and several tools. He placed the clay on the table and began to work it, powerfully, expertly. When he had worked a few minutes he asked her to bring him a large pan of warm water and began again to work the clay. He washed his hands, then said, "Now get a chair and sit here and let me see what you look like."

She did and his fingers examined her, her head, her ears, face, neck, shoulders. His fingers were like fire. Hot probes reaching through the surface of her body and into every hidden corner of her being. His being here, touching her, talking like this brought back memories long suppressed, the child Rick Morgan, his painting her. Then she thought of her father and that horrible day, and her marriage and her crippled soul. And like a flood came the newly awakened lust for completeness and the pounding realization that this was the man who could do it all for her, could make her whole, could with his expert fingers and grand soul turn this cold lump of female clay into a woman.

When his hands went back to the clay he was barely aware that she had gotten up and gone into the house, but when she returned moments later his hands went into the warm water again, then dried themselves on the towel. He reached out to examine the curve that swept from below the ear to the shoulder down to the top of her blouse and his fingers found no blouse, only shoulder. He paused. She noticed a slight trembling in his hand. He looked toward her, surprise on his face, then his jaw set and his hand moved lower and swept down over her shoulder and then to a bare breast. He held the breast and felt the nipple blooming under the warmth of his hand.

He stood up and pulled her up to him and held her. His voice was deep. "Why do you do this?"

"Will you?" she asked. "Please?"

He said nothing. His mind raced. How do I tell her? What now will it do to her?

Her hands reached up and pulled his head down to hers. "I have wanted you for years," she said. And then she kissed him. He met her kiss with his and squeezed her to him.

"There is something you have to know first," he said. "Then we will decide. Something very strange and very cruel. I'd hoped you wouldn't need to know.

"Do you remember the old man I sculpted at the hospital?" he asked.

"Your grandfather," she said. "I remembered later that I'd seen him with you on television."

"My grandfather," he said, "Frank Hyde."

"Hyde?" she breathed.

"My grandfather," he said again, "and yours."

"Mine?" He felt her muscles stiffen. She sat down in the chair beside the clay. "I don't understand."

"Come inside," he said. "Come inside and put your clothes on and I'll tell you about it and how I came to know it." And so he told her, about Frank Hyde and Jonathan Hyde, about the farm at Hidalgo, about little Ricky and about the river and the sheriff and the preaching. And then he told her about that day in the church with the crazed preacher and the razor blade. He told her how the vision came to him in his cage in Vietnam and how strangely at the moment the bullets were tearing through his body he realized that Jonathan Hyde was really his father.

She was dazed. Her body was rigid against him and then she broke and cried out. He held her as she wept and trembled. She cried, "All these years I have loved you and dreamed about you and wanted you. From the time I first saw you in school, when you painted me and when I loved you. . . . " She was still then, "You are my father's son."

"Yes."

"He raped me," she said quietly. "That day."

"Yes," he said, "I suspected it."

"And ever since then I've been messed up. I have not been right since then, Rick. That's what my holy father did to me."

"And you thought I could do it for you?" he said. "You thought you could make love to me?"

"Yes." She sighed. "I thought I could."

"Then why not?" he asked.

"Rick," she breathed.

He lifted her from where she sat and laid her down on the

336

carpet, and with sure and tender hands he led her through the portals of physical love, and it was more, far more beautiful even than she'd dreamed.

Later she lay beside him as he slept and saw the still-red scars of war on his back and knew that he was not yet well. Yet he had healed her. Dare I hope to have him? Then the sobering thought, "My brother!" Her head swam, dizzy with the truth of it. Then her thoughts turned to her father. What kind of man is he?

The next day he finished the bust. "It's me," she said. "It's really me!

"I want you to do a full-size sculpture," she said.

"Of you?" He smiled.

"Of course," she said. "It'll be your first commission as a sculptor. It'll make you famous. Can you do it in bronze?"

"I can do it in clay and cast it," he said. "That's how it's done. That's one way."

"Will you do it?" she asked.

"Of course I'll do it. I always wanted to be famous."

"I'm not kidding," she said.

"I know."

So he got more clay and some forms and began work. They worked on the patio. She got a man to rig a canvas cover, an awning, over them so the summer sun wouldn't bake the clay.

She stripped and stood nude before him for two days as he worked, both of them enjoying it. She loved his hands as they delved and explored and measured, and so did he. And they talked and they made love and they talked.

"Would Melissa mind?" she asked as he made love to her.

"Mind? This?"

"Yes."

"She would hate me if I didn't, under the circumstances," he said.

"She's some woman, then," she said.

"You're right about that," he chuckled.

She laughed. "Can I come see you in Texas?"

"You'd better."

"Rick?"

"Yes?"

337

"I think I can do it now."

"What?"

"Screw."

"You're doing a pretty good job of it." He laughed, pinching her breast.

"No, I mean with somebody else. I mean I think I'm okay now."

He cupped her face with both hands. "Look, Angela, be careful. Find a good man."

"I think I can now, Rick. I know I can. I've learned some things, finally."

"Such as?"

"That I'm whole by myself just like I am; that I don't need my father, or my father's wild god."

"I heard Grandfather Hyde say something like that once. 'There's a silence in Eden, Rick, and it suits me just fine.' "

"Me too," she said, "it suits me just fine, too."

She squeezed him. "I love you, big brother."

"And I love you, Angel. I love you very, very much."

Death came in the winter to old Frank Hyde. On a Thursday morning during the onion harvest he began having pains in his chest and by afternoon when the hurting increased Ellen insisted upon driving him to the hospital. He died at four.

The telegram reached L.A. on Sunday morning and was delivered by a pimply-faced kid on a motorbike. An usher handed it to the reverend who sat behind the pulpit just before he was to deliver his sermon. He took the envelope and without comment opened it and read the contents. He put the paper between the pages of his Bible and looked out over the believers. If there had been anyone in that crowd who really knew the preacher they would have seen that the look in his face was actually one of triumph, of satisfaction. When he stood he was above them all. He looked down upon them and read to them from his Bible, a text on the cruelty of God toward his enemies.

At that moment in a little family cemetery in South Texas the first staccato shovelful of gravelly dirt rained down upon the lid of a simple coffin. A wizened old Mexican man worked steadily, solemnly. After a bit he stopped, stood up, and wiped sweat out of his eyes. A few feet away stood the tall, dark-haired man who had stayed behind when the others had gone back to the house. A faint smile invaded the tear-streaked face as the young man remembered something that had happened a long time ago. He walked around his grandfather's half-filled grave and took the shovel from the little old man. The old Mexican said, "He was the best man I ever knew, Ricardo."

Rick shoveled slowly, respectfully, "I know, Emilio." After a while he gave the shovel back and as he stood watching the little Mexican shape up the rounded top of the grave he thought that that might be a good thing to paint, that little laborer standing alone with his worn old shovel staring through tear-rimmed eyes out over the new grave and back through the past.

"We got the memories," the Mexican told the young man as they turned to walk back toward the house.

He took the old man's shovel and put it over his shoulder and carried it for him. "That's right, Emilio, by God, we got the memories."